Praise for *Oscar Wilde and the Candlelight Murders*

'One of the most intelligent, amusing and entertaining books of
the year. If Oscar Wilde himself had been asked to write this book
he could not have done it any better' Alexander McCall Smith

'Wilde has sprung back to life in this thrilling and
richly atmospheric new novel' *Sunday Express*

'Gyles Brandreth and Oscar Wilde seem made for one another . . .
the complex and nicely structured plot zips along' *Daily Telegraph*

'Brandreth has poured his considerable familiarity with London
into a witty *fin-de-siècle* entertainment, and the rattlingly elegant
dialogue is peppered with witticisms uttered by Wilde well before
he ever thought of putting them into his plays' *Sunday Times*

'Brandreth knows his Wilde . . . He knows his Holmes
too . . . The plot is devilishly clever, the characters are
fully fleshed, the mystery is engrossing, and the solution
is perfectly fair. I love it' *Sherlock Holmes Journal*

Praise for *Oscar Wilde and the Ring of Death*

'Hugely enjoyable' *Daily Mail*

'A cast of historical characters to die for' *Sunday Times*

'A carnival of cliff-hangers and fiendish twists-and-turns . . .
The joy of the book, as with its predecessor, is the rounded and
compelling presentation of the character of Wilde' *Sunday Express*

'Wilde really has to prove himself against Bram Stoker and Arthur
Conan Doyle when a murder ruins their Sunday Supper Club.
But Brandreth's invention – that of Wilde as detective – is more
than up to the challenge. With plenty of wit, too' *Daily Mirror*

'I can't wait until the next one' *Scotsman*

Praise for *Oscar Wilde and the Dead Man's Smile*

'The murders begin. Highly theatrical ones . . . An
entertaining and meticulously researched piece of pop
fiction about Wilde and his circle' *Washington Post*

'An entertaining yarn – easy and pleasing to read – with
an extensive set of vivid characters' *Gay Times*

'Very funny' *Independent on Sunday*

Praise for *Oscar Wilde and the Nest of Vipers*

'Gyles Brandreth's Oscar Wilde murder mysteries get
better and better . . . Positively dazzling. Both witty and
profound, it's also devilishly clever' *District Messenger*,
newsletter of the Sherlock Holmes Society of London

Praise for *Oscar Wilde and the Vatican Murders*

'Literary and theological references merge easily into a
skilfully crafted story that goes all the way to meet the
standards set by his two eminent protagonists' *Daily Mail*

'Hugely enjoyable . . . a story that reminds us just how enjoyable
a well-told traditional murder mystery can be' *Scotsman*

Praise for *Oscar Wilde and the Murders at Reading Gaol*

'What sets the novel apart is Brandreth's talent for conveying
time and place. The barbarism of close confinement has rarely
been so graphically and movingly portrayed' *Daily Mail*

'The Oscar Wilde Murder Mysteries just get better and
better . . . and this is the best so far.' *Sherlock Holmes Journal*

Also by Gyles Brandreth

Oscar Wilde and the Candlelight Murders
Oscar Wilde and the Ring of Death
Oscar Wilde and the Dead Man's Smile
Oscar Wilde and the Nest of Vipers
Oscar Wilde and the Vatican Murders
Oscar Wilde and the Murders at Reading Gaol

Oscar Wilde

and the

Return of

Jack the Ripper

Gyles Brandreth

PEGASUS CRIME

NEW YORK LONDON

OSCAR WILDE AND THE RETURN OF JACK THE RIPPER

Pegasus Books, Ltd.
148 West 37th Street, 13th Floor
New York, NY 10018

Copyright © 2019 by Gyles Brandreth

First Pegasus Books hardcover edition April 2019

ISBN: 978-1-64313-021-7

10 9 8 7 6 5 4 3 2 1

Printed in the United States of America
Distributed by W. W. Norton & Company, Inc.

For Michèle
always

Principal characters in the narrative

Oscar Wilde
Arthur Conan Doyle

Jimmy, bellboy at the Langham Hotel, London
Martin, waiter at the Langham Hotel

Melville Macnaghten, Chief Constable, Metropolitan Police
Criminal Investigation Department

Constance Wilde, Oscar Wilde's wife
William Wilde, Oscar Wilde's brother
Lily Lees, William Wilde's fiancée

Mina Mathers, artist
Ivan Salazkin, ringmaster, the Russian Circus
Olga Ivanov, acrobat
Tom Norman, showman
Stella Stride, prostitute
Henry Labouchere MP
The Marquess of Queensberry
George R. Sims, journalist
Alec Shand, writer
James Barrie, playwright
Bram Stoker, theatre manager

Charles Dodgson, 'Lewis Carroll'
Festing Fitzmaurice, former courtier
Sir Frederick Bunbury, Bt.
Major Ridout
Dr Gabriel, superintendent, Surrey County Lunatic Asylum
Dr Rogerson, superintendent, Colney Hatch Lunatic Asylum

The acknowledged victims of the Whitechapel murderer

Mary Ann Nichols, body found 31 August 1888
Annie Chapman, body found 8 September 1888
Elizabeth Stride, body found 30 September 1888
Catherine Eddowes, body found 30 September 1888
Mary Jane Kelly, body found 9 November 1888

Macnaghten's suspects

Montague John Druitt
Aaron Kosminski
Richard Mansfield
Michael Ostrog
Walter Wellbeloved

Note

I prepared this narrative in 1924, at the time of writing my memoirs. I knew it could not be published during my lifetime, for reasons that will become clear to any future reader. It may be that it cannot be published for many years to come. However, in the fullness of time, I trust it will see the light of day. Any truth is better than indefinite doubt.

Arthur Conan Doyle

New Year's Eve, 1893

He thrust his knee into her belly and held her head hard against the brick wall. The palm of his left hand pushed up against her mouth and nostrils and he pressed his fingers into the sockets of her eyes. In his right hand he held a small butcher's knife and, with the force of a hammer blow, he jabbed it into the right side of her neck, just below her jaw. She made no sound; nor did he, as he pulled out the knife and struck again, this time tearing a line across her neck, from one side to the other, slitting her throat from ear to ear, plunging in the knife so deep that the tip of the blade reached as far as her vertebrae.

Blood trickled from her and he stepped back to let her body slide down the wall and slump to the ground. Bending forward, he rolled the woman over, tore open her coat and jacket and blouse, pulled up her skirt and petticoats, and stabbed her repeatedly in the chest and stomach and groin. In all, he struck her thirty-nine times.

I

1 January 1894

'It was the best of crimes, it was the worst of crimes.'

'What are you saying?'

'That's your opening line, Arthur. "It was the best of crimes, it was the worst of crimes."'

'I don't need an "opening line", thank you very much, Oscar.'

'Oh, but you do, my dear fellow.'

'What for?'

'For your new book. It must open with that line, it really must—'

I interrupted: 'What new book?'

'The one you are starting today – tonight, when you get home. Your account of our latest adventure – the most remarkable of all our extraordinary adventures, Arthur.' He raised his glass to me. His bright eyes brimmed with tears.

'You're drunk, Oscar.'

'I hope so,' he beamed. 'I have made an important discovery, you know. Alcohol taken in sufficient quantities produces all the effects of intoxication.'

Oscar Fingal O'Flahertie Wills Wilde leaned back against the mantelpiece and laughed. He was thirty-nine years of age and looked both older and younger. He had the moonlike face of an ageing cherub, with full pink lips; waxy, pale cheeks; dark, arched eyebrows and what he called, proudly, 'a strong Greek nose'. He was over six feet in height and, though running to fat, still a fine figure of a man because he held himself well. He was unquestionably 'someone'. He was unmistakably the celebrated Oscar Wilde. He dressed the part. That Monday morning he wore an elaborately tailored three-piece suit of blue Donegal tweed and a broad silk tie that matched perfectly the indigo-coloured winter rose that was his buttonhole. He claimed that the pearl in his tiepin had once belonged to John Keats.

When first I had met Oscar, four and half years before, at the end of August 1889, at this same London hotel – the Langham in Portland Place – he was already famous, though known more for his flamboyance and wit than for his short stories and his poetry. He was rising thirty-five then and I had just turned thirty. I had published the first of my Sherlock Holmes stories, but was relatively unknown still and earning my keep, inadequately, practising as a doctor in Southsea.

At that first encounter – over a convivial dinner hosted by an American publisher who, happily, commissioned stories from us both – I was awed by Oscar's intelligence and captivated by his personality. His charm was irresistible. His conversation left an indelible impression upon my mind. Intellectually, he towered above us all, and yet he had the art of seeming to be interested in all that we had to say. He took as well as gave, but what he gave was unique. He had a curious precision of statement, a delicate flavour of humour, and a trick of small gestures to illustrate his meaning, which were peculiar to himself. We became friends – at once. And remained friends. And, while we did not see one another regularly, whenever we met there was always an easy and immediate intimacy between us.

That said, as the years had passed Oscar had changed. The gentlemanly delicacy that I remembered from the late summer of 1889 was less evident in 1894. He was as witty as ever (possibly more so), but louder and, it seemed to me, less mindful of others. He gave more, but he took less. There was an aroma of wine and tobacco about him now. His dress was possibly more sober than when we had first met, but his way of life was not. He had become successful as a dramatist. (His play, *A Woman of No Importance*, had just opened in New York.) He had become wildly extravagant. (The Perrier-Jouët we were drinking was the costliest vintage.) As a husband and father, he had become neglectful of his obligations. There was a recklessness about him that was alarming. Being with him, you sensed danger in the air, and even a touch of madness.

But he was still wonderful company, still irresistible. That's why I was there, at noon, on New Year's Day.

'And lunch?' I enquired, pulling away my glass as he attempted to refill it. 'You promised me "lunch and all the news".'

'I did,' he said, filling his own champagne saucer to the brim. 'And I trust you'll not be disappointed by either. I've ordered potted shrimps and broiled lobster. The chef here is very good and he's conjuring up a special mayonnaise.'

'Lobster mayonnaise in January?'

'It's to be a picnic.'

'A picnic?' I repeated doubtfully.

'Yes, Arthur, I know you're a lamb-cutlets-on-a-Monday sort of man, but needs must. We'll be eating on the move. But, fear not, we won't go hungry.' Smiling, he stepped from the fireplace to a side table by the window and picked up a small, dark, glass container. 'Look. Russian caviar, the best beluga – as enjoyed by Tsar Alexander III and the more intimate friends of Oscar Wilde.'

'A picnic?' I said again. 'In this weather?'

He glanced out of the window. The rain was falling steadily. 'We'll be under cover,' he said soothingly. 'I've ordered a four-wheeler – with rugs.' He looked below. 'It's waiting for us.' He turned to me and laughed. 'Where's your spirit of adventure, Arthur?'

I laughed, too. 'What's all this about, Oscar? What's going on?'

'I'll tell you.' He pointed to the clock on the mantelpiece. 'In a minute's time, I anticipate a knock on the door. It will be one of the hotel bellboys – Jimmy, most likely – an amusing lad, cockney and good-hearted. He will be carrying a small silver salver in his right hand and on the salver will be a telegram addressed to me.'

'And what will this telegram say? "Fly at once – all is discovered"?'

'Very droll, Arthur. It will say, "Come at once", or rather, "Come at two o'clock. Bring friend Doyle if you can. He should prove invaluable." Signed, "Macnaghten." I shall then give Jimmy sixpence, which he will most probably drop, and we will be on our way.'

'How do you know the boy will drop the sixpence?'

'He is very clumsy.'

'And how do you know what the telegram will say?'

Oscar narrowed his eyes and drained his glass. 'I have my methods, Dr Doyle.'

As my friend carefully placed his empty champagne saucer

back on the mantelpiece, there came a double-knock on the door. 'Enter!' cried Oscar. A red-haired, freckle-faced boy of about thirteen years of age came into the room. He was indeed holding a small salver in his right hand.

'Telegram for you, Mr Wilde.'

'Happy New Year, Jimmy,' said Oscar. 'You may give the telegram to Dr Conan Doyle. Have you heard of him, Jimmy?'

'Who, sir?'

'Dr Conan Doyle.'

'No, sir.'

'Have you heard of Sherlock Holmes, Jimmy?'

'Course, sir. Who hasn't?'

'Dr Conan Doyle invented Sherlock Holmes, Jimmy. Sherlock Holmes is a figment of Dr Doyle's imagination.'

'Pleased to meet you, sir,' said the boy, holding the silver salver before me.

'"*Honoured* to meet you" is what you mean, Jimmy. Take the telegram, Arthur. And you, Jimmy, take this.' Oscar gave the lad a silver sixpence and the boy dropped it immediately. It rolled under the side table. 'Retrieve your sixpence, Jimmy, and go!'

The bellboy did as he was told – with some alacrity – and Oscar chuckled happily. 'Now, Arthur,' he continued, 'open the telegram. What does it say?'

'"Come at two o'clock. Bring friend Doyle if you can. Macnaghten ."'

'Is that all?'

'Yes,' I said, smiling and holding up the telegram for my friend to inspect. 'There appears to be no mention of my contribution proving "invaluable".'

'I apologise,' he said, taking the telegram from me and scrutinising it with hooded eyes. 'Macnaghten's a policeman. I suppose one can't expect too much.' He dropped the telegram on the side table, picked up the jar of caviar and looked out of the window and down into the street. 'Come, Arthur, our carriage awaits. We must be on our way. As you'd have it: the game's afoot.'

2

'The toast is warm!'

Our four-wheeler lurched out of the Langham's ornate portico and turned south into Regent Street. With a schoolboy's glee, as though it were a tuck box, Oscar opened the picnic basket that the hotel porter had placed on the banquette between us. He handed me a large linen napkin and a china dish.

'The toast is warm!' he exclaimed delightedly, scooping a spoonful of caviar onto a piece of it. 'Eat up, Arthur. We'll be there in forty minutes, even in this weather.'

'Where are we going?' I asked.

'Tite Street.'

'Tite Street, Chelsea?' I said, surprised. 'Tite Street – where you live?'

'Yes, Tite Street where I live – when I am at home.'

'And you are not at home at present?'

'No. As you see, I am staying at the Langham for a while. The hotel is full of strangers and foreigners. There's nothing more comforting.'

I raised an eyebrow. 'Does Mrs Wilde know where you are staying?' It was a question I felt I knew him well enough to ask.

'Of course. I keep nothing from Constance. No man should keep a secret from his wife. She invariably finds it out.' He sucked noisily on a lobster claw. 'Besides, I was at home for Christmas and it's well known that too much domesticity is debilitating. It ages one rapidly and distracts one's mind from higher things.'

I laughed, as he hoped I would. 'How was Christmas? How are your boys?'

'Christmas was charming in its way.' He looked at me directly and there were tears once more in his eyes. 'The Christmas story is so lovely, but how can one enjoy it when one knows how it will end? Is there to be a crucifixion in all our lives?'

'And the boys?' I said again, not feeling there was anything to be gained by prolonging another of my friend's increasingly frequent maudlin moments.

'The boys are well, thank you. But exhausting. Now they're seven and eight they lead such active lives I don't like to get in their way. The truth is, fathers should be neither seen nor heard. That is the proper basis for family life.'

I wondered if he might enquire after my wife and small ones, but he did not. 'Christmas was good,' he murmured, 'or, at least, untroubled.' He peered inside the picnic basket and pulled out a silver flask. 'Do you think this might contain a passable white Burgundy?' He undid the stopper and sniffed. 'It does!' He filled a small beaker and handed it to me. 'Happy New Year, Arthur. Thank you for answering my summons.'

'I am always pleased to see you,' I said truthfully, raising my beaker to my friend. The carriage juddered to a halt. We had reached Piccadilly Circus. Even on New Year's Day, at lunchtime in the rain, street girls were gathered in small clusters plying their trade. One looked up at me waving a handful of lavender in my direction and called out, 'Happy New Year, guvn'r.' The four-wheeler jolted forward and rumbled on.

'I take it Lord Alfred Douglas is away,' I said lightly.

'Yes, Bosie is in Egypt. He's spending the winter working as private secretary to the consul-general in Cairo. The sun will be bad for his complexion, but the work will be good for his soul.' Oscar leaned towards me and tapped me gently on the knee. 'You must call him Bosie, you know. Everybody does. He likes you very much, Arthur, even though you don't like him.'

'I don't dislike him,' I said. 'I don't really know him, that's all.'

In truth, I felt I knew enough of him not to trust him. Bosie Douglas was a young man of twenty-three, fair-haired, thin-lipped, good-looking (in a very English, weak sort of way), the third son of the 9th Marquess of Queensberry, a spoilt child, a mother's favourite, a self-styled poet, a young idler who had left Oxford without taking a degree: effete, effeminate, ineffectual – and, in my estimation, a ruinous distraction for Oscar who was infatuated with the boy and lavished time, attention and money on him to a degree that was embarrassing. Certainly I would not have been embarking on this adventure with Oscar now had Bosie been in town. When Lord Alfred Douglas whistled, Oscar Wilde would drop everything to run to his side.

'I have been very worried about Bosie, Arthur. He has so much promise, but it's going nowhere. He does nothing. His life seems aimless, unhappy, absurd.'

I helped myself to a spoonful of caviar and glanced out of the carriage window. We were moving south through Trafalgar Square.

Oscar continued earnestly: 'I gave him my French play to translate last year. *Salome.* I thought the story would appeal to his fascination with the sacred and the macabre.'

'And did it?' I asked.

'Oh, yes, very much so. He produced a fine translation, but that was months ago. And since then, he's done nothing. Nothing at all. And empty days lead to sleepless nights, with his health suffering terribly in consequence. He's become nervous – almost hysterical.'

'It's a phase,' I said. 'He's very young. He'll grow out of it.'

'Or kill himself.'

'Now who's getting hysterical?' I asked.

'Suicide runs in families, Arthur. Bosie's grandfather took his own life, you know – shot himself. And his uncle cut his own throat – with a butcher's knife.'

'I thought his uncle was a clergyman.'

'That's another uncle – Lord Archie Douglas. Lord James Douglas is the one who cut his own throat – only a year or so ago. He was in love with his twin sister, Florrie, and when she got married it broke his heart and he went off the rails. He tried to abduct a young girl as a sister-substitute, but that went awry, to put it mildly, so he turned to drink and eventually he killed himself.'

'They're an odd family,' I said, not knowing quite what else to say.

'Anyway, with my encouragement, and his mother's, Bosie's gone to Cairo to work for Lord Cromer. The change of scene, and proper employment, will do him good, I trust.'

'I trust so, too,' I said, without much conviction, adding, with somewhat more sincerity, 'And now Bosie's away, you're free to get on with some work of your own.'

'Precisely,' Oscar answered eagerly. 'And that's what I plan to do – what I need to do, in fact.' We had reached the Thames Embankment and Oscar, looking out of the carriage window and up at the sky, while dramatically waving a forkful of potted shrimp towards the river, suddenly declared: 'I am overwhelmed by the wings of vulture creditors, Arthur. I need money. I am hopelessly in debt.'

'But you've had two plays in town this year,' I protested. 'You've made a fortune.'

'And spent one.' He looked at me and smiled. 'Without regret. Pleasure will be paid for. And pleasure must be had. An inordinate passion for pleasure is the secret of remaining young.'

'As I've heard you say before.'

He offered up a theatrical sigh. 'You see what I am reduced to, Arthur? Repeating my own lines! I need to buy time to create some new turns of phrase. It's very difficult to be original when one is in debt.'

'And you have a plan?' I suggested.

'I do.'

'And it involves me?' I asked.

'It does.'

'And Mr Macnaghten?'

'And Chief Constable Macnaghten – yes, indeed. Macnaghten is to lead us to our crock of gold, Arthur.'

'The chief constable is a neighbour of yours? Tite Street is an unusual address for a policeman.'

'Macnaghten is an unusual policeman. He's intelligent. He's cultivated. He's educated.'

I laughed. 'Does that mean he was at Oxford with you?'

'No, he went to Eton – that's a start. And then he went to India to manage his father's tea estates in Bengal.'

'He's a planter turned policeman – that's a curious kind of career development.'

'He's a polymath, with private means. He could do anything. Apparently, he was spotted by a district judge in Bengal who recognised his potential and when Macnaghten decided to come back to England with a view to being of some service to his country, the good judge pointed him in the direction of the Criminal Investigation Department of the Metropolitan Police. He's now their Chief Constable – and only just turned forty.'

'Is he a family man?' I asked, fearing for a moment that Macnaghten might turn out to be one of Oscar's good-looking enthusiasms suddenly brought into play because of the absence of Lord Alfred Douglas.

'A family man? Very much so. He has fourteen brothers and sisters.'

'And isn't in love with any of them, I hope?'

Oscar giggled. 'He is happily married to a very pretty girl called Dora, the daughter of a canon of Chichester, and I believe they have several small and no doubt delightful children. The family is a model of respectability.'

'You like him?'

'I think I do.'

'And trust him?'

'Absolutely. He has a walrus moustache, Arthur, to rival your own.'

'And this Chief Constable Macnaghten is to help us make our fortune?'

'Correct, my dear friend. You're as sharp as Sherlock Holmes today. I need money and you need money.' He looked at me slyly, his mouth half full of potted shrimp. 'You have a poorly young wife at a nursing home in Switzerland, do you not? She requires

16

care and attention, I'm sure – and that comes at a price.' He took a sip of wine and smiled at me solicitously. 'How is Touie, by the way?'

'She is bearing up, thank you – and asks to be remembered to you. And to Constance.'

'And you have children, don't you, one of each?'

'Yes,' I said, smiling. 'Mary and Kingsley. Well remembered.'

'And they need nursemaids – and education. Obviously nothing that is worth knowing can be taught, but, even so, schools must be found and paid for. You could bring in more money by writing another of your Sherlock Holmes stories, but you appear disinclined to do so . . .'

'I've had enough of Holmes.'

'Very good. But you still need an income.'

'Indeed.'

'Exactly. I reckon you need a story that will outsell all that you have done before – and I need a play that will draw the town.'

'And somehow your Chief Constable Macnaghten can supply us with both?'

'I believe so,' murmured my friend, almost purring with pleasure at the prospect.

'And how exactly, Oscar, will he do that?'

'By the simple expedient of helping us to identify the most celebrated, the most vile, the most notorious, the most repugnant, the most *popular* criminal of the age – Jack the Ripper. Was there ever a more promising start to a new year?'

3

Paradise Walk

I rapped my beaker of white Burgundy down on the picnic basket and laughed out loud. 'We are to unmask Jack the Ripper?'

Oscar glanced up anxiously towards our coachman. Above the rattle of the metal wheels on the roadway, and through the steadily streaming rain, there was no possibility of him overhearing us. Nevertheless, Oscar lowered his voice and leaned in towards me conspiratorially. 'We are to assist the police with their inquiries,' he confided, 'and our reward will be to discover all that they know.'

I gazed at my friend in astonishment. 'But the police know nothing, Oscar,' I protested. 'If they knew anything, they'd have made an arrest by now. They've been searching for this so-called Jack the Ripper for five years – longer – and they've got nowhere. They don't know who he is or where he comes from, they don't know if he's alive or dead, they don't even know for certain how many murders he may have committed. They have no idea what his motives might have been. Remember, the most difficult crime to track is the one which is purposeless. The police know nothing, Oscar – nothing!'

'They know more than you think, Arthur.'

'Oh, really?' I said doubtfully.

'My man Macnaghten is now in charge of the case.'

'As you say.'

'The point is: he's new to it. He was still in Bengal in 'eighty-eight when the murders started. He's come to it with a fresh mind.'

'And fresh information? That's what wanted, surely?'

'He's exploring "a range of possibilities", he tells me. He's been charged with producing a definitive report to put an end to all the lurid speculation – and to get at the truth. And when he does, you will want to write it up, Arthur.'

'If he gets to the truth, it will certainly be a story,' I conceded.

'"It was the best of crimes, it was the worst of crimes" – that's your opening line.'

'As you keep telling me,' I laughed.

'It has a ring to it.'

'A Dickensian ring, Oscar.'

My friend drained his beaker of wine. He had now emptied the flask. 'I never rated Dickens, as you know. One must have a heart of stone to read the death of Little Nell without laughing. But there's no denying Mr Dickens' popularity. His books have sold in their hundreds of thousands. With *Case Closed – The Truth about Jack the Ripper*, or whatever we call it, we can do likewise. You will write the book. I will write the play. The public loves a blood-curdling melodrama. Look at the stage adaptation of *Dr Jekyll and Mr Hyde*: standing room only in London and New York.'

'Your man Macnaghten is the officer in charge of the case?'

'Yes.'

'And if and when he uncovers the truth, he has agreed to share it with us – exclusively?'

Oscar was peering out of the window. We had reached Chelsea Hospital on our right: Tite Street was approaching. 'Not exactly – but we're near neighbours and fast becoming firm friends. He's told me a little about the case – and about the report he's writing – and asked for my assistance – so I am seizing the opportunity. Hence our two o'clock appointment.'

'Your two o'clock appointment, Oscar. He's not expecting me, I think.'

'What do you mean?' My friend looked at me, perturbed.

'That telegram just now,' I said, 'the one purporting to come from Macnaghten. It wasn't from him at all, was it?'

'What do you mean, Arthur?'

'You sent it to yourself, didn't you?'

Oscar had replaced his empty beaker in the picnic basket. His hands fluttered before him like moths trapped in a bottle. He was evidently embarrassed. 'How did you guess?'

I laughed. 'I recognise a charade when I see one, Oscar. That nonsense of the bellboy dropping the sixpence. You set it up too elaborately. He did it too obviously. You'd primed him.'

'He's not a very good actor, I'm afraid.'

'Nor are you.' I smiled. 'For a moment I was almost taken in by your display of Holmesian omniscience, but it was all too pat. I smelled a rat. And now I've worked it out. The telegram was a ploy to intrigue me, wasn't it? A device to get me involved? Macnaghten isn't expecting me at all, but for some reason you don't want to see him on your own. Am I right?'

Oscar dropped his hands in his lap and shook his head in

contrition. 'You're quite right, Arthur. I didn't think you'd agree to come with me to meet Macnaghten and talk of murder if you hadn't been invited – hence my playful subterfuge. It was just one of my little games.'

'Murder isn't a game, old friend.'

'I don't know,' he answered airily, packing up the remnants of our picnic and returning them to the basket. 'There's nothing quite like an unexpected death for lifting the spirits.'

'You've said that before, too.'

We both laughed. 'Thank you for coming,' said Oscar. 'I'll confess I have been oddly anxious about seeing Macnaghten on my own.'

'Did he ask you to come on your own?'

'Not in so many words. He said he wanted to talk about the case "confidentially". But if we arrive together, he can have no objection to your presence. He will be happy to meet you, I'm certain – and who knows where the interview may lead?'

'Are we here?' I asked, as the four-wheeler juddered once more to a stop.

We had reached the corner of Dilke Street and Tite Street, residential thoroughfares just off the embankment, fifty yards from the river's edge. Our coachman jumped down from his driver's seat and opened the carriage door. 'Something's up, sir,' he said. 'The street's closed.'

We peered out into the rain. A knot of shadowy figures was standing on the pavement and a line of four or five uniformed policemen was straddled across the roadway. There was a hubbub of men's voices and, in the distance, the shrill sound of short, sharp repeated blasts from a police whistle.

I recognised the signal. 'They're calling for a Black Maria,' I said. 'It's either an arrest or a body.'

'Wait here,' said Oscar to our driver, as we clambered out of the four-wheeler. I opened up my umbrella and, huddled beneath it, we made our way towards the line of police.

'Is Tite Street closed?' asked Oscar.

'Not if you're a resident, sir. It's Paradise Walk that's closed. There's been an incident.'

'There's been a murder, Mr Wilde,' said a voice from behind us, 'in the alley that leads to the back of your house – and mine.'

We turned towards the voice and I raised the umbrella so that we could see the figure addressing us. He was a tall, handsome man of about forty years of age, with strong, clean features, a firm jaw, an unfurrowed brow, sandy, somewhat receding hair, startlingly clear blue eyes – and, as Oscar had told me, a moustache much like mine. He wore a khaki-coloured greatcoat that glistened in the rain and brown leather gloves. He raised his hat as he shook Oscar by the hand. He nodded to me. 'Melville Macnaghten,' he said, 'Chief Constable, Metropolitan Police CID.' I liked his manner immediately.

'Arthur Conan Doyle,' I replied, 'Doctor.'

'I know the name, Doctor,' he said pleasantly. 'Is it doctor of medicine?'

'It is.'

'May I impose upon you for a moment, Doctor?' He did not wait for my reply. He was a man accustomed to command. 'Kindly follow me, if you would. I doubt you've seen worse, Doctor. It's an horrific crime. We need to remove the body as soon as possible, but a note from a medical man *in situ* could prove useful – if you don't mind. Come this way.'

Briskly, he led us into Tite Street, beyond the line of policemen and away from the group of gawping bystanders. He stopped at the first corner, by a large red-brick building, where two more policemen were standing guard. 'This is the Shelley Theatre – you'll know it, Mr Wilde. And this is the alley that leads to Paradise Walk. She's down here, poor woman – or what remains of her. It's a messy business, Mr Wilde. You won't want to look. Wait here. I'll take the doctor down.'

We left Oscar standing beneath my umbrella and I followed Macnaghten along Shelley Alley. It was muddy and stinking, littered with refuse, broken orange boxes and old vegetables, some fifty yards long but no more than three feet wide – as narrow as the narrowest *calli* in Venice, and as dark: the buildings on either side rose four storeys high.

At the far end of the alley stood three more policemen, bunched together, hovering over the body of the dead woman. One held an umbrella above her head; another lit a spirit lamp to help me see the full horror of her butchered corpse.

'Careful, Doctor,' said Macnaghten, 'there's blood everywhere.'

'I see,' I said.

'Have you a notebook?'

'I have,' I said, pulling it from my coat pocket. 'Is this where you found her? Has she been moved?'

'A knife-grinder found her. Local man. He sometimes leaves his cart in the alley. No one's touched the body.'

It was a hideous sight – the worst that I had ever seen.

I crouched down and inspected the poor creature's bloodied remains as dispassionately as I could – from head to toe. Her hair was largely hidden by a cheap, black bonnet, but what I could see of it was grey. Her brow was deeply lined; her skin was pale; her eyes were mercifully closed. Her muddied, bloodied face had been slashed three times: from top to bottom, from her nose to her chin, across her mouth; from left to right, from cheekbone to jaw; from right to left in the same manner. The major wound – the one that killed her, cutting through the carotid artery and all but severing her head – was a mighty gash across her neck that ran from ear to ear.

Her clothing – a black jacket that looked too big for her, a long, dark green skirt and brown petticoats – was torn and in humiliating disarray. Her torso, trunk and private parts were cruelly exposed and fouled with congealed blood. Her feet were bare.

On my travels in West Africa, I had heard stories of ritual killings, but nothing had prepared me for the catalogue of cruelty I was recording here: the woman's thin and ageing body had been slashed and cut so vilely. I noted:

6 wounds to the neck and upper torso
5 wounds to the left lung
3 wounds to the right lung
4 wounds to the heart
5 wounds to the liver
5 wounds to the spleen
6 wounds to the stomach
5 wounds to the upper thighs and private parts

'She has been slaughtered and then disfigured,' I said. 'With each wound the entry point suggests a right-handed assailant.'

'A man, I assume?'

'Or a remarkably strong woman. The neck has been cut cleanly – but with tremendous force. It will be a man.' I looked up at Macnaghten. 'It always is.'

'Not quite always,' said Macnaghten.

I closed my notebook. 'It will be a man,' I said, 'I am sure of that. The stabbing is concentrated on the breasts, the belly and the reproductive region. There are thirty-nine wounds in all.'

'Thirty-nine, you say?'

'Yes. Is that significant?'

'It might be.' I glanced up at the chief constable once more. 'And can you smell anything?' he asked.

'Beyond the stench of death and the foul smell of the alley?'

'Yes,' he said. 'A faint smell of lavender?'

I sniffed the air above the poor woman's ruined cadaver. 'No,' I said, 'nothing.'

I stood up and felt a moment's giddiness as I did so. Macnaghten put out a hand to steady me. 'Thank you, Doctor,' he said. 'We'll do a complete examination at the morgue, but this is most helpful.'

'From the state of the blood,' I added, 'and the degree of rigor mortis, given her apparent age and the cold weather, I would reckon the attack took place some twelve hours ago.'

'That's what we'd assumed. Thank you. Will you write up a brief report?'

'By all means.'

The chief constable nodded to his men and I followed him back along the alley to where Oscar was awaiting us, smoking one of his Turkish cigarettes.

'How was it?' Oscar asked.

'Horrible,' I answered. 'The work of the devil.'

Macnaghten looked at Oscar and raised an eyebrow. 'We can forget our two o'clock appointment, Mr Wilde. Shall we meet at six instead? Would that be convenient for you? At my house?'

'I will be there,' said Oscar.

'Good,' said Macnaghten pleasantly. 'We will meet at six, then. And bring Dr Doyle. He could prove invaluable.'

4

16 Tite Street

'Starvation, and not sin, is the parent of modern crime,' said Oscar, lighting another Turkish cigarette from the dying embers of the last.

We were continuing up Tite Street, from the corner at the end of the alley in which the woman's body had been found, towards Oscar's house at Number 16. The rain had stopped and Oscar had given me back my umbrella.

'This crime was not caused by starvation,' I said. 'Depravity not hunger is the author of the horror I've just seen.'

'The perpetrator may not have been starving, but the victim most probably was. What sort of woman was she?'

'Not easy to tell. She had been savagely disfigured. She was quite thin, I grant you, but was that age rather than hunger? Yes, her clothes were cheap and mean, and yet . . . I don't know what makes me feel this, but there was something of the lady about her.'

Oscar laughed. 'You feel it because you are a gentleman, Arthur, and cannot really believe ill of any woman. She will have been a poor bedraggled creature of the night, murdered on New Year's Eve by a vicious, drunken reveller – or by her pimp . . .'

'Her "pimp"?' I looked at Oscar, surprised by the word he used. 'This is a respectable part of town, surely?'

'This is London, Arthur; that great cesspool into which all the loungers and idlers of the Empire are irresistibly drained – as you once told me. All human life is here, the best and the worst of it, side by side.'

'What I meant is: this isn't Whitechapel, this isn't Jack the Ripper country.'

'Perhaps it's worse. In the East End, you know exactly where you are. Everybody is poor in Whitechapel. There are no exceptions. Destitution and crime are evident for all to see. Whereas in this part of town, they're not so obvious. They lurk in the dismal back alleys and hide behind the grandest front doors. Confusion reigns. Who's respectable, who isn't? Who's innocent, who's guilty? Where are you safe? At home or abroad? Nobody knows.' He stopped in his tracks and looked up and down the deserted roadway. 'A High Court judge lives in that house there. Mr Justice Wills, a good man, I'm told, decent and honest, but can we be sure? Friend Macnaghten, Chief Constable, lives down there – next to the Shelley Theatre, built by the poet's son, don't you know? Yes, Arthur, the man whose mother gave birth to Frankenstein gave birth to that little theatre. It's quite beautiful inside – and haunted, they say. And just opposite is the studio of Mr John Singer Sargent. I admire his work, but what do we know of the company he keeps? Not long ago, I saw Lady Macbeth ringing the doorbell.'

I furrowed my brow, as I felt Oscar expected.

'It was the actress Ellen Terry, of course, in costume, coming to have her portrait painted.'

I smiled and gazed along the varied range of handsome, high-windowed red-brick and stucco-fronted houses. 'And a stone's throw away,' he went on, 'at the end of that alley you now know too well, parallel with Tite Street, lies another street, one of the foulest and filthiest in all England.'

'Paradise Walk?'

'So named by one of the masters of irony employed by the borough council, yes. It's a hellhole, a miserable mishmash of slum dwellings, hovels and tenements.'

'Who lives there?' I asked, as we walked on.

'Poor unfortunates like that woman whose body you have just seen. Old prostitutes, old soldiers, old lags. All sorts: refugees from the workhouse, a few Jews from Poland and Lithuania, even the odd gentleman down on his luck. There's a former courtier I know who glories in the name of Festing Fitzmaurice. He took to drink and paid the price. Once he lived at Windsor Castle and Osborne House and danced attendance on the Queen. Now he lives in a rat-infested room in Paradise Walk – above a pigsty. The street is rich in livestock: pigs and chickens, dogs and rats.'

He stopped in his tracks once more. 'And here, in a house that overlooks all that, dwell I.'

We had arrived at 16 Tite Street. I had been to the house before, but did not know it well. It had been Oscar's home since the time of his marriage, some ten years before, and though a building very much of its type and period – four narrow storeys, plus a basement, with just two rooms on each floor – Oscar had had it done up in his own peculiar style. His friend, the artist Whistler, had been closely involved in the decoration – and it showed. I knew that Oscar had once loved the house very much: I sensed now that he felt almost indifferent to the place.

As we stood looking up at the front door, it opened and a tall, portly, bearded gentleman emerged, pulling the door shut behind him. At first glance, he had the appearance of a prosperous, if not entirely trustworthy, Levantine merchant. As he turned to come down the front steps, he noticed Oscar and, touching the brim of his hat by way of salutation, murmured, 'Oscar.' Oscar made no reply and continued to fumble in his pockets, looking for his keys.

The man passed us without further acknowledgement and made his way down the street towards the river.

'I feel I know him,' I said.

'I don't think so,' said Oscar. 'I hope not.'

'He looks familiar.'

'He might well. He is my brother.'

'Your brother?'

'Yes, my older brother. William Charles Kingsbury Wilde. I can't help detesting my relations. I suppose it comes from the fact that none of us can stand other people having the same faults as ourselves.'

By now my friend had found his keys, but he did not need them because, as we reached the front door, it opened again and there stood Constance Wilde, smiling and with her hands outstretched to greet us.

'This is a lovely surprise,' she said. 'I thought it was Willie come back, but it's you. Come in.'

She wore a long, black velvet dress, with a white pageboy collar and white lace cuffs. She looked quite beautiful. Her auburn hair fell down to her shoulders in soft curls. She appeared less tired than when I had last seen her: her eyes sparkled and her cheeks were pink. She was evidently in high spirits.

'What was Willie doing here?' Oscar demanded as we stood together on the threshold.

'He came for lunch.'

'You had lunch with Willie?'

'Well, Oscar, I must have lunch with someone.'

'How much did he drink?'

'Too much, I'm sure. He's a creature of habit.'

'Did you give him champagne?'

'"What gentleman stints his guests?" – as you are so fond of saying. Yes, he had champagne and whisky and soda. He is your brother.'

'You are not my brother's housekeeper.'

She turned to me and drew me into the hallway. 'How are you, Arthur? You look so well.' She took my coat and umbrella. 'How is Touie? Is she gaining strength? I hope so. How are the children? How was your Christmas? There's so much to ask. You were in Switzerland, I know. You must tell me all about it. You have been skiing. I long for Oscar to take us skiing. The boys would love it.'

'Where are the boys?' asked Oscar, removing his own coat and pacing about the hallway like a cat on the prowl.

'In Oakley Street, visiting your mother.'

'My sons are with my mother and my brother is with you. This has all the makings of a tragedy by Euripides.'

Constance smiled. 'Your brother came with a purpose,' she said.

'What? He wants to borrow money.'

'No. He wants you to go to his wedding.'

'I've already told him I can't go to all his weddings. I went to the last and I may go to the next. I shall sit this one out.'

Constance went over to her husband and put her hands on

his shoulders to calm him. 'He came to ask me to intercede on his behalf,' she said soothingly. 'He says you will adore his new wife.'

'I doubt it. From all I hear he doesn't like her very much himself. He's only marrying her because he has to. A not-so-happy event is in the offing, I imagine. He wants me to be there to add a veneer of respectability to the proceedings.' Oscar caught my eye in the hallway mirror and addressed me over Constance's shoulder: 'His first wife was an American lady, considerably older than Willie, considerably wealthier, and *considerably* more energetic. Willie was her fourth husband and she made short shrift of him, throwing him out of the house after eight months and telling the world he was of no use to her, "either by day or by night".' Oscar laughed.

'Come now, Oscar,' said Constance, putting her finger to her husband's lips to hush him.

'You know it's true, my dear. Willie's hopeless and I pity any woman who marries him. This new girl is Irish and frail and penniless. It's a fatal combination. The marriage is doomed before it's started.' Oscar broke away from Constance and gave a heavy, weary sigh. 'I'm not going to Willie's wedding and that's that. I'm going to lie down. You can look after Arthur. I offered him a drink at the Langham, but he said he wanted tea – so we're here. We can't stay long. We have an appointment at six.'

And with that Oscar disappeared up the stairs and into his oriental smoking-cum-dressing room.

Constance watched him go and then turned back to me. 'We had a very happy time at Christmas. Bosie has gone to Egypt, you know – at Oscar's suggestion – and life here has been much calmer as a consequence.' She took me by the hand. 'We shall have tea, Arthur, and perhaps a game of cards, and you must tell me all about the family – and your new book. I'm sure you have a new book. I'm writing one, you know.'

I sat with Constance in the white dining room and we talked. She told me about the book of fairy tales that she was writing and about her boys and their progress at school, and I told her about the book that I had been writing about my life as a doctor and about my small ones – and about my fears for Touie and her tuberculosis. We played no cards: we needed no distraction. We took tea – Constance prepared it for me herself – and we chatted – comfortably, as good friends – and I cannot recall a happier afternoon.

At half past five, as the clock on the sideboard chimed, I asked, 'Should we be rousing Oscar, do you think?'

'He'll be down in a moment, I'm sure,' she said. 'If it's the policeman you are seeing, Oscar won't want to be late. He's been anxious about the interview. I don't know why. Has he anything to fear, do you know?'

'I'm sure not.'

'We have money worries, you know.'

'What author doesn't?'

'He seemed quite content over Christmas and then he got this note from the policeman who lives here in Tite Street and he's been anxious ever since. He moved back to the Langham Hotel on Saturday. He's been quite distracted. It's my birthday tomorrow. I know he won't remember.'

'I shall remind him,' I said.

'Please don't,' she said. 'He doesn't like me growing older.'

5

9 Tite Street

'How has your afternoon been, gentlemen?'

Melville Macnaghten had answered his own front door when we had pulled his doorbell on the very stroke of six. He helped us off with our coats and ushered us immediately into his study: a 'man's room', book-lined, comfortably untidy, lit by gaslight, and smelling, reassuringly, of burning logs and pipe smoke. In Oscar's study the walls were painted pale primrose and the woodwork deep red. Here the predominant colour was brown. Macnaghten himself was dressed all in brown: brown suit, brown tie, brown boots. Even his handsome face had a brown tinge to it. He looked like a man who had spent a good few years in the southern hemisphere.

'I have rested,' said Oscar, accepting a glass of brown sherry from our host – having surveyed the sideboard to ascertain that nothing paler or more interesting was likely to be on offer. 'My friend, Dr Conan Doyle, has been flirting with my wife. He's a married man, but wholly irresponsible. Nowadays I find that all the married men I know behave like bachelors and all the bachelors behave like married men.'

Oscar stood in front of Melville Macnaghten's fireplace as though it were his own. If he was anxious about the forthcoming interview, he betrayed no sign of it.

'And how has your afternoon been, Chief Constable?' I asked.

'Grim,' he answered, indicating a leather armchair at the side of his desk for me to sit in. I took my place and, as I did so, on the desk I noticed a bundle of papers, on top of which was a file marked with one word: 'WILDE'.

Macnaghten perched himself against the edge of the desk and sucked on his unlit pipe. 'Grim,' he repeated, 'grim and unsatisfactory. We've taken the body to the morgue and searched the alley. No sign of a murder weapon. No sign of anything, beyond the poor woman's blood and some buttons from her torn clothing. Nothing else. We'll search some more in the morning, by daylight. We have no idea who she might be. None whatsoever.'

'No wedding ring?' asked Oscar.

'No jewellery of any kind,' said Macnaghten. 'No one has been reported missing and the house-to-house inquiries have yielded nothing so far.'

'I don't believe she is a prostitute,' I said. 'My examination was only cursory, as you know, but there was no obvious evidence of a carnal encounter – at least not a recent one. She had been foully mutilated, but, from what I could tell at a glance, the outward condition of her private parts suggested that she was continent in her personal life.'

Oscar raised his sherry glass towards me. 'You have both a quick eye for detail and a delicate way with words, Arthur. I salute you.'

Macnaghten placed his pipe in the pipe-rack on his desk and drummed his fingers softly on his pile of paperwork. 'You will write a report for me, won't you, Doctor?'

'Tonight, sir. Without fail.'

'Thank you.' He turned to Oscar, smiling. 'And now, Mr Wilde, to business.'

'Yes,' said Oscar eagerly, lighting a fresh cigarette and throwing the spent match into the fire grate with a flourish. 'Jack the Ripper. The curtain rises . . .'

'Yes, "Jack the Ripper" – how I loathe the name,' said Macnaghten, shaking his head wearily. 'But loathe it as I might, it has caught the public's imagination, there's no denying it – and we must either catch the man or prove him dead, or this "Jack the Ripper" business will go on for ever.'

'It's a telling name,' said Oscar, 'that is why it has caught the public's imagination. It has a ring to it – like Oliver Twist. And it touches something deep in all of us, going right back to the mythic figures of our childhood. Jack-o'-lantern, Jack and Jill, Jack the Giant-killer . . . Jack the Ripper, Jack the Ripper, Jack the Ripper. Say it softly. Say it slowly. Say it as night falls. The name tells you everything you need to know.'

'Where does it come from?' I asked, as crisply as I could, sensing that Macnaghten might not be appreciating the relish with which Oscar was repeating the name.

'From a letter and a postcard sent to the Central News Agency at the height of the killings and purporting to come from the killer himself.'

'But not coming from him?'

'We don't know. There's a great deal we don't know.' The policeman drummed his fingers lightly on his file of papers once more. 'That's why I have been charged with producing a report – a definitive report – that eliminates the speculation – of which there is a great deal – and focuses on the facts – which, unfortunately, are very few.'

'You will unmask "Jack the Ripper",' announced Oscar, raising his glass towards the policeman. 'I know it.'

'I will produce a report on the "Whitechapel murders", as we refer to them at Scotland Yard, and I will leave no stone unturned, that's all I know.'

'How many "Whitechapel murders" have there been?' I asked.

'There are eleven in all on the file, committed between the third of April 1888 and the thirteenth of February 1891.'

'And all the work of the same inhuman hand?'

'Probably not. Certainly not, in my view. Five of the murders are remarkably similar in terms of the killer's modus operandi – with deep cuts to the throat, specific knife marks on the face, mutilation of the abdomen and private parts, the removal of internal organs—'

'Enough,' cried Oscar, closing his eyes.

'Grotesque,' I said.

Macnaghten nodded. 'Grotesque and distinctive. That's the point. The other six involve strangulation, decapitation – all kinds of horror – but they don't carry the unique hallmarks of a Jack the Ripper killing.'

'Who was the first victim?' I asked.

'The first two murders on the file are those of Emma Smith and Martha Tabram. Smith was robbed and sexually assaulted in Osborn Street, Whitechapel. That was on the third of April 1888.'

'It was Easter, was it not?' said Oscar, opening his eyes.

'The Easter weekend, yes,' said Macnaghten. 'A blunt instrument was thrust into her private parts rupturing her peritoneum.

She survived the attack, but died in hospital the following day of peritonitis.'

'Was she able to describe her assailant before she died?' I asked.

'She said there were two of them, possibly three. She could not describe them in any useful way, but she was certain there was more than one. Months after the event, the newspapers decided to link Smith's murder to the Jack the Ripper killings – without good cause.'

'I believe nothing that I read in the newspapers,' said Oscar, gazing into his empty sherry glass. 'Journalists get everything wrong, in my experience. Instead of monopolising the seat of judgement, journalism should be apologising in the dock.'

'Emma Smith was brutally murdered,' said Macnaghten, 'but by a gang, not by Jack the Ripper.'

'And Martha Tabram?' I asked.

'She was murdered on the seventh of August 1888, in George Yard, Whitechapel, not far from Osborn Street. She is more likely to have been one of the Ripper's victims, but I do not believe that she was.'

'Why not?'

'The Ripper slashed his victims,' said Macnaghten, lifting his pipe from the rack and sawing the air with it. 'Martha Tabram was stabbed in the throat and the abdomen – repeatedly.' He used the pipe to make a short, sharp stabbing gesture. 'She was stabbed thirty-nine times in all.'

I looked up at the chief constable. 'Yes,' he said, smiling. 'An interesting coincidence, but after more than five years and in a quite different part of town, I don't see that it can be anything more.'

'Really?' I said, both puzzled and perturbed.

'Really,' replied the policeman emphatically. He got to his feet and collected the sherry decanter from the sideboard. 'A little more, Mr Wilde?'

'Thank you,' said Oscar. 'I can resist everything except temptation.'

'And your five undoubted victims?' I enquired.

'Five women, all prostitutes, savagely murdered and mutilated in very similar circumstances, within a few streets of one another, within a few weeks of one another, between the thirty-first of August and the ninth of November 1888: Mary Ann Nichols, Annie Chapman, Elizabeth Stride, Catherine Eddowes and Mary Jane Kelly.'

'You know the names by heart.'

'I do. I know the details of each case by heart.'

'Five murders,' said Oscar. 'And how many suspects?'

'Five dozen – five score. More! Hundreds, if you take into account all the speculative possibilities raised by a sensationalist press. Most, of course, are utterly fantastical and don't merit a second glance.'

'But how many do?'

Macnaghten hesitated a moment. 'About twenty individuals in all, no more.'

'And of those,' I asked, 'how many are on your personal list of chief suspects, Chief Constable?'

'Just five. I'm narrowing the field.'

'Anyone we know?' asked Oscar lightly.

'Yes, Mr Wilde, several that you know. That is the point. That is why you are here.'

6

'Am I a suspect?'

O scar looked about Macnaghten's study as though seeking an invisible audience whose applause he might acknowledge. 'Am I a suspect?' he asked, turning towards our host and widening his eyes. 'I rather hope I might be. There's only one thing worse than being talked about and that is not being talked about.'

'This is no laughing matter, Oscar,' I said reprovingly.

'You are not a suspect so far as I am concerned, Mr Wilde, but I do have to tell you that, as I work on my report and consider each suspect in turn, your name keeps cropping up.'

'I'm intrigued,' said Oscar. 'Tell me more, Chief Constable. It seems I know all the wrong people.'

'Oh no,' said Macnaghten, with a dry laugh. 'From our investigation's point of view, you know all the right people, Mr Wilde.'

'Is my friend Sickert, the artist, on your list? I imagine he is.'

'He was, briefly, but he is no longer.'

Oscar turned to me to explain. 'Wat Sickert lived close to

Whitechapel and walked the streets – wearing a long great coat and a tall top hat. Some children caught sight of him and began shouting, "Jack the Ripper! Jack the Ripper!" That's all it takes. Wat looks the part of a stage villain, I grant you, but he's the sweetest creature underneath that curled and waxed moustache.'

'We ascertained that Mr Sickert was in France at the time of the murders,' said Macnaghten. 'He was never a serious candidate, but we try to follow every lead. We hear rumours: we investigate.'

'I suppose poor Prince Eddy is on your list?' said Oscar.

'The late Duke of Clarence and Avondale does feature on the long list, unfortunately, yes.'

'I barely knew him,' said Oscar. 'He was the heir presumptive so, naturally, I didn't presume. He had a chequered career, I know, and a very weak chin, but I didn't see him as a multiple murderer, did you? He was Queen Victoria's grandson, after all.'

Macnaghten said nothing. He was now holding the file marked 'Wilde' in both hands.

'Beyond Sickert and poor Prince Eddy, can there be anybody else on your list that I might know?' Oscar asked the question looking genuinely puzzled.

'Oh, yes,' said the chief constable.

'Who?'

'You will see.' The policeman leaned forward and presented the file he was holding to Oscar. 'I have prepared these notes for you, Mr Wilde. Study them, if you will – at your leisure. They include the names of those I regard as the key suspects. You will find that more than one of them is known to you personally.'

Oscar took the policeman's dossier and gazed down at it, seemingly bewildered. 'Why are you entrusting me with this?' he asked.

'Quite simply, because I need your help, Mr Wilde. You will

know some of these people and you will know them better than I do. You will know them and their circles. You may even know their secrets. I have read your novel, Mr Wilde: *The Picture of Dorian Gray*. You understand what moves a man to murder. I will be grateful for your thoughts.'

'I am not a detective, Chief Constable.'

'No, but you are a poet, a Freemason and a man of the world. All useful qualifications for the business in hand.'

Oscar made to protest, but Macnaghten stopped him. 'You have a poet's eye, Mr Wilde, and that means you can see the facts and then make a leap of the imagination beyond the reach of us mere plodding policemen. The detectives of the Criminal Investigations Department of the Metropolitan Police are not known for their intellectual acuity, whereas you are considered one of the most brilliant men of your generation. You have won every academic prize open to you and have secured a double first from Oxford University. I have not.' Macnaghten stretched out his right hand towards Oscar. 'Will you help me?'

Oscar took the proffered hand and shook it warmly. 'Of course,' he said with emotion. With his other hand he clutched the chief constable's file to his breast. 'I will study this material carefully and do whatever I can to assist you – though it may not be much.' He glanced in my direction and then added, more hesitantly: 'May I share the contents of the file with Dr Conan Doyle?'

'I very much hope that you will,' said Macnaghten, smiling. 'When I discovered this afternoon that you and Dr Doyle were friends, I'll confess that the notion of having both Oscar Wilde and the creator of Sherlock Holmes on the case seemed almost too good to be true. I will be most grateful for your joint assistance – and I know that I can rely on your complete confidentiality.'

'Naturally, sir,' I said.

'Of course,' said Oscar, more diffidently, adding, after a moment's pause, 'Though perhaps, in the fullness of time, as authors we might be permitted to use some of what we have learned . . .' My friend let his sentence trail off into a nothingness.

'You want to write about all this?' said Macnaghten doubtfully. 'Let us cross that bridge as and when we reach it. We are conducting a murder investigation here, Mr Wilde, not conjuring up a murder mystery.'

'I understand,' said Oscar, duly chastened.

'You may depend on us,' I said, getting to my feet, sensing that our interview was at a close.

'Let's meet again shortly,' said Macnaghten, 'when you have had an opportunity to consider the file. We can meet here rather than at Scotland Yard. It's more discreet.' I nodded our agreement. 'And you won't forget to let me have your notes from this afternoon, will you, Doctor?'

'You will have them tomorrow,' I said, 'without fail.'

Oscar drained his sherry glass and returned it to the sideboard. 'May I ask one question,' he said quietly, 'before we leave you?'

'By all means,' answered Macnaghten amiably.

'Why now? These foul murders took place in 1888, six years ago. Why this sudden renewed interest in them?'

'I don't think the interest in them has ever gone away, Mr Wilde. Our sensationalist press has made sure of that. Are you familiar with Mr George R. Sims?'

'Of course. I know him personally, though not well.'

'He has been the leader of the pack. Week in, week out, in his column in *The Referee* he returns to the subject of Jack the Ripper like a dog to a bone. There's nothing new to be said, but that doesn't trouble him. Gleefully he reports that the police continue to make no progress and then fuels empty speculation with lurid conjecture. Every paragraph he writes undermines the authority of the Metropolitan Constabulary. It's bad and it's set to get worse.'

'Worse?'

'You mentioned the Duke of Clarence. As you know, His Royal Highness passed away two years ago. He was just twenty-eight.'

Oscar shrugged. 'The clap shows no respect for age.'

'It was not gonorrhoea, Mr Wilde. It was pneumonia. There is no doubt about that.'

Oscar smiled.

'But you are right,' the chief constable continued imperturbably. 'There were rumours . . .'

'There always are.'

'And since you cannot libel the dead, now the young prince has gone, people are free to say whatever they choose about him – however outrageous. His Royal Highness's thirtieth birthday would have fallen next week, on the eighth of January, and our understanding is that the *Sun* newspaper is planning to run a scurrilous series of articles to mark the anniversary. The Prince of Wales is understandably concerned that newspaper stories linking his eldest son with Jack the Ripper could tarnish the crown . . .'

Oscar raised an eyebrow. 'And might even threaten the throne?'

'Look at France,' said the policeman solemnly. 'Look at Russia. We live in uncertain times, Mr Wilde. Even the oldest monarchies can take nothing for granted.'

'The Prince of Wales has shared these concerns with you?'

'No, he has shared them with certain senior politicians who have shared them with the Metropolitan Police Commissioner who has instructed me to discover the truth of the matter – if I can. Or, if I cannot, at least to produce a report detailing exactly what we do and do not know, narrowing the field of suspects and eliminating all those we know for certain cannot possibly be this "Jack the Ripper" – the late Duke of Clarence being one such. "Eliminate all other factors, and the one which remains must be the truth." Isn't that one of Sherlock Holmes's maxims?'

'It is, indeed,' I said, as Macnaghten escorted us into the hallway. He handed me my overcoat and helped Oscar on with his.

'May I ask a question?' he added, as he opened the front door to see us on our way. 'I know it was your little joke, Mr Wilde, but why, earlier, did you say, "Am I a suspect?" What made you think of such a thing?'

Oscar looked Macnaghten directly in the eye: 'A man has been following me for several months past. He has kept his distance. I have not seen his face. I do not know who he is, but he has something of the manner of a policeman about him. I thought perhaps he was one of your detectives, Chief Constable.'

'No, Mr Wilde; whoever he is, he's not one of mine. I can assure you of that.'

The heavy rain had stopped, but a drizzly fog had now descended on the darkened street. By the smudged pale yellow light of its lamps we found Oscar's four-wheeler waiting for us exactly where we had left it five hours before. It took us forty minutes to travel back to the Langham Hotel.

'Stay the night,' said Oscar as the cab pulled away. 'You will be my guest, old friend.' Beyond that, he said nothing.

7

Five only

We stood in the gas-lit lobby of the hotel and bade one another goodnight. My friend, so exuberant for most of the day, looked weary.

'Forgive me, Arthur. I am not in the giving vein tonight. We can talk it all through in the morning, can't we?'

'We can.'

'You will stay the night, won't you? As my guest.'

'If they have a room, I'll stay the night, of course. But not as your guest. You're wanton with money, Oscar. You over-tipped the cabman quite ludicrously. Your extravagance will ruin you.'

He smiled wanly as we shook hands. 'Surely, it is the ruins the tourists most want to visit.'

The Langham had a room and I took it. I ordered myself a simple supper of bread and cheese and pickle, and a glass of beer, and, as I had promised the chief constable, set about writing up my notes on the body of the murdered woman that I had examined at the beginning of the afternoon. As I worked, the poor unfortunate wretch's scarred and bloodied face settled in my mind's eye. I found the only way to shift the dreadful image was instead to picture the smiling face of Constance Wilde. I was reflecting on her uncomplicated loveliness – and on the sweetness of her nature – when there was a sharp knock on my bedroom door. It was Oscar.

He looked brighter than he had done an hour before. 'Macnaghten's file,' he said, handing it to me. 'I've read it.'

'Already?'

'I'm a quick study, as you know.'

'You've read it all?'

'I am leaving the details to you. I have the colour of it.' He grinned and revealed his none-too-gainly teeth. 'And perhaps an answer to one of the mysteries, too.'

'You amaze me.'

'I have nothing to declare but my genius,' he said complacently. '"It was the best of crimes, it was the worst of crimes", as you'll see. Goodnight, Arthur.'

I closed the door on my friend, sat back on my bed and opened the policeman's dossier.

To: OW
From: MM
Date: 01/01/94 <u>STRICTLY CONFIDENTIAL</u>

<u>WHITECHAPEL MURDERS</u>

<u>Background</u>

Whitechapel is the poorest parish in London's
East End. Drunkenness and vice are rife.
Respect for the law is low and good policing
consequently difficult to achieve. Violence
is commonplace and murder far from unknown.
Brewing, distilling, iron-founding, floor-
cloth manufacture, dyeing and prostitution
are the local industries. There are four
churches in the parish and sixty-two known
brothels. Some 1,200 women work the streets,
notably in the areas close to the bathhouses,
the sailors' home, the workhouse, the boys'
refuge and the Jews' orphan asylum.

Human life is cheap in Whitechapel. Women
are the victims of assault on an everyday
basis. Even when crimes are reported, most
remain unsolved. Rightly or wrongly, the
killing of a dozen females within a matter of
months would not have been considered out of
the ordinary in this district, but for two
factors:

- the brutal nature of the killings and the degree of mutilation involved
- the notion that the killings were the work of one man, the so-called 'Jack the Ripper'

My report is to be concerned with eleven deaths in all, but it is my firm belief that five of the murders – and five only – were committed by the same hand.

THE FIVE VICTIMS

MARY ANN NICHOLLS

Body found at 3.40 a.m. on Friday 31 August 1888 in Buck's Row, Whitechapel.

Throat severed by two cuts; abdomen ripped open; assorted abdominal knife wounds.

No worthwhile witnesses.

ANNIE CHAPMAN

Body found at 6.00 a.m. on Saturday 8 September 1888 at the rear of 29 Hanbury Street, Whitechapel.

Throat severed by two cuts; abdomen ripped open; private parts mutilated; uterus removed; entrails placed around victim's neck.

Witness saw a dark-haired man of 'shabby-genteel' appearance with the victim at about 5.30 a.m.

ELIZABETH STRIDE

Body found at 1.00 a.m. on Sunday 30
September 1888 in Dutfield's Yard, off Berner
Street, Whitechapel.

Throat severed by one cut only and no
mutilation to abdomen. It would seem that the
murderer was disturbed by some Jews who drove
up to a Jewish club nearby and that he then,
mordum satiatus, went in search of a second
victim — see below.

Witnesses give differing accounts of seeing
Elizabeth Stride on the Saturday night —
some say with a fair-haired man, some with a
dark, some say he was well-dressed, some say
shabbily dressed; estimates of his age also
vary.

CATHERINE EDDOWES

Body found at 1.45 a.m. on Sunday 30 September
1888 in Mitre Square, City of London.

Throat severed by one cut; abdomen cut
open; uterus and left kidney removed; severe
mutilation to body and face.

Witness claimed to have seen victim in
the square with a fair-haired man of medium
height, aged about thirty, dress suggesting
a sailor, not long before the murder, but
his two companions at the time could neither
confirm nor deny.

Part of the victim's clothing — a bloodied
piece of her apron — was found later in

Goulston Street, Whitechapel, with near it, on a wall, a message written in chalk: 'The Juwes are The men That Will not be Blamed For nothing'.

On 1 October, a postcard claiming responsibility for these two murders and referring to them as a 'double event' was received at the offices of the Central News Agency in New Bridge Street, Ludgate Circus, London EC. It was signed 'Jack the Ripper'. It followed an earlier letter to the Central News Agency, also claiming to be from 'Jack the Ripper', received on 27 September, though dated 25 September. It was this letter and postcard – published in facsimile by the Metropolitan Police in the hope that a member of the public might recognise the handwriting – that gave common currency to the name 'Jack the Ripper'. (I shall include the facsimile among the papers in this file.)

MARY JANE KELLY
Body found at 10.45 a.m. on Friday 9 November 1888 on Kelly's bed in her room at 13 Miller's Court, off Dorset Street.

Throat severed to the spine; abdomen cut open; abdominal organs removed; heart removed. Mutilation of the most horrific kind.

No useful witnesses.

Attached you will find the coroners' reports
for each of these five murders. They make grim
reading. You will notice that the fury of
the mutilations increased in each case, the
appetite seemingly sharpened by indulgence.

Also attached are the more relevant
'witness statements' secured by the police —
such as they are.

THE INVESTIGATION

In the history of policing in this country,
I do not believe any investigation has been
conducted as exhaustively as in the case
of the Whitechapel murders. The husbands,
lovers, relatives, clients and associates
of the women have all had their stories and
alibis tested. Because of the nature of the
mutilations, butchers, slaughtermen, surgeons,
physicians and medical students have been
questioned. (The London Hospital is located
in Whitechapel.) All types and conditions of
men have been interviewed — from gentlemen
known to frequent the locality after hours to
vagrants, Poles, Russians and sailors passing
through — upwards of 2,000 individuals
in all. More than 300 potential suspects
have been investigated. Of those, eighty
were detained for detailed examination. No
stone has been left unturned — and yet no

worthwhile evidence of any kind has been
found to link anyone with these horrific
crimes.

Of all the material I have considered while
preparing my report, the most useful, in my
estimation, has been the following from Dr
Thomas Bond, the police surgeon who conducted
the post-mortem examination of the last
victim, Mary Kelly. One of my predecessors in
charge of the matter, Assistant Commissioner
Robert Anderson, provided Dr Bond with the
papers relating to the earlier Whitechapel
murders and asked for his considered opinion.
This was his reply:

> 7 The Sanctuary, Westminster Abbey
> November 10th '88

Dear Sir,
Whitechapel Murders

*I beg to report that I have read the notes of the four Whitechapel
Murders viz:*

1. Buck's Row.

2. Hanbury Street.

3. Berner Street.

4. Mitre Square.

*I have also made a Post Mortem Examination of the mutilated
remains of a woman found yesterday in a small room in Dorset
Street —*

1. *All five murders were no doubt committed by the same hand. In the first four the throats appear to have been cut from left to right. In the last case, owing to the extensive mutilation, it is impossible to say in what direction the fatal cut was made, but arterial blood was found on the wall in splashes close to where the woman's head must have been lying.*

2. *All the circumstances surrounding the murders lead me to form the opinion that the women must have been lying down when murdered and in every case the throat was first cut.*

3. *In the four murders of which I have seen the notes only, I cannot form a very definite opinion as to the time that had elapsed between the murder and the discovery of the body.*

In one case, that of Berner Street, the discovery appears to have been made immediately after the deed — in Buck's Row, Hanbury Street and Mitre Square three or four hours only could have elapsed. In the Dorset Street case the body was lying on the bed at the time of my visit, 2 o'clock, quite naked and mutilated as in the annexed report.

Rigor mortis had set in, but increased during the progress of the examination. From this it is difficult to say with any degree of certainty the exact time that had elapsed since death as the period varies from six to twelve hours before rigidity sets in. The body was comparatively cold at 2 o'clock and the remains of a recently taken meal were found in the stomach and scattered about over the intestines. It is, therefore, pretty certain that the woman must have been dead about twelve hours and the partly digested food would indicate that death took place about three or four hours after the food was taken, so one or two o'clock in the morning would be the probable time of the murder.

4. *In all the cases there appears to be no evidence of struggling and the attacks were probably so sudden and made in such a*

position that the women could neither resist nor cry out. In the Dorset Street case the corner of the sheet to the right of the woman's head was much cut and saturated with blood, indicating that the face may have been covered with the sheet at the time of the attack.

5. In the four first cases the murderer must have attacked from the right side of the victim. In the Dorset Street case, he must have attacked from in front or from the left, as there would be no room for him between the wall and the part of the bed on which the woman was lying. Again, the blood had flowed down on the right side of the woman and spurted on to the wall.

6. The murderer would not necessarily be splashed or deluged with blood, but his hands and arms must have been covered and parts of his clothing must certainly have been smeared with blood.

7. The mutilations in each case excepting the Berner Street one were all of the same character and showed clearly that in all the murders, the object was mutilation.

8. In each case the mutilation was inflicted by a person who had no scientific nor anatomical knowledge. In my opinion he does not even possess the technical knowledge of a butcher or horse slaughterer or any person accustomed to cutting up dead animals.

9. The instrument must have been a strong knife at least six inches long, very sharp, pointed at the top and about an inch in width. It may have been a clasp knife, a butcher's knife or a surgeon's knife. I think it was no doubt a straight knife.

10. The murderer must have been a man of physical strength and of great coolness and daring. There is no evidence that he had an accomplice. He must in my opinion be a man subject to periodical attacks of Homicidal and Erotic Mania. The character of the mutilations indicate that the man may be in a condition sexually, that may be called satyriasis. It is of course possible that the Homicidal impulse may have developed from a revengeful or brooding condition of the mind, or that Religious Mania may have been the original disease, but I do not think either hypothesis is likely. The murderer in external appearance is quite likely to be a quiet, inoffensive-looking man, probably middle-aged and neatly and respectably dressed. I think he must be in the habit of wearing a cloak or overcoat or he could hardly have escaped notice in the streets if the blood on his hands or clothes were visible.

11. Assuming the murderer to be such a person as I have just described he would probably be solitary and eccentric in his habits, also he is most likely to be a man without regular occupation, but with some small income or pension. He is possibly living among respectable persons who have some knowledge of his character and habits and who may have grounds for suspicion that he is not quite right in his mind at times. Such persons would probably be unwilling to communicate suspicions to the Police for fear of trouble or notoriety, whereas if there were a prospect of reward it might overcome their scruples.

I am, Dear Sir,
Yours faithfully,
Thos. Bond

THE SUSPECTS

Dr Bond is a police surgeon of considerable experience and a shrewd observer of human nature. My instinct is that our killer will prove to be some such individual as he describes: male, middle-aged, physically strong, solitary, eccentric in his habits, without a regular occupation but with a small income, inoffensive in appearance, possibly living among respectable persons, though committing his crimes without an accomplice.

Who are our principal suspects? After considering scores of possibilities, I have reduced the list to just five – and I would very much like to be able to eliminate one or two of these before presenting my report to the Metropolitan Police Commissioner.

The five are as follows:

- MONTAGUE JOHN DRUITT
- AARON KOSMINSKI
- RICHARD MANSFIELD
- MICHAEL OSTROG
- WALTER WELLBELOVED

Attached you will find a separate file on each of these men. Your thoughts – and any additional information – regarding any of the above will be much appreciated.

Also attached are notes on certain other murders that took place in Whitechapel (and beyond) between April 1888 and February 1891, including the notorious 'torso killings'. I do not believe they are relevant to this inquiry, as you know, but I supply them as background for reasons of 'completeness'. Also attached are notes relating to two other suspects: HRH the Duke of Clarence

and John Pizer, the man known locally as
'Leather Apron'. I have included these for
your interest, not because we consider
them likely suspects, but in case you have
additional information that could assist us
in eliminating them altogether from our list
of possibilities.

8

Breakfast at the Langham

'A larmingly, I think I may know them all.'
'All five of Macnaghten's suspects?'
'Certainly four. I was at Oxford with one of them.'

I had come down to the hotel dining room just before nine o'clock and, to my astonishment, found Oscar already ensconced at a window table, smoking one of his Turkish cigarettes, with the detritus of a full breakfast before him. He was not naturally an early riser, but there he was, bright-eyed and newly shaved, sporting a cream-coloured shirt, a lilac tie and a white amaryllis in his buttonhole.

'I have eaten for both of us,' he declared happily. 'Poached eggs, bacon, kidneys, mushroom, the works. I had no dinner. I was famished.' He dropped his copy of the *Daily Chronicle* onto the floor beside him and beckoned me to sit down. 'There's coffee in the pot, my friend, and fresh toast is on its way. The marmalade may be a little bitter to your taste, but I know you like a challenge to rise to.'

Oscar was fond of saying that 'only dull people are brilliant at breakfast', but I have to report that on this particular morning he was on sparkling form – and far from dull.

'It is my wife's birthday today. I have sent her a telegram.'

'I am happy to hear it,' I said, taking my place opposite him and pouring myself some coffee. 'Shouldn't you be having breakfast with her?' I asked.

'Oh, heavens no. A husband and wife should never share breakfast ... those tedious tête-a-têtes that are the dream of engaged couples and the despair of married men ... that eternal duologue about bills and babies.' He drew deep on his cigarette. 'I want to have breakfast with you, Arthur, and talk about murder.' He said the word with relish. 'Besides, I am seeing Constance tonight.'

'I'm glad to hear it.'

'I am taking her and the boys to the circus.'

'Excellent, Oscar. Does she know?'

'When she receives my telegram, she will. It's the Russian Circus at Olympia.'

'I've read about it,' I said approvingly. 'Apparently, it's "the greatest show on earth".'

'I thought *Aladdin* at Drury Lane was supposed to be that. But never mind. I hope the boys will enjoy it. There are tigers and knife-throwers. And Constance likes anything Russian. You must come, too, Arthur. There'll be clowns.'

'I enjoy the circus.'

'I have a box.'

'A box?' I repeated, impressed.

'I have friends in high places.' He chuckled and narrowed his eyes conspiratorially. 'Well, I know the ringmaster. In life, I've found, it's always useful to know the ringmaster. This one kindly supplies my caviar.'

A rack of fresh toast arrived and, as I took a piece and began to butter it, I noticed Oscar glance suddenly out of the window. 'Are you looking for the man who has been following you?' I asked.

'Yes,' he replied, 'and he's not there. He was there last night, but he's not there now.'

'Are you sure you're being followed?'

'No,' he said, stubbing out his lighted cigarette and immediately reaching inside his cigarette case for an unlighted one. 'Far from it. I have a vivid imagination and a guilty conscience.' He struck a Vesta and smiled at me. 'I see you've brought Macnaghten's file. Good. Let us forget the spectres that may or may not be haunting me and speak of murder . . . murder most foul.'

I looked around the dining room. The tables were gradually emptying. The waiters were moving to and fro, busying themselves at a safe distance.

'Open the file,' Oscar instructed. 'Who's top of his list? Is it Druitt? He's the one I knew at Oxford. What does Macnaghten say?'

I opened the dossier and read as discreetly as I could: 'Montague John Druitt, said to be a doctor and of good family—'

Oscar interrupted. 'I don't think he was a doctor. I think he was a lawyer. The police know nothing.' He shook his head.

I continued reading: 'Druitt disappeared at the time of the Miller's Court murder. His body, which was said to have been upwards of a month in the water, was found in the Thames on the thirty-first of December or about seven weeks after that murder.'

I hesitated. 'Go on,' urged Oscar, clearly recalling what came next.

I read on: 'He was sexually insane and from private information I have little doubt but that his own family believed him to have been the murderer.'

'Sexually insane,' mused Oscar, a little too loudly for my liking, while exhaling a thin plume of purple cigarette smoke and looking around the dining room. I sensed he hoped someone would hear him and be suitably shocked. 'What on earth does Macnaghten mean by "sexually insane"?'

'I don't know,' I said, *sotto voce.*

'I do, I fear,' said Oscar. 'I remember Druitt. He was a good-looking young man and a fine sportsman, but he was not – how shall I put it? – of the marrying kind.'

'He was an invert?'

'He was a man who loved other men. I think if we do a little bit of investigating, Arthur, we shall find that is what drove the poor fellow to throw himself into the Thames. Who's next?'

I looked down at Macnaghten's notes. 'Aaron Kosminski.'

'Ah, yes. He is the one I don't know. At least, the name rings no bells. I believe I did once get my hair cut in Whitechapel, so, who knows, I may have made his acquaintance. One of the advantages of being known for over-tipping is that you don't feel vulnerable in the barber's chair. Read on.'

'Aaron Kosminski, a Polish Jew, resident in Whitechapel where he worked as a hairdresser. He became insane owing to many years' indulgence in solitary vices. He had a great hatred of women, especially of the prostitute class, and was removed to a lunatic asylum around March 1889.'

'The police are so predictable. They find a lonely lunatic who happens to be a hairdresser as well as a misfit and, suddenly, without a shred of evidence, he's "The Demon Barber of Whitechapel".'

'The killings are clearly the work of a disordered mind,' I protested.

'Are they? If they are, there's method in the madness.'

I read on: '*There are many circumstances connected with this man that make him a strong suspect.*'

'Indeed,' cried Oscar. 'I read them. He was about the right height and about the right age and he appears to have been resident in East London on the relevant dates – but so were hundreds of other men, so were thousands! There's "circumstance", there's no evidence.'

'He had a hatred of prostitutes that was well known.'

'I grant you that,' sniffed Oscar. 'Move on.'

'Richard Mansfield, actor.'

'I know him – and I believe his fondness for prostitutes is well known. It's absurd that he features on Macnaghten's list.'

'*Born in Germany.*'

'He must be guilty!'

'*American by nationality.*'

'Hang him!'

'*In New York in 1887 he played the title role in the stage adaptation of Dr Jekyll and Mr Hyde, a performance that made such a profound impression on the public he was invited to bring it to the Lyceum Theatre in London in 1888. As an actor, Mansfield is celebrated for the manner in which he inhabits every part he plays and he is known to have been within a mile of Whitechapel and to be without an alibi at the time of each of the five principal Whitechapel murders.*'

'He has also played the Lord High Executioner in *The Mikado* and King Richard III. It must be him.' Oscar picked up his table napkin and threw it down again. 'Next!'

I laughed and waited for the waiter who had come to clear our table to be out of earshot before continuing.

'Michael Ostrog.'

'Ah, yes,' said Oscar. 'This one's much more promising and neither an invert nor prone to solitary vices, but a proper homicidal maniac.'

'*A mad Russian doctor, a convict, unquestionably a homicidal maniac, said to have been habitually cruel to women and known to have carried about with him surgical knives and other instruments. His antecedents are of the very worst and his whereabouts at the time of the murders could never be satisfactorily accounted for. He was committed to the Surrey County Lunatic Asylum in 1891.*'

'We must pay him a visit.'

'Do you know him?'

'I'm not sure. I recognised the likeness, that's all. Show me.' From the back of Macnaghten's file, I produced the photograph of Ostrog. It was the drawn face of a man who looked fearful of life: his dark hair receded over a broad, lined brow, above deeply sunken eyes.

'Yes,' said Oscar, 'I know him. Without a doubt.' He returned the picture to me. 'Go on. The last of Macnaghten's candidates I know I know and I know I know him well.'

'Walter Wellbeloved.'

'Yes. Walter Wellbeloved. He's the reason for Macnaghten's reference to Freemasonry yesterday. You noticed it?'

'I did,' I said. 'It struck me as curious. If Macnaghten's a Mason—'

'He must be – all senior policemen are.'

'Well, if he is, why did he not signal as much when you introduced us? Why – since there were only three of us in the room – did he not address us as "brother"?'

'Perhaps he is as lapsed as we are, Arthur. Or perhaps I'm wrong and he isn't a Freemason, but he wanted to find a way to indicate to me – and to you – that he knows all my secrets ...' Oscar held up his cigarette between his thumb and his forefinger and studied the tip of smouldering ash. 'Leastways, Walter Wellbeloved is a Master Mason of the third degree.'

'And is that how you know him?'

'I know him through the Hermetic Order of the Golden Dawn.'

'He belongs to it?'

'He is one of the founders. The Order was conjured up by a small group of Rosicrucian Masons to allow – for the first time – men and women to work together *as equals* in magical ceremonies whose purpose was "to test, purify and exalt the individual's spiritual nature so as to unify it with his or her Holy Guardian Angel".'

'You know the mantra.'

'I was a member of the Order – for a brief while. Constance joined first and she persuaded me to follow. Some of the rituals were quite charming.'

'The Order is involved in magic?'

'And human sacrifice, if Macnaghten is to be believed. Read what he says.'

I turned back to the chief constable's file: '*Wellbeloved is a self-styled poet and philosopher who lives not far from Whitechapel and is the owner of a magic shop in Great Russell Street, close by the British Library. He professes to have powers of necromancy and is rumoured to conduct pagan ceremonies involving sexual perversity and (possibly) human sacrifice. He has been interviewed on several occasions, but has refused to give his whereabouts at the time of any of the Whitechapel murders.*'

Oscar sighed and shook his head wearily. 'Macnaghten has nothing to offer but the odd bit of circumstantial evidence, wild conjecture and his own curious obsession with sexual perversion, sexual insanity and solitary vice! I had hoped he was going to lead us to the unmasking of Jack the Ripper.' He gestured towards Macnaghten's file with a languid hand. 'Here he's simply set us off on a wild-goose chase – and I fear there won't be a golden egg at the end of it.'

I leafed through Macnaghten's papers. 'Should we consider what he's got to say about the Duke of Clarence and this man known as "Leather Apron"?'

'He's got nothing of substance to say about either of them. "Leather Apron"? What sort of sobriquet for a murderer is that? It's not quite in the same league as "Bluebeard" or "Jack the Ripper", is it? Poor John Pizer was another unfortunate Polish Jew. He was a bootmaker, so he wore a leather apron. Yes, he had a record of minor assaults against prostitutes, but he also had a copper-bottomed alibi for each murder.'

'I've read the notes. He was arrested.'

'And then released because there wasn't a shred of evidence against him. If you've read the notes, you'll recall the name of the policeman who arrested him.'

'I do. PC Thick.'

'Exactly.'

I closed Macnaghten's file. 'So, what are we to do, Oscar?'

'Discover what we can and share it with the chief constable. I suppose it is our duty as good citizens to do so. I am not hopeful that we will discover much.'

'You said last night that you thought you had an answer to something.'

'I say a lot of things, Arthur. As you should know by now, between me and life there is a mist of words always. I throw probability out of the window for the sake of a phrase, and the chance of an epigram makes me desert truth.'

'Well,' I said, folding my napkin and pushing my chair away from the table, 'in that case, I shall make my way over to Scotland Yard now. I must go to Macnaghten's office and give him the notes I've written up on the body I examined yesterday.'

'Ah, yes. That poor wretch in the alley.' Oscar leaned over and picked up his newspaper from the floor. 'She only merits a paragraph in the *Daily Chronicle*. Had she been killed in Whitechapel, there would have been headlines proclaiming "the return of Jack the Ripper" and page after page of lurid detail.'

I stood to take my leave. 'I will join you at the circus tonight,' I said.

Oscar banged the table with a show of delight. 'I'm glad. Constance will be glad. We'll meet you at seven o'clock by the box office.' He stretched out a hand to shake mine. 'And if you see Macnaghten, can you ask him if we might borrow the piece of torn apron that belonged to Catherine Eddowes? It was found in Goulston Street, I think. I assume the police will have kept it. Ask him if he can let us have it for twenty-four hours, no more.'

'I will, of course.' I picked up Macnaghten's file from the table. 'May I ask why?'

He smiled at me and gently tapped the side of his nose like a conspirator in a penny dreadful. 'I have my reasons, Dr Doyle.'

I looked at my friend doubtfully. 'This is not another of your games, is it, Oscar?'

He grinned. 'I think you'll approve of this one, Arthur.'

9

The Russian Circus

'I am always astonishing myself,' Oscar used to say. 'It is the only thing that makes life worth living.'

During the several years that I knew him, my friend never ceased to astonish me. He was a man full of surprises – and contradictions. He boasted of his lack of physical courage, but, on more than one occasion, proved very useful with his fists. He professed to despise 'the outdoor life', yet he joined me on long walks over the South Downs and, once, took me all the way to Sandwich in Kent to play a round of golf with him. He was a neglectful husband, and unfaithful to his wife, yet he loved her, beyond question, and, while often absent, when present he was a devoted father to his boys.

When I arrived at the circus that evening I found Oscar in the middle of the foyer, down on his haunches, sporting a clown's nose, and introducing his sons to a pair of bear cubs.

The boys were dressed, somewhat absurdly, in frilled shirts and velvet knickerbockers, in the manner of Little Lord Fauntleroy. The bears were standing on their hind legs and tethered by rope to an iron trivet overseen by a beautiful young acrobat in a sequin-covered leotard who, as I approached, bowed to me and then immediately bent over backwards and, with her head between her legs, greeted me with the words: *'Dobry vecher,* Dr Doyle.'

Oscar stood up, laughing, and pulled off his cardboard proboscis. 'This is Olga,' he said. 'She seems to know you, Dr Doyle.'

'I don't know how,' I said, bowing towards the young lady, who was upright once more. 'I am delighted to meet you,' I said, taking her hand.

'Dobro pozhalovat,' she replied, with a gentle smile and a tilt to her head that, I confess, I found wholly captivating.

'You will be seeing more of her later,' said Oscar teasingly. 'We are invited to join the company for a post-performance glass of tea – or vodka.'

'Can we come?' Cyril asked, pulling on his father's hand.

'No,' said Oscar, not unkindly. 'It's an invitation for gentlemen only. No boys.'

'Or wives?' asked Constance quietly.

I had not noticed her until then. She had been standing a little apart from the group. I turned towards her. She stepped forward, smiling. 'I am so pleased you could join us, Arthur. Oscar says you love the circus.'

'Happy birthday,' I said eagerly, tucking the parcel I was holding under my arm and taking both her hands in mine. She was wearing canary-yellow lace gloves and a bottle-green costume cut in the style of a huntsman's coat. 'You look wonderful,' I said.

She laughed. 'Well, it is the circus.'

A bell was being sounded. We looked around the foyer: a variety of the smaller animals from the circus's menagerie were on display, supervised by more young female acrobats in sequined leotards, some standing sentinel, two, I noticed, balancing on their hands on top of a cage that contained a sleeping leopard. A huge man, bearded and in uniform, dressed, it seemed, as Tsar Alexander III himself, was striding through the crowd on stilts, waving a handbell.

'It's extraordinary,' said Constance.

'It is rather splendid,' I agreed.

'It is time to find our seats,' said Oscar. 'I know the way, follow me.' He nodded towards our acrobat. '*Uvidimsya*, Olga.'

'*Uvidimsya*, Mr Wilde.'

'Oscar comes here all the time,' said Constance, taking my arm. 'I believe he is having a liaison with the lady lion tamer.'

Oscar was leading the way, holding one of his sons' hands in each of his. Over his shoulder he asked, 'Is it you who has set this detective on me, Constance?'

'There is no detective, Oscar. You smoke too many cigarettes. You can't see properly any longer.'

We reached Oscar's box. It was the royal box. It was palatial, in the manner of a children's fairy tale, decked out in red and gold, with cushioned seats for eight, though there were only five of us. We took our places – with Oscar and Constance in the central, canopied thrones – and looked out over the vast arena. 'This is the largest room in Europe,' explained Oscar to his boys. 'It can seat nine thousand people.'

'It's a three-ring circus,' I said, looking down at the huge circles of sawdust below us. High above, mighty chandeliers, ropes, ladders, trapezes and what appeared to be a life-size replica of the Montgolfier brothers' hot air balloon hung from the barrel-roof.

'I am glad you're impressed, Arthur. I believe we're in for a treat.'

We were. From the moment the Montgolfier balloon was lowered to the ground to the sound of guns and trumpets and the circus ringmaster – known as Ivan the Terrible, 'the presiding genius', Oscar called him – emerged from its cradle *riding on horseback*, for three hours, without pause, we were presented with a cavalcade of excitement, colour, skill and surprise, the like of which I had never seen before and never expect to see again. African lions, Siberian leopards, Indian elephants, dancing bears and prancing horses, brass bands and balancing acts (in one of which the performers were all sea lions; in another, all chimpanzees), trapeze artists and sword-swallowers, tumblers, tightrope walkers, jugglers, clowns, fire-eaters, dwarfs: it was indeed 'the greatest show on earth'. Towards the end, the boys began to weary, but I was held throughout. And so was Oscar. 'I love the circus, don't you?' he said, as we rose to sing the National Anthem at the close. 'It is so much more real than life.'

When it was over, exhausted and exhilarated, we escorted Constance and her sons onto the street. Oscar had a brougham waiting for them.

'That was a wonderful birthday present, husband,' she said to Oscar, kissing him on the cheek. 'Thank you.'

'I think Arthur has a little present for you, too,' said Oscar, indicating the brown-paper parcel I had been clutching close to my side all evening.

'No, no,' I said quickly. 'I shall bring Constance a present another day. This is something else.'

'What is it?' demanded Oscar, reaching out and feeling the paper parcel with his fingers. 'It's a lady's handkerchief. It must be for Constance.'

'No,' I insisted, embarrassed.

'It was for Constance, but now you've decided to give it to your young acrobat?'

'Stop teasing him, Oscar,' said Constance. 'Goodnight, Arthur. Thank you for sharing my birthday treat with me.'

'What is it?' Oscar persisted.

'It's for you,' I said. 'It's what you asked for.'

'For me? What did I ask for?'

'It's the dead woman's apron.'

Constance bustled the boys into the carriage. She climbed in herself and looked back through the window. 'I don't know what you two are up to, but please take care. Please, I beg you.'

'I can explain,' I said.

'No, no,' said Oscar earnestly, 'don't. Please don't. Nowadays we have so few mysteries left, we cannot afford to part with even one of them.' He called to his sons: 'Goodnight, boys. Look after your mother.' He looked into his wife's eyes steadily. 'Goodnight, Constance. I shall see you later in the week. I have work to do, you understand.'

'I understand,' she said, smiling sadly. She blew a kiss towards me as the brougham began to move away.

'And now,' announced Oscar, '*na pasashok!*'

'What does that mean?' I asked.

'"One for the road", I think. I'm not entirely sure. What little Russian I have I've picked up from Salazkin.'

'He's our host?'

'And the ringmaster. And the knife-thrower.'

'Ivan the Terrible?'

'Yes, it's a good name, isn't it?'

'And is he a good man?'

'You can judge for yourself. He is certainly generous. And he has beautiful manners. And he speaks perfect English. It's just a touch too perfect. That's how we know he isn't English. He's quite difficult to read. More Count Tolstoy than Mr Dickens.'

Oscar led me back into the Olympia Hall, through the throng emerging from the circus, back up the grand staircase to the second floor. Given his bulk, the ease and speed with which he moved often surprised me.

'Where are we going? I thought circus people lived in caravans.'

'They do. The caravans are in the field behind the hall, with cages for the animals. But after the performance, Ivan the Terrible holds court up here – in the Prince's Apartments.'

We had reached a long, narrow corridor, on the north side of the building, with a set of ornate double doors at the end of it. Above the doors, in gilt lettering, a notice read: *The Prince's Apartments.*

'Yes,' said Oscar, 'named in honour of the Prince of Wales – with his approval, for his use. The excellent directors of the National Agricultural Hall Company, owners of Olympia, thought His Royal Highness might like to entertain his mistresses here – and they were right. He does.'

Both doors swung suddenly open and there stood Ivan the Terrible – barely recognisable without his moustaches. His face was smooth and featureless, covered in a layer of make-up so thick that it was impossible at a glance to reckon his age. He was wearing a dressing gown and carpet slippers and seemed shorter and much slighter than he had appeared in the circus ring.

'And his late son,' he said in a clear, clipped, light voice, 'the lamented Duke of Clarence and Avondale, liked to come here, too. He used the apartments to entertain his young gentlemen friends. I've never believed that he was Jack the Ripper, have you?'

He took Oscar's hands in both of his. They were quite small hands, I noticed. 'Welcome, Oscar,' he said warmly. He smiled at me knowingly. 'I have perfect hearing, perfect eyesight and, yes, I speak perfect English – but only because my mother, who was Hungarian, was an ardent Anglophile and engaged an English governess to give me my education. The good lady came from Cheltenham. She found circus life quite a trial.' He returned his gaze to Oscar and looked at him admiringly. 'So here you are, Oscar, gossiping as usual, but looking well – and with the great Arthur Conan Doyle with you, as you promised.' He beckoned us over the threshold. 'Welcome to the Prince's Apartments. Welcome to the Russian Circus. It is good to meet you, Dr Doyle. The company is excited that you are here. We all love Oscar. Why? Because he is good enough to love us.'

We stood for a moment in a small ante-room. We could hear a hubbub of men's voices in the room beyond. 'I am pleased to see you, Ivan,' said Oscar. 'The performance was perfection – as ever. In fact, I think it was better than ever. Thank you for your hospitality.'

'I am relieved to see you, Oscar. I read about the murder in your neck of the woods. Was it very violent? A lady of the night, I assume?'

Oscar caught my eye. 'You see. Mr Salazkin has all our English idioms on the tip of his tongue. "Neck of the woods", "lady of the night". And he loves a good murder.'

The ringmaster smiled. 'It's in the blood.'

'He claims to be descended from Countess Elizabeth Báthory,' said Oscar, 'the lady who, notoriously, killed some six hundred and fifty girls so that she could take baths in their blood.'

Still smiling, our host murmured, 'She had a wonderful complexion.'

'And for a Russian of Hungarian descent, he has a very English sense of humour, don't you think?' Oscar touched the ringmaster on the arm. 'Since you ask, was it very violent? Yes, the poor woman was stabbed thirty-nine times and virtually dismembered – but, thus far, no one seems to know who she is.'

'But you are safe, Oscar,' said our host, opening the inner door. 'That is what counts. And the creator of Sherlock Holmes is with us and that's exciting. Now, gentlemen, you must have a drink and meet the company.'

'We must *salute* the company,' said Oscar emphatically.

We proceeded to do exactly that. There were perhaps twenty of them in the room and I saw at once that the number did not include Olga, the young acrobat. These were all men, and mostly older men, burly, almost brutish in appearance, and, while several spoke French, none had a command of English remotely on a par with that of the ringmaster. Conversation was consequently limited. We shook hands enthusiastically. We said 'Bravo!' repeatedly. I nodded acknowledgement when they boomed at me, 'Sherlock Holmes! Sherlock Holmes!' and slapped me on the back.

I accepted a glass of acrid black tea from the samovar. I saw Oscar throw back three glasses of vodka in quick succession and was grateful to see him decline a fourth. Our host left us to our own devices, so we mingled as best we could. We did not stay long.

As we left the party, and were descending the grand staircase, now shrouded in darkness, Oscar whispered to me: 'You saw him, didn't you?'

'Saw who?'

'The man who was serving the vodka – the man who fetched you your tea.'

'What about him?'

'It was Ostrog – Michael Ostrog – Macnaghten's "homicidal maniac". I know now why I recognised his photograph. He is the man who delivers my caviar.'

10

The Surrey County Lunatic Asylum

'Every man would like to have a mistress.'

Once again Oscar was in puckish form at the breakfast table. I had spent a second night at the Langham Hotel and on this Wednesday morning – it was now 3 January 1894 – I had arrived in the dining room only moments after my friend. He was standing by a window table, looking out into the street. He was dressed in the same suit as on the day before, but wore a fresh buttonhole (a Christmas rose) and a pale pink tie to match. I took his evident ebullience to indicate that his mystery follower was nowhere to be seen.

'Every man would like to have a mistress,' he repeated, grinning at me impishly while taking his place at the table, 'and, in my view, should be encouraged to do so.'

'You don't mean it, Oscar,' I said, taking my place opposite him and determined not to rise to his bait.

'I do. Every great piece of music has its grace notes. Every great work of art calls for light as well as shade. For any marriage to survive beyond seven years the monotony of monogamy needs to be enlivened by the occasional caprice.'

'This is dangerous talk, Oscar,' I said, holding up my hand to silence him while the waiter took our breakfast order.

'It's common sense. What's good enough for my friend the Prince of Wales is good enough for my friend Arthur Conan Doyle.'

'What on earth do you mean?'

'I mean that you should return to the Russian Circus, find that delightful little acrobat of yours and take her out to supper.'

'Please, Oscar!' I protested.

'You know you want to – and you know you can. Your wife is in Switzerland. Your offspring are with her. You are in London, alone, footloose and fancy-free. *Carpe diem*. Seize the day. Seize the girl!'

'This is a ridiculous suggestion, Oscar – unworthy, shameful.'

'It's neither, Arthur, and you know it. I saw the way Olga looked at you and I saw the way you looked at her. It was altogether charming.'

'The girl can't be more than twenty.'

'Exactly,' cried Oscar, his eyes suddenly ablaze. 'And how old are you now, Arthur? Thirty-four, thirty-five going on forty. You are old before your time, my friend. I know how it is. I am five years older than you. The pulse of joy that beats in us at twenty becomes sluggish as time passes. Our limbs fail, our senses rot.' He picked up a spoon from the table and studied his own reflection in it. 'We descend into hideous puppets, haunted by the memory of the passions of which we were too much afraid and the exquisite temptations that we had not the courage to yield to.' He waved his spoon at me admonishingly. 'Youth! Youth! There is absolutely nothing in the world but youth! Olga is twenty, a slim gilt girl, as perfect as a lily, as supple as a leopard, and yours for the asking, Arthur.'

'Enough of this, Oscar,' I hissed at him. 'Pull yourself together, man. We have work to do.'

Oscar put down the spoon and looked up at the young waiter who had just arrived with our breakfast. 'The tragedy of old age, Martin, is not that one is old, but that one is young.'

'Yes, sir,' said the waiter, pouring Oscar his coffee.

My friend looked across to me, took a deep breath, sighed slowly and smiled benignly. 'You are quite right, Arthur, we have work to do.' He pulled out his pocket watch to inspect it. 'Indeed, we have an appointment to keep. At twelve noon. In Tooting, of all places.'

'Tooting?'

'We are going to the Surrey County Lunatic Asylum.'

'We are expected?'

'I have sent the superintendent a telegram.'

'Has he replied?'

'No, not yet, but I have told him to expect us at noon. He will be pleased to see us, I am sure. You are our calling card, Arthur.'

'I rather think Sherlock Holmes is our calling card, but never mind.' The Langham breakfast was a good one: devilled kidneys with fried bread and roasted, sliced tomatoes. 'The Surrey County Lunatic Asylum is where Ostrog was detained – yes?'

'Precisely. And we are going there to discover when he was released and why.'

'And how he comes to be working now at the Russian Circus.'

'That's not so surprising. It is a Russian circus and he is Russian. His release from the asylum is what's curious. I'd understood from Macnaghten's notes that he was to be detained indefinitely.'

Oscar put down his knife and fork to light a cigarette. 'I take it you saw Macnaghten yesterday?'

'I did.'

'And how was he?'

'Frustrated,' I said. 'They have made no progress in identifying the body from Shelley Alley.'

'None at all?'

'The police doctor who examined the poor woman in the morgue confirmed what I thought – she is an older woman and not a prostitute. The hue and texture of her skin suggest that she was well-to-do, not a working woman, but her clothing and her bonnet suggest otherwise.'

'So she had fallen on hard times – and recently?'

'So it would seem. But as to who she might be, as yet there are no clues. No one has been reported missing whose appearance remotely matches hers.'

Oscar contemplated his Turkish cigarette as I finished my breakfast. 'And did you discuss the Whitechapel murders with Macnaghten?' he asked.

'Only briefly. He is anxious to complete his report as soon as may be. Rumour is rife at Scotland Yard that our friends in Fleet Street are about to run a whole series of newspaper articles deriding the police's failure to apprehend Jack the Ripper and naming suspects "hitherto unknown". Macnaghten wants to have all his facts lined up before the gentlemen of the press do their worst.'

'He made no objection to letting you have the piece of the apron that had belonged to Catherine Eddowes?'

'None whatsoever. He did not even enquire why you wanted it.' I had finished my devilled kidneys. I looked at my friend. 'Why do you?'

Oscar smiled enigmatically. 'You shall see,' he said, blowing a thin plume of pale purple smoke into the air above him. 'All in good time.'

Breakfast done, and Martin the waiter over-generously tipped, we repaired to our rooms. I wrote a note to send to my wife in Switzerland, giving her a partial account of my adventures since my return to England at the weekend. (You suppose correctly: I did not mention the young acrobat, Olga, or Oscar's absurd proposition regarding her.) I also scribbled a note to Mrs Stocks, the good lady who had been keeping house for us in South Norwood since my wife had been taken ill, forewarning her that I might yet be delayed a day or two further on business in town.

At 11.00 a.m., as agreed, I met up with Oscar once more in the foyer of the hotel. I found him deep in conversation with the bellboy, Jimmy. The moment I arrived, the lad ran off.

'I have just been giving Jimmy his New Year present,' said Oscar.

'And what did you give him?' I asked.

'A silver cigarette case.'

'That was somewhat extravagant.'

'Oh yes. It was absurdly expensive. I had it inscribed.'

'Was that wise?'

'I hope not.'

My friend laughed his teasing laugh and said, 'Come. I am looking forward to saying to the cab driver, "To the lunatic asylum, my man, and don't spare the horses."'

As it turned out, there was only one horse, but it took no more than fifty minutes for our two-wheeler to convey us from the heart of town in Portland Place to Springfield Park on the Tooting–Wandsworth borders, the near-rural setting for the Surrey County Lunatic Asylum. During my training and early years as a doctor I had visited a number of such grim establishments, but this one, at least in appearance, was much less forbidding than I might have expected. The grounds were generous, gracious almost, with wide gravel walkways around well-kept lawns. The asylum itself featured twisted chimneys and variegated brickwork, all designed in the Tudor style, so that it looked uncannily like Hampton Court Palace. The superintendent looked uncannily like King Henry VIII.

Dr Gabriel was the good man's name – and I sensed at once that he was indeed a good man who had his patients' interests at heart. He was tall, broad and bearded, with a cheery, rubicund face, a benevolent manner and a trick of winking jovially by way of punctuating his conversation. He had large hands, with tufts of reddish hair above his knuckles, and a strong handshake – which I appreciated, but at which I noticed Oscar wince visibly. He was awaiting our arrival on the front steps of the asylum and appeared delighted to see us.

'Welcome, welcome,' he said, in a booming voice. 'It is always good to have the sane among us. We have a thousand lunatics here and the first of the idiot children will be arriving in the spring. We are going to have two hundred of them. We are building extensions all the time. We are very popular with the frail and the foolish, but less so with the unafflicted – which is why your visit is all the more welcome. Come inside.'

Dr Gabriel escorted us into the building, through a spacious, galleried entrance hall (the walls hung with what appeared to be large, indifferent portraits of his predecessors) and down a long but light, high-ceilinged corridor towards his office. To our left, through tall windows, we could see some of the patients wandering about or sitting on benches in an inner courtyard. They were a mixture of men and women of assorted ages and, at first glance, looked like anyone one might expect to see in a public park.

On closer inspection, however, their abnormality was evident: they were wearing overcoats over nightshirts or pyjamas; their hair was unkempt; they were either completely still, standing or sitting like statues, or moving their limbs awkwardly, jerkily, like marionettes; their eyes were either utterly vacant or staring wildly. What was most unnerving was that, though there must have been several dozen of them, each one seemed to be in a world of his or her own.

On our right, as we paced the corridor alongside the amiable superintendent, we passed a series of closed doors. From one of them, an elderly woman emerged and, suddenly seeing us, emitted an awful cry, like the sound of a fox at bay, and immediately scurried back from whence she came.

'Do your inmates roam free?' asked Oscar.

'Some do,' boomed Gabriel. 'Others – like your man Ostrog – the homicidal maniacs and the like – are kept under lock and key, strictly confined, for their own protection as well as ours.'

'You are familiar with the details of Ostrog's case?'

'Oh yes, I know all about Ostrog.' Gabriel chuckled. 'I've got his file out to show you. From your telegram, I gather that's what you're after. As you know, the police believe he may be Jack the Ripper.'

We had reached the last door in the corridor. Dr Gabriel produced a ring of keys from his waistcoat pocket and used two of them to unlock the door. 'This is my office,' he said, gesturing to us to step inside.

The room we entered was gloomy and airless, not so much the office of a superintendent of a lunatic asylum as the library of a university professor. There were crowded oak bookshelves from floor to ceiling on three sides of the room and above the wooden mantelpiece what appeared to be Holman Hunt's *The*

Light of the World, his celebrated painting of Christ standing at a long-unopened door preparing to knock.

'I know that picture,' I said.

'It's a copy,' said Gabriel, 'the work of a lunatic, but rather well done and not without its resonance in a place like this.'

Oscar and I peered up at the painting.

'We have just had electricity installed throughout the asylum,' continued Dr Gabriel. 'Look, I can press a button here and illuminate *The Light of the World.*'

The room was suddenly ablaze with electric light. Dr Gabriel chuckled at his own joke and indicated two leather chairs to the side of his desk. 'Let me get you a sherry and tell you what I can.'

Oscar winced once more as he accepted the superintendent's generous glass of brown sherry. 'Most kind,' he said.

'And we're most honoured,' said Gabriel, raising his glass to each of us in turn and seating himself behind his desk. 'I don't really know your work, Mr Wilde. I don't get to the theatre as much as I'd like. I have to content myself reading the reviews. I read your brother's stuff in *Vanity Fair.* He's a drama critic, is he not?'

'Those who can do,' Oscar murmured into his sherry glass, 'those who can't criticise.'

'Of course,' continued our host cheerfully, 'it goes without saying that I am an *avid* reader of the *Strand Magazine* and a *great* admirer of Mr Doyle and the adventures of Sherlock Holmes.'

I did not look in Oscar's direction for fear he might be wincing yet again, but I acknowledged Dr Gabriel's compliment with a small bow. He winked at me and lifted a sheaf of papers from the top of a stack of paperwork on his desk. 'I telephoned Macnaghten at Scotland Yard when I received your telegram and he tells me he is more than happy for me to give you whatever assistance I can.' He winked once more. 'What do you wish to know?'

'Everything,' said Oscar.

'Well,' said Gabriel, tugging gently on his beard and looking down at the papers, 'we can start with Ostrog's history – or as much of it as we have here.' He picked up the top sheet and studied it. 'He was born in 1833, according to the records. He is Russian by birth, but apparently speaks several European languages – Russian, Polish, German, French, English – and, while we know him as Michael Ostrog, he appears to be known to the authorities – and to have operated – under a host of aliases. Bertrand Ashley, Ashley Nabokov, Max Gosslar, Max Sobieski, *Count* Sobieski, Dr Grant ... to name but a few.' The superintendent lowered the paper he was holding, looked up at us and smiled. 'I think we can take it he is neither a count nor a doctor.'

'Is he a "confidence man" then,' asked Oscar, 'or merely a man who suffers from delusions?'

'Both, I think it's safe to say,' answered Dr Gabriel, with another wink. 'He first comes to the attention of the police in 1863 – in Oxford. Under the name of Max Gosslar he is found guilty of a theft from an Oxford College and sentenced to ten months in prison. He comes out and moves to Cambridge, where we find him sentenced to three months in prison. In July 1864, he turns up in Tunbridge Wells, now under the name Count Sobieski. This time he is sentenced to eight months.'

'These are light sentences,' I suggested.

Dr Gabriel nodded. 'And minor crimes. Petty stuff. Small-time theft.'

'No sign of homicidal mania?' asked Oscar.

Dr Gabriel chuckled. 'Not yet.' He scrutinised the papers once more. 'It gets a little more serious in January 1866 when Ostrog is in court again, this time on charges of fraud. Interestingly, he is acquitted. But he isn't out of trouble for long. On March the nineteenth that year he steals a gold watch and other items from a woman in Maidstone.'

'Is there any violence?' enquired Oscar. 'Did he assault the woman?'

'No, no violence. At this stage in his criminal career, he appears to be a mild-mannered man, quietly spoken, respectably dressed.' Gabriel returned to the paperwork. 'Where are we? 1866. He isn't caught until August, it seems, by which time he had committed a string of similar thefts, as a consequence of which he is sentenced to seven years in prison.'

Oscar sniffed. 'This sounds more like Mr Dickens' Fagin than our Jack the Ripper.'

Dr Gabriel nodded. 'There's no indication of mania thus far. But seven years' incarceration can change a man. In 1873 Ostrog is released from Chatham Gaol and, when he is next arrested, he is found to have a gun on him.'

'Does he use it?' I asked.

'He *threatens* to use it as he's being arrested and, as a consequence, in January 1874, he is sentenced to ten years in prison. He's out again in 1883 and we don't hear anything more of him until 1887 when he is arrested once more – this time for stealing a metal tankard – and sentenced to six months' hard labour. This is the first time we find the word "mania" cropping up in the police reports.'

'What exactly is "mania"?' Oscar asked.

'It's a form of madness characterised by bursts of great excitement, euphoria, delusions ... '

'It sounds rather delightful.'

'A mild burst of mania can be exhilarating,' said Dr Gabriel, with a wink, 'but heightened mania leads to over-activity, loss of control, loss of reason, frenzy, hysteria and, ultimately, violence. The problem is that it comes and goes and we don't quite know what triggers it or how to keep it under control.' He turned back to his paperwork. 'On March the tenth 1888 Ostrog was released from prison, apparently "cured". He then went missing for nine months. The next we hear of him he is in Paris where he is arrested for theft and sentenced to two years' imprisonment on November the eighteenth 1888.'

'So,' said Oscar, sitting forward, 'between March and November 1888, at the time of the Whitechapel murders, nothing is known of Michael Ostrog or his whereabouts.'

'Correct, Mr Wilde, but because he is reckoned to be a dangerous man, a serial offender, a violent criminal and has apparently been sighted in the East End of London, police begin to wonder if he might not be the elusive Jack the Ripper.'

'The police suspect him,' I said, 'but they cannot prove anything.'

'There is no evidence of any kind against him.'

'What about the bag of knives and surgical instruments he is said to have carried about with him and his record of violence against women?' I asked.

'Rumour and hearsay. None of it can be substantiated.'

Oscar asked: 'Why does Macnaghten call him a homicidal maniac?'

'He once threatened the police with a gun – and he is subject to bouts of mania. There is no doubt of that. And because of that, when he comes out of prison in Paris and returns to London in 1890, the Metropolitan Police decide to keep an eye on him – and the next time he is in trouble – it's another petty theft – the authorities decide that enough's enough – and Michael Ostrog is arrested, taken off to the magistrates' court, found "incapable and insane" and committed here to the Surrey County Lunatic Asylum. That was almost three years ago, April 1891.'

'But he's not a homicidal maniac – in your view, Doctor?'

'There's no evidence that he is – or ever was – but once the tag had been attached to him, it suited the police to think of him as such. He was a petty thief, a fantasist, probably delusional, possibly dangerous. He was certainly a nuisance when he was at large. It was arguably for the good of the community to have him locked up here – homicidal maniac or not.'

'And when was he released?' asked Oscar.

Dr Gabriel put down his papers. 'He hasn't been released. He's in our asylum at Her Majesty's pleasure. I imagine he will be incarcerated here until the day he dies.'

II

Face to face

'Can we see him?'

'May we speak with him?'

Oscar and I spoke at the same time – and with an almost comical urgency.

Dr Gabriel laughed and pushed back his chair. 'I can take you to see him now, but he won't speak to you. He won't speak to anybody. He hasn't spoken a word since he arrived.'

'What?' cried Oscar. 'He's not uttered a word in three years?'

'Not a word.'

'He's become dumb?' I asked.

'No. He makes noises. He whimpers. Sometimes he laughs. Not often. If he's in pain, he cries out.'

'In Russian? In Polish?'

'In no discernible language. He makes noises – as an animal might. He's like an animal – like a wretched old dog whose spirit has been broken. You'll see.'

Dr Gabriel got to his feet and, with a cheerful wink, said, 'Shall we?' He turned off the electric lights (bringing darkness to *The Light of the World*) and we followed him out of the gloom into the corridor once more. He doubled-locked the office door and led us back to the main entrance hall and then down a steep and narrow flight of stone steps.

As we descended, Oscar whispered to me, 'Don't say a word.'

The steps led directly onto a second long corridor that must have been immediately beneath the corridor above. Here there were no windows on the left-hand side, just a whitewashed stone wall bleakly illuminated by half a dozen electric light bulbs that hung from wires in the ceiling along the length of the corridor like so many hangman's nooses. The doors on the right-hand side were similar to those on the floor above, except that these appeared to be made of iron or steel, painted dark green, and, at eye-height, each one had a small square window in it, no bigger than a clenched fist.

'Ostrog's in cell three,' said Gabriel. 'He's probably asleep. He usually is. We don't need to go in. You can see him through the spyhole.'

To my surprise, Oscar stepped forward first and looked through the tiny window into the cell. 'Mary Mother of God!' he cried. 'Jesus wept.'

I pulled him away at once and put my own eye to the window – and gasped. Within three inches of my eye, staring directly into it, was the man's right eye. It was a hideous sight: the cornea clouded and milky, the sclera speckled and yellow, the eyelid red-rimmed and encrusted with mucus.

'What is it?' asked Dr Gabriel.

'He is standing right by the door,' I explained, lowering my voice to a whisper.

Dr Gabriel took my place at the spyhole. 'Oh yes, it's lunchtime. He's waiting for his food.' The superintendent banged on the metal door with the palm of his hand. 'Not yet, Ostrog. Soon. Din-dins coming soon. Back to bed now.' He continued to beat the door. 'Shoo! Shoo!' He turned back to us. 'He's retreated to his bunk. You can see him better now.'

Oscar and I took it in turns to inspect the man once more. He sat on the edge of his bed, gazing directly at us, making no noise, betraying no emotion.

'A broken dog, as you say,' murmured Oscar.

'What age would he be?' I asked.

'Sixty or thereabouts.'

'And the mania, has it subsided?'

'There have been no episodes of mania since he was admitted.'

'Not one?' asked Oscar.

'Not one.'

'You don't consider him a homicidal maniac, then?'

'No. That was the police surgeon's diagnosis, not mine.'

'So why is he locked up?'

'It's what the court ordered. But I wouldn't release him now, even if I could. He's not fit to fend for himself. As you can see, he's a helpless imbecile.'

'Thank you, Dr Gabriel.'

'Thank you, gentlemen.'

We climbed the steep steps back into the hallway and bade our genial host farewell.

He beamed at us, shook my hand heartily and, I noticed, offered Oscar a friendly salute rather than a handshake. He was more sensitive than his bluff manner suggested. 'If there is anything else I can do for you, gentlemen, I shall be only too pleased to help.'

'There's one thing,' said Oscar, as we stood by the open door, a chill January wind suddenly whipping into the hallway. 'Do you have photographs of Ostrog?'

'Only the ones taken here on the day of his admission. I can unearth them quite quickly. I know the date: the first of April 1891 – All Fools' Day. We'll take another set in 1901 – should the poor devil live that long. We photograph each inmate every ten years.'

'You've not got any earlier photographs?'

'I didn't know there were any. I've not seen them. The police might have some. Macnaghten may be able to help you there.'

'Thank you,' said Oscar.

'Is there anything more I can do for you?' asked the superintendent.

No. Thank you. Thank you so much.'

We clambered aboard our waiting two-wheeler. 'Simpson's-in-the-Strand,' ordered Oscar, looking out of the cab window and offering Dr Gabriel a final farewell wave. The good man stood on the front step of his asylum, watching, winking and waving, until we had turned out of the gates towards Tooting High Road.

'That's not Ostrog,' said Oscar emphatically, settling back into the corner of the cab and opening his cigarette case.

'Or that *is* Ostrog,' I countered, 'and the man you saw at the Russian Circus is someone else.'

'No, the man I saw at the circus – the man who has been delivering caviar to me in Tite Street – is the man in the photograph in Macnaghten's file. He is Michael Ostrog. This poor unfortunate imbecile is someone else altogether.'

'What do we do now?' I asked.

'Have lunch,' said Oscar, sucking slowly on his cigarette. '"Have lunch" is always the best answer to a difficult question.'

'Shouldn't we return to the Russian Circus?'

'All in good time. There's no hurry. You know my maxim: "Men of thought should have nothing to do with action."'

I raised an eyebrow. 'Fools rush in, et cetera . . . '

'Exactly. And, my God, the Metropolitan Police are fools!' He exhaled a cloud of purple cigarette smoke and, leaning towards me, spoke through it like an oracle appearing through the clouds at Delphi. 'Macnaghten's brief told us Ostrog was a Russian doctor whose "antecedents are of the very worst". Macnaghten knows nothing of Ostrog's antecedents! There's no evidence that Ostrog's a doctor of any kind! And I doubt very much that he's even Russian. He's more likely to be Polish or Lithuanian.'

'Why do you say that?'

'Ostrog liked to call himself Count Sobieski. The Sobieskis were kings of Poland and Grand Dukes of Lithuania – in the good old days.'

'I didn't know that.'

'You did. You've just forgotten.'

I smiled. Oscar continued earnestly: 'Macnaghten and the Metropolitan Police will never solve the mystery of the Whitechapel murders. Never! They know *nothing*. I do believe, Arthur, it really is down to us.' He turned and looked out of the cab window again. After a moment or two's silence, he said slowly: 'I shall have roast beef from the trolley and, given the weather, I think we should both allow ourselves the onion gravy.'

In the distance, a clock struck the hour. 'Big Ben comes from Whitechapel, you know. Until these horrible murders occurred, the Whitechapel Bell Foundry was the district's principal claim to fame. The bell that is Big Ben is more than seven foot tall and nine foot wide and weighs at least thirteen tons – as much as a baby elephant. Macnaghten knows none of this!'

I laughed. 'How do you know it?'

'I have two sons. As you'll discover as your children grow, Arthur, it's the sort of information a father needs at his fingertips if he is to have any hope of being respected in his own household.'

'Very good, Oscar.'

He sat forward suddenly. 'What time is it?'

'Two o'clock.'

'Damnation. We're late.'

'You have reserved a table? They know you at Simpson's.'

'I have invited a guest.' My friend was now anxiously peering out of the cab's side window. 'There he is.' He called up to the driver: 'Whoa! Stop!'

We were already in the Strand. Oscar pushed open the door and jumped down from our carriage. A few yards from us, on the pavement's kerb, outside the Savoy Hotel, adjacent to Simpson's restaurant, scowling at his timepiece while waiting to cross the street, stood the distinctive figure of Richard Mansfield. I recognised him at once, but even if you had never seen his well-favoured, clean-shaven, finely contoured face before you would have known this was an actor – and one who considered himself a leading man. There was a crowd waiting to cross the street with him and most certainly did Mansfield stand out from it. He wore a long, black opera cloak (with ornate silver clasp); he sported a monocle in his right eye and he carried a silver-topped cane in his right hand. He was not especially tall, but he seemed it because he wore the kind of high black hat that everyone wore in the 1850s but only an actor-manager of the old school would wear today.

The moment he caught sight of Oscar coming from our two-wheeler towards him, he called out dismissively: 'It's too late, Wilde! I have another appointment.'

Oscar, arms outstretched, pressed on, offering profuse apologies. Abruptly, Mansfield turned away. 'It's too late, I say.'

As he reached the actor, Oscar put out a soothing hand. 'Don't touch me, man!' cried Mansfield, in a sudden rage. 'How dare you?' He turned and raised his cane. For a dreadful moment I thought he was about to strike Oscar a blow, but instead he held his stick mid-air in a theatrical, threatening gesture that would have been laughable had it not been accompanied by a vehement outburst that chilled the blood. 'You are contemptible, Wilde. First you insult me by sending me a telegram bringing up vile and unfounded allegations that were laid to rest years ago. Then, when, foolishly, I agree to meet you to discuss the matter, you leave me standing in the street like one of your disgusting Mary-Anns. I've waited here almost an hour. How dare you? What business is it of yours anyway? Who the devil do you think you are?'

'I don't know what to say,' said Oscar.

Mansfield said nothing, but lowered his cane, turned and stepped off the pavement into the roadway. Darting elegantly through the traffic, holding his hat against the wind, he crossed the street and disappeared from view.

Oscar came back to where I was still standing by the two-wheeler. He lifted his head and narrowed his eyes: 'I think a really fine Burgundy is what we need with our roast beef and onion gravy, don't you?'

We had a most excellent lunch. We followed the beef with Simpson's celebrated apple pie and custard, and after one bottle of fine Burgundy felt equal to another. We talked of Mansfield and his sudden anger. 'He's famous for it,' said Oscar. 'He's half-American: they're quick to take offence. And I believe he's currently playing Napoleon on stage – that may have something to do with it.'

'It's curious,' I mused, 'that a man who simply murders another man is regarded as a common criminal, but a man like Napoleon – responsible for thousands of cruel deaths – becomes a national hero.'

'There's glory in numbers,' said Oscar. 'In France, they've erected statues of Gilles de Rais, companion-at-arms to Joan of Arc and the self-confessed murderer of little children. He slew them by the score, by the hundred – sodomised them first, then cut them up and preserved the heads of the prettiest ones in aspic.'

'How can a human being do such a thing?'

'Easily, if he has the power and the will, and the stomach and the soul for it.'

'He had a soul of darkness.'

'Indeed. Nothing can cure the soul but the senses, just as nothing can cure the senses but the soul. And, like it or not, he's joined the ranks of the great immortals.'

'Do you think so?'

'Oh, yes, thanks to that jet-black hair with the cobalt hue. As Bluebeard, he's world famous. And the hero of one of our favourite Christmas pantomimes.'

When lunch was done, Oscar paid the bill – despite my protestations – and we returned in our two-wheeler to the Langham Hotel. 'I'm going to take a rest now,' he said, 'and ponder why it is that a man turns to murder and to mutilation. We'll only solve the mysteries of the Whitechapel murders if we think them through. Action is limited and relative. Unlimited and absolute is the vision of him who sits at ease and watches, who walks in loneliness and dreams.'

I smiled and recalled that my friend had ordered a large brandy to accompany his coffee after lunch. 'And I shall go shopping,' I said. 'If I'm to stay in town for a day or two more, I need a fresh shirt.'

'Don't change for dinner tonight,' said Oscar.

'What are we doing tonight?'

'We're going back to Tite Street.'

'Is Constance expecting us?'

'Not at present. I shall go in advance to prepare the ground. You can arrive around seven. Bring Catherine Eddowes' apron with you. We shall need it.'

I waved my friend off to his room and set off down Regent Street towards the bazaar at Regent Circus. I was standing there, at the corner of Oxford Street, looking into the window of a small gentleman's outfitter when, in the reflection in the glass, I saw two figures pass by that I recognised: one was Oscar, unmistakably; the other was Martin, the young waiter from the Langham Hotel.

12

Oysters

For a while I had sensed that all was not well within the Wilde marriage. Oscar was frequently away from home and I could see how easily he was beguiled by the company of young men. But until I caught sight of his reflection in the glass of that shop window at the corner of Oxford Street, it had not – for a single moment – occurred to me that my friend was a man who might have carnal relations with another man.

I was not overly shocked by the notion (I am a man of the world and a doctor), but I was surprised. When I first saw Oscar and Constance together, five years before, they seemed to me to be so ideally matched and their affection – their *love* – for one another was palpable. But beyond surprise, as I stood outside the gentleman's outfitters on that gusty January afternoon, I felt a twinge of anger. My friend had said that he was planning to take a rest, when in fact he was planning to take to the streets with this young man . . . He had told me one thing and done another.

I felt deceived – and aggrieved as a consequence. I decided that I must question my friend on the matter – and as soon as possible. We could not continue this investigation together if there was not to be openness and honesty between us. A friendship without frankness is not worthy of the name.

I proceeded into the store and bought two shirts. I chose neither wisely nor well. (I am old-fashioned: I believe a gentleman's shirts are best chosen by his wife.) When I got back to the hotel, Oscar was not there, of course. An hour later, still he had not returned. I decided to make my way to Tite Street earlier than I had planned, with a view to arriving a little before the agreed hour and securing a private word with my friend.

My stratagem failed. Even as I stood on the doorstep at 16 Tite Street I could hear raised voices within. An altercation of some kind was taking place in the hallway. The moment that I rang the bell, the front door swung open. Oscar stood there, his face flushed, irritation in his eyes.

'Oh, it's you. I was showing my brother out. You are earlier than I expected.'

'I apologise.'

He leaned towards me urgently. 'Did you remember the apron?'

I indicated the brown parcel tucked underneath my arm.

'Very good,' he whispered. 'Don't mention it until I ask you for it and on no account say what it is or where it comes from.'

'What's all this about, Oscar?' I said quietly.

'I'm laying a trap.'

'Who for?'

'Walter Wellbeloved.' Stepping back from the doorway, my friend suddenly raised his voice and called over his shoulder, 'My brother is just leaving.'

'No, he isn't,' said Willie Wilde, emerging from beneath the kitchen stairway arch at the far end of the hall. He was smoking a cigar and holding what looked like a tumbler of whisky. 'He's only just arrived and he's looking forward to a jolly evening. Mrs Wilde has promised a few oysters and some Chablis and a game or two of cards.' He walked towards me, brushing past Oscar. 'If you won't play with us, brother, perhaps your friend will.' He put his cigar in his mouth and put out his hand to shake mine. 'We've not been introduced. My brother doesn't know the meaning of manners. But I know exactly who you are. You are the celebrated Dr Arthur Conan Doyle. I envy you. You have created the great Sherlock Holmes.'

'You envy everybody, Willie,' murmured Oscar. 'Come in, Arthur,' he said to me. 'Let me take your coat.'

'I used to envy you your lovely little wife, Oscar,' boomed Willie, 'but I don't any more because now I have my own.' He turned to me to explain. His manner was disconcertingly like Oscar's, but his beard and waxed moustache gave him the appearance of a Spanish grandee. 'I am marrying this month, Dr Doyle. I only proposed at Christmas. I don't believe in long engagements.'

'Or long marriages,' said Oscar tartly.

'That is not friendly, brother.'

'You are a journalist, Willie. I am not on friendly terms with journalists. I don't trust them.'

'I'm a leader writer,' Willie explained to me. 'And I sell the occasional freelance paragraph when I can.'

'This is my house,' said Oscar. 'I will choose who I invite here. I choose not to entertain journalists.'

Willie raised his glass defiantly towards his brother. 'It's your wife's house also. I am here as her guest at her invitation. We are here to play cards. I am not leaving until and unless Constance instructs me to do so.'

Oscar looked at his timepiece. 'Stay if you must,' he said wear-ily, 'but we are not playing cards. I have other plans for this evening.'

'Oh, God, you're not going to read us one of your plays, are you? Constance tells me that now Bosie's away, you're getting back to work.'

Oscar gazed at his brother with cold eyes. 'We are conducting a séance here this evening – a psychical experiment. Perhaps you and your fiancée, Willie, would care to take part. I understand from Mrs Mathers that seven is the ideal number of participants. I thought we would be five. Since you are here, you can at least serve some useful purpose.'

'A séance?' Willie began to rumble with delight. He polished off his whisky. 'A séance!' he repeated. 'That's much more fun than cards. Did you know that was the plan, Dr Doyle?'

'No,' I said, 'I had no idea.' I looked towards Oscar, somewhat perplexed.

'Have you ever taken part in a séance before?' asked Willie.

I hesitated. 'Yes,' I said, 'yes, I have. In Southsea. It was a some-what laborious process, as I recall. Sitting in the dark, spelling out words, letter by letter.'

'This will be different,' said Oscar. 'Mrs Mathers is able to speak directly to the other side and whoever may be there in the spirit world can speak directly through her to us – or so I understand.'

'Mrs Mathers? Mina Mathers? Mina Bergson as was? This is wonderful,' cried Willie. 'This calls for a drink. Lily! Constance! Come down, ladies.' He turned towards the staircase. 'The present Mrs Wilde and the future Mrs Wilde are upstairs in the nursery.' There was a flurry of skirts on the landing. 'No they're not. They're on their way to join us – and don't they look charming?'

Constance was dressed in her favourite primrose yellow, her hair tied up with yellow ribbons. The future Mrs William Wilde was all in green velvet. A tall, willowy lady, with a long, thin bird-like face, she had large dark eyes, thick black hair and her height, already considerable, was accentuated by a green feather tucked inside a velvet band that ran around her dark brown brow. She gave the immediate impression of intelligence and nerviness, of being a curious cross between a Red Indian squaw and the type of young lady we would soon be calling a 'New Woman'.

'It's to be a séance,' Willie continued enthusiastically, 'with Mrs Mathers putting through the calls. Forget bezique, ladies. We are going to be communicating with "the other side". Perhaps Joan of Arc will be in touch.' He turned to me, beaming. 'It's usually Joan of Arc, isn't it, Dr Doyle? We all speak French, don't we?'

'You didn't tell me about this, Oscar,' said Constance, not unkindly, coming down the stairs and welcoming me with a squeeze of the hand.

'The opportunity suddenly came up,' said Oscar.

'I'd have prepared sandwiches had I known. Are oysters appropriate for a séance?'

'Oh, yes,' gurgled Willie, now leading the way out of the hall and into the dining room. 'Oysters are notorious as aphrodisiacs. Bringing the dead to life is their speciality.'

Oscar barked a hollow laugh.

'Oscar, Arthur,' said Constance, 'may I present Miss Lily Lees, Willie's fiancée? She comes from Dublin.'

'I know,' said Oscar, taking the lady's hand and bowing his head. 'I'm sure we've met before. I know we will have friends in common. I'm only sorry they don't include my older brother.'

'Oscar!' Constance scolded. 'Pay no attention to him, Lily. Willie gave my husband's last play a disobliging review and I'm afraid Oscar cannot bring himself to forgive and forget – quite yet.'

Oscar said nothing. I said, 'I'm pleased to meet you, Miss Lees.'

'Who is Mrs Mathers?' she asked. Her voice was unexpectedly resonant and her accent suggested New England rather than Dublin.

'Mina's lovely,' said Constance. 'We know her through the Order of the Golden Dawn. She is an artist and a seeress and a prophetess – and altogether wonderful. I love her.'

'She's a character,' said Oscar. 'Indeed, I thought she might be a character in a play I am planning to write.'

Willie called from the dining room: 'Oh no, not another one.'

Constance put her forefinger to Oscar's lips. 'Don't say a word, Oscar. Don't rise to it.' She turned to me and to Miss Lees. 'We are in for a treat, I know. Mina has a very special gift. Let us help Willie prepare the room.'

Setting the scene did not take long. In a matter of moments, with the curtains drawn and the candles lit, with its pure white walls, white carpet and white chairs, and with a fresh white damask cloth spread out over the table, the Wildes' dining room was suddenly transformed into the council chamber of an ice palace in a Nordic fairy tale.

'This is magical,' said Lily Lees.

'I will look after the drinks, if I may, Constance?' said Willie. 'Champagne?'

'We can't have champagne for a séance,' said Oscar. 'Unless you've brought some with you, Willie?'

'Don't start bickering, you two,' said Constance. 'We need a calm atmosphere. We need serenity.'

'Something German, then?' suggested Willie.

'We don't want Schiller coming through, do we?' said Oscar.

Willie chuckled. 'That's quite funny, Oscar. You can put that in your play. And you're right. It's got to be French.'

'Alsatian,' said Oscar softly, 'if you're expecting Joan of Arc.'

'What time is Mina coming?' asked Constance, tidying her hair. I was watching her in the mirror above the fireplace. Her face looked so lovely in the flickering yellow candlelight.

Oscar consulted his timepiece as the doorbell rang. 'Half past seven. This will be her.'

'Is she bringing Bergson?'

'No,' said Oscar. 'She is bringing Walter Wellbeloved.'

'Oh my God,' cried Willie, 'the Jack the Ripper suspect?'

'Yes,' said Oscar, 'but we won't dwell on that, if you don't mind, Willie. There are some things a gentleman does not talk about before dinner.'

13

The Séance

In recent years I have become increasingly fascinated by psychic phenomena. I have taken part in psychic experiments across the globe, from America to Australia. I have communed with spirits from the world beyond and done so frequently and through the good offices of mediums young and old, male and female. Here and there, I have encountered false mediums, of course. I have been the occasional victim of trickery. There are charlatans in every walk of life. But over time I have come to accept that what Hamlet told Horatio is true and there are indeed more things in heaven and earth than are dreamt of in our philosophy.

In 1894 I was younger, less experienced and more sceptical. I was no doubt prejudiced, too. The Wildes were Irish and everyone knows that the Irish believe in fairies. Oscar and Constance were poets also, and a poet's view of life tends to the romantic and the fanciful. I am a Scotsman and a scientist. I deal in facts. I write in prose.

You, my reader, must make what you will of what occurred in the Wildes' dining room on the night of Wednesday 3 January 1894. Here are the sceptic's notes I wrote up later that same evening, presented as I penned them in my room at the Langham Hotel, without alteration or benefit of hindsight.

Séance held at Tite Street, Chelsea, 3.i.94

Present

Mina Mathers (née **Mina Bergson**), our medium. A young woman, not yet thirty, full of vitality and intelligence. No great beauty: a pointed nose and narrow chin. Dressed like a Romanian gypsy, she moved with a dancer's grace and, as she spoke (quite softly), she painted pictures with ever-flowing hands and arms. When we were introduced, she said: 'We have met before, in another time. I was once the goddess Isis. I believe you may have known my brother, Osiris – before I married him, before we had our child, Horus. Am I right?' I was lost for words, but (I confess it) oddly charmed.

Walter Wellbeloved. 50, medium height but thin, almost cadaverous. Receding hair, small moustache, piercing eyes, considerable 'presence' and (to my surprise) a most musical voice. Apparently a medium himself ('more an evoker of spirits' than a seer, he explained), he had come as Mrs Mathers' chaperone. 'I am also her lover,' he announced, without embarrassment. 'When we have enjoyed congress, we find that the spirits are much more forthcoming.' I was lost for words once more – but less charmed. In a whispered aside, Oscar instructed me to keep 'the closest eye' on Wellbeloved in case, during the séance, he should 'give himself away'.

William Wilde. 40s, appears older. Oscar's brother and very like him – but, I fear, a slave to the demon drink.

Lily Lees, 30s, William Wilde's fiancée. She said little. I could not fathom her. She watched her future husband become increasingly intemperate and smiled at him, offering no reproof. Throughout the evening, her features told no tales. Had she taken a powder to steady her nerves?

Oscar. Constance. Self.

There were no servants present. Before the séance, Constance fetched a large dish of oysters and bread and butter from the kitchen and Oscar allowed his brother to bring up copious quantities of white wine from the cold room, but Mrs Mathers and Mr Wellbeloved took nothing but water for refreshment. We stood for a while in the candlelit dining room, picking at the food and exchanging pleasantries in a low murmur until a little before eight o'clock when Mrs Mathers lifted her arms slowly above her head and cooed, 'I feel the spirits calling. Let us be seated.'

Mrs Mathers placed herself at the head of the table and, arranged by Oscar, we sat thus:

Mrs Mathers

Wm Wilde	Oscar
Lily Lees	Constance
Mr Wellbeloved	ACD

The ritual

Mrs Mathers held her arms aloft and invited us to join her in 'the sacred circle'. She chanted 'a prayer of peace' and, from the far end of the table, every word she spoke was underscored by a melodious humming supplied by Mr Wellbeloved. She invited us to close our eyes and hold hands. Constance's hand was warm to the touch; that of Mr Wellbeloved ice cold.

After several long minutes of chanted conjurations, invoking 'ancient gods and spirits manifold', Mrs Mathers told us we could let go of one another's hands and open our eyes. During the chanting, someone – Mr Wellbeloved, I assume – had blown out all the candles in the room, bar the one that stood on the table immediately in front of Mrs Mathers. In the gloom, her face shone, radiant yet pale and ghostlike.

'The spirits are here,' she said softly. 'They are waiting for us at the gates.'

'Who is there?' Walter Wellbeloved asked the question.

'So many,' said Mrs Mathers.

'Who are they? What are they?'

'They are women. They are sad. They are weeping.'

'Who are they seeking?' asked Wellbeloved. 'To whom do they wish to speak?'

'I will ask them,' said Mrs Mathers. She straightened her back and lifted her head so that her sharp nose pointed almost to the ceiling. She closed her eyes. 'Spirits at the gate, why do you weep? Whom do you seek? Is there someone here for whom you have a message?' She paused. I noticed Willie Wilde stir impatiently. Mrs Mathers, though her eyes were shut, sensed his movement and stilled him by gently laying her hand on his. 'Hush,' she said, 'hush.' And then, slowly, lightly, she began to toss her head from side to side. 'They are speaking,' she murmured. She raised her voice: 'They are speaking all at once.' She held up her hands as if to calm the multitude. 'One at a time, please, ladies!' She smiled. 'That's better. Thank you, my child.' She laughed. 'Who is it you seek? What? Your brother? My brother? Os ... Osiris? Not my brother, Osiris? Not Osiris. No ... Oscar! It is Oscar to whom you wish to speak?'

'I am here,' said Oscar.

Mrs Mathers opened her eyes and looked directly at Oscar. 'Who are you seeking, Mr Wilde?'

Oscar turned to me. 'Arthur, would you fetch Mrs Mathers the apron?'

Quickly I left the table and brought in my parcel from the cloak stand in the hallway. I gave it to Oscar who unwrapped it and handed Mrs Mathers the folded piece of cloth.

'What is this?' she asked.

'It belonged to the young woman I am seeking,' said Oscar, passing the material to Mrs Mathers.

'Good,' said the medium eagerly. 'Very good.' She did not unfurl it. She did not examine it. First she placed it beneath her nostrils and breathed in deeply and then, with both hands, she pressed the folded material to her forehead – hard – and, as she did so, began to rock to and fro. 'Yes, yes,' she cried, with ever-deepening intakes of breath, as if reaching a kind of ecstasy. 'Yes, this is yours, my dear, is it not? It is yours. It is yours! I knew it. Your shawl is returned to you now. Oscar has brought it for you. He is here.'

'I am here,' said Oscar.

'Can you hear him, my child?'

Mrs Mathers was now rocking forward and back, the folded apron still held to her head. 'She hears you, Mr Wilde. Her sisters hear you. They are holding out their arms towards you in greeting. It is beautiful to behold.'

'How many are there there?' asked Oscar. 'How many wish to speak to us?'

Mrs Mathers leaned forward and, eyes tight shut, looked about her. 'I can see just three of them now. The others have stepped away from the gate. These are the three you have summoned.'

'Are there not five of them?'

'No, just the three that I can see. There are others, but they are standing behind. Speak to these three, Mr Wilde. What do you wish to ask of them?'

'How did they die?'

Mrs Mathers lowered the apron from her forehead and, opening her eyes, looked directly at Oscar. 'They are not "dead", Mr Wilde. They are living in a world beyond ours, that is all.'

William Wilde shifted in his seat. Constance said gently, 'Oscar understands. We all understand.'

'How did they leave this world?' asked Oscar. He spoke calmly, considering Mrs Mathers carefully as he spoke. 'Can they recall? Can they tell us? Can they speak of the brutality of their parting?'

Suddenly Mrs Mathers was rocking once more, moving forward and back, breathing deeply. 'They are crying out to you, Mr Wilde. They are saying that what you say is true. They were taken before their time – cruelly taken.'

'Were they taken together by the same man? Can they tell us that? What do they know?'

'You can speak to them directly, Mr Wilde. They can hear you through me. They will answer through my mouth.' Mrs Mathers lifted Catherine Eddowes' apron to her forehead once more. It covered her eyes. 'They are answering you now, Mr Wilde. They want to share their sorrow with you.'

'What are they saying?'

Mrs Mathers paused and held out her left hand to halt Oscar's flow of questions. 'They will answer you, Mr Wilde. Be patient.' She threw her head back so that her covered face was pointing at the ceiling. 'Two of them died on the same night ... One died alone. Does that make sense? They are speaking all together now. They are so pleased that you care for them. They are grateful for your love.'

'Can they tell me who took their lives?' Oscar asked.

'It was God's will,' Mrs Mathers answered at once.

'It was the devil's work,' said Oscar sharply. 'They were violated, ripped apart.'

'No,' said Mrs Mathers, rocking once more, her head facing forward. 'The girl whose shawl this is says there was no pain. You need feel no pity for her. She felt nothing at the moment of passing. She was overwhelmed in the darkness and then woke in the light of heaven. She is at peace now. She is content.'

'I am glad to hear it,' said Oscar. 'Do the others recall anything of the moment when they were taken? Can they describe what happened?'

Mrs Mathers gave a sudden shriek, violent and piercing, a cry of pain so real that I started. Wellbeloved reached across the table with a restraining hand. 'It is the women,' he said. 'It is their pain. Mina is quite safe.'

William Wilde shifted in his seat once more. No one else at the table responded.

Mrs Mathers took a slow, deep breath, as if to calm herself. 'They died in agony, Mr Wilde. They are shrinking away in terror as you ask your question.'

'What happened to them? Can they tell you?'

'They are raising their hands in horror. They are covering their faces. They are crying out.'

'What happened?'

'They were consumed.'

'By whom? Who did this to them?'

'They were consumed by fire.'

'Stop!' cried Willie Wilde, pushing his chair away from the table. 'These are our sisters, Oscar!' Angrily, he turned towards Mrs Mathers. 'This must stop, madam. This is grotesque. Let's have some light and let the dead rest in peace.' Steadying himself, he got to his feet and taking the candle that stood in front of Mrs Mathers he lit the other candles on the table. 'I need a drink,' he said. 'I'm sure we all do.'

'I think we should go home,' said Miss Lees, getting to her feet.

'I'll have one drink,' said Willie Wilde, 'and then we'll go.' He leaned on the table and looked at Oscar. 'You realise that those were our poor dead sisters, Oscar. Let them rest in peace.'

Oscar sat, strangely silent, his hands laid out on the white tablecloth, his fingers splayed.

Walter Wellbeloved pushed his chair back from the table. 'Who were you expecting, Mr Wilde?' he asked. 'The victims of Jack the Ripper?'

Oscar smiled. 'Possibly,' he said, still gazing down at his own hands.

'They were all fallen women, Mr Wilde – of the worst sort. You're hardly going to find them at the gates of heaven, are you? They'll all have gone to hell.'

14

Kippers

'D id you keep your eye on Wellbeloved throughout?'

'It was a little difficult in the dark, but yes. I did as you asked.'

'And what did you make of him?'

'I didn't warm to him, but I can't say that I saw him do anything to suggest he might be Jack the Ripper.'

'Unfortunately, the séance did not proceed quite as I had hoped.' Oscar poked at the orange kipper that sat untouched on the plate in front of him. 'What did you make of it all?'

'I am not sure,' I said.

'I am,' said my friend emphatically, pushing his breakfast away from him and opening up his cigarette case. 'I concede that for a moment or two I was lulled, carried away by the candlelight and the chanting – just as the idea of these kippers seemed a tempting one ten minutes ago. And then the reality dawned – the kippers came and didn't smell quite right. When Mrs Mathers began sniffing at the poor dead girl's apron it was a theatrical touch too far for me. I smelled a rat.'

'You're mixing your metaphors now, Oscar,' I laughed. 'That's not like you.'

'I'm having a cooked breakfast at nine o'clock in the morning. That's not like me either. These are confusing times, Arthur, but I think we can be clear about last night.'

'Whether or not Wellbeloved is Jack the Ripper, as communers with the spirit world he and Mrs Mathers are charlatans?'

'Or very, *very* eager to please.'

'Your brother appeared to be convinced.'

'Willie has always been a credulous soul. He'll believe anything except what's worth believing.'

'Why conjure up the spirits of your dead sisters, of all people?'

'Because I had asked for a séance and when people request a séance it is almost invariably because they wish to reconnect with a lost loved one. Mrs Mathers knows I had a sister who died when we were children. I've told you the story, Arthur.'

'I remember,' I said. 'She was ten and you were twelve. Isola – that was her name. You published a poem in her memory.'

'Exactly. My poem is published. The story is in the public domain.' Oscar drew on his cigarette and half-turned to gaze out of the dining-room window onto Langham Place. 'And Mrs Mathers comes from Ireland, so she also knows the tragic tale of my two half-sisters, consumed by fire on the terrible night when their ball gowns were accidentally set alight. She takes these long-ago tragedies and uses them to considerable effect – at least so far as Willie is concerned.'

'But could not your sisters genuinely have been trying to contact you from the other side?'

'They could, most certainly – but why should they? Last night, when Mrs Mathers and Mr Wellbeloved arrived at Tite Street no one had the Wilde girls on their mind, did they? Willie had mentioned that Wellbeloved was one of the Jack the Ripper suspects. I had arranged the séance thinking entirely of the Whitechapel victims. We gave Mrs Mathers poor Catherine Eddowes' apron. If we were summoning anyone, it wasn't Isola and Mary and Emily. It was Catherine Eddowes. I wanted to confront Wellbeloved with one of his victims. Instead, he and his accomplice turned the tables and confronted me and Willie with our dead sisters.'

'Why do you think your brother brought the séance to such a sudden close?'

'Because he believed they were indeed our sisters and he has never come to terms with the reality of their deaths. Some drink to drown their sorrows. Willie drinks to avoid sorrow altogether.'

A silence fell between us. Oscar continued to gaze out of the window and draw slowly on his cigarette. I poured myself some more coffee and wondered what best to say next. 'I liked his fiancée,' I volunteered at last – admittedly, without a great deal of conviction.

'I did, too,' said Oscar, with surprising enthusiasm. 'She admired my coat – and didn't mention her own wedding. You could not ask for much more in a woman.' He chuckled. 'They're staying with my mother in Oakley Street, you know.'

'Did you go back there with them last night?'

'Oh, no,' said Oscar. 'My brother does not interest me. I interest him a great deal, I fear. That is one of his life's tragedies. What interests me at the moment, Arthur, is our case.' He turned his chair back towards the dining table and addressed me through a swirl of purple smoke. 'Who was Jack the Ripper? That is the question.'

'And are we any closer to the answer?'

'When you returned to the hotel last night, I gave Mrs Mathers a lift back to her flat and then joined Wellbeloved for a nightcap at his club.'

'And what did you learn?'

'That he only drinks water or blood.'

'Good God.'

'Indeed – though he was perfectly happy for me to have a brandy and soda.'

I laughed. 'Should I be taking notes?' I asked.

'Possibly,' said Oscar. 'Walter Wellbeloved believes in human sacrifice, but only when it is self-sacrifice. The ancient gods require a human offering from time to time, but, according to Wellbeloved, they're quite fussy. Killing someone at random won't appease them. It seems the pagan deities Wellbeloved worships need a knowing sacrifice – and they need innocent blood to be spilled in their honour. Sacrificing a sinner is a worthless gesture. He knows people have accused him of being Jack the Ripper. He sees how his writings about pagan sacrifice, insufficiently carefully read, have led the ignorant to make wild allegations, but he denies being Jack the Ripper absolutely. He assured me that he would only be involved in killing someone if that person was a true believer and wanted to be killed – and then he would need to be certain that the person concerned was worthy of the office. To kill a common harlot by way of sacrifice would be to insult the gods, not honour them.'

'So do we eliminate Wellbeloved from our inquiries?'

'We're in no position to eliminate anyone yet. Walter Wellbeloved was in London at the time of each of the Whitechapel murders and doesn't deny the occasional sortie to Whitechapel during 1888.'

'For what purpose?'

'To visit a friend of his, so he told me last night – a showman by the name of Tom Norman. Have you heard of him? He's well known in certain circles. He has an emporium in the Whitechapel Road where he exhibits freaks of nature. Wellbeloved fell in love with one of them, it seems – a mermaid called Rosie.'

'Oh my God,' I exclaimed, shaking my head in disbelief.

'There's no accounting for taste when Eros spreads his wings,' said Oscar, smiling. He stubbed out his cigarette and looked about the dining room. 'I think we need these kippers cleared away, don't you?'

'So Wellbeloved remains on the list of suspects?'

'For the time being, yes. And I think we should go to Whitechapel to visit Mr Norman.'

'And the mermaid?'

'She's dead. Wellbeloved is distraught. He's taken up with Mrs Mathers by way of consolation.'

'How did the mermaid die?' I asked, marvelling at the words I spoke even as I uttered them.

'We shall discover when we get to Whitechapel. We need to go there anyway.'

'We should be pursuing Ostrog, shouldn't we?'

'Oh, yes. Circuses, freak shows, lunatic asylums – this is the murder mystery that has it all, Arthur. "It was the best of crimes, it was the worst of crimes." Your fortune is made.'

I tapped the table with my pencil. 'It will only work as a story, Oscar, if we discover who did it. No one wants to read of a mystery that's unresolved.'

'*Courage, mon brave.* We'll get there eventually. First, we have a second lunatic asylum to visit. In Colney Hatch, wherever that may be.'

'It's in North London, not far. Is this where Aaron Kosminski is incarcerated?'

'Supposedly. But when we get there, we may discover that he has run away to the circus, too. I have sent a telegram to the asylum superintendent requesting an interview.' He looked up and beamed at the white-jacketed waiter who had just arrived at our table. 'Perhaps Martin has his reply?'

The young man was holding a silver salver on which sat a telegram addressed to Oscar. 'It's for you, sir,' said the lad.

Oscar looked at me and winked. 'I've told him not to call me "Oscar" when he's at work. The maître d'hôtel might not understand.'

I said nothing, but thought to myself: the maître d'hôtel might understand all too well.

'Now, Martin,' continued Oscar gaily, 'before you clear away these foul smelling kippers and bring us some fresh toast and hot coffee, tell Dr Doyle what we were doing yesterday.'

'When, sir?' asked the boy.

'Yesterday afternoon, Martin – when you took me off on that wild-goose chase into Soho and Dr Doyle caught sight of us in the shop window and became so alarmed.'

I looked at Oscar, embarrassed. 'I didn't know you'd seen me . . .'

'Of course I saw you, Arthur – and I saw what you were thinking, too.'

'No, please, Oscar,' I protested. 'There's no need to explain.'

'There's every reason to explain. You thought I had deceived you, did you not?'

'How did you know?'

'Because you are a good, honest, open fellow, Arthur. And you are my friend. Friendship is love without his wings. You don't

deceive me and I would never deceive you. You should know that.'
He looked up at the young waiter once more. 'Now, Martin, what
were we doing?'

'Following the gentleman, sir.'

'Which gentleman?'

'The gentleman who has been following you, sir.'

'Thank you, Martin.' Oscar took the telegram from the
silver salver. 'You may clear the kippers.' The boy set about his
duties and Oscar lit another cigarette. 'Someone is pursuing
me, Arthur – following me, trailing me, waiting outside whatever theatre or restaurant or club I happen to be visiting. He's
waiting outside the hotel here for me every night and he's here
again each morning. I saw him out of the window just now.' I
sat forward and looked out onto the hotel's empty forecourt.
'He's gone,' he said. 'He doesn't linger. He keeps a watchful eye
and follows me, but always at a distance. I've tried to surprise
him, turning back on him suddenly, but each time he's slipped
away. He's too quick for me – so I've set Martin on to him. I've
shown him to the lad and promised the boy a guinea if he can
catch him for me.'

'Have you any idea who he might be?' I asked.

'None whatsoever. He looks neither intelligent nor interesting.
That's why I took him for a detective.'

I laughed. 'I'm glad we've cleared the air, Oscar. "Friendship is
love without his wings." I like that.'

'You did not recognise it?'

'No.'

'It's not mine. It's Byron's line. I've just borrowed it for the
season.'

We looked at one another, easily. I felt comfortable in my
friend's company once more.

He tore open the telegram and read it.

'Is this a genuine telegram?' I asked.

'Yes. And it's not what I expected. It's from Macnaghten. They've found another body in that alleyway off Tite Street.'

15

The Mortuary

Within the hour we found ourselves in the basement mortuary at New Scotland Yard, gazing down at the savagely disfigured body of a young woman. She was naked. Her large brown eyes were wide open; her short brown hair was smeared with blood. Her brow, her cheeks, her chin, her neck, her breasts were criss-crossed with knife markings: sharp lines drawn across the flesh, not deep incisions. The real violence had been inflicted below her waist: she had been disembowelled: her abdomen and uterus lay on the examination table next to her.

'She's no more than twenty,' I said, staring bleakly at the poor, scarred creature.

'Yes,' said Macnaghten, with a brief, professional sigh, 'she's young.'

'But she was strong,' I said, puzzled by the contradictions the corpse presented. 'Look at her arms – the well-developed biceps . . . the triceps, too. And here, look at the calf muscle . . .'

'She was strong, she was fit,' said Macnaghten, 'so why didn't she fight back?'

'Exactly.' I looked up and down the wretched remains. 'It's very strange. The extremities are unscathed. Her face and torso have been cut and slashed, but the shoulders, the arms, the hands, the feet are untouched. There's no bruising there, no signs of a struggle.'

'Yet her eyes are wide open, so she was not killed in her sleep.'

'Would that she had been, poor child.'

'She's not a child,' said Macnaghten drily. He stood across the body from me and took off his hat as he peered down into the dead girl's face. 'It's a young woman's face, but it's not an innocent woman's face, is it?'

'Can you tell?' I asked, suddenly (and curiously) affronted on the dead girl's part.

'Yes,' said Macnaghten, standing upright. 'I believe one can.'

'Has she been examined yet?' I asked. 'Are there indications of recent sexual activity?'

Macnaghten shrugged. With his eyes he indicated the girl's nether regions: 'Given the injuries, is it possible to tell?'

'May I examine her?' I asked.

'That's why you're here, Dr Doyle.'

Macnaghten nodded to the uniformed police sergeant who had brought us down to the mortuary when we arrived. The man was standing three feet or so away from the head of the table, gazing steadfastly ahead of him. At a glance I could tell that he was a decent man, with a good heart, who must have seen much that was shocking in his years on the beat, but had not seen a horror such as this before. He stepped forward and, without catching my eye, took my hat and coat and, from a shelf and a hook on the wall, fetched gloves and a surgical apron for me to wear.

'And why am I here?' asked Oscar.

My friend was standing awkwardly by the door to the room. As we had arrived he and the police sergeant had led the way down the stairs and Oscar had marched briskly towards the mortuary as the man very much in command of the situation and then, like a steeplechaser suddenly refusing a jump, had balked at the sight of the naked and dismembered body laid out on the table. We had moved past him into the room; he had remained fixed where he was in the doorway, one hand resting on the door handle.

Macnaghten turned towards him. 'You are here, Mr Wilde, because, perhaps after all, there is a connection between these murders in Chelsea and the Whitechapel murders of six years ago.'

'Do you think so?' asked Oscar. 'Do you really think so?'

Macnaghten paused before replying. 'I do not know how I cannot think so now,' he said eventually.

'Surely,' said Oscar, 'scores of women are murdered in London every year . . .'

Macnaghten moved away from the examination table and towards the door. 'Yes, Mr Wilde, but very few are murdered in a manner such as this. The appalling savagery is very terrible – I'm not surprised you cannot face it. It is also quite distinctive – and echoes those brutal murders of 1888. The woman whose body we found in Shelley Alley on Monday night had been stabbed thirty-nine times.'

'I recall,' said Oscar.

'Martha Tabram, killed on the seventh of August 1888, was also stabbed thirty-nine times.'

'On Monday night you considered that no more than a coincidence.'

Macnaghten gave a curt, joyless laugh. 'I now consider that I may have been wrong.'

'You surprise me,' said Oscar. 'When you gave us the file on the Whitechapel murders, you were most emphatic that Tabram was not one of the so-called Ripper's victims. You distinctly said: "Jack the Ripper had only five victims and Martha Tabram was not one of them."'

'Yes,' said Macnaghten, shrugging his shoulders once more. 'That's what I said. That's what I believed. Then.'

'This poor woman has not been stabbed,' I said, looking up from my grim work at the examination table. 'She has been cut to pieces with some care. A sharp knife has been used – possibly a surgical knife, certainly a knife at least six inches long – and it has been used by someone with some anatomical knowledge. The girl's pelvic organs have been removed with one clean sweep of the knife. The intestines, neatly severed from their mesenteric attachments, have been lifted out of the body, whole. And from the pelvis, the uterus and its appendages, the vagina and the bladder, have all been cut out as if a perverse surgeon had been at work. The rectum is untouched.'

'You will write this up, Doctor?' asked Macnaghten.

'Please,' pleaded Oscar, from his station by the door, 'spare us the anatomical details.'

'I cannot,' I said, standing back from the table for a moment, 'and for a reason.'

'I know the reason,' said Oscar. 'I read the police surgeon's post-mortem report on Annie Chapman. These wounds are similar.'

'They are identical,' I said.

'I thought they might be,' said Macnaghten, with satisfaction. 'I am grateful to have it confirmed, Dr Doyle.'

'As I recall,' added Oscar, wincing at the recollection, 'in the case of Annie Chapman, the intestines had been removed from her body and placed on the shoulder of her corpse.'

'It was the same in this case here,' said Macnaghten. 'When this girl's body was found, the organs that had been removed were laid out on her shoulders – almost as though they had been placed on display.'

'Do we know who this poor woman is?' asked Oscar, still not looking towards the table where the girl's body lay.

'No.'

'And we still have no idea who Monday's victim was?'

'None whatsoever.'

'The Whitechapel victims were all women of the street,' said Oscar, 'whereas . . .'

I completed his thought: 'I do not believe Monday's victim was a prostitute. She was malnourished. Her skin was withered, but it was not rough. Her fingernails were well cared for. She was not a working woman. She was a lady – I'm sure of it.'

'And this young woman?'

'She has a working woman's hands,' I said. 'Her nails are not so well cared for. And there appear to be traces of seminal fluid on her lower thigh, suggesting sexual activity not long before her death.'

'She might be a prostitute?' asked Macnaghten.

'Yes,' I said reluctantly. 'And yet she looks well fed. She looks healthy. When we have examined her organs more carefully, I will be surprised if we find anything to suggest excessive use of narcotics or alcohol. The photographs of the Whitechapel victims all show pale-faced, bedraggled women who have been broken by life – ruined long before their ghastly murders.'

'This one is young, as you say, Dr Doyle,' said Macnaghten. 'Perhaps her way of life had not yet had time to destroy her.'

I considered the cadaver once more. For a reason I could not quite understand, I did not want this poor murdered wretch to have been a prostitute. I said: 'Her face and hands are a little darker than her body, wouldn't you say? That suggests she spent some time out of doors and worked by day rather than by night.'

'Possibly,' said Macnaghten.

'What do her clothes tell us about her?' asked Oscar from the doorway.

'There are no clothes,' said Macnaghten.

'No clothes of any kind? No shoes, no stockings, no undergarments?'

'Nothing at all. No rings, no jewellery. She was discovered in the alley, naked, like this.'

'And there were no garments nearby?'

'No garments of any kind: no coat, no covering, nothing at all.'

'Not a shred of a thread? And no signs of a struggle?'

'Her body was discovered lying in the middle of the alley, just where we found the body on Monday. She was laid out on her back on the ground – as she is now, but with her innards resting on her shoulders.'

I saw Oscar close his eyes. 'It is grotesque,' he whispered.

'Were there any marks on the ground?' I asked.

'The earth was dry. There were old boot prints, of course. It's a busy alley by day.'

'But no prints of note?'

'No.'

'No prints of a naked foot? No signs of her heels being dragged across the ground.'

'No, nothing of the sort. Just the body placed on the ground – carefully, it would seem, not dropped or thrown down.'

'And was her blood still wet?' I asked.

'It was sticky to the touch,' said Macnaghten, 'but ice cold. It was a cold night. She was discovered soon after five this morning.'

'By the knife-grinder who keeps his cart in the alley?' asked Oscar, looking at the chief constable once more.

'Yes, the same man.'

'And at what time do you reckon the murder took place?'

Macnaghten turned to me. 'What does the rigor mortis tell us, Doctor?'

'She died twelve to fifteen hours ago,' I said.

Macnaghten pulled out a half-hunter from his waistcoat pocket. 'So, perhaps ten o'clock last night?'

'Were we still in Tite Street then?' asked Oscar.

'You were at home last night, Mr Wilde?' enquired Macnaghten. He sounded surprised. 'I thought you were staying in town – to work.'

'I was. I am. But I was in Tite Street last evening. Dr Doyle was with me.'

'So you were there at the time of the murder?'

'I was. And if you were at home last night, Chief Constable, you were there also.'

'I was not – as it happens.' He smiled. 'But I might have been.'

'I need some air, gentlemen,' said Oscar. 'Would you excuse me?'

16

The Westminster Alhambra

'Forgive me,' said Oscar, bowing his head in shame.

'There is nothing to forgive,' I said sincerely.

'But there is,' he protested. 'I stood like a toothless Cerberus at the gates of hell. I could not go in. I could not face the horror of that poor girl's mutilated body.'

'I am not surprised. I do not blame you.'

'I have made a fetish of beauty, Arthur, to the extent that I cannot face the reality of the grotesque.'

'I understand,' I said.

'I believe you do.' He looked at me and smiled. 'You are a good friend.' He clapped his hands together lightly to herald a change of mood. 'And while you have been examining the remains of that unfortunate young woman, please know that I have not been entirely idle. I have been considering the evidence and conducting an interview.'

'Here?' I asked, surprised.

'Yes, here, on this very marble slab.' He gave one of his characteristic little giggles. 'And what's more, without benefit of luncheon.'

It was now gone two o'clock in the afternoon and I had joined my friend at Nevill's Turkish Bath, off Trafalgar Square, at the Whitehall end of Northumberland Avenue. He had left me a note at the front desk at New Scotland Yard telling me where I might find him and, in truth, having completed the grim and bloody business of the post-mortem examination, I welcomed the idea of stripping off my clothes and steam-cleaning my body from head to toe.

The baths were recently opened and handsomely appointed in an amusingly mock-Moorish style. At the entrance, the payment kiosk was surmounted by an onion-shaped cupola, painted midnight blue and decorated with a star and crescent moon. The attendant was dressed as Ali Baba, though his demeanour was more suggestive of one of the Forty Thieves. 'Mr Wilde's expecting you,' he said, in an accent that spoke of New Bermondsey rather than Old Baghdad. 'He's paid. Keep going till you find him.'

I descended the winding staircase to the changing room, disrobed and, wrapped in a towel, did as I had been instructed, moving along mosaic-covered passageways, from one subterranean chamber to the next, each hotter than the last. In every room, seated on benches, were men, middle-aged or elderly in the main, wrapped in towels, lost in contemplation – either of their stomachs or their destinies: it was not possible to tell.

I found Oscar in the fifth room. It was the hottest room by far.

'This is the *calidarium*,' he explained, beckoning me to sit on the marble by his side. 'We're not likely to be disturbed here.

Only the hardiest souls venture this far. The temperature can reach 250 degrees.'

My friend looked remarkably at ease in the extraordinary heat. 'Forgive this semi-recumbent posture,' he said, beads of perspiration bespangling his brow. 'It is not very elegant, but it is comfortable.' He looked like the Walrus perched on the rocks in one of Tenniel's drawings from *Alice in Wonderland*. Having apologised for his abrupt departure from the mortuary, his mood was suddenly sunny.

'No lunch and an interview?' I asked, seating myself alongside him. 'What has been going on?'

'Progress – of sorts. Michael Ostrog is indeed at large, but he was not in London last night. He was in Paris.'

'How on earth do you know this?'

'I have been interviewing his employer.'

'His employer? The man from the circus?'

'Yes, my friend Salazkin – Ivan the Terrible, circus owner, ringmaster, knife-thrower, lion tamer and spy.'

'Spy?'

Oscar smiled. 'I assume so. Every Russian in London is a spy. It's well known. Why else are they here? It can't be for the *cuisine*. The English have no feel for beetroot.'

I laughed. 'Are you sure he's a spy?'

'No. But I've long thought he might be, with his circus moving from capital to capital around the western world – and I assume that's why he comes here rather than going to a Turkish bath on his side of town. This is the Westminster Alhambra . It is where all the European spies come to meet the politicians and the diplomats.'

'Salazkin was here?'

'He left moments ago. He may still be in the building, cooling off in the plunge pool.'

'Did you have an appointment?'

'No, it was a chance encounter. He was with another friend of mine – an acquaintance, really. Henry Labouchere MP. Labby. Do you know him?'

'No.'

'You will. He's one of the parliamentarians making Macnaghten's life a misery, incessantly demanding to know, "Who was Jack the Ripper?" Labby's gloriously censorious – which, of course, makes him wonderfully suspect.'

'And Messrs Labouchere and Salazkin were here together just now?'

'Yes, Labby and Ivan the Terrible, *à deux* in the *tepidarium*. Naked. Not a pretty sight.' He pulled his own towel more closely about him before going on. 'Curiously, they have a good deal in common. Labby, bizarrely, once worked in a circus. He was an acrobat, a tumbler. Dressed in pink tights, he was billed as "The Bounding Buck of Babylon".'

'When was this?'

'In younger and happier days – a lifetime ago. His is an interesting story, though he's not a very interesting man. He is predictable in a way that Ivan the Terrible is not.'

'And you talked to them about Ostrog?'

'Fortuitously, Labby had a lunch to go to – with the Foreign Secretary, as he told us with an affectation of insouciance that was truly nauseating.' Oscar's portly body rumbled with suppressed laughter. 'Labby does not know that I know all there is to know about Lord Rosebery. Bosie's brother is the Foreign Secretary's private secretary.'

I smiled. It was good to see my friend back on song.

'I'm in touch with Bosie again, by the way,' he added. 'Constance approves. Indeed, last night she suggested I take a little holiday with Bosie before I start on my new play.' I said nothing. 'Anyway,' he went on merrily, 'with Labby dispatched to the Foreign Office, Salazkin and I moved ourselves into here. That's when I asked him about Ostrog.'

'It is definitely Ostrog?'

'He calls himself Michael Ostrov now, but it's the man in the police file. I recognised him in the photograph. I recognised him at the circus the other night. He is the man who has kindly delivered Salazkin's gifts of caviar to me in Tite Street. According to Salazkin, he's been his trusted assistant for several years.'

'Does he vouch for him?'

'He says he's loyal, hard-working, taciturn – which Salazkin likes. At the circus, Salazkin does the talking. Ostrov does the errands. Salazkin says he's not very bright, but he's willing, relatively reliable and reasonably able.'

'Did you tell him that the police suspect the man of being Jack the Ripper – and that they believe he is locked up in a lunatic asylum?'

'I did – and Salazkin roared with laughter. He said he'd assumed Ostrov had a doubtful past – he'd not enquired too closely. One way or another, he said, "all circus folk walk the tightrope". He has an amusing way with him, Salazkin. But he knew nothing of the lunatic asylum, though he said that from time to time Ostrov "disappears for a day or two" – but, as he put it, "that's a Russian failing brought on by an excess of vodka". He said the man was incapable of murder. He has neither the strength nor the courage, according to Salazkin. As we shall discover when we question him.'

'We are to question him?'

'Salazkin will arrange it – as soon as Ostrov is back from Paris. He went on the boat train yesterday, on circus business, taking publicity material to the French printers. The circus moves on to Paris shortly.'

'And where do we go next?' I asked.

'Bed,' said Oscar, with a mighty yawn. 'I'm drained, aren't you? You must be, after the horrors of the morning. Bed and then dinner and a stroll.'

'I must get back to work, Oscar,' I said. I felt a sudden knot of anxiety forming in my stomach. 'I have a living to earn. Deadlines to meet. Stories to write.'

'This will furnish you with a story,' he said, sitting up and resting his hand on my arm.

'There's no story without a satisfactory ending, Oscar. You know that. Who was the Whitechapel murderer? Unless we can name him, what have we got? A journey and no destination. That won't work in a book.'

'We're getting there.'

'Are we? Macnaghten has five suspects. We've met just two of them and neither seemed particularly suspect to me.'

'Macnaghten knows nothing.'

'Do we know more?'

'I believe I've solved the greatest part of the mystery already,' said Oscar. He beamed at me and with his large, soft hands smoothed out his towel complacently. The Walrus was now taking on the demeanour of the Cheshire Cat.

'Really?'

'Yes, "really". And Salazkin's going to give us Ostrog to interview. And tomorrow I'm planning to take us to the Colney Hatch Lunatic Asylum to see Kosminski – if he's to be found. And tonight, after dinner, I thought we should take a stroll round Whitechapel – walk the course, as it were. We're charged with winkling out the truth of the Whitechapel murders. Apparently, I secured the most brilliant First of my generation. Undeniably, you created Sherlock Holmes. If we can't solve the mystery, Arthur, who can?'

'Are you going to tell me what you think you've already discovered?'

'Not yet. I'm not quite certain.'

'And what about these new murders?' I asked.

'What about them? They are not part of our remit, Arthur. You know my motto: "Don't dabble, focus."'

I laughed. 'That has *never* been your motto, Oscar.'

'Come now, Arthur, do you really think we are seeing the return of Jack the Ripper?'

'It's possible.'

'But not likely. Or, at least, not if any of Macnaghten's suspects is indeed a guilty party. If the poor girl whose body you examined this morning in the mortuary was murdered in Chelsea last night, it can't have been Walter Wellbeloved because he was with us. It can't have been Richard Mansfield because he was strutting the stage as Napoleon – and I reckon the audience would have noticed if the emperor had gone missing during the second act. It can't have been Ostrog because he is in Paris. And it can't have been Montague Druitt or the Duke of Clarence because they're both dead. I suppose Kosminski could have slipped down from Colney Hatch under cover of darkness to do the dreadful deed, but it does seem a bit unlikely. Kosminski was an East End barber. Chelsea really isn't his patch.'

'Yes,' I ruminated, 'why are these murders suddenly happening in Tite Street?'

'They're not "happening" in Tite Street. The bodies are being discovered in Shelley Alley, off Tite Street, that's all.'

'It's significant, Oscar. You can't deny it. Macnaghten, charged with producing a report on the Whitechapel murders, invites you to assist him and suddenly two bodies, mutilated in a manner disturbingly reminiscent of the Whitechapel murders, turn up on your doorstep.'

'Shelley Alley is marginally closer to Macnaghten's doorstep than mine. I don't believe Oscar Wilde has anything to do with the *mise-en-scène*.'

'Don't you?'

'I don't. The first body was discovered before our meeting with Chief Constable Macnaghten, remember – before I was involved in the matter in any way.'

'But you knew what Macnaghten wanted to discuss with you, didn't you?'

'I had an idea, yes. But no one else knew. Macnaghten told me that he had not mentioned it to any of his colleagues and wouldn't do so. I'd only mentioned it to you – and to Constance.' He got to his feet. 'Our task is to concentrate on the Whitechapel murders, Arthur.'

'But we keep being pulled back to Tite Street.'

'Perhaps it is Constance, then? Do you think she's contriving these murders to lure me home?'

'Don't be absurd. Even as a joke that's a horrible thing to say.'

'Love will find a way through paths where wolves fear to prey.'

I looked at him. His face was flushed and covered in sweat. I saw tears in the corner of his eyes. 'You are a strange fellow. You say something quite horrible and then you come up with a lovely line like that.'

He smiled. 'I'm glad you like it. It's one of my favourites. I stole it from a dead man. I steal a lot of my lines, you know. It's one of my smaller secrets.'

'Do you have many secrets?' I asked.

'We all have secrets.'

'I hope I don't have secrets,' I said.

'You may not now, Arthur, but you will have one day.'

17

Whitechapel

Woe did not dine in town, after all.

'We'll find something in Whitechapel,' said Oscar, as we climbed up into the two-wheeler he had ordered for us. 'There's a stall I know by the docks that sells cockles and mussels. And gin. It's close by my favourite opium den. Wonderful silks on the walls.' My friend was in a teasing mood, but somehow, although I'd taken to my bed for an hour's rest in the afternoon, I hadn't the energy to rise to his bait.

It was a cold evening, and not yet seven o'clock. The day had been a dreary one and now a dense, drizzly fog lay low upon the great city. As we drove east down the Strand the lamps were but misty splotches of diffused light that threw a feeble circular glimmer upon the slimy pavement. The yellow glare from the shop windows streamed out into the steamy, vaporous air, and threw a murky, shifting radiance across the crowded thorough-fare. There was, to my mind, something eerie and ghostlike in the endless procession of faces that flitted across these narrow bars of light – sad faces and glad, haggard and merry. Like all human-kind, they flitted from the gloom into the light, and so back into the gloom once more. I am not subject to impressions, but the dull, heavy evening, with the strange business upon which we were engaged, combined to make me nervous and depressed. I was conscious, too, of missing Touie and my children, and feeling that if I could not be with them in Switzerland I should then, at least, be at home in South Norwood earning their keep, writing a publishable story – with a satisfactory ending.

Oscar's mood was very different. He was ebullient, gaily filling the cab with his favourite aphorisms and purple cigarette smoke. 'A cigarette is the perfect type of a perfect pleasure,' he declared. 'It is exquisite and leaves one unsatisfied.'

'The fog in here is worse than the fog out there,' I said dourly.

'This is not your best mood, Arthur, but happily moods don't last. It is their chief charm.'

'I'm sorry,' I said. 'I'm thinking about these poor women. All so brutally murdered. For what?'

'Is that a rhetorical question?' he asked, smiling at me slyly, drawing slowly on his cigarette, his head half turned away.

'It was – probably,' I answered. I was not inclined to conversation, but Oscar would persist.

'All so brutally murdered,' he repeated. 'For what? Not for money, that's for sure. All of the Whitechapel victims were prostitutes. None was worth robbing for what she possessed. And the police explored the sad history of each of them and there is no reason to believe that any one of them was killed because someone – husband, lover, rival – wanted them dead and was ready to pay to have them dispatched. So, if not for money, then for what? For pleasure?'

I shuddered at the thought. 'Could there be any pleasure in such perversity?'

'Oh, a great deal, I fear, Arthur. You're a moderate man. You don't touch the extremes, but there are others for whom life is unfulfilled if they have not experienced every experience that life has to offer. These are murders most foul and to the murderer that is what makes them most delicious.'

I looked out of the cab window. The streets were darker and emptier now. I only gave half an ear to Oscar as, with a mellifluous fluency that was quite maddening, he continued to expound his philosophy of the perverse. 'You contain your baser impulses, Arthur. You keep them well-buttoned within your tweed waistcoat, but you have had passions that have made you afraid, surely? Thoughts that have filled you with terror? Dreams where mere memory might stain your cheek with shame—'

'No,' I said emphatically. 'No, Oscar. No.'

He lit another cigarette and grinned at me through the light of his flaming Vesta like a latter-day Mephistopheles. 'I hear you, my friend,' he said soothingly, 'but others sing a different song. To us every impulse that we strive to strangle broods in the mind and poisons us. The only way to get rid of a temptation is to yield to it. Resist it and your soul grows sick with longing. And nothing can cure the soul but the senses, just as nothing can cure the senses but the soul.'

'Sometimes, Oscar, I believe you talk too much.'

He laughed. 'I am merely setting out the case for the new Hedonism. We have to consider every possibility.'

'So Jack the Ripper is one of your new Hedonists, is he?'

'Well, it's an avenue I doubt the fellows at New Scotland Yard have explored. And if he is, then I suppose Richard Mansfield could be our man – playing all the parts, tasting all the fruits of all the gardens in the world.'

'I think a loner and lunatic with a grudge against prostitutes is more likely to be our man.'

He lowered the carriage window and threw out a half-smoked cigarette. 'I agree. I was just filling the night air with sound.' He looked at me benignly and brushed his gloves across my knee. 'I need to talk myself out sometimes.' He laughed. 'I was going to say, "Pay no heed, Arthur", but I don't believe you did.' The cab came to a halt. 'We're here now.'

'Where are we?'

We clambered down from the two-wheeler. 'Buck's Row, Whitechapel,' said Oscar, 'where it all began.' He called up to the cabman. 'Meet us in two hours at St Katharine's Dock – at Harry's whelk stall. Do you know it?' The man nodded. 'If we're not there, look for us. We won't be far away.' The cab drove on. The air was cold. The street was strangely silent.

'We should have brought a map,' I said, looking about me. The driver had dropped us off at the end of a narrow, sloping cobbled street. It was deserted and unlit. At the far end from us, there was a faint glow of yellow light coming from a ground-floor window. At our end, there was darkness. If there was a moon up above, it was not set to penetrate tonight's pea-souper.

'I have one,' said Oscar, pulling a folded paper from his coat pocket, 'but it may be of little use.' He peered up at the black brick walls to either side of us. 'The streets appear to have no names.' He beckoned me to follow him. We left the cobbled roadway and turned right, down a small dirt track.

'I smell horses,' I said.

'Yes, there's a stable at the end. It's by the gate to the stable yard that she was killed, I think.'

In the gloom, through the fog, I could just see the black shadow of Oscar's heavy frame as he moved along the track. 'Mary Ann Nichols, known as Polly, struck down, then cut to pieces.'

'Poor woman. May she rest in peace.'

'Christ almighty!' cried Oscar, suddenly stumbling forward, toppling to the ground, reaching out for the wall as he fell.

A woman's shrill voice rang out. It was less a cry of alarm than a yelp of pain. Oscar pushed himself up from the ground and, as he did so, in the dark, came face to face with a bedraggled beggar woman, dressed in rags, squatting on the ground.

'Forgive me, madam,' he said, breathing hard. 'I did not see you there.' He stood over the woman, recovering his balance, fumbling in his pockets for change. He found some coins and dropped them into her lap. 'Get yourself some sustenance – and then a room for the night,' he said.

The pathetic creature looked up at him and said nothing. I could not see her face. She held up her hands. Oscar reached into his coat for more change.

'Come, Arthur,' he said quickly, turning away from her. 'We don't need to see the yard where the hapless Polly died. We have seen enough. We can imagine the rest.'

Swiftly, our eyes now curiously adjusting to the gloom, we marched back down the alley into the street and turned left, up the slope towards the house at the far end whose window gave off a faint light. As we reached it, Oscar took his paper from his pocket. 'Where are we?' he said, holding it up to read. 'It's a small corner of hell, isn't it?'

'It's bleak, certainly,' I said.

'Ever the realist, Arthur. But you're right. If it was hell at least there'd be fires to keep us warm and some amusing company.'

He held the paper against the window pane. 'This is where we are and each cross marks the spot where one of the murdered women was found.'

'Where next, then?' I asked.

'Here, Hanbury Street. Half a mile as the crow flies, but through these dark alleys and backwaters, God knows how long it will take us.'

In fact, it took us no more than twenty minutes. The alleys and passageways were all unlit. We scuttled through them as quickly as we could, stepping over occasional bodies lying in our path, making way for drunken figures that lurched past us, avoiding darkened doorways in which stood the shadowy figures of men in working clothes, smoking pipes, and women of the night, dressed in little more than rags, pitifully plying their trade.

Hanbury Street itself was, by that night's standard, a busy, almost wholesome, thoroughfare. Young women sat on door-steps, chatting, making paper flowers. Dogs ran across the cobblestones. A handful of young men – sailors and carters, by the look of them – stood around a roasted chestnut vendor's brazier. It was a long street and mostly dark, so that figures kept making entrances and exits through the shadows. Every hundred yards or so a street lamp threw down a murky pool of gaslight. Beneath one of them stood two policemen. Each touched his helmet as we approached.

'Good evening, gentlemen,' said the older of the two. He had broad shoulders, mutton-chop whiskers and a boxer's face. 'Mind how you go now.'

'Thank you, Officer,' said Oscar. 'We're looking for number twenty-nine.'

'Where the girl was done in?'

'Yes,' said Oscar. 'Annie Chapman.'

'It's down there,' said the policeman, 'on the right, past the lodging house. There's nothing to see. But people still come.'

'Did you know her?'

'I knew all the Ripper's victims, sir. We all did.' His companion nodded. 'I call her a girl. She was a woman. Nearly fifty. Fat and drunk and stupid.'

'You didn't like her?'

'She was all right. They're all the same. They drinks too much. They gets in to fights. Their men beats them. They drinks some more.'

'Did her man beat her?'

'Her actual hubby was dead. She had two regulars, though, who paid for her services.' He chuckled, not unkindly. 'They didn't pay much. They didn't have to.'

'"Harry the Hawker" and "The Pensioner",' said Oscar.

'You've read all about it, then? There's been plenty to read. Only "The Pensioner" wasn't an old soldier like he said. He was a brickie of sorts. And a brute. Ted Stanley. He used to beat her black and blue.'

'Did he kill her?'

'No. She died for the want of fourpence. Like Polly Nichols.'

'Meaning?' I asked.

'They lived in one of the lodging houses – fourpence a night for a bed. We got 146 lodging houses in this square mile, common beds for six thousand souls in all. The sheets are changed every week and there's a cup of tea every morning. But if you ain't got the fourpence, you don't get the bed. They was both turned out, Polly Nichols and Annie Chapman, and had to spend the night on the street. That's where he found 'em, the Ripper, and did his stuff.'

'Do you know who he is?' asked Oscar lightly.

'I know who he isn't,' said the policeman firmly. 'He isn't any of the lads round here. They drink, they're rough, they're crooked. Some of them is evil. But none's the sort to go round killing women and carefully cutting out their privates. That's not Whitechapel.'

'You know your patch well,' said Oscar disarmingly. 'Five murders in ten weeks within one square mile, yet you didn't get close to finding the man?'

'We arrested a hundred of 'em. And more. Any man those women knew, any man seen anywhere nearby on any of the nights in question, we had 'em in. The long, the short and the tall. The lame, the halt and the lunatic. The lot. They all had a sorry tale to tell, but most of 'em had solid alibis too. We couldn't make it stick on any of 'em. Not one.'

'It'll be a stranger,' said the second policeman. 'An outsider. Got to be. A foreigner most like.'

'Could be a gentleman,' said the older policeman, 'Look at you two.' He enjoyed his little joke. Oscar smiled obligingly. 'Someone who comes and goes and no one thinks to stop. Someone with a hat and cloak to hide behind. Someone who can afford a hansom to get away from the scene of the crime. I was on duty at the inquests.'

'We both was.'

'It could be a doctor. That would explain the way they was all cut up. Maybe the doctor what drowned himself.'

'Druitt,' said Oscar.

'Him,' said the policeman with finality. 'He drowned himself and the killing stopped.'

'Well, thank you, officers,' said Oscar. 'That's most interesting. We're much obliged. We'll be on our way now.'

'Go carefully. Avoid the alleys. Don't stay too late.'

'May we ask who you are?' said the younger policeman. 'Just for the record, just in case.'

'Of course,' said Oscar. 'I am Henry Labouchere, Member of Parliament. And this is my friend Lord Rosebery.'

The policeman touched his helmet. 'I thought you looked familiar.'

18

Darkness

'Why the devil did you do that?' I asked him, in an exasperated whisper, as soon as we were far enough away.

'I thought it prudent.'

'And why those names?'

'I thought it amusing.'

'You're a curious fellow, Oscar Wilde,' I said, shaking my head. A boy with a metal hoop had just brushed past us, but there was no one else near us on the pavement where we stood. 'We are investigating murders of the most horrific kind – unspeakable crimes – and you're telling lies to the police while trying to be amusing.'

'And if I laugh at any mortal thing, 'Tis that I may not weep.'

He looked up at the building we had reached: 29 Hanbury Street. It was made of red English brick, four storeys tall, a narrow terraced house of no consequence. It stood in darkness, all shuttered up. 'Unlit, unloved, unlovely,' murmured my friend. He put his boot on the doorstep. 'Is this where she died?'

'No,' I said, 'I think it was at the back of the building.'

We walked on past the house and found the side-alley that led to the back-alley than ran behind the terrace. It was a narrow dirt track, no wider than three feet, muddy under foot, and littered with old newspapers, broken boxes and vegetable peelings. Each house had its own small yard, with shed and privy, enclosed by a wooden fence. 'This'll be it,' I said. Oscar, some inches taller than me, stood on his toes to peer over the paling. He stepped back at once, as if losing his footing. It was his turn to whisper now. 'Come away. Come!'

'What is it?'

He pulled me back along the slippery, littered path. 'A man and a woman – against the wall – rutting. I saw her vacant eyes and his heaving body. That was enough.' He shook his head and reached into his pockets for his cigarettes. 'They made no noise. The squalor of it, Arthur. This is a vile world.'

'Would you recognise the man again?'

'No, of course not. I only saw his back. He was hunched over the poor creature.'

'When Annie Chapman was murdered, it was just before dawn. A man next door, at number twenty-seven, heard a woman's voice call out "No" and then heard what sounded like someone falling against the fence.'

'And he did nothing. As we've done nothing now.'

'And twenty minutes later a carter on his way to work discovered Annie's mutilated body lying in the dirt by the doorway to the yard.'

Oscar drew deep on his cigarette.

'Did the woman you've just seen appear to be in danger?'

'She looked dead to all sensation,' he said, 'but I doubt that she's in mortal danger. Who knows?' He dropped his cigarette in the gutter and pointed west. 'This way.' We continued along Hanbury Street, Oscar setting a brisk pace. 'If we cross Commercial Street, we should reach Miller's Court. It's not far. At least we're learning what we need to know.'

'What's that?' I asked.

'That this is the vilest part of town where poverty and prostitution are rife, where the main thoroughfares are few and poorly lit, and between them are myriad passageways, backstreets, lanes and alleys through which rats of every kind may run.' He stopped in his tracks. 'Where are we now?'

There was a street sign fixed to the railings. I could barely read it through the murk. 'It says "Commercial Road",' I said.

'We have come the wrong way.' He struck a Vesta and in the flickering light peered at his map. 'Down here, fourth on the right and we should be at Dutfield's Yard. We'll go there first.'

As we paced along the roadway, counting the side streets, he said, 'I am beginning to understand how the police have failed. We see the shape of people as they pass us by, but in the darkness we don't see their faces. No two witnesses offered the same description of any one suspect. Now we know why.'

'This is Berner Street,' I said.

'And this alley here leads to Dutfield's Yard. It's a black hole.'

'But the killings occurred in August and September. Perhaps there was no fog. There might have been a moon.'

'Yes,' he said, moving slowly along the alley, his gloved hand touching the wall as he went. 'Yes, there must have been a moon. The murderer saw what he was doing. The crime was brutal, but the surgery curiously precise.'

'Except here. This is where Elizabeth Stride was killed, isn't it? Her throat was cut – her left artery severed – but there were no other incisions, no abdominal mutilations.'

We had reached the end of the alley. We sensed the absence of walls to either side of us, we knew there was an open space before us, but still we could see nothing.

'Why are we here?' I asked.

'Because the darkness tells its own story.' He reached in his pocket once more and lit another of his Vestas. A blue flame burst into life and suddenly we saw her, standing immediately in front of us – a middle-aged woman with a painted face and a feather boa wrapped around her neck. She appeared quite unperturbed.

'Hello, dearie,' she said, smiling.

'Mary Mother of God,' cried Oscar, stepping backwards. 'These women are everywhere.'

'Please excuse us,' I said lamely. I took Oscar's arm to pull him away.

'Come to see where poor Lizzie died?' enquired the woman. She put the question almost cheerfully.

'Did you know her?' asked Oscar, holding up his matchstick above the woman's face.

'She was my sister. This was her patch. Now it's mine.'

'How can you bear to come here?' asked Oscar, as the light flickered and died in his hand.

'I gets a lot of business on account of poor Lizzie. There's a lot of men likes the idea of having their way with the sister of one of Jack the Ripper's girls. They want to do it where poor Lizzie died.'

Oscar lit another of his Vestas. His hands were trembling, but his voice was steady. 'It can't be safe for you.' He handed me the light and felt in his coat for his wallet. 'Here,' he said, producing a pound note. 'Here, please take this.'

'It's too much,' she said, shaking her head. And then she laughed and grabbed the note. 'Or is it for the two of you?'

'Oh my God,' said Oscar. 'Please don't misunderstand us. We're . . . '

'We're concerned for your safety,' I said.

'I can look after myself,' said the woman. Clasping Oscar's money tightly in the palm of her left hand, with thumb and forefinger she pulled her feather boa away from her neck. In her right hand, just below her chin, she held an unsheathed knife that looked quite sharp enough to kill a man.

'Do you know who it was who murdered your sister?'

'It was Jack,' she said. 'He killed another girl that night.'

'Yes,' said Oscar. 'Catherine Eddowes – in Mitre Square.'

'Poor Kate. He ripped her apart all right. He cut out her kidney. With Lizzie he had to stop.'

'He was disturbed?'

'It was only one o'clock, wasn't it? There was still people in Berner Street. He must have heard a noise and scarpered.'

'Did anyone see him?'

'Some say they did, but they didn't. All we know is that it wasn't one of her regulars. They've been accounted for.' She smiled. 'I see some of them now.'

'Do you have many regulars?' I asked. She chuckled and I realised how awkwardly I had phrased my question. 'I mean, does one have many regulars in your line of business?'

'A few. But here, 'cos we're down by the docks, we get a lot of sailors. And foreigners. Russians, Poles, Jews. There's not a lot of chit-chat, but some of the English ones like to talk about Lizzie first. The gentlemen that is, not the locals. Strangers, like you two. Funny that. Jack the Ripper's been good for business.'

'I'm sorry about that.'

'Don't be. There's no point in being sorry about anything.' She laughed again. 'We all ends up dead anyway.'

'It's a philosophy, I suppose,' said Oscar. His Vesta died once more and we stood in silence in the black night. 'We must be going,' he added. He put out a hand and took my arm.

'Is that it, then?' asked the woman.

'Yes,' said Oscar, 'thank you. May I ask, what is your name?'

'Stella,' she said. 'But if you want me and I'm not here, just ask for Lizzie Stride's sister.'

'And you've no idea who he might have been?'

'No,' she said, 'but I has an idea about it all the same.'

'Yes?' said Oscar eagerly.

'If you want to know, and nobody does, I think there might have been two of 'em.'

'Two assailants?'

'Yeah. Two Jacks for the price of one.'

'Why do you say that?' I asked.

'I don't know, really. It's just a working girl's hunch, that's all.' As she laughed we could see nothing but her breath in the night air. 'It wasn't you two, was it?'

19

Opium

We continued our walk through the murky streets of Whitechapel. Poverty and squalor were everywhere. At one street corner a drunken man stood pissing in a doorway. As we veered off the pavement to avoid him, in the fog I collided with a woman who was pulling a small handcart along the gutter. She was dressed as a washerwoman, and her cart was piled high with bloodied rags. The stench was overwhelming.

We quickened our pace and hurried on. 'Life is never fair,' said Oscar, as we passed by an old soldier sitting on the kerbstone with a wooden crutch and an empty begging bowl at his side. 'Perhaps it is a good thing for most of us that it is not.' He looked at me and smiled and then turned back and emptied all the coins from his coat pocket into the begging bowl. The old soldier touched his cap, but said nothing.

'Have we seen enough?' I asked.

'Probably. And what have we learned from what we've seen?'

'That the streets are dark and the fog is thick and it's little wonder that the police have failed to find their man,' I said, somewhat bleakly.

Oscar laughed. 'You're getting hungry, aren't you, Arthur? Let's make for the docks.'

'The docks?'

'Harry's whelk stall?'

'It's a bit cold for gin and whelks,' I said.

'You'd prefer a glass of stout and a ham sandwich, wouldn't you?'

It was my turn to laugh. 'I would,' I said.

'Follow me,' he said.

We were now on Back Church Street, travelling south towards the river. There were street lamps here and Oscar paused beneath one of them to consult his map. 'There's Pinchin Street to our left . . .'

'Where the torso was found?'

'Yes, but let's not be distracted. "Don't dabble, focus." The torso belongs to an entirely different case, according to Macnaghten – remember? You need your supper and there's a club of sorts near here where they'll serve you a passable sandwich.'

'You've been here before?' I asked, surprised.

'Once or twice. I am a man of the world, Arthur, as you know. I get about. And the club has a highly respectable clientele.'

The 'club' was an opium den and as seedy and disreputable an establishment as I have encountered.

It stood between a slop-shop and a gin-shop in a vile alley underneath the railway arches off Pinchin Street. A lamp flickered above the wooden front door, but there was no outward indication of what lay within. 'Here we are,' said Oscar cheerily, lifting the latch on the door and making his way into the gloom beyond as comfortably as a man might do returning to the cosiness of his beloved hearth and home.

At once we found ourselves in a long, low room, thick and heavy with brown opium smoke, and terraced with wooden berths, like the forecastle of an emigrant ship. Through the poisonous mist one could dimly catch a glimpse of bodies lying in strange fantastic poses, bowed shoulders, bent knees, heads thrown back and chins pointing upward, with here and there a dark, lack-lustre eye turned upon the newcomer. Out of the black shadows there glimmered little red circles of light, now bright, now faint, as the burning opium waxed or waned in the bowls of the metal pipes. Most lay silent, but some muttered to themselves, and others talked together in a strange, low, monotonous voice, their conversation audible in snatches and then suddenly tailing off into silence, each mumbling out his own thoughts and paying little heed to the words of his neighbour.

As we entered, a sallow Malay attendant hurried up with a pipe in each hand, beckoning us towards an empty berth. 'Thank you,' said Oscar. 'But we have no time to smoke today. We're simply after a bite to eat and a little warmth. Is there any room in the captain's cabin?'

The Malay attendant offered Oscar an obsequious bow and, with a fawning, crablike, sideways gait, led us along the narrow passageway between the double row of sleepers, and through a heavily curtained doorway into a second, smaller chamber beyond. Here the air was clearer, the light was brighter and the furnishings more comfortable. The walls and floor were covered with Turkish rugs; around the room were assorted stools, chairs and divans, some empty, some occupied. In one corner was a small brazier of burning charcoal, beside which, on a three-legged wooden stool, there sat a tall, thin old man, with his jaw resting upon his two fists, and his elbows upon his knees, staring into the fire. A boy, no more than sixteen or seventeen years of age, sat at his feet resting his head against the old man's thigh. In another corner, in a high-backed armchair, sat a surly looking individual, a man of perhaps fifty years of age, of medium build but strong physical presence, immediately noticeable because of the sneer on his lips and the thick black bushiness of his eyebrows. He held a horsewhip in his hand and beat it rhythmically across his knees. It was clear at once that Oscar recognised the man.

'We'll sit here,' said Oscar softly, indicating a sofa close to the doorway.

'Should you greet your friend?' I asked.

Oscar ignored my remark and said to the Malay: 'Sandwiches, Mamat, please, and beer. Chop-chop.' The attendant hurried away and Oscar leaned towards me conspiratorially. 'I have read *The Man with the Twisted Lip*, Arthur. I know you have been to places such as this before.'

'Only the once,' I said truthfully, 'for the purposes of research. I have read *The Picture of Dorian Gray*, Oscar. I think this is more your *milieu* than mine.'

'There are gentlemen here, as you can see,' he continued, his voice barely above a whisper, 'and fundamental to the rules of a place like this is that no one acknowledges anyone else and no one tells tales.'

'It is the Freemasonry of the damned,' I murmured.

'Exactly,' whispered my friend, with a knowing smile.

'What are you saying?'

'That if Mansfield or Druitt or Wellbeloved or anyone else had taken refuge here, no one would have spoken of it.'

'Even if they had been covered in blood?'

'*Especially* if they had been covered in blood. This is a secret garden, Arthur. The weeds and flowers that grow here do so undisturbed, unreported, unobserved.'

The Malay returned with a tin tray on which stood two tankards of beer and a plate of meat and cheese sandwiches. As he placed the tray on the floor between us, beyond his stooping figure I caught sight of the boy sitting by the brazier at the feet of the thin old man. The youth looked directly at me and then, closing his eyes, reached up with his hands and pulled the old man's head towards his and kissed him on the mouth.

'Tuck in, Arthur,' said Oscar happily. 'I think you'll be surprised.'

'It is a night for surprises,' I said drily, but I drank the ale and ate the sandwiches and they were indeed unexpectedly good.

'One of the many mysteries of this case,' continued my friend, between mouthfuls, *sotto voce*, 'is that each of the killings was as bloody a business as you may imagine and yet no one – no one at all – appears to have seen anybody within the vicinity of the crimes whose hands or clothes betrayed the least signs of blood. How come?'

Assuming the question was rhetorical, I said nothing. 'How come?' repeated Oscar, in a hoarse whisper, waving a crust towards me.

'The perpetrator wore a cloak,' I suggested lamely, 'an all-encompassing cloak, and was spirited away from the area by a waiting hansom cab in the immediate aftermath of the crimes.'

Oscar sipped at the warm beer. 'That's possible, though I don't recall Macnaghten's report making mention of any heavily cloaked figures having been seen in this part of town on the nights of the murders. And every licensed cabman known to ply for trade in the East End was questioned by police and none provided any evidence of value.'

'Well,' I said, finding it not easy to maintain my concentration in our bizarre surroundings, 'as we know, one of the best ways to hide is in full view, so perhaps the murderer made no secret of his bloody hands and clothes.'

'Indeed – the very reason PC Thick and Co. began by arresting every butcher and meat-market porter to the east of Smithfield. To no avail. They moved on to doctors, surgeons ... Anyone who might have reason to have blood on their hands. Again, it led them nowhere.'

'So you think that the murderer could have come here?'

'To wash and change and destroy his incriminating clothes in one of the many fires that burn here by day and night ... Yes, I think it's a possibility.'

'I suppose so.'

'No clothing of any kind bearing bloodstains of any kind was found among the possessions of any of the suspects. The clothing must have been destroyed.'

'Or cleaned?'

He nodded. 'Yes, we must consider every possibility.' He leaned closer to me and lowered his voice still further. 'What did you make of poor Lizzie Stride's sister? Everyone has assumed that the Whitechapel murderer was a lone wolf: they've only been looking for a man on his own. But what if Stella Stride is right? What if these are crimes perpetrated by two men, not one?'

'Or by a woman?' I suggested – a wild thought suddenly springing into my distracted mind. 'Did you notice the woman we passed, dragging her handcart through the gutter? Did you smell her? I recognised the stench. She is a practitioner of foeticide.'

Oscar's brow furrowed. 'She procures abortions?'

'I fear so. A crime punishable by death and yet, in this godforsaken part of town, a calling so commonplace that the wretched woman can walk the streets with her bundles of bloodied rags and raise no comment whatsoever.'

Oscar reached into his waistcoat pocket for his half-hunter. 'What time is it? You've put me off my sandwich, Arthur.'

I looked about the room. I felt a giddiness in my head. I turned away from the sight of the old man and the boy by the brazier, now in one another's embrace, and saw, for the first time, lying on a divan nearby them, what appeared to be a clergyman. I looked into the pin-point pupils of his wide-open eyes. I considered his yellow, pasty face, his drooping eyelids, his half-open mouth. I felt a mixture of horror and pity as I gazed at the wreck and ruin of a noble man.

'This is a beastly place,' I said. 'Let us go.'

Oscar pressed a consoling hand upon my knee. 'Do you not see how necessary a world of pains and troubles is to school an intelligence and make it a soul?' he said.

As he spoke, the man with the black eyebrows and the sneer strode past us, swishing his horsewhip as he went. He disappeared through the curtained doorway, letting in a gust of foul fumes.

'You know that man?' I asked.

'Quite well,' said Oscar, getting to his feet.

'Who is he?'

'This is a private club. I should not tell you, but we must have no secrets, Arthur, so I will. He is the ninth Marquess of Queensberry.'

I laughed. 'And I am Lord Rosebery. Who is he really?'

'He is who I say he is. He is Lord Queensberry.'

'Your friend Bosie's father?'

'The very same.'

'Why is he here?'

20

Questions

'Why was Lord Queensberry there?'

It was my fourth breakfast in a row at an hotel I could not afford in pursuit of a mystery I could not see being solved – but I was on parade yet again in the dining room of the Langham that Friday morning, 5 January 1894, because there was something irresistible about the company of Oscar Wilde.

I had not slept well. The opium fumes and the beer had taken their toll on my system. Oscar, by contrast, was in fine form, bubbling with bonhomie and dressed in a fresh pink shirt and pale yellow tie, with a matching pale yellow gardenia in his buttonhole.

'Did you know that the gardenia is named after a Dr Garden? Names really are everything. He was a Scotsman, like you, Arthur.'

'Why was he there?' I repeated, pouring myself a cup of black coffee.

'Queensberry? Last night?'

'Yes. Why was he in that dreadful place?'

'It's a place where a man may go to ruin himself – and fulfil himself. To beat or to be beaten.'

'Meaning?'

'Queensberry is a brute. You saw his ape-like appearance, his bestial, half-witted grin, his stableman's gait, his twitching hands.'

'I think you exaggerate a little, Oscar. I noticed his heavy eyebrows and I know he is the man who's codified the rules of boxing.'

'I don't exaggerate one little bit,' said my friend earnestly, while turning his boiled egg around in its eggcup. 'Queensberry's a brute and a blackguard. You saw the riding crop he was holding?'

'Yes.'

'He uses it with equal violence on his dogs, his horses, his servants and his women.' As he spoke, Oscar beat the top of the shell of his boiled egg with almost comical vigour. 'And as to the celebrated Queensberry Rules, outside of the boxing ring the man has no concept of the notion of fair play.'

'I hear what you say, but I still don't understand why we found him sitting alone in that ghastly backroom in Whitechapel last night.'

'He's a member of the club.'

'He smokes opium?'

'I doubt it. Opium is only one of the delights on offer underneath the railway arches of Pinchin Street. There's a room beyond the captain's cabin where release of a different kind is on offer.'

'You're talking in riddles, Oscar.'

'You're even more innocent than you look, Arthur.' My friend plunged his teaspoon into his boiled egg. 'The Marquess of Queensberry takes pleasure in beating others. He also derives pleasure from being beaten himself. He goes to the club to be stripped naked by the amiable Mamat and beaten black and blue.'

'Goodness,' I exclaimed.

'Goodness has nothing to do with it.'

My friend devoured his egg with relish and wiped his mouth with his napkin. 'The first Lady Queensberry – Bosie's mother – divorced him because of his brutish ways and his adultery, and the second Lady Queensberry, as I understand it, left him at Christmas. I assume he was in Whitechapel last night in search of distraction and the kind of light relief no longer available to him at home.'

'And he found you.'

'Yes, that will have spoiled his evening somewhat. The mad marquess does not approve of me – and the more his wife and children like me, the greater his dislike grows.'

'Has he any reason to dislike you?'

'He thinks my interest in Bosie is unnatural.'

I looked at my friend over the edge of my coffee cup. I did not say, 'And is it?', but he read my mind.

'I adore Bosie. He is young and he is beautiful. There is nothing of the gardenia about him. He is quite like a narcissus – so white and gold.' He turned away from the table and looked out of the window onto Portland Place below. 'He lies like a hyacinth on the sofa and I worship him.'

'Yes, well, I can see how a boxing man might find your flowery enthusiasm for his son a tad disconcerting.'

'Exactly. A brute is never going to see eye to eye with a poet, is he?' He turned back to the table and raised his coffee cup towards me. 'But I think you do understand, Arthur, and I am grateful for that.' He leaned forward and tapped the dossier of papers I had brought with me to the table. 'Never mind Queensberry. Are these Macnaghten's notes about the torso?'

'They are.'

'Thank you. Just what we need.'

I picked up the folder and rifled through it. It was a mixture of handwritten memoranda, typewritten copies of autopsy and coroners' reports and newspaper cuttings. 'There's material here about several unsolved murders coincidental with the Whitechapel killings – but Macnaghten is adamant that the five Whitechapel killings stand alone.'

'I know. But just because Macnaghten is adamant does not mean that he is correct. What do the notes tell us?'

I glanced around the dining room. The hotel residents at other tables appeared engrossed in their breakfasts and their newspapers. I opened the folder and, *sotto voce*, read out the salient points: '*On September 10, 1889, at 5.15 a.m., a female torso was discovered by PC William Pennett under a railway arch in Pinchin Street. It was hidden beneath some sacking and partially covered by an old chemise. The body, missing both head and legs, was already heavily decomposed, and it was the stench of the remains that attracted the policeman's attention.*'

I paused and looked anxiously around the room once more. 'Carry on,' said Oscar. 'I shall eat my toast noisily during the less savoury parts of the narrative.'

I continued: '*PC Pennett immediately summoned assistance and proceeded to arrest three men who were found sleeping under nearby arches. They were subsequently cleared of any involvement in the crime. Bloodstained female clothing was later found in Batty Street, but whether or not it was connected with the murder was never established. Sergeant William Thick was in charge of the investigation.*'

'Ah,' said Oscar, eyebrow raised, 'Thick is moving up the ranks, I see. He'll be a chief inspector ere long.' He plucked another piece of toast from the rack and began to butter it. 'Were there any clues to the woman's identity?'

'No clues of substance, but there was press speculation. The newspapers named Lydia Hart as the victim – a prostitute reported missing at about the same time.'

'The story is a tragic one, but the names are undeniably enchanting. The dead girl is called Hart and Sergeant Thick is looking for evidence in Batty Street. *Nomen est omen.* And what was the good sergeant's conclusion?'

'A curious one,' I said, turning to the final page of Macnaghten's memorandum. '*The police decided that the woman was probably a factory worker – despite the fact, according to the autopsy, that "her arms and hands were well formed and showed no signs of manual labour".*'

'That's intriguing,' said Oscar. 'That may be the answer to the entire mystery!' He put the last corner of toast into his mouth and laid his hands on the table triumphantly.

'What on earth do you mean?' I ask, amazed.

'I'm not quite sure,' he said. 'I'm in the throes of making one of those leaps of the imagination Macnaghten told us were beyond the reach of mere plodding policeman.'

'Tell me more.'

'Not quite yet. I need to be sure. If I am right, it may be painful for you, Arthur.'

'What on earth are you talking about, man? I don't follow you. You're speaking in riddles again.'

'And probably barking up the wrong tree as well.' He laughed. 'Now I am speaking in clichés. Ignore all I have just said and let's get to the nub of the matter. Why does Macnaghten maintain this Whitechapel murder has nothing to do with the earlier Whitechapel murders?'

'Because it's a whole year later and because of the nature of the mutilation in this case. With the 1888 murders, the victims were cut about the face and chest and had their innards removed, but there was no decapitation, no limbs were cut off.'

'But wasn't another torso found somewhere along the Thames in 1888 – at the same time as the so-called Jack the Ripper killings?'

'Yes, according to the notes, a torso was found hidden below ground, in a vault in Whitehall, during the building of the police headquarters at New Scotland Yard. It was a young woman again – *of large stature and well-nourished.*'

'That's interesting. That's what it says in the post-mortem?'

'It is.'

'And had the poor creature been disembowelled?'

'Her uterus had been removed. And a right arm and shoulder believed to belong to the same woman were found washed up from the river in Pimlico.'

'Not far from the southern end of Tite Street?'

'Yes.'

'When was this exactly?'

'September to October 1888.'

'And Macnaghten insists this has nothing to do with the Whitechapel murders?'

'He does.'

'If the torso was discovered in Whitehall and the victim's arm and shoulder were washed up in Pimlico, why does Macnaghten include this material in his dossier on the Whitechapel murders?'

'I don't know. For "completeness", as "background"?'

'He's hedging his bets, Arthur. He doesn't know a thing.'

'Do we know much more?'

'We know a great deal, my friend.'

'Do we?'

'We do,' he cried exultantly. 'And we're about to discover yet more. Drink up your coffee, Arthur. Our carriage awaits.'

21

Freaks

It was not yet ten o'clock in the morning and already we were back in another two-wheeler. As we climbed aboard, Oscar called up to the cabman: '123 Whitechapel Road, John – and as speedily as your fiery-footed steeds will take us.'

The cabman chuckled and grunted, 'Righto, sir.'

'I thought we were going to the Colney Hatch Asylum this morning,' I said, 'in search of Aaron Kosminski?'

'We are. But something you mentioned at breakfast, Arthur, suggests that a detour via Whitechapel may be to our advantage. Freaks first, lunatics later.'

'I am confused,' I said.

'Indeed.' He grinned at me mischievously as he settled back in his seat, laying Macnaghten's file carefully upon his lap and taking out his cigarette case. 'I do believe "confusion" may be what this is all about.'

The streets of London were curiously quiet and the smog

had not yet descended on the city. Our journey east was a swift one and the crisp January air blowing in through the carriage windows helped to clear my head. As we travelled, Oscar leafed through Macnaghten's dossier, occasionally letting out a mild snort of derision or a gentle gurgle of satisfaction, and I gazed out at the passing scene and did my best to order my thoughts. When I asked Oscar why we were going where we were going, he did not look up but said simply, 'All will become clear when we get there.'

'I hope so,' I replied, rather doubting it.

When I asked him how he knew the name of our cabman when we had merely climbed into the first carriage in the rank, he said: 'I didn't. I don't. But John is by a long way the most common Christian name among men in this country, so the odds were in my favour. I don't hedge my bets. He seemed happy enough to be called John.'

'But if his name is Tom or Dick or whatever it may be—'

'William is the second most common name in England.'

'Yes, whatever. It's an amusing trick, but if you get it wrong, the effect is rather spoiled and he won't be so happy.'

My friend turned and looked at me steadily, widening his eyes. 'I grant you that, Arthur. Every effect that one produces risks giving one an enemy. To be popular one must be a mediocrity.'

We travelled on in silence.

Whitechapel, when we reached it, looked more hospitable than it had the night before. The shops were open; the pavements were more crowded; and the people going about their business moved with an energy and sense of purpose that, I suppose, surprised me.

'Are we going to the London Hospital?' I asked, as we travelled down the Whitechapel Road and the familiar porticoed front of the building came into view. Until this adventure, my only forays into this part of town had been to meet up with medical colleagues at the hospital here.

'No, we are going to Tom Norman's Exotic Emporium – just opposite, just here.'

Our two-wheeler drew to a halt on the north side of the street. Oscar jumped down. 'Thank you, John,' he called up to the cabman. 'It is John, isn't it?'

'Yes, sir.'

'And your wife is Mary. Am I right?'

'You are, sir. And it is Mr Wilde, isn't it?'

'It is.'

'We all know you, sir. Best tipper in town.'

'Thank you, John. Please wait for us. We won't be long.' Oscar smiled at me. 'That's not a bad reputation to have, is it, Arthur? Though, of course, in the fullness of time, it can lead a man to ruin.'

He laughed gently and, taking me by the elbow, turned me towards the 'emporium'. It had the look of a store in a story-book. With its thick mullioned windows framed in dark wood, it reminded me of the Maclise drawing of Mr Dickens' Old Curiosity Shop.

'Why are we here?' I asked.

'To see Tom Norman.'

'Is he expecting us?'

'No – and for that reason I think an oblique approach is called for. "Softly, softly, catchee monkey", as the saying goes. Let's not let him know the truth of why we've come to see him.'

'Why have we come to see him? His name doesn't feature in any of Macnaghten's notes, as I recall.'

'Perhaps it should,' said Oscar, looking at me with a knowing smile. 'Tom Norman is a friend of Walter Wellbeloved and we don't yet know enough about him. We are here to make inquiries the police have failed to make.'

'We may fail also,' I replied. 'The shop is closed.' There was a handwritten sign to that effect hanging inside the door.

Oscar pressed his nose to the glass. 'But it's not empty. Somebody's at home.' He rapped his knuckles against the pane. Almost at once, the front door swung open and there stood a curious-looking character who might have been Dickens' Mr Jingle. He was tall and lean, with a sallow complexion and a head of luxuriant jet-black hair half-hidden beneath a silk top hat that appeared to have known better days. He wore a cut-away frock coat of shabby black velvet, a silk waistcoat to his neck, and full-length narrow black britches above buckled evening shoes. Beyond the tarnished silver of his buckles and coat buttons, the only relief from the blackness of his appearance came from his yellow cheeks and pale grey spats.

'You are Tom Norman,' said Oscar warmly. 'I am Oscar Wilde.'

The man in black said nothing, but pushed back his hat the better to inspect us. He had small, round eyes with small, black pupils.

'And this is Dr Arthur Conan Doyle,' continued Oscar, making the announcement as if playing a trump card.

The figure in the doorway raised an eyebrow. 'I know. The Sherlock Holmes man.'

Oscar was not finished. 'I am a friend of Phineas Barnum,' he went on.

'Ah,' said the man.

'And a friend of Walter Wellbeloved.'

'His spirit guide was one of my artistes,' said Tom Norman. 'You'd better come in, but I haven't got long.'

He stepped back to allow us into his shop. It was cavernous, dark and cold, and filled, from corner to corner and side to side, with display cases and cabinets of every size, each one covered with a blanket.

'So you knew Barnum,' he said to Oscar. His voice was high-pitched; his way of speaking, precise. 'A good man.'

'A remarkable man,' echoed Oscar. 'I went to his circus in New York and he introduced me to Jumbo the Elephant.'

'Yes,' said Mr Norman, curling one of his locks of black hair around a thin, pale forefinger, 'Barnum had the elephant and I had the Elephant Man.'

'I remember,' said Oscar.

Norman looked at me with both eyebrows raised. 'Did you ever see him, the Elephant Man?' I shook my head. He shrugged his shoulders and giggled mirthlessly. 'Well, that's how I billed him. Said his mother had been frightened by an elephant during her pregnancy. Joseph Merrick. Hideous deformities. I gave him a home and a means of earning his living. He was grateful. He lived in there.' Norman nodded towards the rear of the shop. There was a doorway covered by a beaded curtain and a sign above it that read, in gold and red lettering, *A Penny a Peep.* 'He had to sleep sitting up, poor fellow. We were good friends – until some busy-bodying doctor from across the road came along and decided he knew best what was good for the Elephant Man.'

'Dr Treves,' I said. 'I know him.'

'I'm sorry to hear it,' said Norman lightly. 'No doubt your friend meant well, but Joseph didn't like being taken from here to there to be poked and prodded by the medical students. He had to wear a hood and cloak to cross the road. They stripped him naked and displayed him like an animal in a cattle market. I had him properly dressed and treated him like a star.'

'Was he your chief attraction?' Oscar asked.

Norman giggled once more. It was a peculiar sound and seemed the more unnatural because the man never smiled. 'I did well with The World's Ugliest Woman, too.' Norman shuddered with apparent pleasure at the memory of her. 'She didn't disappoint.' Oscar chuckled obligingly as the man in black continued his nostalgic reverie. 'Did you ever see John Chambers, the Armless Carpenter?' he asked. 'He was ever a favourite.' He looked around the darkened room. 'And he built most of these cabinets, too.'

'I remember your Man in a Trance,' said Oscar.

'Do you? Do you really? He was a bugger. I had to get rid of him. He kept asking for more and more.' Norman giggled again. 'He had too much time to think about things. Money became his obsession.'

'Money is in some respects life's fire,' said Oscar, tilting his head to one side and studying our host. 'It is a very excellent servant, but a terrible master.'

'You did know Mr Barnum, didn't you? That was one of his lines. He taught me the tricks of the trade, did Barnum – the need for novelty as well as variety. For years my top attraction was Electra, The Electric Lady. There was so much electricity in her she could light a lamp. As she got elderly, poor old bird, she lost her spark. I was going to replace her with her daughter – The Electric Girl. Barnum said, "No, you need something different." Rosie the Mermaid – that was his idea.'

'Rosie was Electra's daughter?'

'Yes. She was a little charmer was our Rosie.'

'What happened to her?' I asked.

'She died. Went to Ramsgate with Walter Wellbeloved – dirty weekend. He said she was his spirit guide. They'll call it anything, these old buggers, won't they? Anyway, he took her for a dip and she drowned. She couldn't swim.'

Oscar began to laugh.

'I thought she was a mermaid,' I protested.

'She was – in the bath here.' He began to giggle once more. 'Poor girl. I was very fond of her. And to be fair to Wellbeloved, I think he was fond of her, too.' He sighed and looked around his emporium, as if conjuring up the spirits of all the acts and turns he had been proud to present across the years. 'I've had 'em all,' he cooed, 'Mermaids, midgets, savage Zulus.'

'And now you've had enough,' said Oscar briskly. 'You're moving, I see?'

Norman returned from his reveries. 'How do you see that, Mr Wilde?'

'Well, there's dust on your forearms and when you kindly opened the door to us there was a line of perspiration across your brow, which suggested unaccustomed exertion. You've been moving heavy items that have not been moved for a while.'

Norman tittered. 'Picking up some of Mr Holmes's tricks, eh? Yes, I'm cataloguing the collection prior to my departure – for Chicago.'

'Oh,' said Oscar. 'When are you going?'

'As soon as possible.'

'Are you going alone?'

'I'm not taking any of my artistes with me, if that's what you mean. I shall be recruiting new talent in Illinois. They have taller giants and shorter midgets there than we do. I'm just taking my cabinets with me – about a hundred cabinets in all, that's more than enough.'

'Featuring?'

'The collection of a lifetime!' Norman moved across the shop to the nearest cabinet and lifted its blanket covering slowly – as if he had been a child raising the curtain on a toy theatre. 'Behold,' he said.

'What's that?' I asked.

'It's the world's smallest whale,' he breathed, his voice thick with wonder.

'Really?' said Oscar, going over to the cabinet and peering in at the specimen. 'It looks more like a bloater in aspic to me.'

'You may well be right, Mr Wilde.' He dropped the blanket over the glass case and lifted the curtain on the adjacent cabinet. 'This may be more to your liking.'

'Good grief,' cried Oscar. 'It's an ass's head.'

'It is all that remains of the donkey that carried Our Lord into Jerusalem on the first Palm Sunday.'

'That certainly is remarkable,' said Oscar.

Tom Norman covered up the animal's head and fixed his beady eyes on Oscar. 'My father was a butcher. I began in the butcher's trade. I keep his knives still. They come into their own now and then.'

'Do you have human specimens?' I asked.

'Oh, yes,' answered Norman eagerly. He stood, with his hat well pushed back on his head, toying with his black locks while surveying the room, pondering which case or cabinet to unveil next. 'Mr Barnum had the Siamese Twins, of course, and the advantage that they were living and breathing creatures. I have the Trowbridge Triplets. The disadvantage is that they died at birth. However, there are three of them and they're conjoined in a most interesting fashion. If I can remember where they are, I'll show you.'

'No, no thank you,' protested Oscar. 'Please don't trouble yourself.'

'No trouble,' said Norman, squeezing himself between cabinets. 'And no charge, either.' He moved like a dancer. 'It's good to meet people who appreciate the exotic. Not everyone does nowadays. Back here I have some wonderful novelties – not just freaks of nature, but intriguing parts of the anatomy. Somewhere I have an amusing case featuring the private parts of well-endowed young men.'

'How on earth have you come by those?'

'Medical students used to bring them over. Young doctors have a lively sense of humour. One offered me a female head not long ago. Said it was Mary, Queen of Scots and he'd found it washed up by the Tower of London. We all know Mary wasn't beheaded at the Tower. She was executed up at Fotheringay. Funny folk, doctors.' Norman looked at me and giggled coldly. 'Am I right, Dr Doyle?'

I did not know what reply to make, so I deflected his question with an enquiry of my own. 'And how do you preserve your specimens?' I asked.

'Formaldehyde,' he said. 'It's a chemical that's quite transformed the art of embalming.' He was turning to and fro within his maze of cabinets, lifting and dropping the blanket coverings of his cases as he spoke. 'We may have to leave the mummified members for another day,' he said. 'It's all a bit of a muddle back here, I'm afraid.'

'It's an extraordinary collection,' said Oscar admiringly. 'I am sorry you are closing.'

'Business is not what it was. You really need a good story to sell a show.'

'I don't believe you can have run out of those,' said Oscar amiably.

'Indeed, not,' replied Norman, gazing steadily at Oscar. 'I have a perfect story right on my doorstep. You've heard of Jack the Ripper, have you not?'

'We have. Of course.'

'He was partial to eviscerating his victims – removing their entrails, don't you know.'

'Quite so.'

'And he was local. If I'd been able to display some of his trophies here – the Ripper's off-cuts, as it were – I'd have had the public lining the street from Whitechapel to Ludgate Circus.'

'I can imagine,' said Oscar.

'I asked the police about it, but they were most unhelpful. Said the body parts had been buried with the victims' remains. No guts, no show.'

'Indeed.'

'We must go,' I said, suddenly feeling that I had enjoyed more than a sufficiency of the company of this queer showman who laughed but never smiled.

'Just before we do, Mr Norman,' said Oscar, as we stepped towards the door, 'I have a favour to ask. It's the reason for our visit, in fact.'

'I thought there must be one.'

'I have written a play.'

'Another one?'

'This is in French and on a biblical theme.'

'Ah,' sniffed Norman, 'you are not planning to draw the town.'

'But I'd like to,' said Oscar. 'What playwright wouldn't?'

'Forgive me, Mr Wilde, but yours does not sound like an obviously popular piece.'

'Oh, but it might be – if well translated and with the right leading lady. And your assistance.'

'My assistance? I am going to Chicago.'

'The play tells the story of Salome, the daughter of King Herod.'

'I know who you mean. She's the one who asked for the head of John the Baptist – on a plate.'

'Exactly. And to help "draw the town", as you'd have it, I am in want . . . '

' . . . Not of the plate, but of the head of John the Baptist?'

'Can you help me? Can you supply the head – preserved in formaldehyde?'

Tom Norman giggled. 'I can't supply you with the original, I'm afraid.'

Oscar looked imploringly into Tom Norman's yes. 'Walter Wellbeloved thought you might be able to assist me,' he said earnestly. 'He told me you'd helped him in the past.'

'Walter's made some improbable requests in his time for his rituals – but always animals, never humans. You need a human head, do you? Male? What sort of age?'

'Twenties, thirties, handsome, hirsute. There's a fine Caravaggio in the National Gallery that will give you an idea.'

'I'll do what I can, Mr Wilde – since you're a friend of Mr Wellbeloved. I make no promises, but I'll see what I can do.'

'Thank you,' said Oscar, extending his hand towards Tom Norman. 'Don't say a word, Arthur.'

'I wasn't going to,' I said. I was too bewildered to know what to say.

'You'll be in touch, then?' said Oscar, pulling open the shop door.

'I will be,' said Norman. 'If I make progress, I'll send you a note to agree terms. You're still in Tite Street, I presume?'

22

Colney Hatch Lunatic Asylum

'What on earth was that about?'

Oscar chuckled as, complacently, he settled himself back into our two-wheeler and carefully placed his yellow gloves across his knees. 'On to Colney Hatch Lane, John,' he called out to the cabman. 'I was testing the temperature of the water, Arthur, that's all.'

'You were asking a man to supply you with a severed head,' I hissed. 'You were as good as commissioning a murder.'

'Don't be absurd, Arthur. Have a cigarette. These come from Algiers. They are rough and smooth at the same time – an intriguing combination. Tom Norman's not a murderer.'

'How do you know?'

'Because if he had been, he'd have protested at once that he couldn't supply me with a severed head. Have a cigarette. It'll soothe your nerves.'

'I won't have a cigarette, thank you. My nerves do not need soothing. I'm simply confused by your line of inquiry.'

'Don't be. If you'll forgive me for adding a commonplace to a platitude and mixing my metaphors, as well as testing the water, I was scattering bread on the water in hope of getting a clearer picture of how the land lies. Tom Norman preserves body parts in formaldehyde. Does that have any bearing on our case?'

'I don't know. Does it?'

'Tom Norman lives and works in Whitechapel. Business is not what it was. Could he have commissioned the Whitechapel murders to create a sensation in the hope of exploiting that sensation with a Jack the Ripper show for his emporium?'

'That seems unlikely.'

'But not impossible. The police have got nowhere, Arthur. We must look everywhere. I was merely lifting up a few stones to see what crawled out.'

'I can't say I took to the man,' I said. 'I didn't care for his mirthless laugh.'

'The vulgar only laugh, but never smile,' said Oscar, drawing slowly on his Algerian cigarette, 'whereas well-bred people often smile, but seldom laugh.'

I shook my head. 'He's a queer fish.'

'No, he's a showman. He trades in queer fish – and mermaids.' He smiled at his own joke. 'Don't concern yourself, Arthur. I was sounding him out, nothing more.'

'You were playing a dangerous game at the end there, Oscar,' I said, taking out my pipe. 'How did he know your address?'

Oscar pondered for a moment. 'He knows Walter Wellbeloved. Constance and I are friends of Walter Wellbeloved. People talk about me. If there is one thing worse than being talked about—'

'Don't say it. I know the line.'

'Tom Norman will have learned my address from Walter Wellbeloved.'

I considered the point. 'Yes, I suppose that's possible.'

'And we learned a little bit more about the nature of Walter Wellbeloved, did we not, Arthur? Wellbeloved sought animal parts from Tom Norman, but never human ones. That's useful to know – and in Wellbeloved's favour.'

'We certainly learned that Wellbeloved's another queer fish. A love affair with a mermaid? What was going on there, I ask myself.'

'Not a great deal, I imagine,' said Oscar, grinning mischievously. '*L'amour de l'impossible* . . . it's a well-known phenomenon. Men yearn for what they know they cannot have.'

My friend exhaled a blue-black cloud of cigarette smoke and rapped me gently over the knee with one of his yellow gloves. 'Close your eyes, Arthur, and picture that unknown land full of strange flowers and subtle perfumes, that land of which it is a joy of all joys to dream, that land where all things are perfect and poisonous.' He closed his own eyes as he spoke.

'I think I'll smoke my pipe,' I said.

It took us more than an hour to reach the Colney Hatch Lunatic Asylum, travelling due north from the slums of Whitechapel through the suburbs of Islington towards the countryside. For much of the journey Oscar slept, holding his cigarette between his fingers all the while. I smoked my pipe and looked out at the passing scene and, when the motion of the carriage allowed, I read. I had brought with me a pocket edition of Robert Louis Stevenson's novel, *The Strange Case of Dr Jekyll and Mr Hyde*. For some time I had been intending to reread it for professional purposes: the better to understand the secrets of its extraordinary popular success. I chose to reread it now in case it should have a bearing on our case. One line in particular struck me: 'All human beings, as we meet them, are commingled out of good and evil: and Edward Hyde, alone, in the ranks of mankind, was pure evil.'

'I have been thinking,' I said to Oscar, as we clambered out of the two-wheeler at our journey's end, 'these crimes – these Whitechapel murders – are acts of pure evil, are they not?'

'One cannot think of them otherwise,' he said, blinking in the sharp January sunlight and stamping his feet on the ground to return some life to them after our journey.

'So whoever is responsible is a creature of pure evil?'

'Yes,' said Oscar, 'or a madman. And if he's a madman, of course, it does make the story less interesting.'

We were standing on a gravel drive at the foot of a broad flight of shallow steps leading up to the high arched doorway of the asylum – the largest institution of its kind in Europe, we later learned. The building was huge and formidable – a curious cross between Wandsworth Prison and Blenheim Palace, but seemingly larger than either. The drive from the gates of the establishment to these front steps must have been at least half a mile long.

'We are expected,' I murmured.

Alone, at the top of the steps, gazing down at us, stood a figure in a frock coat that I took at once, and correctly, to be the asylum superintendent. He was a genial-looking man of about sixty, of medium height, portly, largely bald but heavily bearded. His benign appearance was belied by a brisk, businesslike manner.

'Are we late, Dr Rogerson?' cried Oscar, climbing the steps, hand extended.

'You are here, Mr Wilde, and you are welcome,' said the superintendent. 'And you are welcome, too, Dr Conan Doyle. You trained in Edinburgh, I know. We must talk of that another time. I have Kosminski in the visiting room waiting to see you.'

'Thank you,' replied Oscar, as the superintendent led us

through the main door into a large marble-floored hallway. We looked about us and marvelled at what we saw. The grandeur of the surroundings was overwhelming and the quietness of the place unsettling.

'This is impressive,' I said.

'Yes,' replied Dr Rogerson. 'Prince Albert didn't entirely approve. He came to open us. He couldn't really complain. He chose the architect. This way.'

'You received my telegram,' said Oscar. 'You understand what we're about.'

'Perfectly,' said Dr Rogerson. 'Follow me.'

The superintendent marched us across the empty, echoing hallway and, taking a small bundle of keys from his waistcoat pocket, unlocked an elegant side door that led immediately to a second, plainer, sturdier inner door. He unlocked this with two further keys. 'Go through,' he commanded, 'cross the corridor and wait by the door that faces you.'

We did as we were instructed while Dr Rogerson locked the doors we had come through behind him.

'Oh my,' murmured Oscar, 'we have stepped from the anteroom to Elysium onto the pathway to Hades.'

The corridor we crossed did indeed resemble a hellish highway of sorts. It stretched out to either side of us – apparently infinitely – and along it walked and wandered, ambled and jigged, strolled and strode, a multitude of madmen. Each seemed lunatic in a different way. One marched by, with wild staring eyes, muttering menaces. Another ran forward on tiptoes, then stopped, bent down to kiss the ground, rose again and ran on in silence. A third stood close by the door where Dr Rogerson had instructed us to wait, banging his head rhythmically against the whitewashed brick wall.

The superintendent rejoined us, still sorting his keys. 'Miss Terry said the problem with our lunatics is that they are all far too theatrical. If you tried playing them like this on the stage, no one would believe you.'

'Ellen has been here?' asked Oscar, wide-eyed. 'Not as a patient, surely?'

Dr Rogerson laughed. 'No. She came when she was studying to play Ophelia. She wanted to see for herself the reality of madness. She decided it would be too much for the paying public to cope with.' He held up a key. 'Kosminski is in here. Are you ready, gentlemen? I don't think this will take long.'

Oscar stayed the superintendent's hand. 'Does he know why we have come?'

'I have told him, but what he understands and does not understand is difficult to tell.'

'But he was ready to meet us?'

'He made no objection.'

I looked into the face of Dr Rogerson and sensed that I recognised the eyes of an honest man. 'May I ask your professional opinion, Doctor?'

'By all means.'

'Could this man Kosminski be the notorious Jack the Ripper? Does the nature of his madness suggest to you the characteristics of a homicidal maniac?'

'No. At least, not now.'

'Then why is he here?' exclaimed Oscar.

'Where else is he to go?' said Dr Rogerson simply. 'He is certainly not in his right mind. He was in the workhouse until they could manage him no more. He was committed here by the local magistrate at the instigation of the police.'

'Was he violent?' I asked.

'He had been, apparently. And he had filthy habits. Self-abuse was the worst of them.'

'The police believe he may be the Whitechapel murderer,' said Oscar.

'I know,' said the superintendent. 'But on what grounds I don't know. He was questioned, but never charged.'

'He lived and worked in Whitechapel,' I said, 'and because he worked as a barber he had ready access to an assortment of blades and scissors and knives.'

'I believe I visited his barber's shop on one occasion,' said Oscar.

'I wonder if you'll recognise him now,' said Dr Rogerson, putting his key in the lock and turning it.

He pushed open the door and ushered us into a large, light-filled room. The sun poured in through tall, wide windows covered with a lattice of white-painted grilles. It was an elegant room, sparsely furnished but with a fine Adam-style fireplace and a small Murano glass chandelier hanging from the ceiling. Arranged around the room were half a dozen occasional tables with a pair of upright wooden chairs on either side of each of them. Seated on one of these chairs, dressed in striped pyjamas reminiscent of a convict's uniform, was Aaron Kosminski.

'Oh,' whispered Oscar, 'he's not run away to the circus. That's him. Without a doubt.'

'He's strapped in,' I said, appalled to see that the hapless creature's arms were pinioned to the back of his chair. I looked to the floor and saw that each of the chairs in the room was fixed where it was by lock and bolt.

'He might be Jack the Ripper,' said Dr Rogerson quietly. 'We don't know.'

'But if he is,' said Oscar, 'he is not going to harm us, is he? We are not women of the night. And he's an old man.'

'He's not yet forty.'

'Look at him,' said Oscar. 'He's a broken man.'

He was certainly a forlorn figure. His lank black hair was streaked with grey. His moustache drooped around his half-open mouth. He seemed to have no teeth. He seemed to have no life. He sat, as slumped on his chair as the tethers allowed, his eyes cast down, his beaky nose pointing towards the ground.

'We secure all patients with a history of violence like this,' explained Dr Rogerson.

'But does he have a history of violence?' I asked.

'Not a recent one, no. He has been consistently placid since his arrival here. If he were admitted today, he'd be classed as a harmless imbecile. But, by definition, mania comes and goes. Five years ago, he will have been a different man. The magistrate who committed him believed he was a threat to others as well as to himself.'

'He looks very weak,' I said.

'He eats very little.'

We looked at him. We stepped towards him. We introduced ourselves. We asked him his name. We asked him if he remembered his life in Whitechapel. We asked him a dozen questions and more.

He did not move. He did not say a word.

Eventually, Oscar turned to the asylum superintendent. 'Does he ever speak?'

'Rarely,' said Dr Rogerson. 'Sometimes at night he calls out in his sleep, but we can make no sense of what he says. None of us speaks Yiddish. By day he is as you see him now.'

'As if in a trance,' I said.

'Exactly so,' said the superintendent, stroking his beard reflectively while gazing fixedly at Kosminski's impassive face.

'He's not registering our presence,' said Oscar.

'He's not registering anything,' said Dr Rogerson. 'Watch.' Suddenly, the superintendent leaned forward and clapped his hands together loudly in front of his patient's face. 'Not the flicker of an eyelid.'

'How long has he been like this?' I asked.

'Since he arrived.'

'And will he be like this always?' asked Oscar.

'There is no reason to suppose not,' said Dr Rogerson. 'I think we can assume he will be like this until the day he dies.'

'Thank you, Doctor,' said Oscar quietly. 'This has been most helpful.'

23

Olga

'I'm not sure I'd call that interview "helpful", Oscar,' I said, as we climbed back into our two-wheeler. 'We learned nothing.'

'On the contrary, Arthur. We learned a great deal.'

'Did we?' I protested. 'I don't think so. The wretched man is dead to the world.'

'Yes. And firmly under lock and key – and consequently incapable of committing this week's killings in Chelsea. At least we learned that.'

'True enough,' I conceded. 'But we learned nothing about his life in Whitechapel.'

'Not so,' purred my friend complacently. 'I visited his barber's shop in Whitechapel once, as you know, and I remember nothing about it. What does that tell us?'

'That you have a poor memory?'

'No. It tells us that nothing occurred that was out of the ordinary. Kosminski was simply a nondescript Whitechapel barber.

Now he's a wreck of a man, dead to the world, locked in a trance. What trauma was it that induced so great a change in him?'

Having asked his question, Oscar closed his eyes and left me to ponder it. I did so, as we journeyed back from Colney Hatch to central London. Was Kosminski our murderer? Had an eventual realisation of the horror of his crimes brought him to his present state? I did not know the answer. Nor, I reckoned, did Oscar.

As finally we reached our hotel once more, my friend, beaming blithely, evidently refreshed by his further sleep on the homeward journey, announced that he had 'business to attend to' and, without further explanation, proposed that we meet, 'after dinner, at around ten o'clock'.

'What's happening then?'

'Our promised interview with Michael Ostrog. Kosminski told us nothing and everything. What will we learn from Ostrog, I wonder?'

'Where's this interview to take place?' I asked.

'At the office of Ivan the Terrible.'

'Where's that?'

'Somewhere at the circus. Up in the rafters of the Agricultural Hall, I suppose. Olga will show you the way, I'm sure.'

Until that mention of her name, I had had no more than fleeting thoughts of the young Russian acrobat who had so charmed me at our first brief encounter at the circus on Constance's birthday a few days before. Now, all of a sudden, and to my amazement, I could not get the beguiling girl out of my mind's eye! It was six o'clock: I heard the church clock in Portland Place strike the hour. I went up to my hotel room and failed to settle. I ordered a glass of ale and a sandwich and thought to read some more of Stevenson's novel. Before the refreshments had arrived, I had tossed the book aside. I began a letter to my darling Touie, but abandoned it even as I was writing her dear name. I decided that work would be the answer – as it so often is – and took out the notes of a story I had in mind and began to write. I had done with Sherlock Holmes. 'The Final Problem' had appeared in *The Strand Magazine* before Christmas. Now I was planning something in a different vein. The opening sentences pleased me:

> It is hard for the general practitioner who sits among his patients both morning and evening, and sees them in their homes between, to steal time for one little daily breath of cleanly air. To win it he must slip early from his bed and walk out between shuttered shops when it is chill but very clear, and all things are sharply outlined, as in a frost. It is an hour that has a charm of its own . . .

I stopped. I reread the phrase: 'It is an hour that has a charm of its own . . .'

I laid down my pen, I picked up my coat. Without pausing, I left my room, ran down the stairs and out into the street. On the rank outside the hotel, a two-wheeler was waiting.

I called up to the cabman: 'John – do you know the way to Olympia?'

'That's not my name, sir. I'm Bill, but I knows the way to Olympia.'

'Take me there, please, as fast as you can.'

It was not long after six. We reached the circus at a little before seven. I paid off the cab and, with a pounding heart I did not try to comprehend, pushed my way through the press of public arriving for the Friday-night performance. This was London's alternative to the pantomime and the gathering crowd was in holiday mood. Children's faces shone with anticipation. Fathers (proud and satisfied) held tickets aloft as they led their broods into the teeming entrance hall. Mothers (happy yet anxious) followed behind, clucking, scolding, praying the treat might work out as well as planned.

Inside the foyer the swirl of circus-goers moved hither and yon: finding and losing one another, seeking out the doorways leading to their seats, queuing for programmes, oranges and ices, gathering in clusters around the daises on which stood or lay assorted circus animals. At once, to my right, at the back of the foyer, I saw the bear cubs tied to their trivet and pushed my way towards them, but as I got close the sequined acrobat standing over them, hoop and whip in hand, turned towards me. It was not her.

Where was she? I had to find her! I stopped as the crowd churned about me. For a singular, queer moment I felt I was a man drowning in a whirlpool of heaving humanity. I rose up onto my toes and turned and turned about again – and then I saw her.

She was no more than ten feet away, standing on a stool at the foot of the main staircase. Her figure was an enchantment. She had the poise of a dancer and the vigour of an athlete. She was looking out over the heads of the crowd. Her shining dark hair was swept back and tied on top of her head in a bun. Her loveliness was not of the obvious kind. Her face had neither regularity of feature nor beauty of complexion, but her expression was sweet and amiable, and her large blue eyes were singularly spiritual and sympathetic. Simply looking at her I could see her strength and her intelligence. Suddenly, she saw me and, laughing, she waved. I pushed through the throng towards her. She jumped down from her stool, still laughing, and held out her hand towards me.

'Olga,' I said.

'Doctor,' she said.

'You remember me?'

'I remember.'

'You speak English?'

'*Malenkly*. A little.'

'You speak good English.'

'No, I speak bad English.' She shook her head and turned away, as if embarrassed. For a moment, a silence fell between us. There must have been five hundred people swarming through the circus foyer that night, but in that moment's silence there were just the two of us – and on a round raised dais, in a small roped-off enclosure no more than four feet wide and no more than two feet away from where we stood, a black panther cub. The animal (the size of a large dog) was lying down, resting its huge head on its mighty paws. It gazed balefully at us and yawned, its black tongue lolling out of its mouth, exposing its white teeth, as long as kitchen knives, as sharp as icicles.

'Is he friendly?' I asked.

'No,' she said, 'but he won't move from there. You are safe.'

'Your English is so good,' I said. 'How long have you been here?'

'This time? One month. But I have been to England many times.'

'Always with the circus?'

'Yes, always with Ivan. He is not so terrible. He looks after us.'

'How long have you been with the circus?'

'Always.'

'Always? You are from a circus family?'

'No. We have no families. We are orphans.'

'You are orphans?'

She laughed and looked around. 'Yes, all the girls here are orphans – all the acrobat girls. All of us. Ivan is like a father to us. He comes to the orphanage each year and chooses the best – the girls who will be strongest. We are lucky. Life in Russia is bad. Life in the circus is good.'

'You have no parents?'

She laughed again. 'No parents, no brothers, no sisters, no cousins, nobody. But I have the circus. I have work. I have food. And I travel the world. London, Paris, Berlin. Next year we will go to New York. That's what Ivan says.'

'Will you stay with him always?'

'I don't know. He does not like us to go. He owns us. We are his serfs. It is the Russian way.'

'Not any more,' I said earnestly. 'Serfdom has been abolished. You are free.'

She laughed. 'Of course,' she said. 'It is a joke. It is Ivan's joke. He says he is our Tsar and he owns us. But not all the girls stay. Some girls run away. We don't see them again.'

'Will you run away?' I asked.

She smiled. 'If I find the right man, perhaps.'

'You need a man to run away with?'

'Of course,' she said seriously. She tilted her head to one side and looked up at me with smiling eyes. 'How old are you?'

'I am too old for you,' I said.

'How old are you?' she repeated.

'I am thirty-four,' I said.

'That is perfect,' she said. 'You are ten years older than I am. That is the correct difference.'

I laughed. 'Who says?'

'Everyone knows it. And I need a man who is strong. And brave. You are a strong man. And you are brave. I know that. You are a doctor.'

'Yes, I am a doctor. I am a writer, also.' I hesitated. 'And I am a fami—'

She put her finger to my lips. 'I know. You are a famous man. You are the man who invented the great Sherlock Holmes. In Russia, everybody loves Mr Sherlock Holmes.'

'Thank you,' I said, 'but there's going to be no more Mr Holmes. I have written my last story about him.'

'I understand,' she said. 'You want to be free. You want to fly.'

'You do understand, don't you? Yes, I want to be free. I am going to write different stories now. I will write a story about the circus and about you and your animals.' She smiled at me and, leaning across the rope barrier, stretched out her arm and scratched the panther cub behind his large cup-like ears. The animal lifted his head and shook it. His long whiskers twitched.

'He is very good,' I said.

'I have hypnotised him. It is quite easy. Ivan teaches us. I can teach you.' She looked into my eyes. I said nothing. She smiled. 'You do not believe me?'

'Oh, I believe you, Olga.' I returned her gaze. I had never seen eyes so blue. 'Yes,' I said, 'I know you are a hypnotist.'

Above us on the stairs, a clown appeared ringing a bell. On the dais the panther got to his feet and stretched. His tail swished from side to side. Olga put her hand on mine. 'We can talk tomorrow. We can make our plans. I will see you here at twelve o'clock. Yes? Remember, I am a hypnotist.'

'I will be here,' I said.

'And now – for the circus?' she asked. 'Have you got a ticket?'

'No,' I said. 'I am meeting Mr Wilde later – afterwards – "in Ivan's office", wherever that is.'

'I will show you,' she said. 'You can watch the show. We are not full tonight. I will find you a seat. And when I come on I will know where you are and I will bow to you and you will cheer for me.'

The seat that she found for me was right by the ringside, at the end of a row, alongside a family who engaged me in conversation, but of whom I recall nothing, except that they were fellow Scots (I think) and happy to be there. I watched the circus in a daze. Clowns and tumblers, jugglers and men on stilts, chimpanzees and fire-eaters, elephants and bears, sea lions in portable lagoons and African lions in cages – on they came, off they went. It was an extraordinary cavalcade of colour and excitement – but looking back, now, all I can recollect are two moments: when Ivan the ringmaster made his extraordinary entrance, emerging on horseback from the cradle of the balloon that had been lowered from the roof, and when Olga came on – at the head of a line of a dozen sequined acrobats. The girls – all identical in height and build and costume – marched directly across the sawdust-covered ring towards my seat and, together, all at once, to a sudden burst of trumpets, lifted their right hands high into the air and then swept them down before them to touch the ground in an elaborate bow. Their acrobatic routine involved jumping, leaping, twisting, tumbling, climbing vertical ladders on their hands and turning somersaults along bars balanced thirty feet above the ground. It culminated with Olga climbing onto a giant swing that was wheeled by the other acrobats into the centre of the ring. There she stood, her feet planted on the seat of the swing, her arms holding the ropes to either side of her. As drums rolled, with legs and arms she pumped the swing back and forth until, slowly, gradually, it began to swing in high arcs, forward and back, higher and further, until ultimately it rotated 360 degrees. Round and round and round she went, faster and faster, until suddenly, she let go of the swing at the peak of its arc, and she flew . . .

Into the air she flew, twisting and turning as she rose higher and higher, and then, with her arms outstretched, like a diving swallow, she swept down into the arms of her fellow acrobats who stood in formation on the ground ready to catch her.

When the performance was over, I waited in the foyer at the foot of the stairs leading up to the Prince's Apartments. She found me there.

'I heard you cheering, Dr Doyle.'

'You must call me Arthur,' I said.

'You saw me bowing to you?'

'Of course,' I said. 'I did not take my eyes off you. You were wonderful. You are wonderful. You have hypnotised me, without a doubt.'

She laughed. I laughed, too. 'I will take you to Ivan's office now,' she said. 'Come with me.'

She took me by the hand and led me out of the foyer and into the street. The departing crowds were already thinning on the pavement. In the roadway hansoms and four-wheelers were rattling up, taking on their cargoes of shirt-fronted men, beshawled, bejewelled women and weary, happy children. Olga held onto me as she took me around the side of the building.

'Look,' she said, as we emerged from the side-alley into the field at the back of the Agricultural Hall, 'look up into the sky. In London you cannot usually see the stars, because of the fog, but tonight the sky is clear. Look at the stars, Arthur. They are shining for us. They are happy for us.'

I turned to look into her face, but in the darkness all I could see was the glimmer of her eyes. 'Over there,' she said, 'that is Ivan's office – up those steps.'

I looked to where she was pointing and then turned back. She was gone.

24

Ostrog

The 'office' of Ivan Salazkin, ringmaster and owner of the Russian Circus, turned out to be his caravan. On the outside, silhouetted in the darkness, it looked like a traditional gypsy wagon: a fairy-tale cottage carried on giant wheels, with high sides that sloped outwards as they rose towards the eaves. Inside, it looked like the private dining room of the St Petersburg palace of Catherine the Great.

The room was entirely lit by candles – there were scores of them: in two chandeliers hanging from the ceiling, in sconces on each wall, in gilt candlesticks on every surface – and it seemed so vast because on the long side walls and on the far wall facing the door were *trompe-l'oeil* windows filled with mirrored glass. In every direction the room appeared to continue to infinity. Above the gilded window frames were elaborate wooden carvings – not of fruit and flowers or harps and lyres, but of jugglers and acrobats, performing elephants on their hind legs and costumed dancing bears. On the ceiling, between the chandeliers, was a mock-baroque painting depicting what I took to be the sun god Helios and his sister Eos, the goddess of dawn. He looked not unlike Salazkin and her face was the face of Olga – or so it seemed to me. The whole extraordinary room might have been designed by Rastrelli himself in the mid-eighteenth century – with finishing touches supplied more recently by P. T. Barnum. I stood in the doorway, bemused, amazed.

Oscar was already there – and in wine, I thought.

He was seated at the head of a table at the end of the room, dressed in evening clothes, sporting the green carnation in his buttonhole that was a favourite affectation. ('It means nothing,' he liked to explain, 'which is why people believe it must mean everything.') He had a saucer of champagne in one hand and a lighted cigarette in the other. His face was flushed – and appeared orange in the candlelight. His eyes were glistening with tears. When he grinned at me I thought he looked like a pumpkin at Hallowe'en.

Ivan Salazkin sat next to him at the head of the table. It can only have been a quarter of an hour since the ringmaster had taken his final bow in the centre of the sawdust ring – magnificent in his black riding boots, scarlet tailcoat, tall top hat and waxed moustaches. Now, the facial hair was all gone, his strong features had turned to putty and he cut a diminished figure, wrapped in a quilted dressing gown, with a towel around his neck, and carpet slippers on his feet. He, too, held a glass of champagne in one hand and a cigarette in the other. Looking at the pair of them seated before me, the image of the Hallowe'en pumpkin vanished, replaced by Tweedledum and Tweedledee out on the razzle.

And behind them, like the Frog Footman waiting at table,

stood Michael Ostrog. Oscar had been right. This was certainly the man in the photograph in Macnaghten's file.

'Come in, Dr Doyle,' cried Salazkin. 'Did you enjoy the show? We saw you there.' He looked up at his servant. 'Ostrov – fetch Dr Doyle a glass.'

'We have been having a political discussion, Arthur,' said Oscar merrily. 'Salazkin is remarkably well-informed.'

'I know nothing about politics,' protested our host. 'Nothing at all.'

'He doesn't seem to know much about British politics for sure. He thinks that I should become a member of parliament. He doesn't appear to realise that only people who look dull ever get into the House of Commons and only people who are dull ever succeed there.'

'You are a public figure, Mr Wilde, and much admired. Your voice should be heard in the counsels of the land. England is the mother of parliaments, after all. England needs you. You would be an adornment to any government.'

'I'm flattered, I'm sure,' said Oscar, chuckling. 'But I am Irish and an artist.'

'And what difference does being Irish make? Are you not allowed to vote?'

'Oh, I can vote, but do I want to? England is full of Irishmen, but we are all outsiders. Artists should be outsiders, I believe.'

'And tell me,' asked Salazkin, 'what form of government is it most suitable for an artist to live under?'

'There is only one answer to that question. The form of government that is most suitable to the artist is no government at all.'

'You believe that?' said the ringmaster, sitting up and looking at Oscar carefully, an eyebrow raised.

'I do,' answered Oscar solemnly.

'You are an anarchist, then?'

'I am,' said Oscar, offering a modest bow at the accolade. 'I even belong to the Anarchists' Club. I know you know it. I have seen you there.' He turned to me and explained in an aside: 'It's in Soho. Somewhat *louche*, but I think you'd like it. I will take you sometime. The conversation's lively and it's surprisingly well organised.' He giggled at his own joke and then added: 'I am a royalist as well, of course.'

And a little tipsy, too, I thought to myself. Feeling I should contribute to the conversation but not, in truth, much interested in it, I asked Salazkin: 'Are you involved in politics at all in your own country?'

The ringmaster smiled. 'Who said, "What the people want is bread and circuses"?'

'Juvenal,' murmured Oscar, closing his eyes and laying his champagne glass on the table.

'I give them circuses ... ' Salazkin paused and looked directly at me. His eyes told me nothing.

'When what they need is bread?' I suggested.

'Yes,' he said, nodding, and gesturing to Ostrog to pour out more champagne. 'Life in Russia is hard for many people. There is starvation. We have the highest infant mortality in Europe. Life expectancy is little more than thirty years. We are still recovering from the great famine that killed more than half a million of my fellow citizens.'

Oscar opened his eyes. 'You see, Arthur. He is alarmingly well-informed. And he calls them "citizens", not "subjects". What would the Tsar make of that? He's probably an anarchist himself, if not a Socialist.'

'I am not one for politics, Mr Wilde, I do assure you.'

'I don't believe you, my friend. I saw you yesterday at Nevill's

Turkish Bath hobnobbing with Henry Labouchere MP. I've seen you there before, gossiping with the great and not-so-good. You're steeped in politics.'

'Enough of this nonsense, Mr Wilde,' said the ringmaster, sitting forward again and slapping the table with his hand. 'You are here to interview my man Ostrov. You'd better get on with it.' Oscar made no effort to rouse himself. 'Sit, Ostrov,' said Salazkin, 'and answer Mr Wilde's questions. He has been told that you could be the notorious Jack the Ripper.'

'I know,' said the servant. He seemed curiously unperturbed by the suggestion. He stood at the other end of the dining table, facing Oscar and his master. I considered his face: it was undoubtedly the face of a man defeated by life, but in his deeply sunken eyes I recognised a glimmer of defiance. He held his arms at his side and looked straight ahead, as though he were a man in the dock.

'Sit,' insisted Salazkin. Ostrog sat. 'Proceed,' said Salazkin.

I glanced at Oscar and, realising that my friend was either too weary or too far gone in drink to conduct the cross-examination himself, reached into my jacket pocket for my pen and notebook.

I looked down the table towards Ostrog. 'Thank you for agreeing to talk to us,' I began. The man said nothing.

'May I start by asking your name?'

'Yes,' he said.

Silence fell. I looked at the man through the flickering candlelight. His face was immobile, his gaze seemingly fixed on Oscar and Salazkin – but, in fact, I suddenly realised, fixed on himself. He was staring straight ahead at his reflection in the mirrored glass. 'So, what is your name?' I asked.

'Michael Ostrov.'

'Also known as Michael Ostrog?'

'Yes.' He smiled – not at me, but at himself. And added: 'And Michael Hanneford and Bertrand Ashley and Ashley Nabokov and Claude Clayton and Max Gosslar and Count Sobieski and Dr Grant.'

'You have many names,' I said.

'Not now. Now I am Michael Ostrov.' His accent was thick, but his English was remarkably good.

'But you have had many names?'

'Yes.'

'May I ask why?'

'Because I have been many people.'

'Ah,' I said – not knowing what to say. I glanced towards Oscar. His eyes were half-closed, but there was a smile on his lips. He appeared amused by my predicament.

'To begin with, who were you? Where do you come from? Where were you born?'

'I was born in 1833 in Ostrog in the Ukraine. I am Ukrainian Jew.'

'And when did you come to England?'

'When the Russians burned down our house. They killed all the Jews, except for me. I escaped. On my horse.'

'On your horse?'

'My family were horse traders – for a thousand years. The Russians burned our house and our stables. They killed every Jew in Ostrog – except for me. I was in the hills on the morning that they came.'

'And you escaped?'

'I escaped. I was young. And I was strong. And I was clever.' He smiled at himself in the mirror. 'I am a Jew.'

'How did you get to England?'

'It took a year – two years. I came with the circus.'

I glanced towards Salazkin. He was studying Ostrog with apparent satisfaction, as a master might a star pupil. 'Not this circus,' he said quietly.

'The Hanneford Circus,' said Ostrog. 'They had a horse-riding show. Thirty years ago. I was a stable lad.'

'A Jewish stable lad?' murmured Oscar. 'This is sounding a touch improbable.'

Ostrog's head turned suddenly. For a moment, I thought he was going to spit. 'Yes,' he said, his dark eyes suddenly blazing, 'a Jewish stable lad. You don't have that in England, do you? You have a Jew for prime minister but he has to call himself a Christian. We got to England and the Hannefords said they didn't need me any more.'

Oscar roused himself. He sat forward at the table and moved one of the candlesticks the better to see Ostrog. 'And so you turned to a life of crime?'

Ostrog said nothing and looked away once more.

'I have read the police file,' said Oscar. 'In Oxford, as Max Gosslar, you worked as a College servant until you were arrested for theft and imprisoned for ten months. In Cambridge, a year later, you pulled the same trick – with a similar result. Next you turned up in Tunbridge Wells – as Count Sobieski.'

'Why Count Sobieski?' I asked.

Oscar put his hand lightly on my sleeve. 'Oh, come now, Arthur, it was Tunbridge Wells—'

Salazkin intervened. 'Ask him if he was guilty of all the offences for which he was imprisoned?'

'A good question,' said Oscar. 'And what is the answer?' He sat forward at the table, resting his chin on his hand, and looked at Ostrog intently.

'I am a Jew. I plead guilty.'

'In 1873,' I said, 'I seem to recall you threatened a policeman with a revolver.'

'And I was sent to gaol for ten years.'

'And when you were released, it started all over again,' said Oscar.

'Did you not learn your lesson?' I asked.

'I learned that no one will give work to a man who tells the truth. No one will give work to a Jew who has been in prison for ten years. Would you? *Would you?*'

'But Mr Salazkin did,' said Oscar. 'I wonder why.'

Salazkin spoke. 'Because I am Russian and because he told me what the Russians had done to his family.'

Oscar turned towards Salazkin and looked at him amiably. 'How did you meet?'

'He came to the circus, looking for work.'

'Here in London?'

'No, in Paris.'

'When was this?'

'Tell them,' said Salazkin.

'I left England on the tenth of March 1888. When I went to prison they said I was a "homicidal maniac" – because I fired that gun at the police. I fired it to protect myself. But when they released me they said I was cured. I left England at once. I wanted to go home. I went to Paris. I looked for work. I speak English and Yiddish and Russian. I went to the Russian Circus.'

'And I took him on,' said Salazkin, 'and he has been with me ever since.'

'I thought he was imprisoned in France,' I said.

'He was,' said Salazkin, 'for two years. But when he came out of prison, I took him on again – and he's stayed on the straight and narrow ever since. He looks after my carriage and my horses and he looks after me. He's an odd-looking fellow, I agree, but I can vouch for him and I do.'

Oscar laid down his champagne and threw up his hands. 'So why on earth is he mixed up in this business of the Whitechapel murders? Why do the police reckon he is Jack the Ripper? Why do they believe that at this moment he is locked up in the Surrey County Lunatic Asylum?'

'I can tell you,' said Salazkin. 'Because when we brought the circus to London in the summer of 1888, Ostrov went to Whitechapel.'

'I had heard about the Jewish market there – and the women. I wanted Jewish food. Bialys and chicken feet. And I needed a woman. And before I found the woman I went for a shave and to get my hair cut.'

'And Kosminski was the barber?' I said.

'Yes.'

'And you became friends?'

'No. Never friends. We were Jews together, that is all.'

'And together you hunted for prostitutes.'

'We did not hunt. We paid. We paid money that we had earned – Kosminski cutting hair and Ostrov working at the Russian Circus.'

'And you called yourself Ostrov here because it sounds more Russian?'

'I can call myself whatever I choose. I can be whoever I want to be.'

'And why do the police think you are Jack the Ripper?' I asked.

'Because I was in Whitechapel when the killings happened and I went with prostitutes and I am a foreigner and a convict and a Jew.'

'But you are not Jack the Ripper?' said Oscar.

Ostrog said nothing.

'Answer,' said Salazkin.

'Jack the Ripper? It's a stupid name,' said Ostrog contemptuously.

'I agree,' said Oscar, now lighting another cigarette. 'But for the sake of clarity: you are not he?'

'No.'

'Then how do you explain the bag of knives you were carrying when the police first arrested you?'

'They were clean knives. There was no blood on them.'

Oscar chuckled. 'Had there been, I imagine you'd have been arrested, charged, tried, convicted and executed by now, my friend.'

Ostrog stood impassively still gazing at his own reflection in the glass.

'What on earth were you doing traipsing through Whitechapel with a bag full of knives?' Oscar persisted. 'According to the police, you were frequently seen in Whitechapel with your bag of knives. What was going on?'

'You told the police you were a doctor,' I said.

'That was a lie,' said Oscar.

'That was to protect me,' said Salazkin. 'They were my knives. They are my knives. You saw them tonight, Dr Doyle – in the show. I threw them at the girl, do you remember? The girl turning on the Catherine wheel.'

I remembered the routine. It was impressive. 'You use real knives?' I said.

'We do. And they need to be sharp – and to shine in the lights. And one of Ostrov's tasks is to keep them sharp and in good repair. He takes them to the knife-grinder for me.'

'And the knife-grinder plies his trade in the back streets of Whitechapel?'

'No,' said Ostrog. 'The knife-grinder is near here in Hammersmith. I took the knives to Whitechapel to show Kosminski. He liked the knives. He liked to look at them and play with them. He used to shave with them. He cut marks in his body with them. He was a strange man.'

'You're not entirely Old Uncle Normality yourself,' said Oscar, smiling.

Ostrog turned again and looked at Oscar. 'You patronise me because I am a Jew. I speak good English, I know I do, but because I have a Yiddish accent, I am a funny foreigner to you. My ancestors were nobles. I could have been a doctor. But my parents were burned to death, Mr Oscar Wilde. I lost my inheritance. I am a servant now. I serve you your champagne. I bring caviar to your house. And from your great height you patronise me.'

'That's enough,' said Salazkin. 'You were wrong to take the knives to Whitechapel and you know it.'

Oscar closed his eyes. 'Is Kosminski Jack the Ripper, do you think?' I asked.

'I do not know,' said Ostrog. 'He is a sick man. Strange and sick. When the police could find no evidence against us, they got the magistrates to put us away as lunatics. With Kosminski, that was the right thing to do.'

'But not with you?'

'I am not mad.'

'And you are not the Michael Ostrog who is now languishing in the Surrey County Lunatic Asylum?'

'No.'

'Who is he?'

'He is a sick man. It is right that he should be there.'

'Who is he?'

'I do not know his name.'

Salazkin got up from his chair and fetched the bottle of champagne from the ice bucket on the sideboard. He came behind me to refill my glass. He put the bottle on the table next to Oscar so that he could refill his own. 'We found the man underneath the railway arches in Pinchin Street. He was more dead than alive. He was a drinker, but he was past drink. He was a beggar, but he was past begging. He had nothing. He was waiting to die.'

'He was a Russian Jew?' I asked.

'Oh, yes,' said Salazkin. 'Whitechapel is full of them. The East End is their home now. Russia does not want them. As our Tsar likes to say, "Let us never forget that it was the Jews who crucified Jesus." There is no place for a Jew in modern Russia.'

'Whitechapel is where they come to die,' said Ostrog.

'At least we saved one of them,' said Salazkin, resuming his seat. 'I knew that Ostrov was not Jack the Ripper. I knew that Ostrov was not mad. He'd been my good and faithful servant – he'd looked after my carriage and my horses, he'd sharpened my knives, he'd delivered gifts of caviar to the homes of my friends. I wasn't going to let him be taken off to the lunatic asylum, so on the day when they came in their Black Maria with their straps and their straitjacket to take him away I handed him over . . . '

'Only the man you handed over wasn't Ostrog at all. It was the man you had found under the railway arch in Pinchin Street.'

'We cleaned him up. We shaved him. We dressed him in Ostrov's clothes. The clothes were too big for him, but it didn't matter. He looked a little like Ostrov, but that didn't much matter either.'

'No one really looks closely when the Jew walks by,' said Ostrog.

'Did the man know what was happening to him?' I asked.

'He knew he was getting food at last. And clothes. And shelter.'

'Could he talk? Did he make sense?'

'He was not in his right mind. He'd ruined that with drink. But he could talk – not in English, but in Yiddish and Russian.'

'Did you ask him his name?'

'No. We told him his name.'

'Michael Ostrog.'

'Yes,' said Salazkin. 'We told him who he was. We told him his whole life story.'

'And he believed you?'

'Yes. He became who we wanted him to be.'

'How did you do it?'

'Very simply,' said Salazkin, with a smile. 'I hypnotised him. It is easily done. It's much easier than knife-throwing. You can buy a book in the Tottenham Court Road that will show you how.'

25

George R. Sims

The interview concluded, I left Oscar at the circus and walked back to the Langham Hotel alone. It was a cold night, but the sky was clear and the moon was full. I maintained a brisk pace through near-deserted streets and managed the journey from Olympia to Portland Place in little more than an hour. I relished the solitary walk – and the silence. I needed time – and peace – to think.

As I lay in bed, my head was filled with a kaleidoscope of images: Ostrog staring at himself in the looking glass, Ivan the Terrible on horseback commanding the circus ring, little Olga swinging towards me on her trapeze. I could not get the girl out of my mind's eye. She was an enchantress and I was spellbound.

In the morning, at breakfast, there was no sign of Oscar. As I left the dining room, I found Martin, the young waiter, hovering by the door. He seemed eager to speak to me. I asked him if he had seen Mr Wilde.

'No, sir,' he said, 'not since yesterday, but I's seen the man who's following him. He was outside the hotel last night and he was here again this morning. When I come on at six, he was already out there, underneath the lamp-post. That's how I saw him. I went out to speak to him. He didn't see me sneak up on him. He was lighting a cigarette. I went right up to him and said, "Who are you? What do you want?" He didn't say a word, just walked away.'

I thanked the lad and told him I'd report his intelligence to Mr Wilde. He grinned mischievously. 'You do that, sir. I know he'll reward me. He's good like that.'

I went up to Oscar's room: there was no answer at the door. I tried it: it was locked. I found the chambermaid: she told me she had already cleaned the room and that the bed had not been slept in. I returned to my own room – the maid had cleaned that, too – and spent the morning seated at the table by the window completing the short story I had begun the night before. When I had finished it, I called it 'Sweethearts'. (If you are inclined to read it, it appeared in *The Idler* in June that year, 1894.)

My work done (and done well, I felt), I returned to Olympia – this time by bus and tram. As I was leaving the hotel, Jimmy, the bellboy, stopped me in the foyer.

'Mr Wilde hasn't collected his flower today,' he said.

'What is it?' I asked.

'I don't rightly know, sir. It's for a lady, I think. It's a pink 'un.'

'Show me,' I said.

It was a pink viola and quite beautiful. 'I'll take it,' I said. 'It would be a shame for it to go to waste.'

Clutching my small bloom, I found Olga waiting for me outside the National Agricultural Hall. As I walked towards her from the bus stop, she walked towards me, smiling broadly, with a firm step and outward composure of manner, but as we met and

I presented her with the flower, her lip trembled and her hand quivered.

It was the first time that I had seen her not dressed as a circus acrobat, not costumed in her sequined leotard. Today she was a young lady, small, dainty, well gloved, and dressed in the most perfect taste. There was, unsurprisingly, a plainness and simplicity about her outfit, which bore with it the suggestion of limited means. Her coat was a sombre, greyish beige, untrimmed and unbraided, and on her head she wore a small turban of the same dull hue, relieved only by a suspicion of white feather in the side.

'You look lovely, Olga,' I said.

'And you look so handsome, Arthur,' she replied. 'Thank you for my flower.'

Arm in arm, we walked down the road to Hammersmith to a small teashop that Olga knew well. We had a pot of tea and poached eggs on toast, followed by more tea and a slice of Victoria sponge, which we shared. 'This is my favourite meal,' she said. It was one of the happiest and saddest meals that I have ever known. We cannot command our love, but we can our actions. Olga captivated me: she was so young and so alive. I wanted to make love to her – so much! But I knew it would be wrong – so wrong!

At two o'clock, Olga had to return to the circus and I made my way back to the Langham Hotel. There was a wire waiting for me from Oscar:

```
YOU WILL ALWAYS BE FOND OF ME ARTHUR. I
REPRESENT ALL THE SINS YOU NEVER HAD THE
COURAGE TO COMMIT. SEE YOU TONIGHT AT SEVEN
PM AT TWELVE CLARENCE GATE LONDON W. SIMS
KNOWS ALL.
```

George R. Sims certainly knew everybody. In 1894 he was at the height of his fame and fortune. He was the highest paid journalist in the land (reputedly earning upwards of £150,000 a year) and, arguably, the best informed. He was also a prolific playwright, popular poet, zealous social reformer, acknowledged criminologist, noted *bon vivant* and ardent follower of the horses, the dogs and the boxing ring. Today, he is probably best remembered as the author of the sentimental ballad that begins, 'It was Christmas day in the workhouse ...' In his day, he was known as a thoroughly good egg, a wholly decent, hard-working, amusing, intelligent, clubbable man.

'Even behind his back, people say nice things about George R. Sims,' said Oscar. 'What's his dark secret, I wonder? He must have one.'

'Hush!' I said.

I had encountered my friend in the entrance hall of Sims' house, just off the Marylebone Road on the south side of Regent's Park. Oscar had stepped out of his carriage just as I was coming up the road from the underground at Baker Street. The Sims' butler was helping him off with his coat. Oscar was looking unusually pink-cheeked and ebullient, freshly kitted out in a well-cut velvet evening suit of bottle green.

'Where have you been?' I asked, taking off my own coat to hand to the butler.

'Never mind that,' said my friend. 'Look where we are now! This is George R. Sims' Twelfth Night party. Everybody who is anybody will be here.'

Together we walked across the parquet-floored hall and into the Sims' drawing room. Footmen on either side of the double doors held trays bearing frosted flutes of gently bubbling champagne. 'It'll be Perrier-Jouët,' murmured Oscar. 'And a good vintage. George is a generous soul.'

The drawing room was beautifully proportioned, high-ceilinged, brilliantly lit and crowded with an equally brilliant assembly. There must have been eighty to a hundred people in the room and, even at a glance, most of them looked familiar. At once, I recognised actresses I knew from picture postcards, politicians I knew from photographs in the daily papers, authors I knew as rivals.

'There's Bram Stoker,' I said.

'With Florrie Balcombe, once the prettiest girl in Dublin, now the loveliest woman in London. You know she turned down my offer of marriage in favour of Bram?'

'So you tell me.'

'So it is.'

'And who are they talking to?'

'The handsome one's Alec Shand. Now *he* was secretly engaged to Constance. Before my time. He's a most unusual fellow with some quite unusual ideas. He has sent me his new book. It's intriguing.'

'And the little old man they're talking to? Is he a clergyman?'

'That is the Reverend Charles Dodgson.'

'Lewis Carroll?'

'Oh yes. Sims knows everybody. *Le tout monde* and *le demi-monde*. Look over there ... Tom Norman deep in conversation with Walter Wellbeloved. And there's Richard Mansfield hugger-mugger with my friend Wat Sickert. Extraordinary. Is this a convocation of Jack the Ripper suspects brought together for our convenience?'

As he spoke, a large hand fell on his right shoulder and another on my left. It was our host coming up behind us and giving us a welcoming embrace. He was as tall as Oscar – over six feet – and as elegantly attired – he sported a black velvet evening suit, with silk trimmings – but he cut a more dapper figure because he was slimmer than Oscar and, unlike Oscar, wore a full beard, carefully cut in the style made fashionable by the Prince of Wales.

'You know I was once mistaken for Jack the Ripper, don't you? My portrait appeared on the cover of a sixpenny edition of one of my books and a Whitechapel coffee-stall keeper who claimed to have had a conversation with the Ripper on the night of the double murder said "That's the man" and took my picture to the police.'

'Were you arrested?'

Sims had a warm, deep voice, which, at all times, carried with it the hint of a chuckle. 'I was pleased to help them with their inquiries,' he answered, smiling, 'and provide them with my rock-solid alibis. Who knows who the coffee-stall keeper was talking to that night? It might have been Jack the Ripper. Or it might not. Whitechapel was and is awash with possible suspects, but there are no known witnesses to any of the crimes. The murderer remains a faceless wonder.'

'Could he be among your guests tonight, George?'

'Anything is possible, Oscar, but, whatever the gossip-mongers say, I don't believe it's going to turn out to be Lewis Carroll, do you? Look at him. Eccentric, I grant you, but I don't think the darling man has the *strength* for it.'

'You know everybody and everything,' said Oscar ingratiatingly. 'Who do you reckon is the Whitechapel murderer?'

'I can tell you that the *Sun* newspaper is about to run a series of articles accusing one Thomas Cutbrush of the crimes.'

'I know the name,' I said.

'You might well do, Arthur. It was in the papers a year or two ago. Cutbrush is a lunatic, already in Broadmoor because in 1891 he was caught red-handed assaulting a woman's buttocks with a kitchen knife – but, *pace* the *Sun,* there's nothing of any substance to link him with the Whitechapel killings of 1888. I'm afraid some papers will say anything in pursuit of sales.'

'Cutbrush is a good name for a murderer, all the same.'

Sims smiled. 'I agree, Oscar. Names do make such a difference, don't they? I was so sorry when Dr Cream was ruled out of the running. Dr Cream! Top hat, black moustache – whiskers you could twirl. He looked the part, he played the part – confessed to killings all over the shop – apparently actually boasted of being Jack the Ripper as he went to the gallows. Unfortunately, it turned out he was in America all through 1888 and his modus operandi was the phial of poison rather than the kitchen knife.'

'You know there's been a Holmes accused of being the Ripper?' I said.

'Indeed,' answered Sims. 'H. H. Holmes, the man who built his own "Murder Castle". I had hopes of interviewing him, but he proved elusive.'

'And where did Mr Holmes build his "Murder Castle"?' enquired Oscar, widening his eyes. 'Not in Whitechapel?'

'No, in Chicago. It was a hotel designed to attract young unattached females attending the Chicago World's Fair and looking for an inexpensive room for the night. Holmes designed it all himself – with secret passageways, dungeons, poisoned gas chambers, acid pits, the works. I thought it would make a marvellous setting for a play – build the actual house on stage. Holmes murdered women by the dozen, apparently. He's still on the run. Maybe we should put your Holmes on his trail, Arthur?'

'My Holmes is a fictional character,' I said firmly, 'and I've done with him, thank you very much.'

'Will we ever be done with Jack the Ripper, I wonder?' mused

Sims. 'H. H. Holmes is in the clear, however. There's no evidence he was in Whitechapel in 1888.'

'And is Prince Eddy in the clear, too?' asked Oscar. 'I see Bunbury is here tonight and in mourning.'

'Bunbury?' I asked.

'Prince Eddy's equerry,' explained our host. 'The Bunburys have been courtiers since time immemorial. Freddie was at Prince Eddy's beck and call to the last – but, while I've no doubt he still misses HRH, he's actually in mourning for his wife. She passed away only this week. I am glad he's come, under the circumstances.'

'I think I should say hello to him,' said Oscar. 'I know him slightly. You'll like him, Arthur. He's most engaging.'

'Mix and mingle, gentlemen,' said Sims encouragingly, pushing us towards the throng. 'Recharge your glasses as you go. I'll catch up with you later. There's something in particular I want to say to you, Oscar. Meanwhile, help me out and work the room – but don't just hover round the actresses.' He laughed as we plunged into the mêlée. 'Your brother's here, Oscar,' he called out after us. 'And the Marquess of Queensbury is here. You know his son, don't you?'

'Queensbury and Willie we can avoid,' murmured Oscar. 'Let's find Bunbury. He's a sweet old thing.'

Having squeezed our way through the multitude, we found him by the fireplace. Sir Frederick Bunbury, Bt., was a tall, lean figure, dressed all in black, with a thin neck that failed to touch his shirt collar but somehow supported an improbably large head that hung forward like a tortoise's. His eyes were hooded; his face was deeply lined; he had long white hair and a drooping white moustache.

'My condolences, Sir Freddie,' said Oscar gently, taking the old gentleman by the hand. 'I feel for you in your loss.'

'Thank you, Wilde,' murmured the baronet softly. 'She had been poorly for some time, so it was not entirely unexpected. And for her, at least, a release.'

Oscar presented me to Bunbury and, inadequately, I added my condolences.

'Thank you,' nodded the elderly courtier. 'The Reverend Dodgson has been reminding me that my dear wife is now in a better place and I believe him. Do you know Mr Dodgson?'

'I know of Lewis Carroll, of course, the author of *Alice's Adventures in Wonderland*,' said Oscar with feeling, shaking the clergyman's small hand with both of his. 'It is an honour to meet you, sir. The Mad Hatter, the March Hare, the White Rabbit, Alice – all yours.'

'Alice is a real person,' said Lewis Carroll, in a small Dormouse-like voice, gazing up at Oscar myopically. 'I take no credit for her.'

'No doubt God and the girl's parents brought her into the world, but you took her into Wonderland and have made her immortal.'

Lewis Carroll blinked at Oscar, but said nothing more.

'I agree,' drawled Bunbury. (He was an aristocrat of the old school: his lips barely moved as he spoke and the sound came from the cavernous roof of his mouth.) 'It's an extraordinary thing to do – create a character that lives beyond the page. Not many can boast as much.'

'Though, curiously,' said Oscar, now in full flow, 'two or three who can are gathered here. Arthur Conan Doyle is the creator of the great detective Mr Sherlock Holmes. And look, here with my brother is one of our finest players, Mr Richard Mansfield, who has successfully brought to life both Dr Jekyll and Mr Hyde.'

Willie Wilde, Richard Mansfield, Bram Stoker and my friend James Barrie were standing in line in front of the fireplace. All but Willie were smiling at Oscar's effulgence. 'To create a name that will live beyond your own lifetime – that's something. You've done it, Mr Dodgson – with a dozen characters and more. Mr Dickens did it with Mr Pickwick and old Scrooge. I reckon Arthur here has done it with Holmes and his friend Watson. I have some hopes for my Dorian Gray. How's your vampire coming along, Bram? Has he got a name yet?'

'Not yet,' said Stoker. 'I'm thinking of calling him "The Undead".'

'That won't do,' cried Oscar dismissively. 'You need a proper name – a name with a ring to it.' Oscar glanced around the little group gathered by the fireplace. 'Pickwick, Scrooge, Humpty Dumpty, Holmes and Watson, Jekyll and Hyde – they're all names that will join the ranks of the great immortals. If you want to capture the public's imagination, you've got to get the name right.'

Willie Wilde spoke up: 'Jack the Ripper is a case in point.'

Oscar placed his champagne flute on the mantelpiece and looked at his brother. 'For once, Willie, I agree with you. Jack the Ripper is a name that could outlast them all.'

26

Stay

Sims' party was a memorable one and convivial in the main. It was marred by two incidents, noticed by none except those involved.

The first was minor. As we broke away from the gathering of writers around the fireplace, Willie remarked to Oscar: 'I notice you're not wearing your customary buttonhole tonight, Oscar. Neglecting your appearance as well as your wife? Where will it all end, I wonder?'

Oscar rose above the slight, but I felt it – and felt responsible for it, too.

The second incident might have been more serious.

'Who is your friend, Arthur?' Oscar asked once we had shaken off Willie and were returning to the fray. 'The young man with the sad eyes and the subaltern's moustache – who is he?'

'James Barrie,' I said. 'A fellow Scot. We wrote a comic opera together, *Jane Annie*.'

'Really?'

'Yes, really. It's set in a girls' boarding school.'

'Oh, Arthur, you do sail close to the wind.' He laughed and turned. 'I'm going back to find him. He looks interesting. I want to talk to him.'

'He is interesting,' I said, 'but he doesn't say very much.'

'That won't be a problem,' said Oscar, turning towards the fireplace. Barrie, I saw, was now standing to one side of it, alone.

I watched Oscar go up to my young friend and introduce himself and, at once, say something that made the customarily solemn JMB laugh out loud. For the next hour, every ten minutes or so, as I moved through the crush of Sims' distinguished guests, I caught sight of them – Oscar and James – standing side by side, talking animatedly.

As I did our host's bidding and 'worked' the room, for some reason (no doubt connected with Olga) I did avoid the actresses. I talked for a while with Richard Mansfield. He said: 'Your friend Wilde is amusing, but please tell him that I haven't played *Jekyll and Hyde* for several years. I'd rather be known for my *Richard III* or, better still, my *Napoleon*.'

'Napoleon is the part you are playing at the moment?' I asked.

'Yes, but I've taken the night off to attend George's party – and to give my understudy an opportunity.'

'I'd enjoy seeing your performace,' I said.

'Thank you,' he replied. 'Come tomorrow, why don't you? We've a special Sunday performance – by invitation only. We'll get Wilde to come, too.' He glanced in Oscar's direction. 'I'd ask him now, but he seems a little preoccupied.' The actor offered me a knowing smile and moved off into the throng.

I sought out Walter Wellbeloved and found him in conversation with Alec Shand. 'I've only just met Wellbeloved,' said Shand disarmingly, 'but we're already close because we have discovered we both have a longing for Constance Wilde. Do you hanker after her, too, Dr Doyle?' I made no reply. 'Ah.' He smiled knowingly. 'I see you do. You say nothing, but your eyes speak volumes. The eyes truly are the mirror to the soul. Everything you feel, they show. You cannot hide it.'

'Is that so?' I said, disarmed.

'It is. And if your eyes look dead it's because your soul is dead. Your eyes are full of life, Dr Doyle. And full of longing, too. You should be pleased.'

'I'm not sure what to say,' I answered.

'Say nothing,' said Shand pleasantly. 'You can read my treatise on the subject if you're interested. I think you'll find the research convincing – and revealing. I've sent Wilde a copy. Borrow it from him.'

We were joined by Henry Labouchere MP who boomed at us: 'When you're with a prostitute, do you think about her or your wife or your mistress or the barmaid down at the old Bull and Bush? Come on, chaps, I want the truth.'

Walter Wellbeloved half closed his eyes: 'I have drunk too much or I wouldn't say this. I think about a girl called Rosie. She was a mermaid.'

'I don't think you've drunk nearly enough, old fellow,' said Alec Shand. 'Let's get you another glass. I want to hear more about Rosie.'

Gradually the room thinned. I looked at my watch. It was nine o'clock. Oscar and James were still standing next to the fireplace, side by side, backs against the wall. I went to join them.

'We've only just begun, Arthur, and you're telling us it's time to leave.'

'It's gone nine,' I said. 'I'm glad you've met.'

'James has been asking me about Dorian Gray,' said Oscar. 'He's taken with the notion of eternal youth. He tells me my book has given him an idea for a play.'

'That's charming,' I said. 'I hope it will be more successful than *Jane Annie*.'

As we were laughing, a voice behind me hissed: 'It's disgusting. The man's a disgrace.' I felt spittle on my ear.

I turned to find the diminutive Marquess of Queensbury glowering at us. His head jutted forward, his shoulders were hunched. He slapped a tight fist into his open palm and leaned in towards Oscar. 'I've been watching you, Wilde,' he snarled. 'I've been watching you with this young man. You're at it again.'

'At what, may I ask?' enquired Oscar coolly.

'Carrying on like a pervert.' Oscar raised an eyebrow. 'I don't say you are it, but you look it. You *pose* as it, which is just as bad.' Queensberry twisted his head towards James Barrie. 'You'll steer clear of this perfumed popinjay if you know what's good for you, sir. He's near ruined my son. He knows no shame.'

'I must protest—' Oscar began, but mildly.

'Wilde,' barked Lord Queensberry, 'if I catch you and my son together again in any public place, I will thrash you. I give you fair warning.'

Oscar stopped lounging against the wall and stood upright. He towered over the snarling marquess. 'I do not know what the Queensberry rules are, but the Oscar Wilde rule is to shoot at sight.'

With a yowl of derision, Queensberry turned and stomped away.

'Bosie is right,' said Oscar gently. 'What a funny little man he is.'

There was a moment's awkward silence before Barrie said: 'I must be on my way. I will write to you, Mr Wilde. I'll see you very soon, Arthur. We must talk cricket.' With a schoolboyish formality, he shook us both by the hand. 'Goodnight, Mr Wilde. I have so enjoyed our conversation.'

We watched him as he crossed the now half-empty drawing room and disappeared into the hall.

'What an interesting young man,' said Oscar. 'He told me dreams do come true, if we only wish hard enough. Do you believe that, Arthur?'

'I'm not sure,' I answered truthfully.

'He did add a caveat. He said you can have anything in life if you will sacrifice everything else for it.'

'He thinks deep thoughts.'

'And he plays cricket.'

'Yes.'

'And yet he's a Scotsman. Quite a conundrum.' As we spoke we were still gazing across the emptying drawing room towards the hallway. 'Look,' said Oscar, 'Labby and Lord Queensberry are leaving together – and Richard Mansfield and Walter Wellbeloved are departing à deux as well.'

I noticed that Labouchere, the member of parliament, had greeted the marquess with a congratulatory arm about his shoulder. 'I wouldn't think it advisable to make an enemy of those two,' I said.

'I choose my friends for their good looks,' replied Oscar, 'my acquaintances for their good characters, and my enemies for their intellects – as a rule. Those two are thoroughly stupid, but I am hearing what you say, Arthur. A man cannot be too careful in the choice of his enemies.'

'Shall we go?' I asked.

'Yes,' said Oscar. 'I'm hungry. I'll take you to Willis's. I know you. Sausage and mash – it's Saturday night.'

We crossed the room, Oscar nodding amiably to a young actress he recognised (Elizabeth Robins) and a champion jockey he didn't (Tommy Loates). As we reached the hallway, George R. Sims broke away from the group to whom he was bidding farewell and said, 'Don't go. There's something I want to say to you.'

'Arthur's hungry,' pleaded Oscar.

'Wait in there,' said Sims, indicating a doorway off the hall. 'I'll be with you in a moment. Almost everyone's gone. We'll have Welsh rarebit. Escoffier's recipe. You can't say no.'

'Escoffier's recipe?' repeated Oscar. 'George knows everybody.'

We stepped through the door that Sims had indicated and found ourselves in a small dining room. There were candles already lit on the table, which was set for three.

'I suppose this is the breakfast room,' said Oscar. 'Look at the paintings.'

'They're very modern,' I said.

'Yes,' mused Oscar, standing in front of a small picture that appeared to me to be a sketch of St Mark's Square in Venice overlaid with a Spanish omelette. 'Modern pictures are, no doubt, delightful to look at,' he said, opening his cigarette case with ostentatious panache. 'At least, some of them are. But they are impossible to live with; they are too clever, too assertive, too intellectual. Their meaning is too obvious, and their method too clearly defined. One exhausts what they have to say in a very short time, and then they become as tedious as one's relations.'

I laughed and peered more closely at the painting. 'Are we looking at the same picture, Oscar?'

He moved to the other side of the room. 'Now this one I do like. I think this is Wat Sickert's work. And really quite whole-some by Wat's standard. Look, it's the young Queen Victoria.'

It was – and recognisably so. 'That I like very much,' I said. 'Very much indeed.'

'By the way,' said Oscar, now leaning across the dining table to light his cigarette from one of the candles, 'my friend Freddie Bunbury has just invited us to Prince Eddy's birthday picnic.'

'But Prince Eddy is dead,' I said.

'I know, but were he alive it would be his thirtieth birthday on Monday and Freddie Bunbury and Festing Fitzmaurice are having a small celebration in his honour. It'll be at Festing's place and fairly squalid, I imagine, but I think we should go.'

'Who else is going?'

'I've no idea, but he was very pressing and, under the circumstances, with the death of his wife and all that, I didn't have the heart to say no. I can't go alone, so you must come, too. Who knows? We might learn something useful.'

'When is this?'

'On Monday.'

'I must get back to work, Oscar,' I said plaintively. 'I have a living to earn.'

'You can go back to work on Tuesday, Arthur. We're nearly there.'

'Are we?'

'Of course we are. And I think we need to eliminate Prince Eddy entirely from our inquiries, don't you? It would be lese-majesty not to.' He blew a cloud of blue-grey smoke into the air and, as the door opened, said happily: 'Good. That's settled.'

'What's settled?' asked George R. Sims, coming into the room.

'Everything,' said Oscar, spreading his arms like an actor about to take his bow.

'Excellent,' said Sims. 'Take a seat, gentlemen. The Welsh rarebit is on its way. And so are the last of my guests, I'm happy to say.'

'Indeed,' said Oscar, taking his place at our host's right hand. 'The only pleasure greater than greeting an old friend is bidding him farewell.'

'There are a few stragglers left,' said Sims, unfurling his linen table napkin with one quick flick of the wrist, like a jockey flourishing a whip, 'but it's wisest to leave them be. If I linger out there, it'll only encourage them to linger, too. Pour the claret, would you, Arthur? It's a poor thing, but mine own.'

'You're growing wine now, George?' said Oscar, in astonishment.

'I have a small share in Tommy Loates's vineyard. Yes, he's a jockey from Derby, but he rides for Leopold de Rothschild who manages his investments. That's the joy of the turf. We're all equal there.'

'Ever the democrat, George!'

Sims smiled at Oscar and looked at him with an amused eye. 'Ever the anarchist, Oscar?'

'Oscar is right,' I said, pouring the wine. (It was a wonderful colour.) 'You do know everybody.'

'I like to mix and mingle,' said Sims, without affectation.

'Lord Queensberry was on form tonight,' said Oscar.

'I'm sorry about that,' answered Sims, frowning. 'He's a rum one. He transformed the world of boxing and I admire him for that. But he treated his wife abominably, as you know, and falls out with almost everybody. He's really at his best with dogs and horses. He has considerable difficulty with human beings. He doesn't like you, I'm afraid, Oscar.'

Oscar said nothing.

'And Labby, for some reason, has turned against you, too.'

'I know,' said Oscar. 'A pity. He was once an admirer, but he came to one of my lectures and took notes. He told me afterwards that I had used the word "charming" seventeen times, "beautiful" twenty-six times and "lovely" forty-three times and, as a consequence, he could no longer trust me.'

'That's very funny,' said Sims. 'Labby's an odd mixture – frightfully amusing and at the same time frightfully sanctimonious. He reprimanded me for inviting Lewis Carroll to the party. Can you believe it? He said, "We've given a knighthood to the man who illustrated Alice in Wonderland, but nothing to the man who created Alice in Wonderland. Why? Because there's a cloud hanging over him. Take note of the weather, Sims." The pomposity of the man! I said, "I thought it was Her Majesty who bestowed the knighthoods, Labby." He said, "It is, but on the recommendation of her advisors . . . " and then tapped the side of his nose, without for a moment realising how preposterous he looked.'

'Labby's a power in the land,' said Oscar reflectively, contemplating the flickering candles through the crimson of his wine glass.

'And the cloud that hangs over Lewis Carroll?' I asked.

'Arthur's very innocent,' said Oscar, look up and smiling. 'The Reverend Dodgson proposed marriage to the real Alice in Wonderland when she was just a child. His interest in little girls is notorious – and regarded as unhealthy by some.'

George R. Sims explained: 'Labby's lasting legacy is the recent Criminal Law Amendment Act. It's raised the age of consent for girls from thirteen to sixteen, outlawed unnatural acts between men of all ages and criminalised brothels. Everyone thought it was a good idea at the time, but it's proved a blackmailer's charter.'

'And what's so amusing,' said Oscar from within a cloud of cigarette smoke, 'is that if you know anything about Labby you'll know that he has been a lifelong and enthusiastic habitué of the brothel.'

'Truly?' I asked, knowing Oscar's weakness for exaggeration.

'Truly. He told me himself that when he was at Cambridge he was always falling foul of the proctors because of it. The university authorities do not approve of the undergraduates consorting with prostitutes. Once, when Labby was walking down Silver Street arm in arm with a local lady of the night, he was confronted by a proctor and asked to explain his companion. "She's my sister," declared Labby boldly. "Nonsense, man," cried the proctor. "She's one of the most notorious whores in Cambridge." Labby looked crestfallen. "Yes, sir, I know, and both Mother and I are very worried about it."'

We all laughed and, at Oscar's prompting, raised our glasses of claret to 'younger and happier days' as a footman arrived carrying a tray laden with dishes.

'Here we are,' said Sims, happily smacking his lips, as the footman began to remove the heavy lids from a trio of large silver salvers. 'Welsh rarebit – and Buck rarebit, too.'

'And devilled kidneys and bacon,' I exclaimed.

'And sausage and mash,' cried Oscar. 'Sausages of different shapes and sizes, too!'

'Beef and pork, sir,' said the footman quietly. 'I'm not sure which is which.'

'The feast will be a journey of discovery,' purred Oscar. He waved a fork towards our host. 'This is perfect, George. And nothing fresh or green anywhere to be seen. You know how to entertain a gentleman. Thank you.'

The footman served me a slice of the Welsh rarebit. The grilled cheese was golden brown and still bubbling like a miniature volcano. I echoed Oscar's thanks.

'Thank you both for staying,' said Sims, dismissing the footman with a nod.

'You were expecting us?' said Oscar, as the door closed behind the departing servant. 'The table was already set.'

'Yes,' answered Sims, tucking in to his food as he spoke. I sensed that he felt awkward about what he wanted to say and was grateful to have something on his plate and in his mouth to help camouflage his embarrassment. 'I don't know you well, Oscar, but I know you well enough to count you as a friend.'

I glanced at Oscar. I saw the flicker of apprehension in his eye.

'And I know that Arthur here is your friend also,' Sims continued, 'and a trusted friend, and I know that he is a good man, too. Young James Barrie says he's the best. I know they play cricket together.'

'Never mind the cricket,' said Oscar. 'Where's this leading, George?'

Our host put down his knife and fork and mopped his mouth with his napkin. 'I'll tell you,' he said.

'Please do,' said Oscar.

'As you may know, as a journalist I mix with members of the Metropolitan Police – and have done for years. I mix with all sorts – the bobbies on the beat and their commanding officers at Scotland Yard, all sorts.'

'Ever the democrat, George,' said Oscar.

Sims took a sip of wine and mopped his lips again. 'As a consequence,' he continued, lowering his voice as he did so, 'I know Melville Macnaghten. I know him quite well.'

'Of course,' said Oscar.

'And knowing Macnaghten as I do, and seeing him quite frequently, I know that he has set you both on the trail of Jack the Ripper. Am I right?'

'You are,' said Oscar.

'I also know,' continued Sims, now looking Oscar quite steadily in the eye, 'that while you are busy investigating the Whitechapel murders at Macnaghten's request, Macnaghten is equally busy investigating you.'

27

'Explain yourself'

'Explain yourself, George,' said Oscar calmly.

'I can't exactly,' said Sims, picking up his knife and fork and turning his attention to his plate once again. 'All I can tell you is that he has you in his sights.'

'Both of us?' I asked.

'No, just Oscar.'

'"In his sights"?' queried Oscar. 'You mean he has people following me?'

'I believe so,' said Sims.

'But he denied it absolutely,' I protested. 'I was there. I heard him. Oscar put it to him. He denied it. And I took him for a gentleman.'

Sims looked up. 'You're right to do so. I believe he is one.'

'This is preposterous,' said Oscar, helping himself to a spoonful more of mashed potato. 'I don't believe it. I think you've misread the situation, George. Unlike you, I agree, but there's a misunderstanding of some kind here. There must be. Macnaghten asked for my help.'

'Indeed. But why? He is the chief constable in charge of the Criminal Investigation Department of the Metropolitan Police – believe it or not, the most respected police force in the world. Why did he ask for your assistance? You of all people?'

'Because I'm a neighbour – and I have a poet's eye.'

'Is that what he told you?'

'Yes.'

Sims shook his head and suppressed a chuckle. 'Macnaghten is a policeman, Oscar. He was a tea-planter in Bengal. Think, man. Is it really likely that what he's after is the assistance of a friendly neighbour with "a poet's eye"?'

Oscar said nothing, but continued eating.

'And why now? You've been neighbours for some years. Your "poet's eye" has long been at his disposal if he'd wanted it. Why ask for your help now? The Whitechapel murders took place six years ago.'

'Ah,' I said, relieved to have something to contribute. 'Macnaghten was clear about that. What would have been the Duke of Clarence and Avondale's thirtieth birthday is imminent. It falls on Monday, in fact. Macnaghten explained that the Palace is fearful that the anniversary will prompt more lurid press speculation – more damaging nonsense about Prince Eddy and the possibility of him being Jack the Ripper. Macnaghten mentioned the series that the *Sun* is planning to run.'

'The *Sun*'s articles will be all about a man called Thomas Cutbrush. They'll have nothing to do with Prince Eddy. Macnaghten knows that. I told him as much before Christmas.'

'Well,' I said, perplexed, 'he told us that the Prince of Wales is concerned.'

Sims shrugged. 'He may be – but without much cause. As far as the press is concerned, the hunt is still on for Jack the Ripper, and Scotland Yard have made a botch of it so far, but Prince Eddy is no longer a hare that anyone is chasing.'

Sims got to his feet and fetched the decanter of claret from the sideboard. He refilled each of our glasses and then left the decanter at Oscar's side. 'Macnaghten gave you his list of suspects?' he asked.

'He did,' said Oscar, 'and I acknowledged that I was familiar with several of the names. Wellbeloved and Mansfield are friends, of sorts. Druitt and I overlapped at Oxford. I didn't know Ostrog's name, but I knew his face. In Whitechapel once I was a customer of Kosminski's at his barber's shop. I was intrigued.'

'Did Macnaghten tell you which of the suspects he suspected most?'

'No,' said Oscar, 'he did not.'

'Far from it,' I said.

'I'm surprised,' said Sims. 'A year ago, Macnaghten told me he believed he knew who had committed the Whitechapel murders – but couldn't prove it.'

'That's not what he told us,' I insisted. 'He gave us his list of five suspects and invited us to explore the possibilities, eliminate the impossibilities and arrive at the truth – if we could.'

'Well,' said Sims, laying down his napkin and pushing his chair back from the table, 'when I discussed the case with Macnaghten – and went through his five principal suspects and a host of others – he gave me the distinct impression that he had come to a conclusion.'

'Which was?' asked Oscar, looking over his wine glass, eyebrow raised.

'That Montague Druitt was the Whitechapel murderer.'

'The man who was found drowned?'

'Yes,' said Sims. 'He's been my favourite candidate, too. I have found the whereabouts of Druitt's sister. I've not interviewed her yet, but I'm in correspondence with her and I believe she will talk to me and, if she does, I may have something to tell the readers of *The Referee* that will see the *Sun* and Thomas Cutbrush thrown firmly out of the ring.'

'And why is Montague Druitt Macnaghten's principal suspect – and yours?'

'Because his drowning coincided with the last of the Whitechapel murders.'

'But so did the incarceration of Ostrog and Kosminski, didn't they?' I said. 'And so did Richard Mansfield's departure for America.'

'The police know nothing,' cried Oscar suddenly, pushing his plate away from him. 'According to Macnaghten's notes, Druitt was a doctor. But I knew him at Oxford. He was a lawyer.'

'And he may be irrelevant, anyway,' said Sims, looking up and gently rubbing his right ear. 'Macnaghten is now not certain it is Druitt after all.'

'Who is it, then?' exclaimed Oscar. 'Is it me? Is that what he has said to you?'

Sims made no reply. He took a gulp of wine.

'And why is Druitt now suddenly out of the running?' I asked.

'Because of the Tite Street murders.'

'But they are different,' I said.

'Yes,' said Sims, 'different, but similar. And they have occurred after Druitt's drowning.'

'Long after,' I said. 'And not in Whitechapel.'

'Indeed. Not in Whitechapel, as you say.'

'But in the vicinity of Tite Street – where Oscar lives.'

'As does Macnaghten,' cried Oscar. 'As does Mr Justice Wills. Are they suspects too?'

'No one is accusing you of anything, Oscar,' said Sims soothingly.

'Aren't they? Aren't they?'

'As I understand it,' I said, 'Macnaghten invited Oscar to help him investigate the Whitechapel murders before the first of the Tite Street killings took place.'

'Is that so?' asked Sims.

'Yes,' said Oscar. 'He mentioned it first before Christmas, though we didn't meet to discuss it until New Year's Day – last Monday. It was the first, wasn't it?'

'It was,' I said.

'But why, George? Why did Macnaghten go to all the trouble of inviting me to his house and giving me his files – and letting Arthur become involved too – if he did not in reality want my assistance at all?'

Sims said nothing, but sipped at his wine once more.

'Why, George, why?' persisted Oscar.

'Because,' said Sims, laying down his glass carefully and positioning it just to the right of his half-eaten plate of mashed potato and devilled kidneys, 'he wanted to keep you occupied – occupied in an enterprise that might incidentally throw up information or intelligence relevant to the Whitechapel murders – that would be a bonus – but essentially occupied in an endeavour of his choosing and occupied in London.'

'He wanted to keep me in London?'

'Yes.'

'What? Not following Bosie to Egypt? Is that what this is all about? Is Macnaghten in cahoots with Queensbury and

Labouchere? Is that the nub of it? Is that what this preposterous charade is all about?'

'I don't believe so. I have no reason to think that.'

'Have you told me all that you know, George? You do know everything, after all.'

Sims smiled. 'I've told you what I know, Oscar. You can trust me, as a friend – as a fellow author. I know that Macnaghten has been following you for some time, keeping you in his sights. I know no more than that. I just thought it right to mark your card – to alert you, in case ever you go to places less enlightened souls might not approve of and consort with people whose personal morality is outwith the law as it is currently constituted.' He paused and looked at Oscar kindly. 'Do you take my meaning?'

'I do,' said Oscar quietly.

'Your private life is your own affair. You are a free spirit and will do as you please. I just felt you should know that Macnaghten's men are watching you. Take care.'

'I understand,' said Oscar. 'Thank you, George.'

'Do you know,' I added, feeling it was time I made a contribution, 'I believe this is the best Welsh rarebit I've ever had.'

28

'I can solve it all'

Oscar Wilde died in November 1900, at the age of only forty-six. At the time I was surprised because when I knew him, just a few years before, he seemed to me to have the constitution of an ox. He was a big man, with a big man's appetite for food, for drink, for life.

When we emerged from George R. Sims' house that Saturday night it was gone eleven o'clock. I was ready for bed. Oscar was not. As Sims closed his front door behind us and we came down the stone steps into the street, Oscar announced, 'We're going drinking, Arthur.' There was a steely defiance in his tone. As he pulled open the door of the two-wheeler that stood waiting for us, I noticed his hand trembling with suppressed rage. 'We're near Baker Street, aren't we? This is your territory, Arthur. Where would Holmes take Watson for a night on the tiles?'

'Holmes is not really a drinking man,' I said unhelpfully, my heart sinking somewhat at the prospect of 'a night on the tiles'.

'Of course not,' laughed Oscar. 'He's a dope fiend.' He climbed up into the carriage. 'How do you get away with it? If I'd created a hero who revelled in his addiction to cocaine I'd be drummed out of town, but somehow you're everybody's favourite author. How do you do it?' He called up to the cabman. 'Take us to the Mermaid in Marylebone Lane.'

'I don't know it,' I said. 'Is it a pub? Will it be open still?'

'For us, it will be. It is a refuge for the angry and the sad.'

'And which are we?' I asked, as our two-wheeler pulled away and trundled steadily along Clarence Gate towards the Marylebone Road. The night was still and the street was quiet: the only sound, the clatter of the iron wheels on the wet cobblestones.

'I am angry and you are sad.'

'If Macnaghten has indeed deceived you, I can understand your anger,' I said, 'but I'd be surprised. He struck me as a gentleman through and through.'

Oscar laughed. 'And you strike me as a model husband, through and through, devoted to your Touie and your bairns, and yet you long for your little Russian acrobat – how you long for her . . . '

'No,' I said emphatically – but without conviction. 'No, you're wrong . . . ' I turned away from Oscar and looked out onto the wet, black roadway.

Did I sigh? I don't believe I did, but, afterwards, Oscar told me that I had. At all events, with his glove he rapped my knee gently and whispered, 'Sigh no more, Arthur, sigh no more. Men were deceivers ever – one foot in the sea and one on shore, to one thing constant never.'

'I shall be constant to Touie,' I said, not looking back at him.

'Infidelity starts in the mind,' he replied. 'It's too late now.'

We sat in awkward silence until the carriage came to a halt.

The Mermaid was a small, traditional London public house, with mullioned windows and oak beams, low-ceilinged, smoke-filled and cosy, with a coal fire burning at each end of its one narrow room. The place was owned, Oscar explained, by a former Metropolitan police sergeant, who 'entertained friends' after hours, 'no questions asked, no money taken, though a Christmas present is always appreciated'.

'Just the one drink,' I said, as we stood at the bar and Oscar ordered what he called his 'usual': a bottle of champagne and a bottle of brandy to go with it. The barman – a young Negro who appeared to be dressed as a sailor – produced the bottles at once and an empty pewter tankard for each of us. Oscar, brooking no argument, poured two fingers of brandy and four of champagne into each vessel. He gave me mine and raised his towards me.

'Welcome to the Mermaid,' he said, 'where those who lead double lives seek consolation.'

The place was entirely lit by candles and in their ochre glow, Oscar, more mellow now, looked like a benign devil hosting a Hallowe'en drinks party for a few of his closer friends. There were no more than twenty people in the room, seated at small tables, standing in alcoves, mostly in pairs and, mostly, I realised at once, older men – professional men – with younger women not of their class.

'And not all the women are women,' Oscar whispered to me, as he watched me watching them. 'Some of these "girls" are tele-graph boys on the spree.'

'I see,' I said, taking a sip of Oscar's heady brew.

''Evening, Mr Wilde,' said a figure who stood alone, lounging against the wall at the far end of the bar. He was tall and lean with a thin yellow face and a curious staring gaze. He wore a dark red velvet suit whose plush was as worn as the covering of one of the bar stools.

'Good evening, Jonah.' Oscar turned to me and murmured: 'This is our host, Arthur. He doesn't look like a police sergeant, does he? He's blind.'

'But not deaf,' answered the landlord, moving away from the wall and coming along the bar towards us. 'We've not seen you for a while, Mr Wilde.' The man set his staring, dead eyes towards my friend.

'I was hoping Walter Wellbeloved might be here tonight,' said Oscar.

The landlord shook his head. 'He's not been here for months. He stopped coming once his own mermaid died. He knew I'd been a copper. I think I made him nervous.'

'Do you think he killed his mermaid?' asked Oscar.

'Possibly,' said the landlord. 'Probably. Most women who get murdered are murdered by their husbands or their lovers.'

Oscar peered into his tankard. 'Does each man kill the thing he loves?'

'It's common, that's all I'm saying,' continued the landlord. 'He's an odd one, that Walter Wellbeloved, and quite capable of murder, in my opinion.'

'Could he be Jack the Ripper, in your opinion?' I asked.

'No,' said the landlord emphatically.

'Who is then?' asked Oscar, looking into our host's blind eyes.

'No idea. I've been out of the game too long. But it won't be an Englishman, that's all I know.'

'Why do you say that, Jonah?' asked Oscar, seemingly amused by the assertion.

'I was in the force for thirty years. I've known my share of murderers and I can tell you this: an Englishman can be a brute.

He'll batter a woman, beat her, break her neck, shoot her in cold blood, throttle her in the heat of the moment, poison her, drown her even – like Wellbeloved drowned his mermaid. But he won't cut her up and leave her entrails all over the place – especially not her private parts.'

'Why not?'

'He's English. He's too squeamish.'

Oscar laughed and refilled his tankard with brandy and champagne.

It must have been four in the morning before we reached our rooms at the Langham Hotel. In truth, I have no recollection of reaching mine. All I recall is being woken at around nine in the morning by a shaft of winter sunlight piercing through the half-closed curtains and forcing its way through my eyelids. It seemed I had managed to undress myself, but had not climbed beneath the bedclothes. As the daylight hit my aching eyes, my ears picked up the sound of scratching – as though a mouse was caught in a cupboard. Slowly, painfully, I rose, pulled on my dressing gown and, searching for my slippers, noticed that a piece of paper had been pushed under the bedroom door. It was a note from Oscar:

I can solve it all. I am in the dining room having breakfast.
Join me when you are ready. O.

Within twenty minutes, I had washed, shaved, dressed and made my way down to the dining room where my bleary eyes were confronted by a quite extraordinary sight: Oscar, bright-eyed, pink-cheeked, *en prince*, sporting a canary-yellow carnation in the buttonhole of a startlingly bright green Harris-tweed suit. He had a cup of coffee in one hand, a piece of toast in the other and a copy of the *Observer* propped up against the coffee pot in front of him.

'Good morning, Oscar,' I croaked. 'I'm impressed to see you looking so fresh and wide awake.'

He looked up at me and smiled. 'Enjoy your breakfast and confound your enemies. Nothing annoys them more.'

I sat down facing him. He poured me some coffee. 'You're keeping notes, I take it?' he asked.

'Yes, but not last night. I'll write them up when I get home this evening.'

'You're not going home this evening, Arthur,' he exclaimed. 'You're coming to the theatre with me. And with Constance. Richard Mansfield has invited us to a special Sunday matinée. It's a private performance for friends and members of the profession only. It would be churlish to refuse.'

'I must go home,' I pleaded.

'Not quite yet. One more night here. I shall pay. And tomorrow we've got our picnic lunch with Freddie Bunbury and Festing Fitzmaurice. We need to eliminate Prince Eddy altogether. I can let you go after that. We should have it all done and dusted by then, don't you think?'

'What on earth do you mean?'

He put down his coffee cup and reached for his cigarette case. 'I'll confess a certain sense of satisfaction,' he said, narrowing his eyes and suddenly looking distinctly like Mr Dodgson's Cheshire Cat. 'The police have been on the case for six years and have got nowhere. We have been at it for barely six days and I do believe we're nearly there.' He struck a Vesta with a flourish.

'What are you talking about, man?' I protested.

'We've got to see the Druitt family, I grant you, and find out if

"Leather Apron" has anything useful to offer, but that done I am hopeful we'll be able to say "Case closed".'

'You are quite extraordinary, Oscar,' I said.

'Thank you,' he replied, beaming. 'You said that with real feeling, Arthur.' He drew deeply on his cigarette. 'Of course,' he added mischievously, 'every portrait that is painted with feeling is a portrait of the artist, not the sitter, but even so, you are the man to write up this story, without a doubt. Can you imagine what a dreary job Henry James would make of it?' He laughed and turned to scan the dining room for a waiter. 'We must get you some eggs and bacon. You're looking quite wan and you're going to need all your strength for the final furlong.'

He waved a languid hand in the direction of the boy Martin, who appeared to be coming towards our table in any event. The young waiter arrived, breathless and smiling. He was carrying a large cardboard box in both hands.

'Good morning, Martin,' said Oscar cheerily.

''Morning, sir,' answered the boy.

'Have you seen him today?'

'Yes, sir. He's out there as usual.'

'And is this a present from him?' asked Oscar, indicating the container the boy was holding out before him.

'No, sir, this is from Mrs Wilde. She's just had it sent over by cab from Tite Street. It's addressed to you. It's heavy.'

'Put it down, boy,' said Oscar, clearing space on the table.

'Take care,' I said, suddenly alarmed. 'It might be a bomb.'

'Don't be absurd,' said Oscar. 'This isn't Paris. This isn't St Petersburg. And I'm Irish and known for my Republican sympathies.'

'Nevertheless, extinguish your cigarette, Oscar,' I said. 'I insist.'

My friend looked at me with a raised eyebrow, but did as I

instructed. He took a knife from the table and used it to saw at the string wrapped around the box. 'It's an educated hand,' he said, peering at the address label. 'It's marked: "Oscar Wilde – for his eyes only".'

'Do you think it is a bomb?' asked the boy excitedly.

'I doubt it very much,' said Oscar.

'What is it?' I asked impatiently.

Oscar had cut through the string and lifted the lid from the box. 'Christ almighty,' he cried, blanching. 'It must be from Tom Norman.'

'Oh no,' I whimpered.

'Oh yes,' said Oscar. 'It is the head of John the Baptist.'

29

The Man in the Street

Within the hour we were seated once more at number 9 Tite Street, in the brown, book-lined study of Melville Macnaghten, chief constable of the Criminal Investigation Department of the Metropolitan Police. Precariously, the policeman held the box containing the severed head on his lap and peered into it, poking at the contents with a pencil.

'Is it wearing a wig?' he asked.

'Yes,' I answered. 'And a false beard.'

'And the hideous eyes?'

'They're made of glass.'

'But the head is human? You've examined it? It's not a waxwork?'

'It's human, without question. The waxy look is due to the embalming process. The head has been preserved in formaldehyde.'

Macnaghten lowered his face further towards the box. 'I can't smell anything,' he said. 'He looks grotesque – like a doll, quite unreal.'

'For a reason,' I said.

Macnaghten looked up. 'A reason?'

'Yes. He isn't a "he". That's not a man's head. It's the head of a young woman.'

'Good God.' Macnaghten sat back abruptly; the cardboard box shifted on his lap; he used both hands to steady it. 'Are you sure?'

'Yes, quite sure.'

'How can you tell?'

'The size of the head, it's quite small. The proportions of the features. Principally, the texture of the skin and the angle and size of the Adam's apple. There is no doubt about it. That is the head of a young woman, aged around twenty, I'd say, at the time of her death.'

'But why is she disguised as a man, for heaven's sake? It's too bizarre.'

Oscar now spoke – for the first time since we had arrived so unexpectedly at the chief constable's front door ten minutes before. 'She is disguised as John the Baptist,' he said quietly. He moved uneasily in his seat, extinguishing his cigarette. 'I'm afraid it is my fault. I am responsible.'

'Not for her death?'

'No. That would be too terrible.' He shuddered visibly. 'But I am responsible for her appearance here, like this – as you see her now. It is my doing.'

'Explain yourself, man,' said Macnaghten. He lowered the box onto the floor and placed it by his feet. He looked at Oscar and widened his eyes. 'What is all this about, Mr Wilde?'

'It's a tale simply told,' said Oscar.

'Then tell it simply, if you please,' snapped Macnaghten.

'We went to visit Tom Norman's emporium in the Whitechapel Road.' Oscar paused. I was unaccustomed to seeing him so hesitant. 'You know the place?'

Macnaghten nodded.

'It was part of our inquiries,' continued Oscar, now waving his hands about distractedly. 'Part of our investigation ...'

'You were wasting your time,' said Macnaghten crisply. 'Norman's a shady character, no doubt, what the Americans call "a huckster" – but he's not Jack the Ripper.'

'Nevertheless, we went to see him and while we were there I asked him – foolishly, I see now – whether he might be able to procure for me the head of Iokannan the prophet, the head of John the Baptist.'

'I am lost, Mr Wilde. And not much amused. Would you explain yourself as simply and succinctly as you can?'

I intervened. 'Oscar has written a play,' I said, 'based on the bible story of Salome.'

'The story features in both the gospels of Saint Matthew and Saint Mark,' added Oscar eagerly. 'Salome is the daughter of Herod and Herodias.'

'I don't need to know about Salome's antecedents, Mr Wilde. I need to know why this young woman's head has been sent to you.'

'Because I asked Tom Norman to supply me with such a head – as a theatrical property. And he has done so.'

'You commissioned this head?'

'After a fashion, yes. But I meant it as a tease, as a challenge ... I did not want the head of a young woman. I wanted the head of John the Baptist.'

'And did you pay for it? Did the package contain Norman's bill?'

'There was nothing in the box beyond the head,' I said.

'So we cannot be certain that the head comes from Tom Norman?'

'No,' I said. 'But the postmark shows the parcel was sent from Whitechapel.'

'To Mr Wilde at his Tite Street address?'

'It must be from Tom Norman,' said Oscar.

'Do you recognise the handwriting in the address?'

'It is written with capital letters.' I was holding the lid to the cardboard box. I passed it to the chief constable. He smiled at me – a conspiratorial smile. His manner made it clear that he regarded me as his sort of man, but now harboured the severest doubts about Oscar.

'I see it all,' persisted Oscar. 'Tom Norman is a collector of curiosities – many of them grotesque. I – stupidly – asked for a head. Either he had one already in his collection or he acquired one.'

'Well, it's a possibility,' Macnaghten conceded. 'We know that in the past he has acquired body parts from the mortuary at the Whitechapel Hospital. This may be one of them. I shall make inquiries.'

He got to his feet. I followed suit. Oscar remained seated.

'Thank you, Dr Doyle,' said Macnaghten, shaking me by the hand. 'You did the right thing bringing this to me right away.'

He moved towards the door and I went with him. 'When do you think this young woman lost her head? Not recently?'

'Certainly not in recent days – or weeks. The head is well embalmed. There's no lingering smell of formaldehyde. She might have died months ago, years even.'

'Yes, I see. Thank you. And the decapitation?'

'Cleanly done, professionally, post mortem.'

'Thank you.' Macnaghten opened his study door and felt in his coat pocket for his pipe.

'Have you made any progress identifying the two women who were murdered this week?' I asked.

'The two women found in the alley here, off Tite Street?'

'Yes.'

'None at all,' said Macnaghten, sucking on his empty pipe. 'No one has come forward asking after them. No one has been reported missing.'

'Is that unusual?'

'Yes.'

Macnaghten and I stood together awkwardly at the doorway of his study. I glanced back at Oscar who sat immobile in the armchair by the fireplace.

'Mr Wilde?' said Macnaghten.

Oscar turned his head in Macnaghten's direction. 'On Monday you asked for my assistance. Today you treat me as an idiot-child.'

'Forgive me, Mr Wilde, but seeking to procure a human head as "a tease" or "a challenge", as you put it, is not responsible behaviour. It is juvenile at best. At worst . . . '

'It is criminal, no doubt,' said Oscar.

'No doubt at all,' said Macnaghten.

Oscar got to his feet and turned towards the chief constable. 'We are neighbours,' he said, 'and I hoped that we might be friends. But I believe that you have deceived me.'

'What on earth do you mean, man?'

'When I asked you if I was being followed by one of your men, you assured me that I was not.'

'And you are not.'

'But I am,' said Oscar. He stepped away from the armchair and moved towards the window. 'Please, Mr Macnaghten, look out of your window and across the street. You will see a man standing beneath a lamp-post. He is watching your house. But he is not watching you. He is watching me.' Oscar beckoned me towards the window. 'Look at him, Arthur. You can get a good view of him here. He looks almost respectable, doesn't he?'

'Whoever he is,' said Macnaghten quietly, neither looking at Oscar nor out of the window but tapping the bowl of his pipe gently against the palm of his hand, 'I am not responsible for his presence. He is not there at my behest. He does not report to me.'

There was a moment's pause.

'But we do,' said Oscar lightly, turning on his heel towards the policeman and smiling broadly. His mood appeared suddenly to have changed: his smile was like a burst of sunshine breaking through black clouds. 'I apologise for my misdemeanour. Tom Norman's a rogue and I was wrong to encourage him. Dr Doyle was right – as he always is. We have brought you this dismembered head and if it is of any use in your inquiries that will be to the good. If it is not, at least it will now get a decent burial – or as decent a burial as the resources of the Metropolitan Police will allow.'

Macnaghten looked bewildered. Oscar's sudden transformation of manner quite disarmed him.

'This head,' continued Oscar, pointing with a languid hand towards the cardboard box on the floor, 'appears to have drawn us down an unpleasant cul-de-sac. We must now return to the highway. I sense we are nearing the end of the road.'

'I am confused, Mr Wilde,' said Macnaghten, shaking his head and pocketing his pipe.

Oscar laughed. 'I can see that, sir.' He crossed the study to join the policeman by the door. I turned away from the window and followed. 'Have no fear,' my friend continued gaily, 'Wilde and Doyle are on the case. We are doing as you asked – eliminating those prime suspects of yours and even finding a few new ones of our own.'

'We did investigate Tom Norman, I assure you,' said Macnaghten, nodding and leading us out of his study into the hallway. 'He is a doubtful character and I know that butchery was in the family line, but he had watertight alibis – witnesses who could prove he was elsewhere at the time of the majority of the Whitechapel murders.'

'And what about the Marquess of Queensberry?' asked Oscar.

'What about him?' replied Macnaghten, looking astonished.

Oscar glanced back towards the policeman's study. 'That man in the street – the one who follows me – if he is not in your pay – and I accept your word on that – perhaps he is in the pay of Lord Queensberry? I am a friend of his son, you know.'

'Of Lord Alfred Douglas? Yes, I know that.'

'And Lord Queensberry does not approve. He feels that I am not a proper or fit person for his son to know. That could be why the noble marquess has me trailed. He hopes to find evidence of immoral behaviour on my part.'

Macnaghten said nothing.

Oscar smiled. 'Never mind that.' He touched the policeman lightly on the arm. 'You were right to point out that I have been acquainted with a number of the suspects in these Whitechapel murders. I am acquainted with the Marquess of Queensberry, also. You have not considered him as a possible "Jack the Ripper"?'

'Not for a moment.'

'Ah,' said Oscar, picking up his gloves from the side table in the hallway and pulling them on. 'Queensberry is a noted woman-beater, a known frequenter of Whitechapel and, without a shadow of a doubt, utterly unhinged. You should be investigating him, Mr Macnaghten. Leave no stone unturned.'

'I don't know what to say, Mr Wilde.'

'You are an Englishman, Mr Macnaghten. You should say something about the weather.'

Macnaghten opened the front door and looked up at the sky. 'Well, yes, at least it isn't raining.'

As we stepped into our waiting carriage, I noticed that the man in the street had disappeared. As he sat back in his seat, Oscar laughed. 'I think I negotiated the rapids there quite successfully, don't you, Arthur? I need a drink. How about you?'

30

The Club

'I don't need a drink, Oscar. I need an explanation.' The carriage was turning in a circle and making its way down Tite Street towards the Thames Embankment. 'Where are we going?' I asked. 'Since we're here in Tite Street, shouldn't we call in on Constance?'

'We will be seeing Constance later,' said Oscar, settling himself back in his seat and gazing calmly out of the window. 'She is joining us at the theatre.'

'Must we go to the theatre?'

'Mansfield sent me a wire overnight saying you had expressed a desire to see his Napoleon. He's arranged tickets for us. It's your doing, Arthur.'

'I must go home,' I pleaded. 'I have work to do.'

'This will be work – and hard work, too, if the reviews are anything to go by. It's a poor play, by all accounts, but given the leading man is one of Chief Constable Macnaghten's principal suspects it is our duty to attend.'

Our four-wheeler was now rattling along past the Chelsea Physic Garden. Oscar continued: 'Walter Wellbeloved, evoker of spirits and mermaid-fancier of this parish, another of Macnaghten's murderous possibilities, is joining us – along with Constance. It should be an instructive afternoon. And before it, we're having a drink.'

I shook my head despairingly. 'Tomorrow, I am going home,' I said emphatically.

'After the birthday picnic – if you must,' said Oscar. 'That is up to you, *mon ami*. But our mystery is almost unravelled. It would be a pity to miss the *dénouement*.'

'"Miss the *dénouement*"? You do talk a lot of tosh at times, Oscar,' I said. I sat back and looked across at him. I was simultaneously exasperated and amused. 'And what was all that in there about the Marquess of Queensberry? Explain yourself.'

'It was a diversionary tactic,' answered my friend smugly.

'You don't seriously think Lord Queensberry is Jack the Ripper? It's an absurd notion.'

'No more absurd than it being Lewis Carroll or the Duke of Clarence.'

'You were just making mischief, Oscar.'

'And if I was, it was a case of fair-dealing. The Marquess of Queensberry is not a pleasant person. He's a brute, a blackguard and, I reckon, quite capable of murder.'

'But why would he murder five women in Whitechapel?'

'Why would anyone? That is the nub of the matter.'

'Do you think it might be one of Queensberry's men who is following you?'

Oscar looked at me. 'I accept that it is not one of Macnaghten's men. I know that your instinct is that the chief constable is a good man, Arthur, and, given his repeated assurance, I am ready to take him at his word.'

'I am glad.'

'But that means that George R. Sims must have been mistaken – which is not like him.'

'It's a complex case,' I said gravely.

He leaned towards me. 'But we are getting there.'

'Are we?'

'We are.'

I could not share my friend's confidence, but I sensed that he spoke from the heart. 'At least we have eliminated Tom Norman,' I said, in an effort to be positive.

'More or less.'

'Macnaghten was adamant. Norman has alibis.'

'Indeed. And the very fact of sending the head suggests a clear conscience – of a sort.'

'It was not a pretty sight.'

'You say that,' said Oscar, 'and, of course, I only glanced at it briefly when you took it out of the box to examine it, but beneath the wig and whiskers I caught sight of what seemed to me to be a pretty face.'

'You noticed?'

'Yes. And I noticed the high cheekbones, too.'

Charing Cross station approached and, as we reached it, the four-wheeler turned left up Craven Street towards Trafalgar Square. 'Three may keep a secret if two of them are dead,' murmured Oscar, peering out of the carriage window once more.

'What's that?'

'One of Benjamin Franklin's lines,' said Oscar. 'He was full of good ones. He lived here – in this street.'

'Is that where we're going?'

'Oh no. I don't think Benjamin Franklin would approve of where we're going.'

'And where are we going?'

'The Anarchists' Club in Windmill Street. We can walk to the theatre from there. It's not your usual London club. The decor's not up to much, but I know you'll enjoy the company. There should be a little friend waiting for you.'

In truth there was no decor to speak of. The club – correctly termed 'Club Autonomie' – consisted of a series of four or five shabby rooms on the ground floor of a narrow, nondescript house in a side street off the Tottenham Court Road. The flooring throughout was made up of bare boards, ill-fitting, unvarnished, covered with patches of oil-cloth and linoleum. The walls were peeling plaster painted a dingy green and covered with newspapers pinned up for the members to read. In the main room – Oscar called it 'the club room' – there was a bar at one end where an elderly Sicilian barman served wine and beer and spirits and, in the centre of the room, dominating it, a long, low refectory table. On either side of the table, crowded on wooden benches, talking, arguing, eating, drinking, reading pamphlets, writing notes, gazing into the middle distance, sleeping head in arms, was a curious assortment of people, some evidently in clusters, others in pairs, a number on their own, ranging in age from twenty to seventy. The air was thick with yellow smoke and the hubbub of conversation. The people, as I glanced at them, appeared to be in costume – as though they were supernumeraries in an Italian opera.

'None of them looks English,' I whispered to Oscar as we walked the length of the room towards the bar.

'None of them is English. You won't find the weather being discussed here. They only talk of revolution. They made me a member when I published *The Soul of Man under Socialism*. I read a paper here – in this room. In German. It was an evening short on laughter. German, French and Italian are the principal languages spoken here, though I sense that Russian is gaining ground.'

'Why are we here?'

'I like it. The drink is good and inexpensive. The conversation is challenging. Curiously, Constance likes it too.'

'They have lady members?'

'Oh yes. Look.'

We had reached the bar and there, standing at it, half-turned towards us, was Olga.

'Hello,' I said. I know that I spoke awkwardly. I fear that my face may have reddened.

'*Dobro pozhalovat*,' she replied. She smiled and put out a hand to touch mine. 'I wasn't sure that I was going to see you. I thought I might, so I came.' Her fingers rested over my hand. I could not think what to say. 'I know I look strange. I am wearing my costume underneath my coat.' She laughed and stood back. She was wearing the same sombre coat she had worn when we had had tea together, but it was unbuttoned now and the way it hung around her slim frame made it look curiously like a dressing gown. 'Do I look ridiculous?' she asked.

'You look lovely,' I said, smitten.

'Good afternoon, Dr Doyle.' Ivan Salazkin was also at the bar. He, too, was wearing his circus costume, with, over it, a capacious black cape. Without his top hat or his elaborate waxed moustache, he looked magnificent but real, like a handsome hussar in a painting by Sir Thomas Lawrence. 'You are arriving just as we are leaving,' he said in his impeccable English. 'We expected you an hour ago.'

'This is the Anarchists' Club,' said Oscar. 'We thrive on confusion.'

'I did not know we were expected,' I said.

'Olga wanted to say goodbye,' said Salazkin, nodding towards her. 'The circus moves on to Paris at the end of the week. Oscar proposed that we meet here for a farewell drink.'

'I shall now organise a farewell dinner instead,' said Oscar.

'There will be no time,' said Salazkin. 'We have a performance every afternoon and every evening and then, next Sunday, in the early hours, we depart.'

'There will be a post-show supper,' Oscar insisted. 'You will have time for that. I will arrange it.'

'I have to get back to work,' I said.

'More Holmes, I hope?' asked Salazkin pleasantly.

'I don't think so,' I replied. 'I have other plans.'

'And responsibilities?' said Salazkin.

'Yes.'

'You have a family?'

'Yes.' There was a moment's pause.

'You have children?' asked Olga. We were standing side by side at the bar. Her fingers were no longer resting on my hand, but our arms were touching. I was aware of that.

'Yes,' I said, looking down at her. 'I'm sure I told you. A girl and a boy.'

She smiled at me. 'You did not tell me, Arthur. Do you have a photograph of them? Are they very young?'

'Yes,' I said awkwardly, 'they are young.'

'How old are they?'

Absurdly, I struggled to recall their ages. 'They are four and two,' I said. 'They are with their mother and their nurse in Switzerland.'

'And do you have a picture of them?' she asked again. Her eyes sparkled. In them I saw no reproach.

'He does,' boomed Oscar from behind me. 'Show her, Arthur.'

I reached inside my coat for my wallet and pulled from it the small photograph I carried with me of Kingsley as a baby resting on little Mary's lap. It was a lovely picture, full of hope and joy and innocence.

Olga looked at the photograph and smiled. 'He looks like you, Arthur. He is handsome, too. And he looks so happy.'

'He looks nothing like Arthur,' cried Oscar. 'He's a beautiful baby. Don't you agree, Ivan?'

Olga held up the photograph for Salazkin to consider. The ring-master looked at it coolly, nodded and said, 'Charming.' He felt beneath his cape for his timepiece. 'We must go,' he announced. 'We are cutting it fine, as you English like to say.'

'I am Irish,' said Oscar, shaking Salazkin by the hand.

'Goodbye, Arthur,' said Olga, holding up her face for me to kiss. 'Think of me now and then.'

I kissed her and she turned away at once, as if to hide the tears in her eyes. She ran after Salazkin who had already reached the door where Michael Ostrog was waiting, holding his master's cane and hat. She did not look back and, suddenly, she was gone.

All that afternoon and evening I thought of her. As I stood with Oscar at the bar of the Anarchists' Club, drinking small glasses of flavourless spirit, eating small wedges of beetroot doused in vinegar, while my friend filled the air with sound, Olga filled my head. Even as Constance arrived with Walter Wellbeloved and Oscar's brother Willie in tow, and Oscar's torrent of words became louder and more turbulent, I heard the hubbub, but I was not listening.

As we left the club to walk across Oxford Street and on through Soho towards the theatre, I was conscious of Oscar's fury at Willie's unexpected presence and his alarm that 'Queensberry's spy', as he now called him, was observing our departure from across the street, but when Constance put her arm through mine and whispered, 'You're in a dream today, Arthur, and Oscar's in a bate,' I simply smiled at her vacantly, and answered, without thinking, 'Yes, I suppose so.'

At the theatre, Richard Mansfield had arranged a box for our party. I sat at the back of the box, on the banquette, alongside Willie, who made the occasional sardonic remark, to which I failed to respond. The auditorium was far from full, but the audience – friends of the company and other members of the theatrical profession – was enthusiastic and attentive and, while I did not focus on the plot of the drama or the detail of the dialogue, I felt the force of Mansfield's portrayal of Napoleon. The actor had undeniable 'presence'.

As soon the curtain fell at the end of the first act, reckoning I should make some sort of contribution, I said, 'He's playing it well, is he not?'

'He's a brutal murderer,' barked Oscar, 'notwithstanding the veneer of sophistication.'

'Who?' I asked. 'Mansfield?'

Oscar laughed. 'Bonaparte, Arthur. His wars cost some six million lives. He was callous. He was cruel. He was arrogant. He led men to the slaughter while smirking at his own epigrams.'

'He came up with some choice ones,' said Willie. '"Never interrupt your enemy when he is making a mistake" is a wonderful line. It's one of my favourites.'

'Quotation is a serviceable substitute for wit,' said Oscar.

During the second interval I said nothing. I returned to my reverie as Oscar turned the conversation from 'mass murder of the Napoleonic kind' to 'our own capacity to kill' and enquired of a bewildered Wellbeloved under what circumstances he would be ready to slaughter someone and what means he would use and whether his preference would be to take the life of a man or of a woman.

'I don't know what to say,' answered Wellbeloved. 'Those stories of human sacrifice and drinking blood . . . '

'Ignore Oscar,' said Constance soothingly. 'He is in one of his provocative moods.'

'Could you kill a man, Oscar?' asked Willie.

'With my own hands? I doubt it. I lack the courage. I might give the order to another, I suppose.'

'Don't say that, dearest,' said Constance, leaning over to her husband, 'even in jest.'

'If you want a thing done well, do it yourself,' said Willie.

When the performance was over, Oscar led us out of the box and down the corridor towards a baize-covered door that opened immediately onto the side of the stage. We were plunged from bright light to half-darkness. 'I know this theatre,' he declared. 'Follow me.' With his right arm raised like a tour guide escorting visitors around St Peter's in Rome, he pushed his way through a small crowd of chatting supernumeraries and stagehands smoking cigarettes, and took us across the wings, through another door and down a narrow flight of metal steps.

'Let the path be open to talent,' murmured Willie as our party followed in Oscar's wake.

'Is that another of Boney's bons mots, brother? You appear to have swallowed the Dictionary of Quotations whole.'

'Hush, you two,' scolded Constance.

'We are here,' announced Oscar triumphantly.

'And you are expected,' cried Richard Mansfield. The actor, in his dressing gown, stood in the doorway to his dressing room holding an open bottle of champagne in his hand. 'Perrier-Jouët, Oscar. I got it in for you especially. There's another in the bucket.'

'Thank you, my friend. And thank you, too, for the performance of a lifetime. I had thought of Napoleon as a poisonous pygmy. You made him a giant – heroic in the first act, human in the second, and in the third, a fallen demi-god. You were magnificent!'

Mansfield, his face glowing through a mask of sweat and Pond's cold cream, beamed at Oscar and tossed his head lightly from side to side like a frisky pony. 'Come in one, come in all. Did the performance live up to your expectations, Dr Conan Doyle? I hope so. *Entrez*. My dresser will pour the champagne.' He handed over the bottle to a handsome young Malay who served each of us with glasses that I noticed were engraved with a Napoleonic 'N' surmounted by an imperial crown.

'What did you really think, Oscar?' asked the actor, now wiping his face with a towel and addressing my friend through the looking glass above his dressing table.

'You were Napoleon,' said Oscar with conviction.

'What did you make of the play?' asked Mansfield, raising an eyebrow and looking in my direction.

Oscar answered for me. 'The play is nothing,' he declared. 'You, Richard, are everything!'

'Too kind,' breathed Mansfield contentedly, and then, slowly, carefully, reverentially, with both hands and each finger extended, he lifted his wig off his head and held it up before him as though he were a priest raising the host before his congregation. He placed the wig on top of a skull that stood on the dressing table next to an open cigar box that served as the container for sticks of make-up. As he did so, he caught my eye in the mirror and winked. 'Yorick's skull,' he said. He turned towards me and picked it up to show me. It looked quite hideous: a gaunt, grey death's-head sporting Napoleon's distinctive pate lopsidedly. 'The skull is actually that of John Wilkes Booth,' he said.

'The man who assassinated Abraham Lincoln?'

'The very same. He was an actor, too, of course – though less well known than his celebrated brother, Edwin.'

'Perhaps not now,' said Oscar, peering down at the skull.

'You used it for your Hamlet?' asked Constance.

'I did.'

'How did you acquire it?' asked Oscar.

'I bought it from Tom Norman. He specialises in these things. Do you know him?'

'I know him,' volunteered Walter Wellbeloved from the back of the crowd in his curious, musical voice. 'A good man.'

'I agree, sir,' said Mansfield. 'He is leaving the country, you know. He is not appreciated here – but I love him. Look at this!' From within the cigar box, the actor scooped up a glass phial half-filled with a reddish-brown liquid. He held it up to one of the gas lamps at the side of his looking glass.

'What is it?' Constance asked.

'The blood of the Emperor Napoleon!'

'Good grief,' cried Wellbeloved.

'Can you be sure?' asked Oscar.

'You saw the performance, Oscar. What do you think? I take a sip of the blood before the curtain rises every day.'

I raised an eyebrow, but said nothing.

'Tom Norman acquired the blood from the grandson of Sir Hudson Lowe, governor of St Helena when Napoleon died.'

'I imagine it cost you a pretty penny,' said Oscar.

'And not only in the cash I handed over to Norman – but more so in the cost to my reputation. It was because of my repeated visits to Norman's emporium that I gained a reputation as a

Whitechapel habitué and consequently was accused of being Jack the Ripper.'

'Ah.' Oscar nodded sympathetically.

'Would you like to play him on stage?' asked Willie.

'Jack the Ripper? Oh, yes!' cried the actor. 'What a part! Immortal Jack! I would kill for the role.'

'Would you now?' said Oscar playfully.

Mansfield laughed. 'You know what I mean, Oscar. Napoleon, Richard Crookback, Dr Jekyll and Mr Hyde – these are the parts for me. The name is known, but the man isn't. By playing him, I would reveal him. Who is he, this inhuman human? "Who is Jack the Ripper?" That should be the title. You must write the play, Oscar.'

'Perhaps I will,' answered Oscar, raising his glass in Mansfield's direction.

'More champagne, Haziq – and the photographs!'

Mansfield's dresser emptied the remains of the second bottle of Perrier-Jouët into our champagne flutes and then, with some ceremony, presented each of us with a handsome quarto-sized card containing a signed photograph of our host in his costume as Napoleon.

'Oh,' cried Oscar happily, 'I love photographs like these. When I went to America to lecture, you know, I had to have two secretaries, one for autographs, one for locks of hair. Within six months the one had died of writer's cramp and the other was completely bald.' We all laughed. Oscar turned to me. 'Oh, Arthur,' he said, 'do show our friends that charming picture of your children. It is so delightful.'

'Please, Oscar,' I protested, 'this is hardly—'

'I'd love to see a picture of your little ones, Arthur. Do show us.'

Pressed by Constance, I produced my photograph and passed

it around the group, murmuring embarrassed apologies as I did so. Each in turn studied the small picture and made gently appreciative noises.

'A boy and a girl,' said Mansfield good-humouredly. 'You're a lucky devil.'

Willie surprised me by remarking, 'It is only for the quality of his wife and the fact of his children that I envy Oscar. Nothing else.'

When we left the theatre, accompanied to the stage door by Haziq the dresser, Oscar, now in high spirits, proposed dinner at Kettner's: '*Foie gras* and *sole Careme*, followed by *soufflé a la Josephine* – something light yet Napoleonic, don't you think?'

I professed exhaustion, made my excuses, kissed Constance, saluted Willie and Wellbeloved, promised Oscar I would not be late for our appointment in the morning, and, alone (mercifully alone!), walked down Shaftesbury Avenue, around Piccadilly Circus and along Regent Street, back to the Langham Hotel.

I had a beef sandwich and a glass of beer in the hotel buttery and then retired to my room and went directly to bed. It can't have been later than eight o'clock.

I pressed my face into the pillow and willed myself to sleep. I wanted to dream of Olga.

31

Paradise Walk

I slept soundly until nine o'clock on Monday morning. As I awoke, unbidden, one of Oscar's favourite lines came into my head: 'They've promised that dreams can come true – but forgot to mention that nightmares are dreams, too.'

I got up, dipped my face into a basin of cold water, shaved and dressed. For once, I did not join my friend for breakfast. Instead, I rang the bell and ordered coffee in my room. It was strong and welcome. As I drank it, I sat at the table by the window and wrote a letter to my wife. I told Touie how much I loved her and how greatly I missed her and the children. I told her something of my week's adventures, but not everything, of course. (Some doors are best left forever closed.) I shared with her my frustration at having spent a week in town – and seven nights at an expensive West End hotel – on what felt now like a wild-goose chase in pursuit of fool's gold. I told her how much I was looking forward to returning to our home in South Norwood that afternoon and to getting back to my own desk – 'my dear old desk'– and to proper work. As I signed and sealed the letter, I repeated out loud the words that I had said to myself on the afternoon I had taken tea with Olga: 'We cannot command our love, but we can our actions.'

I took the letter down into the street to catch the mid-morning post. I could have given it to one of the porters or the bellboy, but I wanted to post it myself –the postbox was no more than thirty yards from the hotel's front entrance and the day was a fine one. The sky was clear, the air bracing.

My small task done, as I turned back from the postbox, feeling curiously exhilarated, I found myself almost face to face with the man who had been set to spy on Oscar. We were walking towards one another. Our paths crossed. His eyes did not meet mine and it took me a moment to realise who he was. When I did, I turned back and called out to him: 'Good morning, sir.' He stopped, but said nothing. 'May I ask what your business is?' He neither turned nor spoke. 'You are making a nuisance of yourself, sir,' I continued, 'loitering here as you do, following my friend as you have been.' Still the man said nothing. Nor did he move. I walked back towards him. He stood stock still, almost to attention. From the way in which he held his arms and shoulders I recognised a military bearing. I walked beyond him and turned back to confront him. His features were clean-cut; his hair was fair; his eyes were blue; there was a small scar across his forehead. 'What's going on?' I asked.

'I cannot tell you, sir,' he replied, in a voice much more measured than I expected, 'but it is for the best, I do assure you.' He nodded, touched the brim of his hat and walked briskly on. I watched him until he turned into the first side street and disappeared. The moment he was gone, I felt as if I had been in the presence of an apparition.

I returned to my room, packed my few things into my overnight bag, settled my bill (which was far smaller than it should
have been) and, at twelve noon, as the clock struck, found Oscar
lounging in the hotel foyer, with his hat and coat across his lap,
ready to set off for our picnic in Paradise Walk. He was wearing a
suit of charcoal grey, and sporting a purple bow tie, loosely worn,
with an amaryllis buttonhole to match.

'You're dressed in your Sunday best,' I said admiringly.

'It's a picnic in honour of royalty,' he replied, rising slowly from
the couch and taking a bow. 'I'm glad you approve.' He held out
his arm. 'Feel the quality of the cloth, Arthur. It's from Kashmir.
Made entirely of goats' hair, if you please. But doesn't smell of
goat at all.' He giggled. 'Isn't it wonderful?'

It was certainly soft to the touch.

'And you,' he continued, looking me up and down with a
doubtful eye, 'appear to be wearing exactly what you were wearing yesterday.'

'The shirt is fresh,' I protested.

'And are you going somewhere?' He prodded my bag with his
ebony cane. 'What is the meaning of this?'

'I'm going home after lunch, Oscar. I must. You know that.'

'You haven't paid your bill, have you?'

'I've tried, but I fear you anticipated me. You must let me know
what I owe you.'

'You should not have paid your bill, Arthur.' He waved his cane
at me reprovingly. 'It is only by not paying one's bills that one can
hope to live in the memory of the commercial classes.' He smiled.
'I never pay my bills – on principle.'

'But you appear to have paid most of mine,' I protested.

He laughed. 'That is different. I've involved you in this business. I should take care of any expenses that you might incur in

the process.' He donned his hat and turned towards the door. 'Our carriage awaits. Bring your bag if you must. I don't know how you can consider abandoning the field as we stand on the very brink of victory, but there it is. *En avant!* To be late today really would be lese-majesty.'

When we were ensconced in the back of the two-wheeler and on our way to Chelsea, I looked at my friend as he sucked happily on his Turkish cigarette and observed, 'You seem remarkably mellow this morning, Oscar.'

'I had a good dinner. Constance was charming. Willie was almost bearable. And I'm thinking we can eliminate Walter Wellbeloved from our inquiries. He is a sentimental milksop and virtually a vegetarian.'

'I thought he believed in human sacrifice.'

'Only when "absolutely necessary" to appease the gods – and in his experience, apparently, it has never been remotely necessary. At all the rituals he masterminds it seems the gods are quite satisfied with a standard Old English hen – well plucked and lightly broiled.'

'He eats chicken, then?'

'No, that's what he offers up to the gods. He doesn't touch meat himself. And he confessed, when we were well into the third bottle of Mr Kettner's finest Meursault, that whatever he might have said in the past to impress young acolytes, he has never even seen a chalice of human blood, let alone drunk from one.' Oscar grinned at me mischievously. 'And the poor fellow's gone off fish entirely since he lost his beloved mermaid.'

'The hapless Rosie? Do you think he drowned her?'

'It's possible – they were alone at sea together in a beautiful pea-green boat. But why would he? It's clear that he loved her and she – poor deformed creature – doted on him. He misses her dreadfully and Mrs Mathers, for all her psychic prowess, is no substitute.'

'He's an odd one, all the same. And known to have been in and around Whitechapel at the time of each the Ripper murders.'

'Indeed – but the same could be said of so many. Our thespian friend, Mr Richard Mansfield, among them ...' Oscar turned eagerly towards me. I was amused to see him so relishing our conversation. 'What did you make of Mansfield, Arthur?'

'He's a fine actor.'

'Undeniably. One of the best. But what of the man?'

'I was confused. As I recall, the first time we encountered him he was consumed with rage and about to beat you black and blue. But at Sims' party and yesterday at the theatre ...'

'Yes,' Oscar chortled. 'He could not have been friendlier, could he? It was as if, having shown us his Mr Hyde, he was determined we should see his Dr Jekyll.'

'Of course, you disarmed him at the theatre with your avalanche of praise.'

'Women are never disarmed by compliments. Men always are. That is the difference between the sexes. But even before I spoke, he was wanting to endear himself to us. He had the champagne open and the signed photographs waiting.'

'He certainly gave the impression of being pleased to see us.'

'Giving a convincing impression is, of course, the actor's stock-in-trade. But I agree. And he would have been pleased to see Willie. He likes Willie.'

'How so?'

'Willie is a critic – of sorts – and his notices of Mansfield's work have always been generous to a fault. Unqualified praise is all an actor ever really wants.'

There was a pause, and it was a comfortable one, so I asked the question that had long puzzled me: 'What is your problem with your brother, Oscar?'

His reply came without hesitation. 'My problem with him is his problem with me. Willie envies me, Arthur, and envy is the ugliest of sins. It twists men's mouths and tortures their souls. In Willie's case, it also drives them to drink. He was a good-looking child. Look at him now. I have a horror of ugliness.' He took a deep breath and contemplated the dying embers of his Turkish cigarette. 'It is a beautiful day,' he said, turning to look out of the window. We were now on the Chelsea Embankment, not far from our destination. 'We should talk of beautiful things.'

'Tell me about our hosts,' I said.

'Festing Fitzmaurice and Sir Frederick Bunbury? They're hardly beautiful, but they are amusing and that's the next best thing.' Oscar looked directly at me and I saw the devil had entered his eye. He lit another cigarette and grinned as he extinguished his match with a small flourish. 'You don't know the story of Festing Fitzmaurice?'

'No,' I said, 'I don't.'

'Festing Fitzmaurice was a courtier – long-serving and much loved, a particular favourite of the Princess of Wales until ... ' Oscar removed a speck of tobacco from his lip.

'Until?'

'Until he was caught buggering a goat.'

'Good God,' I spluttered. 'Can this be true?'

'All too true, alas.'

'When was this?'

'Oh, eight, ten years ago.'

'Couldn't it have been hushed up?'

'Not really. It was the Princess of Wales who caught him. She found him *in flagrante* in the royal stables at Windsor.

Unfortunately, there were two ladies-in-waiting with her, an equerry and a stable lad. Even more unfortunately, it was a male goat and the regimental mascot of the Prince of Wales's 3rd Dragoon Guards to boot – a descendant of one of the goats brought back from the regiment's triumphant tour of India in the sixties. Come to think of it, the poor animal was probably a forebear of the goat that supplied the wool for my suit.' Oscar burst out laughing. 'I'm even more appropriately dressed for the picnic than I realised!'

'What an extraordinary tale,' I said.

'Yes, too good not to retell. I'm sure Her Royal Highness never breathed a word, but ladies-in-waiting, equerries and stable lads all live by gossip. Festing knew that. He was a dreadful gossip himself. He fled at once – he had no choice. He withdrew imme-diately – first from the goat, then from the castle. He was gone within the hour. He paid a high price for his passion.'

'It was a perversion, Oscar.'

'To him, it was a passion – and it cost him his place, his position in the world, his grace and favour lodging, everything. One day he was sitting pretty at the court of Queen Victoria. The next he was an outcast, eking out an existence of sorts in a wretched room in a backwater in Chelsea.' Oscar looked out of the carriage window once more. We had reached Fitzmaurice's address. 'Here we are. As you can see, the poor fellow lives above a pigsty.'

Paradise Walk was a bleak thoroughfare, part city road, part country track, where ramshackle dwellings and outbuildings for livestock butted against one another, providing a community of sorts for the human flotsam that washes up on the shore of many a great metropolis. Lithuanians, Russians, Poles, latter-day Dick Whittingtons from all corners of the British Isles who had failed to find the streets of London paved with gold lived here in squalor, feeding off what food their animals provided and drinking whatever alcohol came their way. It was exactly parallel with Tite Street, where the Wildes and Melville Macnaghten had their fine houses, but there was nothing remotely appealing about Paradise Walk – other than its name. We stepped down from the two-wheeler onto muddy ground, littered with the detritus of poverty: dirty, sodden hay; broken bottles; filthy rags; strewn newspapers trampled into the ground. The stench of animal ordure filled our nostrils.

'I call it "a wretched room",' Oscar continued, wincing at the stink that assailed us. 'I've never been inside before. I just see Festing now and then in the street – and greet him for old times' sake. I suppose that's why we're here now. To be friends to the fallen.'

'Why is Bunbury here?'

'Freddie and Festing were close – and Freddie's a decent fellow. The best of the Old School. Most of the court abandoned Festing altogether, but Freddie didn't. They shared a special affection for the Princess of Wales's eldest son. When he was a boy, they were charged with keeping an eye on young Prince Eddy.'

'Perhaps they share a secret?' I pondered, looking up at the grimy tenement building that loomed over us.

'And if they do,' said Oscar, bracing himself as he made to lead the way, 'we shall uncover it.' My friend looked at me and smiled grimly. 'I need you on board for this, Arthur. I'm glad you're here.'

Using his cane, he pushed open the wooden gate that took us from the public path into the yard that led to the building itself. The pigsty – three stinking stalls covered with a dilapidated roof and containing a sad-looking swine asleep in its own mess – stood like a guardhouse alongside the front door. Oscar pushed at the door with his cane. It was unlatched and opened onto a dark and filthy stone stairwell. Together we stepped inside. 'Festing's room is on the first landing, I believe.'

'It is indeed,' called out a thin, fluting voice from above us. We looked up the stairway and there, just visible in the half-light, leaning over the iron banister, we saw the drooping figure of Sir Frederick Bunbury, Bt., his tortoise head nodding like a metronome.

'Good to see you, Sir Freddie,' cried Oscar amiably. He began to trudge up the steps. I followed. 'Actually, I can only just see you in the gloom. But perhaps the gloom's a blessing. Paradise Walk this may be, but the staircase to heaven this ain't.'

'Thank you for coming,' drawled the baronet. He patted Oscar on the shoulder by way of welcome. He felt the quality of Oscar's suiting with evident pleasure. 'I'm glad you've dressed for the occasion. I have, too.'

'So I see,' exclaimed Oscar, stepping back in wonder.

I shook the elderly courtier's languid hand. He was costumed in full court attire: tail-coat, waistcoat, breeches, lace cuffs, lace jabot, silk stockings, buckled shoes, cocked hat, white gloves and sword. He noticed me noticing it. 'It's Prince Eddy's sword,' he said proudly. He gestured towards the open doorway leading to what I assumed were Festing Fitzmaurice's quarters. The room was lit by candles. 'Festing's dressed for the occasion, also – as you can see.'

We could indeed. Festing Fitzmaurice was standing in the middle of his room, holding a posy of paper flowers and wearing a full-length pink taffeta ball gown, once the property of HRH Princess Alexandra, Princess of Wales.

'The jewellery's paste, of course,' drawled Sir Freddie, nodding happily, 'but Festing's the real thing, you must agree.'

32

A toast to Prince Eddy

Oscar rose to the moment magnificently. He stepped into the room, spread his arms wide and, with a voice full of warmth and admiration, declared: 'What a wonderful way to salute Prince Eddy on his birthday – as the mother he loved so well.'

'You understand, Oscar,' trilled Sir Freddie joyfully. 'I knew you would. That's why I wanted you to be here. And your friend, of course.' He smiled at me with his hooded eyes. 'We shall have fireworks later. I have saved some from Her Majesty's golden jubilee. And we have costumes for you both.'

'Is it just us?' enquired Oscar.

'Just you,' replied Sir Freddie. 'You'll have the pick of the wardrobe.'

'Sadly, we can't stay long,' countered Oscar swiftly. 'We won't have time to change – alas.'

'Pity,' said Sir Freddie mournfully. At George R. Sims'

reception on Saturday night, he had reminded me of Lewis Carroll's creation, the White Knight. Today he was Cervantes' Don Quixote – the knight of the woeful countenance. He stroked his dangling moustaches and gazed sadly at the ground.

'A great pity,' echoed Oscar. 'My friend Conan Doyle does a charming turn as Salome. His dance of the seven veils is something to be seen!'

Sir Freddie rallied and winked as he looked up at me. 'I can believe it.' The old gentleman now fixed his gaze on me admiringly. 'Did you ever serve in Africa, sir?' he asked.

'Tell him, Arthur,' said Oscar, relishing my embarrassment.

'Well . . .' I hesitated. 'I was a ship's surgeon on the SS *Mayumba* during a voyage to the West African coast.'

'Ah.' Sir Freddie nodded, apparently satisfied. 'A sailor. Rum, bum and the concertina, eh? If you'd brought your squeeze-box we could have had some music. Festing loves to dance.'

'Does he not speak these days?' enquired Oscar, appraising Mr Fitzmaurice who I realised now was standing like a statue within an arc of candles laid before him on the floor as footlights. He did not move – or make a sound – but his watery eyes sparkled in the candlelight and his rouged lips trembled gently.

'Very little. Not at all, really. There's nothing left to say. I think he still hears. I sing to him sometimes. He still sees – though he doesn't read any more. We're winding down, both of us. Gradually putting out the lights, shutting up shop. It's over for us now. Time's up. Business done.'

'And done well?' asked Oscar.

'In the end, yes,' said Sir Freddie solemnly. 'I believe so.' He smiled at Oscar. 'We're determined to go out with a bang, you know.'

'And why not?' said Oscar, returning the old man's smile.

I looked around the room. There were shutters over the window; the floorboards were uncarpeted; the walls were bare. There was a mantelpiece above the fire grate and on it three photographs in ornate frames. I recognised Queen Victoria and the Prince and Princess of Wales. I assumed the third portrait was of the Duke of Clarence and Avondale: there was a sprig of rosemary set by it.

There was a curious odour in the atmosphere – not the foul stench of the street below, something sweeter. Was it rosemary or lavender? Or a fragrance that Festing Fitzmaurice used to disguise the stink of the neighbourhood? It was familiar, but I could not place it.

I saw Oscar glance over towards the narrow single bed that stood in the corner of the room: there were no chairs that I could see, no sofa or divan. Draped over the end of the iron bedstead was an array of ladies' clothes – dresses, undergarments, petticoats, coats, hats and shawls.

'Does Festing have quite a selection from Her Royal Highness's wardrobe?' asked Oscar lightly.

'Oh no, only cast-offs and hand-me-downs, nothing stolen – items given to him by the princess. And some servants' garments as well – workaday dresses and suchlike. Something for all occasions. They're mostly the worse for wear now, threadbare, moth-eaten. We've been clearing out the wardrobe, burning what pieces Festing can bare to be parted from. My dear wife used to mend and launder everything for him – until she lost her mind.'

'I never knew her,' murmured Oscar.

'Few did,' answered Sir Freddie. 'She was not much at court. And I was away travelling with the prince so much. She stayed at home in Yorkshire. She was not one for the royal round. She was not nobly born – but she was a lady in my eyes. Always.'

'I'm sure.'

'So beautiful when young – a little like your wife, Oscar, if I may say so. *Gamine*. But pitiful at the end – when her mind went. You understand?'

'I understand,' said Oscar.

Suddenly, Festing Fitzmaurice moved. In one movement, like the automated doll on a musical box, he twisted his whole body so that it faced the fireplace. With a separate jerk of his head, he fixed his eyes on the portrait of Prince Eddy.

'Oh, yes,' cried Sir Freddie. 'It'll soon be time for the toast.' He looked about the room. 'It's definitely time for the picnic. I have it all prepared.' With almost balletic steps, he moved to a darkened corner of the room and returned a moment later carrying a plate on which sat what appeared to be a trio of large and lumpen rotten oranges.

'*Nargisi kofta*,' he declared triumphantly, 'Prince Eddy's favourite – Narcissus meatballs!'

'Ah,' sighed Oscar, coming to the rescue once again. 'Scotch eggs – Grecian style. Alas, we cannot. We must not. We've only recently become vegetarians and it's too soon to break our vows.' Widening his eyes, he looked directly at Sir Freddie: 'But the toast we must share. Do you have any of Prince Eddy's favourite wine?'

'Of course,' warbled Bunbury, stepping lightly back into the shadow and returning almost at once bearing a large tray on which stood, unsteadily, a dust-covered brown bottle and three green Hoch glasses. 'Gewürztraminer,' he announced, 'and a good year, too.'

'And opened already,' said Oscar, raising a somewhat anxious eyebrow.

'Fear not,' chirruped Sir Freddie. 'There's a second bottle cooling in the bassinet.'

'Excellent,' said Oscar. 'Shall I pour?'

'By all means – and you may drink for Festing.' The baronet lowered his voice: 'He no longer eats and he doesn't like to drink in company. Because of the dribbling.'

Oscar filled our glasses to the brim. Sir Freddie handed me mine. 'We introduced Prince Eddy to the Gewürztraminer when we first accompanied him to Heidelberg. Forever after, it was his wine of choice.'

'I know Heidelberg,' I said. 'A fine university.'

'We were with him at Heidelberg – and at Cambridge, of course. He was at Trinity. I know Oscar was at Oxford. Were you an Oxford man?'

'Edinburgh,' I said.

'Never mind,' murmured Sir Freddie consolingly. 'You went to sea eventually – that's what counts. We spent three years at sea with Prince Eddy – aboard HMS *Bacchante*. That was before he went to university. He was a midshipman and we were in attendance, along with Dalton, his tutor, who served as the ship's chaplain. We toured the Empire – the Americas, the Falkland Islands, South Africa, Australia, the Far East, Ceylon, Aden, Egypt, the Holy Land, Greece.'

'Ah, Greece,' sighed Oscar, sipping the yellow-green wine. (It was crisp and refreshing, to my surprise.)

'Yes,' responded Sir Freddie brightly. 'It was in Greece that Festing accepted his true nature. In the hills, outside Athens.'

'Say no more,' I murmured.

Bunbury continued, unabashed: 'I remember, Oscar, when I first met you, you were a young man then, and you told me your ambition was "to eat of the fruit of all the trees in the garden of the world". That was our ambition, too. That's what we wanted for Prince Eddy.'

'And Dalton, the clergyman, the tutor?'

'Dalton had other ideas, of course – but ours prevailed. Prince Eddy was our boy. He was Her Majesty's eldest grandson, of course – named Albert Victor after her and her beloved Albert, destined to be sovereign himself one day – but he was always Eddy to his dear mamma and it was she who put him in our charge. From the age of sixteen, until the day he died, he was ours, all ours. We promised the princess we would look after him and we did.'

'You indulged him,' said Oscar, without prejudice.

'We loved him. He was a wayward boy, as princes are, but he was our boy. We indulged him, yes. Whatever he wanted, we gave him. Elephants to ride, tigers to shoot – a Gaiety girl in Brighton, a geisha in Fukagawa, a goatherd in Thessalonica.' He laughed at the recollection.

'Did you set no boundaries?' I asked.

'None at all. In Japan he wanted a tattoo. We had a moment's doubt about that because we knew he would be marked for life – but he was determined, so we let him have his way, as ever, and, given where it was placed, we knew that his mother would never see it – though I fear, as she nursed him on his deathbed, she may have done so.'

'He died very young,' I said.

'Yes,' said Sir Freddie. 'Don't believe any of the rumours, it was pneumonia. He was twenty-eight. He did indeed die very young, but while he was alive, he lived!' He turned towards Oscar and raised his nodding tortoise's head defiantly. 'Yes, sir, we indulged him in everything, I'm proud to say. Whatever he wanted, if it was within our power to grant it, we did.'

'Did you ever let him kill a man?'

'He fought a duel in Heidelberg, but no one was hurt. He wasn't much of a swordsman. He was a good shot.'

'No, I meant kill a man for sport?'

'They were hunting aboriginals for sport in Australia when we were there, but that didn't interest Prince Eddy.'

'Would you have given him the chance to commit murder if that is what he'd wanted?'

'But he didn't. He was a gentleman through and through. And a gentle man.' The baronet bridled and narrowed his eyes. 'I know what you're getting at, Oscar. All that Jack the Ripper stuff. A vile calumny. Intolerable.' His pale face flushed with anger. 'Prince Eddy would never have harmed a woman. Not in a thousand years. People will always believe the worst of someone if they can – most particularly of a prince. The slur about Jack the Ripper has tarnished his memory, I know that. It's been my life's last ambition to clear his name. When the police came sniffing around again last year, when my poor wife was fading, I showed them the log books and the diaries. The prince was five hundred miles away when most of the Whitechapel murders occurred. And so were we.'

'But you took him to Whitechapel on occasion?' Oscar persisted. 'That's how the stories started.'

'We did. He had a taste for the oriental. He had "a soft spot for smooth skin". That was the line he used. Witty, eh? Dalton always downplayed the prince's intelligence – said his mind was "abnormally dormant". Far from it. Prince Eddy wasn't intellectual, but he had an enquiring mind. He truly wanted to "taste of all the fruit". We went to Whitechapel to smoke the occasional opium pipe and to seek out the company of Chinese sailors. They had no idea who he was and he loved that.'

'And you loved him.'

'We did,' said Sir Freddie, gazing wistfully at the portrait on the mantelpiece.

'Were you alone?' asked Oscar.

'How do you mean?'

'Was this special bond confined to just the pair of you – you and Festing?'

'We knew him best, we loved him most,' Sir Freddie nodded, 'but, yes, there was a third – and I think you knew him, Oscar. James Kenneth Stephen.'

'The poet? Yes, I knew him. He kindly supported my candidature for membership of the Savile Club. That was a few years ago. But I remember him. He was a nice man.'

'He was Prince Eddy's tutor at Cambridge. He was only four years the prince's senior, but they became close friends.'

'Were they lovers?'

'I don't know. All I do know is that when Stephen heard the news of the prince's death, he was overwhelmed by grief. He refused to eat and died twenty days later, aged just thirty-two.' The baronet turned to look at his friend in the taffeta ball gown. 'I think that's what Festing is doing now – not eating, just waiting to die.'

'Shall we raise our glasses to the prince?' said Oscar.

'Yes,' said Sir Freddie. He held out his glass towards the picture on the mantelpiece. 'To the memory of His Royal Highness Albert Victor Christian Edward, Duke of Clarence and Avondale – our Prince Eddy. Happy birthday, darling boy.'

33

Home

O scar heaved his body into the back of the two-wheeler and collapsed onto the leather banquette with an exaggerated sigh. 'We should have coupled that with a toast to those that loved not wisely but too well.'

'What an extraordinary experience,' I said, moving my portmanteau from the seat and sitting down next to my friend. 'I'm quite drained.'

'Likewise. Drained. And ravenous. Those hideous Scotch eggs . . .'

'You handled it all superbly, Oscar.'

He laughed wheezily and, letting out a slow, deep breath, he patted me on the arm. 'Thank you, Arthur. You didn't do so badly yourself. For one dreadful moment I thought we were destined to spend the morning *en travestie*, trussed up like a couple of Ugly Sisters from the pantomime.' He took his cane and banged it up against the roof of the carriage. 'Back to the Langham Hotel, driver, if you please,' he called.

'No, not for me. I'm going home now. I must. Drop me at an underground station when we pass one.'

'What, no lunch? You can't seriously be contemplating returning to South Norwood on an empty stomach.'

'I have to go home, Oscar. I've matters to attend to, work to do. I've a living to earn.'

'Write this up and your fortune's made. I'm planning the play already. Mansfield's ready to play the part – eager, in fact. You heard him say so yesterday.'

I laughed. 'I did indeed.'

'We're just tying up loose ends now. We need to see Druitt's sister and then I think we can safely say "case closed".' He turned and looked at me, bright-eyed. 'You can't go home without lunch, Arthur. I won't let you. And the Langham will do us proud. What do you fancy? Lobster bisque, spring lamb, pink, cut slantingly to the bone, with really crisp roast potatoes, buttered carrots, peppery cabbage slightly underdone, and a gravy just like the one your dear old grandmother used to make . . . How does that sound? '

I resisted the temptation. And Oscar, generously, had the two-wheeler take us all the way to London Bridge so I might catch the fast train to Norwood Junction.

As we travelled across town, we reflected on the morning's bizarre encounter. I asked my friend how he had first come to meet these two unlikely courtiers.

'They're not "unlikely" really. They are almost typical, in fact. A royal court's a curious place. Everyone you meet there is a tad improbable. I first met Fitzmaurice and Bunbury many years ago. The Prince of Wales hosted a dinner to which I was invited. They were there. I sat between them.'

'How well do you know the Prince of Wales?'

'He's been to our house – to take part in an experiment in thought-reading, of all things. Lily Langtry brought him. They were close – for a time. But, as you know, nothing lasts. Neither summer nor winter, nor the passion of love. And rides on the merry-go-round of royal romance are customarily of quite brief duration.'

'Are you and the prince still friends?'

Oscar cocked an eyebrow and grinned. 'We were never "friends" in the way you mean. Royalty offer you friendliness, not friendship. There is a difference. You and I are friends, Arthur, and I believe we always will be. I've known a lot of good men in my time, but none, I think, as decent as you. "Steel true, blade straight" – that's what it should say on your gravestone.'

When we reached the railway station, I clambered down from the two-wheeler and extended a hand to my friend. He shook it warmly. 'The moment there's news I'll wire you,' he said. 'And don't forget next Saturday night – it's goodbye to the circus. My farewell supper for our Russian friends. I'll get Mansfield and George R. Sims to join us. Make a bit of a party of it. You can say *au revoir* to your little Russian acrobat then – if you don't slip up to town for a secret tryst meanwhile. But if you can resist the Langham spring lamb you can probably resist anything. Goodbye, old heart.'

As I stepped under the stone archway to enter the station booking hall, I turned back to wave, but the two-wheeler was already gone.

Within the hour I was back home in South Norwood. It was good to be home. In many ways I had enjoyed my week on the trail of Jack the Ripper in the company of Oscar Wilde, but I was exhausted by it, too – exhausted by Oscar, by his wit and his exuberance, by his appetite and his perversity – and dispirited by the fog of London, by the macabre world of police mortuaries and East End opium dens, by the grim spectacle of young women, cruelly disembowelled, and old men absurdly dressed in ball gowns.

When I reached Norwood a light rain was falling, but it did not matter. As I walked down the hill from the station, I felt it washing away the grime of the metropolis. As I turned into Tennison Road I had a spring in my step. It was good see my familiar front door, good to turn the key in the latch, good to find my darling Touie's face smiling up at me from the small framed photograph of her that I kept on my desk in the study. It was especially good to be back at that desk again.

The house was in good order and well-aired. Mrs Stocks, our part-time housekeeper, had everything spic and span, with flowers in the hallway, fresh linen on the bed and my kind of simple fare waiting for me in the larder. As a man eats, so shall he write. I had enjoyed reading my friend Wilde's short stories – they tasted of *foie gras* and lobster bisque. Mine, I fancy, taste more of corned beef and pickled onions.

For the next few days, I ate simply and worked well. I completed my story for *The Idler* and started on another. Now and again I thought of Olga and wondered whether I would indeed see her one last time that coming Saturday. Now and then in my mind I turned over elements of the case we had been investigating, but felt as baffled by it all as Macnaghten and his men seemed to have been. The recollection of Oscar asserting merrily that we were 'just tying up loose ends now' made me smile.

I was alone with my breakfast boiled egg on Thursday morning when I heard from him. The postman called at 8.00 a.m.: Oscar's was the only letter he had to deliver. Over the five years of our friendship, we had not corresponded much, but I recognised his precise, elegant hand at once:

16 Tite Street
10.i.94

My dear Arthur,

*I have news — but before I share it, how are you? Are you
working hard? To work, to work: that is your duty. And your
pleasure, too, I trust. Work never seems to me a reality, but a
way of getting rid of reality! I have returned to Tite Street —
in the interests of economy — but I shall not stay here long.
My boys are delightful, but they are noisy. They make work
difficult and meals impossible. To be able to live at home
I need to send my sons to boarding school and my wife to
Biarritz — or perhaps to Switzerland to join yours? — but, alas,
at present I have not the means. I am in the purple valleys of
despair and no gold coins are dropping down from the heavens
to gladden me. I am overdrawn at the bank and last night a
tax collector called here at the house.*

'Taxes! Why should I pay taxes?' I cried.

*'But, sir,' he said, 'you are the householder here, are you
not? You live here, you sleep here.'*

'Ah, yes, but I sleep so badly.'

*The man simply did not comprehend. I gave him my brother
Willie's address and said I was sure he would give him better
satisfaction than I was able to do. You are so wise to have
retreated to the country, Arthur (I am assuming Norwood
is the country: I have never been) — London is now become
so very dangerous: the barking of tax inspectors at dusk is
distressing, the roaring of creditors towards dawn is frightful,
and I hear this morning that solicitors are getting rabies and
biting people.*

It really is intolerable the want of money. I have concluded that wanton extravagance is the only remedy — and to that end for Saturday's late supper I have ordered the finest wines and the costliest dishes that the Langham's sommelier and <u>chef de cuisine</u> can produce for our delectation. I am also thinking, as it will be the thirteenth, we should have <u>thirteen</u> at table — <u>viz</u>

ACD and OW

Ivan the Terrible and little Olga

Richard Mansfield and brother Willie (because Mansfield admires him and Constance will insist I invite Willie. She is anxious for a 'family reconciliation'. I cannot invite Constance herself, alas, or Willie will expect his fiancée to be invited too — and there are limits!)

George R. Sims and Freddie Bunbury (if he's up to it — we can take it that Festing Fitzmaurice won't be — what <u>would</u> she wear?) — and Labby, perhaps? He is frightfully pompous, but he can be amusing and he knows Salazkin. What do you think?

And Mr Dodgson/Lewis Carroll? I feel the evening needs the sense of a Mad Tea Party and it is always charming to have a 'celebrity' at this kind of gathering, don't you agree? (Sims will bring him if you approve the idea.)

I don't believe the Prince and Princess of Wales will be able to make it at this short notice, so: Wellbeloved and Mrs Mathers?

And then Macnaghten, of course. That's thirteen, I think. I want Macnaghten there because, as my party piece, after we've eaten, I thought I would 'reveal' the true identity of Jack the Ripper. We need to impress Mansfield with a <u>coup de théâtre</u> — so he commits to the play there and then and we can secure an advance on royalties!

I put down the pages of my friend's letter and said out loud, 'The man's gone mad.' I laughed. I got to my feet and cleared away my breakfast things and, briefly, unlocked the back door and stepped into the garden. The air was biting. There was frost on the grass like icing on a cake. I stood, legs apart, hands on hips, head held high, and breathed deeply. I noticed the water-butt frozen over and, suddenly, found swimming into my mind's eye the men I'd known fourteen years before when I was a boy of twenty and had signed on as the ship's surgeon on the whaler *Hope* that took us from Peterhead to the Arctic Circle. I thought of those men and their courage and endurance and of how they risked death by day and night – not just from hypothermia (the cold was excruciating) but from the ever-shifting floes of ice that could slice a man in half. And then I thought of Oscar and Willie and Labby and the rest and roared as I might have done at the music hall.

My head cleared, I returned to the kitchen, poured myself another cup of tea and picked up Oscar's letter once more:

My news – my real news – is quickly told. We can eliminate Montague Druitt from our list of suspects. As you know, he was Macnaghten's prime candidate <u>entirely</u> because his suicide came hard on the heels of the last of the initial Whitechapel killings. Mary Jane Kelly was murdered at Miller's Court on 8 November 1888. Montague Druitt threw himself into the Thames on or soon after 1 December 1888.

That Druitt took his own life is not in question. When his body was recovered there were four large and heavy stones found in each of his coat pockets and when his rooms at Blackheath were searched a suicide note was discovered. It read: 'Since Friday I felt I was going to be like Mother, and the best thing for me was to die.' Mrs Druitt had been committed to the Manor House Lunatic Asylum in the spring of 1888.

Macnaghten's thinking was simple: Druitt was a medical man with a lunatic mother. He could wield a scalpel and had lunacy in his blood. Shortly after the Miller's Court murder Druitt took his own life and the Whitechapel murders ceased. Ergo Druitt is Jack the Ripper!

Druitt, of course, was not a doctor and while he was certainly fearful that his mind was giving way as his mother's had done, he could not have murdered Mary Jane Kelly in Whitechapel on 8 November because he was in Bournemouth staying with his sister at the time! She told me so yesterday afternoon – and can furnish witnesses to the fact should they be required.

As he had promised, George R. Sims supplied me with Miss Druitt's address. She had earlier declined Sims' invitation to provide an interview for publication, but she was ready to meet me – indeed, she was eager to do so. I sent her a telegram on Monday and she travelled up to town on Tuesday. I gave her tea at the Savoy. She is a timid soul – a typical English spinster: unpretty, unpowdered, approaching forty – but with a great appetite for scones! She had refused to meet Sims – and had said very little to the police when Sergeant Thick went to question her four years ago – but she was happy to meet me because her brother had given her my book of fairy stories shortly before his death and 'The Happy Prince' is 'the saddest and most beautiful thing' she has ever read! Her brother, it seems, often spoke of me – recollecting my notoriety at Oxford! – and she was anxious to unburden herself to me because she sensed I would be 'in sympathy' with her brother and his tragedy.

In a nutshell, Druitt was a barrister but not a sufficiently successful one. To supplement his income, he took to tutoring at a boys' school near his digs in Blackheath. He taught Latin and Greek and coached the Cricket XI. (At Winchester and New College he'd been a cricketer of distinction.) Unfortunately, at Blackheath Druitt developed a _tendresse_ for the captain of the school cricket team — a youth by the name of Dickinson. Even more unfortunately, the _tendresse_ was reciprocated and an _affaire_ ensued. Druitt was thirty-one, the boy was seventeen. Druitt knew that it was wrong — knew that it was _madness_ — but could not stop himself. He confessed all this to his sister, his 'only friend in the world' — his mother being confined in the asylum, his father having died a year or two before and his elder brother not being the sort of chap to whom one makes this kind of confession. Miss Druitt did not sit in judgement on her brother's behaviour — 'the heart has its reasons', she said, fluttering her eyelashes — but she urged him 'to take control of himself' and to resign from his post at the school and remove himself from harm's way at the earliest opportunity.

Druitt promised he would do so and arranged an appointment with the school's headmaster for Friday 30 November. What occurred at that meeting his sister does not know — but such was her brother's emotional state at the time, she fears he may have 'told his whole story'. When his body was found he had a cheque in his wallet for £50. Miss Druitt believes the school may have paid him off to ensure his silence.

The school did not want a scandal. And Druitt's family did not want a scandal either. What Miss Druitt told me she had also told her other brother — William Druitt, a solicitor — but he would not believe it ('Monty was a sportsman and gentleman', etc.,) and told her to say nothing 'for the honour of the family'. He preferred the false truth that Montague Druitt was Jack the Ripper to the worse truth that he was a lover of young men!

Miss Druitt keeps a diary and it accompanies her everywhere – she said, rather amusingly, 'one must always have something sensational to read in the train' – and showed me her diary entries for the dates in August and September when the first four of the Whitechapel killings occurred. Montague Druitt was playing cricket in Wimborne on each of the dates in question and stayed with his sister in Wimborne overnight. On the night of the Miller's Court murder, 8/9 November, Druitt was again with his sister in Bournemouth and that evening two of her friends joined them for a game of Russian Whist. She volunteered the names and addresses of these ladies – 'both highly respectable' – should they be required.

So, Arthur, the upshot is: we can forget Montague John Druitt altogether.

Ditto John Pizer, better known as 'Leather Apron'.

Having concluded my interview with Miss Druitt and taken her by hansom to Waterloo to catch her train home, I instructed the cab to take me on to Whitechapel where (so I was advised by Sims) I would find Pizer at the Soup Kitchen for the Jewish Poor. This is where he holds court as the man who was once 'thought to be Jack the Ripper but turned out not to be'! I found him without difficulty: he is well known among the regulars. He was tucking in to a supper of bread and kosher sardines, but did not appear to resent my intrusion and he assured me he would tell me 'anything I wanted to know' in return for a shilling. I gave him half-a-crown and *he proceeded to give me his 'turn'. It was Henry Irving as Shylock done for the halls. He is an ugly-looking brute: small, thickset, with greasy hair and a weasel's eyes — not easy to understand (he has a thick guttural accent) and impossible to trust. He's what your man Dr Watson would call 'a slippery customer'. Indeed, Pizer was a slipper-maker by trade and, when he worked, carried a knife and wore a leather apron as he went about his business — hence his sobriquet. He had had, he acknowledged, a reputation for taunting the Whitechapel prostitutes — they claimed he was an extortionist and threatened violence against them for money: he denies it — and, when the murders started, word spread like wildfire that it was Leather Apron 'what done it'. In fact, he had sound alibis for each and every murder and, though questioned by the police, was never at risk of being charged. But for a brief moment he was the most notorious villain in the land — the Star claimed that 'Leather Apron' had been named as the murderer by at least fifty of the women who worked on the streets of Whitechapel. The sobriquet made him famous — until another, stronger, more sensational sobriquet came along. Pizer concluded his tale, almost wistfully: 'When the letters from "Jack the Ripper" appeared in the papers they lost interest in "Leather Apron".'*

When I asked him who he thought the real murderer might be, he told me he had no idea. 'Nobody knows. Nobody will ever know. It's just Jack the Ripper.'

That is all my news, my friend. I could not write more briefly. I did not have the time.

Ever yours,
Oscar

PS Unless I hear to the contrary, I will assume that my proposed guest list for Saturday night meets with your approval and I will issue invitations accordingly. It is important that <u>Bunbury</u> is with us on Saturday. I believe his life depends on it.

34

Murder

I did not reply to Oscar's letter. Instead, I wrote once more to my Touie in Switzerland, telling her how pleased I was to be back home, assuring her that Mrs Stocks was taking good care of me, and reporting to her on the excellent progress I felt I was making with my new story – one inspired by my adventures with the whalers in the Arctic Circle.

On Friday morning, a little before noon, the telegraph boy arrived with a wire from Oscar:

```
GUESTS INVITED + YOUR ROOM AT LANGHAM BOOKED
+ SUPPER AT ELEVEN + REVELATIONS AT MIDNIGHT
+ OSCAR
```

On Saturday morning I was still undecided. I felt my comrade-ship with Oscar required me to attend the supper party he was holding and I was intrigued to know what 'revelations' he might conjure up for the benefit of his guests, but at the same time the prospect of seeing Olga once more unnerved me. I had fallen in love with the girl – I couldn't deny it, at least not to myself – but there could be no future for us. I knew that. What could be gained by seeing her once more but a renewal of desire followed by regret and heartache?

It was early in the afternoon, at the very moment that I had resolved *not* to go to London that evening and was beginning to word a telegram of explanation that I might send to Oscar – could I claim to have caught a sudden chill? Or should I tell the simple truth? – when, from my study window, I saw the telegraph boy rest his bicycle against the front gate and come running up the path. It was another wire from Oscar:

```
FURTHER MURDER IN TITE STREET + HORROR
UNSPEAKABLE + COME SOONEST + OW
```

By train and hansom cab, I reached Tite Street in little more than two hours. Darkness had fallen and the street lamps gave a poor light, but I could see through the gloom that the entrance to the road was blocked, as it has been twelve days before when the first body had been found in the alley leading from Tite Street to Paradise Walk. A yellow fog swirled down the street and from it – as I paid off the cabman – I saw a shadowy figure emerge and vanish and appear again, like a ghost on the ramparts at Elsinore.

I felt I recognised the silhouette. I called out: 'Is that you, Macnaghten?'

The figure came towards me. So thick was the murk that I did not see his face until he was a yard away. It was one of Macnaghten's men – a sergeant. I knew him from my visit to the police morgue the week before. 'The chief constable's not here, sir,' he said.

'What's happened?' I asked.

'Another murder.'

'Another woman?'

'Yes, sir. Like the last two, but worse. It's Jack the Ripper all over again.'

'Can I see the scene?'

'Not without the chief's say-so, sir. They've taken the body away – what was left of it. The chief was here all morning. Your friend, Mr Wilde, was here too.'

'I'm going to his house,' I said.

'Very good, sir. You know the way?'

I left the sergeant and walked past him into the gloom, past the narrow, black entrance to the alley, now guarded by two policemen, and up the all-but-invisible street. So thick was the fog that I could not tell one house from another and started up the wrong front doorsteps twice before arriving correctly at number 16. I rang the bell. There was no answer. I peered up at the dun-coloured building shrouded in a heavy veil of yellow mist. There were smudges of light at the windows on the upper floors. I rang again. I waited. I was turning over in my mind what best to do next, when I heard the rattle of keys and the pulling of a bolt. An anxious girl's face peeped around the edge of the door. It was Mary, the Wildes' young maid.

'Oh, it's you, Dr Doyle,' she whispered. 'Come in. I thought it might be Mr Wilde. Mrs Wilde said not to let him in.'

'Not let him in?'

'He's the worse for wear.'

'I'm sorry to hear it.'

The girl gave a nervous giggle as she opened the door to let me pass. 'Oh, no. Mr William, I mean. Mr Oscar's with the police. It's been quite a day, all the comings and goings. Mr William was in a bad way.'

The girl took my hat and dropped it as, all jitters, she helped me off with my coat. The gas jets in the sconces on the wall above the hallway table hissed and flared. 'Where is Mrs Wilde?' I asked. 'Is she in?'

'She's changing for dinner, sir.'

As the girl bent down to retrieve my hat, I heard footfall on the landing above and then Constance calling from the top of the stairs: 'Is that you, Arthur? It's you, isn't it? I'm not decent, but you don't mind, do you? You're a doctor, after all.'

Mary dropped my hat once more and scuttled away to the kitchen as I looked up to find Constance coming down the stairs, her hands held out towards me. She looked quite wonderful, in a way I had never seen her look before, with her hair pinned up and her face unpainted. She was wearing a Japanese kimono.

'I look ridiculous, I know,' she said, coming up and kissing me. As her hands touched mine, I felt them shaking. 'It's good to see you, Arthur,' she said. 'We've had quite a day here.'

'So I understand.'

'Willie's been here and made a terrible scene – terrified poor Mary. Oscar's having this supper party tonight and has invited Willie, but not his fiancée. And now Willie's discovered that I'm going, but Lily hasn't been asked and he's incensed.'

'The supper party is still happening?'

'Yes – and Oscar says I have to come, which is why I'm changing now.'

'Where is Oscar?'

'With Mr Macnaghten – at the explosion.'

'The explosion?'

'You've not heard?'

'What explosion? I know nothing.'

'In Paradise Walk, about two hours ago – what time is it?' She looked around at the clock on the wall. 'Around lunchtime, it must have been – just after we got rid of Willie. It was quite a small explosion, but alarming all the same. Oscar went out to investigate. He was gone for an hour. We became quite anxious – Mary started crying. You know what girls are. And then Oscar came back with Macnaghten and they gave me telegrams to send. So much has been happening. I'm quite bewildered.'

'Where are your boys?'

'They're with Oscar's mother, thank heavens. They're safe. Oscar can't cope with them here. He says he can't work with them in the house.'

'How is Oscar?'

'Now?' She hesitated. 'Excited, I think.' She put her hands over mine. 'I know that sounds strange, but, yes, excited. Almost mad.' She looked up into my eyes and I saw tears in the corners of hers. 'I sometimes think he is quite mad and I do not know what to do. I love him so very much.'

'I know,' I said. 'I understand.'

'This morning, when we heard about the murder – the poor girl in the alley . . . You know about that?'

'Yes. Oscar sent me a wire. That's why I've come.'

'When he came back from seeing the poor girl's body he was white as a sheet – so shocked by what he'd seen. I gave him some brandy, and then Willie arrived while we were having lunch and there was this dreadful argument – and then the explosion occurred and the fire . . .'

Behind me, I heard the key turning sharply in the latch. The front door flew wide open and there stood Oscar in a whorl of yellow mist – like a ghastly apparition in an Adelphi melodrama. His cloak was swept back over his shoulder. He was wild-eyed and grinning like a man possessed.

'Ah, here you are,' he cried, laughing and pointing at me. 'In at the kill, eh? And with my wife in your arms!'

I broke abruptly away from Constance. 'What's the matter, Oscar?'

He stepped in to the hallway, but held the door open. The gas jets flared once more. 'Come, man, this is no time for romance. We must go. The carriage is waiting. Where's your bag?'

'I've brought no bag,' I said.

'Have you dropped it at the hotel already?'

'I have no bag, Oscar.'

'Aren't you going to change for the party? We're not in South Norwood now.'

'I can't come to the party, Oscar,' I protested. 'I came now because of your telegram – and Constance was kind enough to welcome me. But I cannot come to any party. You should cancel the supper, Oscar. Please.'

'What?' he bellowed. 'Are you mad?'

'Leastways, I cannot come. I really cannot. You must understand—'

'Oh,' he cried, suddenly clapping his hands. 'Have no fear. She's not coming, your little acrobat. You're quite safe, Arthur. I should have told you. The cast list is changed altogether. Come now.' He stepped back over the threshold beckoning me towards him. I picked up my hat and coat to follow.

Constance called after him: 'What time must I be there, Oscar?'

'Eleven at the latest, my dear – but do change before you come. It's a supper party, not a costume ball.'

We climbed into the two-wheeler that stood waiting at the kerb-side. 'I thought the street was closed,' I said.

'It was,' said Oscar, settling back into his seat with a mighty sigh. 'Macnaghten ordered it open again just a minute ago. He's gone home to change. He's had quite a day.'

'And you, Oscar? How are you?' He made no answer, but began to feel under his cloak for his cigarettes. 'Remember, I am your friend – and a doctor, too. You're overwrought. It's not good for your heart.'

He turned and smiled at me. He appeared calmer now. 'I know the golden rule: "Always behave as if nothing has happened, no matter what has happened." It's sound advice, but so very English and I'm profoundly Irish, I'm afraid.' He lit his cigarette and chuckled softly.

'What has happened?' I asked.

'So much,' he said. 'And there's more to come – much more, "ere midnight's frown and morning's smile, ere thou and peace may meet."'

'Keats?'

'Shelley.' He gave me his familiar, reassuring pat on the knee. 'I'm glad you're here, Arthur. You were here at the start. You should be here at the finish, too.'

'So what has happened today?' I asked. 'Another poor girl was found this morning? As before?'

'Worse. She had been decapitated. And disembowelled.'

'You saw the body?'.

'Only briefly. A glance, no more. It was enough. I'm not a doctor.'

'I understand,' I said.

'The legs had been cut off, too. What was left were the arms and a bloodied torso.'

'Like the torso found beneath the railway arch in Pinchin Street?'

'And the torso found below ground in the vault in Whitehall – yes. The same.'

'Was the head nearby?'

'No – no head, no legs, no clothes, no jewellery, nothing. Just the torso dropped at the end of the alley, as before. The poor creature was lying on her back, her arms outstretched, crucified.'

'Horrible.'

'Unspeakable.'

'And, of course, no one reported missing?'

'Not yet – but I'd not expect it. It's the pattern exactly as before.'

'This is too much.' I sighed. 'Something must be done.'

'Something will be done,' said Oscar, peering out of the carriage window into the darkness, 'and tonight.'

'Tonight,' I repeated. 'Yes, tonight ...' I looked at my friend's turned head, perplexed. 'What are these "revelations" you are promising for tonight, Oscar? Why are you even thinking of going ahead with the party?'

He turned back towards me and said eagerly, 'We must. We have no choice – though, as Constance may have told you, the guest list has been somewhat modified.'

'You told me. Olga is not coming.'

'Nor Mr Dodgson. He declined. Nor Mrs Mathers. She is summoned to a séance in Paddington – for ready money. Quite understandable. And, of course, Sir Freddie Bunbury will not be there.'

'Bunbury is not coming?'

Oscar looked at me through a cloud of cigarette smoke. 'Bunbury is dead.'

'What?'

'Bunbury is quite exploded.'

'I do not follow you, Oscar. Explain, man.'

'The explosion – that was Bunbury. He took his own life – and Festing's. Did Constance not tell you?'

'No,' I answered, shaking my head in disbelief. 'That was the explosion in Paradise Walk?'

'Yes. And now they are at peace – with Lady Bunbury and Prince Eddy. It's what they wanted. I thought something of the sort might occur, but not today – tomorrow. That's why I felt is so essential to have Freddie at the supper tonight. I sensed his life might depend on it. I thought to save him from himself.'

'I am confused, Oscar – utterly confused.'

'Tomorrow, Arthur, is the fourteenth of January – the anniversary of Prince Eddy's death. Last week when we had that dreadful "picnic lunch" with Freddie and Festing, Freddie told us they were nearing their end, did he not? He even told us they hoped to go out with a bang? I should learn to take my friends more literally. I see now it was his little joke. He had it all planned out. And I believe he was so insistent we should be there because, somehow, he wanted to share their secret. He thought I might understand – and I believe I do.'

'Bunbury has taken his own life – and murdered Festing Fitzmaurice in the process?'

'Two heinous crimes, according to English law – but at times "the law is a ass, a idiot".' Oscar lit a second cigarette from the embers of his first and smiled at me. 'As you know, Arthur, I've not much time for Dickens as rule, but in this instance he gets it right.'

'I marvel at your composure, Oscar. Your friends are dead and you are almost making light of it?'

'A moment ago, Arthur, you were telling me I was over-wrought. You really must settle on a single diagnosis.'

I laughed despairingly. Oscar shook his head. 'I am sanguine about Bunbury and Fitzmaurice,' he went on, 'because both were old men. One had lost his wife, the other his wits. There was nothing of worth left for them in this world. They were ready for the next.'

'What does Macnaghten make of it all?' I asked.

'He's all excitement. Here's a crime he could solve at a stroke. I arrived on the scene at the very moment he did. The pigsty was ablaze.'

'The pigsty?'

'That's where the explosion occurred. In one of the stalls. Bunbury and Fitzmaurice tied together with ribbons – mortars strapped to their chests ignited by fireworks.'

'Good God.'

'Macnaghten recognised the *modus operandi* straight away. He'd first seen primitive mortars like these used by the natives in the land riots in India when he was there. It seems there are combustible chemicals of some sort lurking in animal manure—'

'Ammonium nitrate,' I said.

'That's it. Ammonium nitrate. You're the man of science, Arthur. Macnaghten likes to think he is, too. Well, combine a distillation of this ammonium nitrate with a little gunpowder and – boom! Indian rioters, Fenians, anarchists, fading courtiers . . . they're all using it, apparently.'

'I marvel that Bunbury knew how.'

'He was a soldier once upon a time. But, of course, that was many years ago and his home-made mortar wasn't up to much. Macnaghten reckons the shock of the explosion knocked them out and the fumes from the fire asphyxiated them. It was quite a small blaze. The pig escaped, I'm glad to say. And now Macnaghten is merry as a grig because he believes we have found Jack the Ripper.'

'What?' I exclaimed, now utterly confounded.

'Yes, Macnaghten is crying "case solved". He may be a gentleman, Arthur, but he's also a fool. He's misunderstood everything. I don't know why he wasted all those years managing his father's tea estates in Bengal. The man was born to be a policeman.'

35

A true friend

T he Langham was one of several London hotels where Oscar
kept a set of evening clothes in case 'by chance' he'd need
them.

It was eight o'clock when we arrived and, as we did, much
of fashionable London appeared to be criss-crossing the hotel
foyer, bustling this way and that like elegant ants, coming from
dinner, going to dinner, racing to the theatre or the concert
hall, collecting coats and hats and wraps and furs, demanding
hansom cabs, pondering whether or not to take umbrellas in
case of rain. 'It's chaos here,' cried Oscar happily, as we surveyed
the throng.

'Can we find a quiet corner where you can tell me exactly what
is going on?' I pleaded.

'We must secure our rooms first, Arthur. I need to bathe and
change. I must smell like Guy Fawkes on Bonfire Night.'

He forged a path through the teeming crowd. He had the

height and bulk – and presence – for the endeavour. I followed dutifully.

A moment later, as we stood at the reception desk, waiting to be attended to, across the foyer, at the foot of the main staircase, I noticed a man whose face and stance I recognised. He was engaged in conversation with Jimmy, the cockney bellboy. I tugged at Oscar's sleeve. 'Look,' I hissed, 'isn't that the man who has been following you?'

My friend glanced across the foyer. 'Oh yes,' he said. He turned towards the man and raised a hand in benevolent greeting.

The man caught Oscar's eye at once and waved back. Jimmy the bellboy grinned.

'Yes, indeed,' said Oscar lightly, 'That's Major Ridout. You thought he had a military bearing and how right you were.'

'You know him?' I asked, amazed.

'Only since yesterday – but you can trust him, Arthur. It turns out he is our friend.'

'I am utterly confused, Oscar,' I complained. 'I really don't know where I am with any of this.'

He laughed. 'There's nothing stable in the world, uproar's your only music.'

I looked at him despairingly. He raised an amused eyebrow. 'Play the game,' he said.

'Shelley?' I volunteered.

He smiled. 'Keats.'

We reached the front of the queue and collected our bedroom keys. 'Your evening clothes have been pressed and laid out in your room, Mr Wilde,' murmured the manager obsequiously, as he ushered us towards the lift.

We had adjacent rooms on the second floor. 'I shall change and rest,' said Oscar. 'I must. You should rest, too, Arthur – the night may prove unruly.' He turned the key in the lock of the door. 'You have nothing to change into, I appreciate. I suppose one of the waiters might lend you something . . . '

'No, thank you,' I protested. 'There are limits.'

He chuckled. 'Very well – the dining room will be dimly lit, I've no doubt. The ladies prefer it. No one will notice your country costume.'

'I've not come as a Morris Man, Oscar,' I countered. 'This is a perfectly respectable tweed suit. Besides, if Constance is of the party no one will notice the gentlemen anyway. She is looking very lovely.'

Oscar had pushed open his door. 'You're smitten with Constance now, eh?' he said teasingly. 'Have you forgotten little Olga already?'

'No,' I answered solemnly, 'and, as you should know, Oscar, I believe I never shall.'

He stopped and looked at me kindly. 'I know,' he said. 'I know full well.'

'But I am glad she is not coming tonight. There's only so much turbulence a man's heart can take.'

'Fear not for the future, weep not for the past.'

'Keats?'

'Shelley! Did they teach you *nothing* at Stonyhurst?'

We both laughed. From his jacket pocket he produced an envelope and handed it to me. 'This is the new *placement* for our supper. We're in the Winter Room. Martin's our waiter. He should have the cards. Can you make sure it's all in order? I must rest now. I am utterly exhausted.'

Oscar retreated into his room and I made my way into mine. I took off my boots and coat and lay on the bed. In the darkness, gazing blankly at the ceiling, my head filled with thoughts of Olga, of her energy, her youth, her laugh, her loveliness. As I closed my eyes, deliberately, I pushed her from my mind as a croupier sweeps the gambling chips off the green-baize table. I filled my head instead with the awful vision of Sir Freddie Bunbury and Festing Fitzmaurice, festooned with ribbons, being consumed by flames.

I reached the Winter Room, the private dining room where Oscar's supper party was due to be held, well before eleven o'clock. It was, as Oscar had predicted, dimly lit, but the candles on the table and in the sconces on the walls all had crimson shades, so that a pink glow suffused the room. The rose tint of light and the sparkle of the polished silver and crystal glasses on the damask tablecloth produced the effect of a table set for a wedding breakfast in fairy-land rather than a last supper on a day of death and desolation.

Martin, the waiter, was in fine form. 'Mr Wilde's changed the menu at least three times and I've no idea who is supposed to be sitting where.'

'I have the table plan here,' I said.

'It's still set for thirteen, is it, sir?'

'It is,' I said.

'Thirteen's an unlucky number, you know. I hope Mr Wilde knows what he's doing.'

I echoed Martin's sentiment as I wrote out the names of the guests and we set them in their places:

Oscar Wilde

Ivan Salazkin	Melville Macnaghten
Henry Labouchere MP	Walter Wellbeloved
Dr Rogerson	Alec Shand
Dr Gabriel	George R. Sims
Richard Mansfield	Arthur Conan Doyle
William Wilde	Constance Wilde

'The room looks charming, Martin,' cried Oscar, as he swept in a little before eleven, dressed in a bottle-green velvet evening suit, with a pale green tie and matching carnation in his buttonhole. He was newly shaven: his cheeks were pink. He had washed his hair: he had the look of Dionysus on the town. He crackled with energy and good humour. 'It has been a horrid day, Arthur, but it will be a night to remember, I promise. I hope you are happy with the *placement*. By rights I should have put you between the doctors, but I thought you'd prefer to be next to Constance.'

'That's very thoughtful.' I smiled.

'She has to have Willie next to her because he's here at her insistence and Willie's next to Mansfield because Mansfield's about the only man in London who'll tolerate him.'

'Willie is your brother, Oscar.'

'I know. And we look so alike I insist he wears that preposterous beard so we don't get mistaken for one another. We say all the same things, too, you know, but I do believe I say them first.'

'I'm very happy with where I'm seated, Oscar,' I said. 'Now I am here, I am glad I came.'

'Good,' he said with satisfaction, walking around the table, inspecting each setting in turn. 'You see, I've put George R. Sims on your right. He knows everybody and everything and he's the best of fellows. You can tell him your whaling stories and he'll be happy to hear them. Keep an eye on Alec Shand, will you? You met him at Sims' party. You remember? He's the handsome devil to whom Constance was once engaged – secretly, of course.' He lifted one of the glasses by Shand's setting and held it close to a candle. 'This needs a polish, Martin,' he commanded. 'We all have our secrets,' he continued happily. 'Yes, Shand is very handsome and very clever, although I'm not entirely sure I trust him where the ladies are concerned.'

'Why is he here?' I asked.

'Because he's cracked the case, of course – though he doesn't know it.'

'Shand has cracked the case?' I asked, bewildered.

'Of course, you've not read his book. No wonder you're confused.' He laughed. 'Oh, look, here they come.'

And suddenly, into the room, all at once the guests came: George R. Sims and Alec Shand and Henry Labouchere MP leading the parade, followed by Walter Wellbeloved, then Willie and Constance who arrived with Macnaghten – they had shared a four-wheeler from Tite Street, it seemed – and, bringing up the rear, the two asylum superintendents, looking a little stiff in their evening dress but beaming with goodwill. The horror of the day appeared to be unknown to these people, or to have been put aside. The party bubbled with anticipation.

'Welcome one, welcome all,' cooed Oscar, moving smoothly among his guests, shaking hands, pressing shoulders. The moment he saw me, Macnaghten broke away from Willie and Constance and took me warmly by the arm: 'Congratulations, Dr Doyle. And thank you. Case closed – at last.'

'*A table*, gentlemen,' called Oscar, above the hubbub. 'No standing on ceremony and no pre-prandial drinks. It's simply supper and there's a cheese soufflé to start us off, so it's very much like one of George's comedies – timing is everything. Kindly take your places. Martin will then serve the champagne.'

I showed Constance to her place. She was looking quite lovely in a simple midnight-blue evening dress with a collar of white lace.

'Your husband loves you very much,' I said.

She laughed. 'Do you think so?'

'He's certainly jealous of the attention you receive from others. He has told me to keep a close eye on Alec Shand.'

'Oscar is extraordinary, isn't he?' she said, looking up at me as she sat down. 'His mood changes from hour to hour. This morning, after seeing that poor girl's body, he was in despair – then at lunch with Willie he was in a fury – then, after the explosion, he was almost exultant – and now this . . . ' She turned back and surveyed the glittering table. 'It's like a first night!'

'Yes,' called Oscar from the head of the table, 'but without the leading men.'

'Who's missing?' cried Labouchere. 'Bad form. It's gone eleven. We're ready for our soufflé.'

Oscar indicated the two empty places: 'Salazkin and Mansfield.'

'They're performers,' said George R. Sims. 'It's allowed.'

'It's expected,' said Labouchere.

'What time does the curtain come down at the Globe?' asked someone.

'Ten o'clock,' said Willie, 'just after.'

As he spoke, Richard Mansfield was at the door. He could only have been an actor. He was immaculately turned out in white tie and tails. His dark hair was slicked back with oil. His pale face shone like a Pierrot's in the half-light. He struck a pose and held the moment until he had the room's attention. 'Forgive my lateness,' he murmured silkily. 'The ovation was somewhat sustained tonight.'

As he let his monocle fall from his eye, the room rewarded his entrance with a round of applause. 'You are seated over there, Richard,' instructed Oscar, pointing Mansfield towards his place. 'You're between your favourite critic and my new friend, Dr Gabriel. Dr Gabriel looks like Henry VIII, but he's actually the superintendent of the Surrey County Lunatic Asylum. He has a thousand poor crazed creatures in his care, so he's quite accustomed to meeting people who believe they are Napoleon!'

Mansfield laughed obligingly and shook both Gabriel and Willie Wilde by the hand as he took his seat. He looked over at Constance and blew a discreet kiss in her direction.

'I should have introduced Dr Rogerson, as well. My apologies, Doctor. Dr Rogerson hails from the Colney Hatch Lunatic Asylum.'

'The company you keep, Wilde . . . ' muttered Labouchere. He turned to Rogerson and shook his hand. 'Good to meet you, sir. I know you do good work.'

'Dr Rogerson was a friend of the late Prince Albert,' Oscar continued, 'and tutored Ellen Terry for her role as Ophelia.'

'You're very droll, Mr Wilde,' said Rogerson amiably.

'Or very drunk,' said Willie Wilde.

There was a moment's silence. 'Ah,' cried George R. Sims, 'saved by the guest of honour.' Ivan Salazkin had arrived.

Like Mansfield, he too struck a pose in the doorway. It was even more arresting because Salazkin was still dressed in his ringmaster's costume: boots, britches, red frock coat, cape, silk top hat, wig and whiskers – the full fig. He held up his white-gloved hands: 'A thousand apologies! It's our last night. The lions, the tigers, the bears – they sense that we're on the move again. They get restless. And the company – the clowns and the acrobats – they have to bid farewell to the lovers they have found in London.' As he spoke, Salazkin's eyes surveyed the room. When he saw me, he touched the brim of his top hat.

'You've arrived,' said Oscar, beckoning the ringmaster in to the room, 'that's what matters. And you're sitting here beside me.'

Salazkin removed his hat and cape and handed them to the

hovering Martin. 'Would you give them to my man? He's just outside in the vestibule.'

'Do you want a moment to get changed?' asked Oscar solicitously.

'No, no,' said Salazkin, taking his seat. 'I've kept you all long enough.'

'Well,' said Oscar, beaming at his guest, 'you are the star attraction. It's good that you should look the part.'

Salazkin's eye ran round the table once more. He nodded to each of us in turn. We murmured words of welcome. Oscar stood at the head of the table, gazing down at the Russian. 'Shall I begin?'

'By all means,' said Salazkin softly.

Oscar glanced at his timepiece and picked up his champagne glass from the table. 'We have the soufflé arriving momentarily, so I need to keep my opening remarks brief . . .'

'Hear, hear!' cried Labouchere and Willie Wilde in unison.

'But, in lieu of grace, I do want to begin with a word of welcome – and a toast.' He looked down the table. 'Gentlemen – and Constance – may I say how lovely my wife looks?'

'You may,' declared Alec Shand, provoking a susurration of approval from all corners of the table.

Oscar smiled and paused to let the room settle once again.

'A poet,' he continued, 'is a nightingale who sits in darkness and sings to cheer its own solitude with sweet sounds.'

'Shelley?' I muttered quietly.

'Bravo!' said Oscar, smiling. 'But tonight this poet is in company and hoping to throw light onto darkness with his song. After we've eaten, I have a story to tell, a mystery to unravel . . .'

'We all love a mystery,' murmured George R. Sims.

'We all love a soufflé,' muttered Henry Labouchere.

'But first I have a toast to propose to our guest of honour – Ivan Salazkin – Ivan the Terrible!' We banged the table in assent.

'Ivan has been bringing his Russian Circus to London for several years now. This much you know. And you know, too, I hope, that his is a circus without equal. You've been. You've taken your children, as I have mine. What Sarah Bernhardt is to beauty, what Irving is to Shakespeare, Salazkin is to circus! Whatever our American friend P. T. Barnum may claim, Ivan Salazkin's Russian Circus is the Greatest Show on Earth.'

Oscar paused to allow a moment of applause.

I heard Willie Wilde mutter to Richard Mansfield: 'Do you think Oscar's on some sort of commission?' Oscar heard him too and smiled. Willie went on, more loudly: 'And I thought his reference to Irving in your presence, Mansfield, quite uncalled for.'

'The true artist,' Oscar continued, unabashed, 'is a man who believes absolutely in himself, because he is absolutely himself. Watch Ivan Salazkin in command of everything that occurs in the three rings of his circus and you will see a true artist at the height of his powers.'

'Well said, Oscar,' rumbled George R. Sims, lifting his glass in readiness for the toast.

'But what I want to share with you tonight is something even my friend George R. Sims may not know . . .'

'Surely not!'

'I did not know it myself until this past week. Ivan Salazkin is a friend to our country – a true friend.'

'Hear, hear!' growled Henry Labouchere, banging the table with the flat of his hand.

'Labby leads the cheers,' said Oscar, 'because he is a member of parliament – and a senior one: he has the ear of the Foreign Office – and Labby knows more of this than any of us – and I have his permission to share what I now know with all of you. In this uncertain world, gentlemen, where the whiff of revolution is in the air and the possibility of terror lurks in the least expected places, the government needs intelligence – information. And Ivan Salazkin is one of those who provide it. For several years now he has brought news from Russia, Germany, France to the United Kingdom. He has shared what he knows with our government and tonight we can salute him for his contribution to our national safety. Though his English is quite perfect, he is Russian, not British. He cannot receive any honour from the Sovereign, but he can receive thanks from some of her subjects. Can we raise our glasses, please, to our friend and guest of honour, Ivan Salazkin?'

With a cheer, we rose and held out our glasses towards the Russian ringmaster who half-stood and bowed his acknowledgement.

'Well spoken, Wilde,' said Labouchere. 'You understand the niceties.' As he resumed his seat, he put his hand on Salazkin's shoulder. 'You see, Ivan. You are appreciated by your peers.'

'The soufflé is served,' cried Oscar, looking to the door as Martin and a second waiter trooped in to the room bearing trays. Their arrival prompted even louder cheers than Oscar's eloquent toast had done.

'I'm confused,' grumbled Willie Wilde, leaning across the table. 'Is the man a spy?'

'Not exactly,' said Constance in a whisper. 'According to Oscar, Mr Salazkin is what the Foreign Office call "a friendly informer". He collects nuggets of political gossip in the various capitals in which the circus performs and then shares them with Labby when he gets to London.'

'In return for what?' asked Willie.

'Ease of passage, a *laissez-passer* for his animals, no awkward questions asked at customs, no local taxes exacted while he's here, access to those in high places,' I suggested, hazarding the answer.

'Precisely,' said Constance. 'I don't think he gets paid.'

'How do we know he isn't telling our secrets to the Germans and the Russians and the rest?'

Constance, giggling, leaned forward conspiratorially and lowered her voice still further. 'Oh, Oscar's quite sure he is!'

'And tonight is about keeping him sweet, is it?' muttered Willie. 'Making him feel more valued in this country than he might do in others?'

'Yes,' she said, barely audibly, 'and encouraging Mr Sims to write about him as a friend, without giving anything away that isn't in the national interest.'

'How do you know all this, Constance?' I asked.

'Oscar explained it all last night – when he came round with his new friend, Major Ridout.'

'The man who's been following him?' I said.

'Yes, Major Ridout works for the War Office. He's been keeping an eye on Oscar for months now, it seems – ever since Oscar joined the Club Autonomie. They wanted to be sure Oscar wasn't truly an anarchist.'

'Now I've heard everything!' spluttered Willie. 'Oscar Wilde, aesthete and anarchist, dilettante and terrorist – under surveillance from the War Office. I must drink to that.' He looked down the table. Mansfield was engaged with the two doctors. Sims and Shand were hugger-mugger. Oscar was holding court at his end of the table, clearly mid-anecdote. Willie caught Martin's eye: 'Waiter, more wine, if you please. I must drink to the Tite Street revolutionary.'

'Hush, Willie,' said Constance firmly. 'Isn't the soufflé delicious?'

36

Revelations

The soufflé was outstanding. The lamb cutlets that followed exactly right. And to round off the meal, there was a choice: a hot Chester pudding or fresh fruit salad. 'Can't I have both?' demanded Willie.

'Of course, sir,' said Martin. 'They go together nicely.'

'I'll be the judge of that,' said Willie, mopping his full lips with his napkin before taking another gulp of wine.

The combination of Martin, the wine, the food and Constance had succeeded in keeping Willie in check all night. By turns, he was combative and waspish, overbearing and bombastic, but he was amusing, too, and on those topics that interested him – Irish history, the London theatre, the breeding of wolfhounds – he talked with passion and perception. He was evidently obsessed with his younger brother and torn between scorning him and hankering after his respect and approbation. Constance handled him faultlessly, with the firmness of a loving mother and the sweetness of an understanding wife. Each time he appeared to be about to embarrass himself by addressing the table at large, she managed, with an extraordinary lightness of touch, to nip his outburst in the bud.

As pudding was cleared away, I looked around the candlelit table and the array of contented well-fed faces glowing in the dark and I marvelled at the scene. George R. Sims, seated on my right, read my mind. 'I hear from Macnaghten that another unknown girl was cut to death today and two old men were burned alive, yet here we are enjoying a thoroughly civilised evening. A splendid spread, congenial company. Odd, isn't it? Only in London . . .'

As Sims spoke, Oscar was on his feet once more. Gently he struck the side of a wine glass with the edge of a knife to command our attention. 'I think we can agree that the chef and his team and Martin and his colleagues have done us proud tonight . . .' There was a mellow murmur of assent. 'And now, the iron tongue of midnight having told twelve—'

'About twenty minutes ago!' interjected Richard Mansfield.

'Indeed,' said Oscar. 'It is now time for—'

'The Revelations!' cried George R. Sims.

'Exactly, George. The Revelations. There's cheese and port to keep us going – and, gentlemen, you may now smoke.'

Constance discreetly rose in her place and made to leave the table. 'Where are you going, my dear?' called Oscar. 'There's no need to leave – or, if you must for a moment, be sure to return.'

'Shall we have a moment's break, Wilde?' suggested Macnaghten. 'I could use a breath of fresh air.'

'Very good. No more than five minutes, gentlemen.' He considered his timepiece. 'If we resume as the clock strikes the half-hour, as I am an honest Puck I promise to release you all by one o'clock.'

For a moment the small dining room took on the semblance of a provincial assembly room as the last dance was being called: figures rose (some steadily, some less so) and moved from here to there, weaving their way around the room, smiling, bowing, bobbing, exchanging banter, asking after brandy, lighting cigars.

I accompanied Constance across the vestibule and up the small flight of stairs towards the ladies' powder room. 'Do you know what Oscar has in store for us?' I asked.

'I don't,' she said lightly, 'but I reminded him that all these dead girls were real people once, not characters in one of his short stories, let alone a fairy tale.'

'Of course, he is a playwright. He can't resist a touch of theatre.'

And so it proved. When we returned to the dining room, we found that Oscar had moved himself to the other end of the table. He now faced the room. And he had extinguished some of the table candles so that where he stood was bathed in light and his audience was seated in darkness.

'Sit where you please, gentlemen. And, Constance, you come sit by me.'

I escorted Mrs Wilde to her place and resumed my own. The rest of the party gradually returned to their seats. Willie was flushed and shambling as he collapsed into his chair. He had the look of the fallen giant in the last act of *Jack the Giant Killer*. By contrast, Mansfield and Salazkin, still in costume, were the last to return and appeared as spruce now as they had done on their arrival.

Oscar looked at me and smiled. 'Arthur, would you kindly lock the door?'

'You like a captive audience, do you, Oscar?' said Mansfield, taking his place with a chuckle.

'We don't want to be disturbed,' said Oscar smoothly.

When we were all seated and still, Oscar, having removed the shade from a candlestick, held it up to his face to light his cigarette. His pale cheeks shone, his tearful eyes sparkled, his full lips trembled.

'The Book of Life,' he said, 'begins with a man and a woman in a garden. It ends with Revelations.'

Suddenly, I thought of Olga. I felt her hand pressing mine. I looked up. It was Constance. She smiled at me reassuringly and whispered, 'Remember, Oscar's the cleverest man in England.'

I returned her smile: 'I know.'

'You are here this evening, my friends,' continued Oscar, 'because you are my friends – and because each of you, in a different way, has a connection with the tragedy of what Chief Constable Macnaghten of the Metropolitan Police calls "the Whitechapel murders" and the rest of us think of as the hideous case of Jack the Ripper.' He paused and drew slowly on his cigarette.

'You were quite a loss to the stage, Oscar,' murmured Richard Mansfield.

Oscar acknowledged the compliment with the hint of a smile. 'Our drama opens not in Whitechapel, but in Chelsea. We begin with a man and a woman, not in the Garden of Eden, but in Paradise Walk. Who are they, this couple? Not Adam and Eve, surely? No. They are better dressed, for a start. They are an English baronet and his good lady: Sir Freddie and Lady Bunbury. They have been married for nigh on fifty years – since before the Battle of Balaclava. Now he is old and tired. She is older still and at her wits' end. It is two weeks' ago exactly, and Sir Freddie brings his frail and failing wife down from Yorkshire to spend New Year's Eve at the home of the one friend he knows he can trust – an old courtier by the name of Festing Fitzmaurice. There,

Freddie Bunbury kills his wife. It is a mercy killing, for he loves her dearly.'

'It's murder nonetheless,' grunted Willie.

'Quite so. And how does he do it? How does Sir Freddie dispatch Lady Bunbury? Very simply, I suggest. After supper, when she is lying sleeping on Fitzmaurice's bed, he smothers her to death – with a handkerchief suffused with her own lavender-scented perfume.

'Sir Freddie Bunbury is an old soldier, an old courtier and an old gentleman. He has killed his wife to put an end to the misery of her existence – and to serve another purpose, too. He may have regarded it as an even greater good. Having killed his lady, the knight undresses her – removes every vestige of her clothing and every ring and ornament from about her person. Then he dresses her afresh with a serving woman's clothes and bonnet that his friend Festing Fitzmaurice keeps in his curious collection of women's apparel.'

'Can this be true?' muttered George R. Sims.

'I fear so,' I whispered.

'The hours pass until, at around three in the morning, a little earlier perhaps – there was no moon that night – the old soldier dons an apron and lifts the slight body of the old lady and carries it over his shoulder down the stairs, out into the yard and along the street for thirty paces. There he turns into the alleyway – Shelley Alley it's called – and, resting himself against the knife-grinder's cart that happens to be there, he heaves his burden – his dead's wife body – up against the wall. And now he does the dreadful deed – the deed that will lead us ultimately to the identity of Jack the Ripper.'

Oscar paused to draw once more on his cigarette. I looked back at the table. In the near-darkness cigar smoke hovered above the dining table. No one stirred.

'Well?' said Richard Mansfield eventually. 'You can only hold a pause so long, old man.'

Oscar closed his eyes as he continued. 'From out of his pocket, the old knight takes a small butcher's knife and from within his tortured soul somehow he finds the strength to do what he has to do. He thrusts his knee into his poor wife's belly and holds her heavy head hard against the brick wall. The palm of his left hand pushes up against her mouth and nostrils and he presses his fingers into the sockets of her eyes. In his right hand he holds his knife and, with the force of a hammer blow, he jabs it into the right-side of her neck, just below her jaw. He pulls out the knife and strikes again, this time tearing a line across her neck, from one side to the other, slitting her throat from ear to ear, plunging in the knife so deep that the tip of the blade reaches as far as her vertebrae.'

'No, Oscar, no,' murmured Constance, beneath her breath.

'Blood trickles from her and he steps back to let her body slide down the wall and slump to the ground. Bending down, he rolls the body over, tears open the poor woman's coat and jacket and blouse, pulls up her skirt and petticoats, and stabs her repeatedly in the chest and stomach and groin. In all, he strikes her thirty-nine times.'

George R. Sims cried out: 'In God's name, why?'

Oscar opened his eyes. 'To prove, once and for all, that Prince Albert Victor, Duke of Clarence and Avondale, was not and never could have been Jack the Ripper.'

'Is this possible?'

'If the Ripper was still at work, the Ripper could not be Prince Eddy – for Prince Eddy died two years ago.'

'How do you know all this, Oscar?' Willie asked the question.

'Some of this I surmise. Some of it I know. Chief Constable

Macnaghten smelled the lavender-scented perfume first when he examined the poor woman's corpse. Dr Conan Doyle and I smelled it again when we visited Fitzmaurice's room last Monday. That was where we came across Fitzmaurice's curious collection of female attire – much of it large enough to be worn by a man. Dr Doyle had observed that the clothes worn by the woman found in the alley were too large for her – and were a working woman's clothes, while the body of the victim, her complexion and her hands, suggested she was an older lady of some refinement.'

'How could a man do such a thing to his wife?' asked Henry Labouchere.

'To his wife's body, Labby – to a lifeless corpse. Sir Freddie loved his wife, I am certain of that. He loved Prince Eddy, too, and cherished the prince's memory – and used his wife's cadaver as an instrument, a tool, a means to draw a line under the unfounded slurs against the prince he loved and so rescue the prince's honour for eternity.'

'Extraordinary,' said Labouchere.

'I believe Bunbury planned all this with care,' continued Oscar. 'He wanted Jack the Ripper to strike again in the run-up to Prince Eddy's thirtieth birthday in anticipation of the lurid press specula-tion that the anniversary might reignite. He chose New Year's Eve.'

'But why did he choose Chelsea and not Whitechapel?' asked George R. Sims.

'There, I think, he had no choice. He was an old man: he could struggle from his friend's room in Paradise Walk to dump the body in a darkened alley close by, but he couldn't get a carriage to take it from Chelsea to Whitechapel – at least, not undetected. That is why, I am sure, he felt the need to replicate so carefully, so precisely, the exact murder of Martha Tabram. He wanted there to be no misunderstanding. This was to be the handiwork of Jack the Ripper – a living monster, not a dead prince. Bunbury had read the horrific details of the killing of Martha Tabram in August 1888. We all had. The newspapers had been full of them. Every savage stroke had been detailed in the coroner's report. Bunbury knew them all by heart.'

'Forgive me, Oscar,' said Sims, 'but some of us in the press later concluded that Martha Tabram's murder was not the work of the Ripper. I recall Macnaghten telling me that Jack the Ripper was responsible for just five killings – and Tabram's wasn't one of them.' Sims turned towards the chief constable. 'Isn't that right, Melville?'

'That's what I thought once,' replied the policeman quietly.

'But Bunbury was not privy to Chief Constable Macnaghten's thinking,' said Oscar. 'Nor, George, to yours. What he recalled was what he had read in the press – a poor woman in a dark alley, brutally cut to pieces and stabbed thirty-nine times. It was the number that lodged in his memory. . . So, with precision, counting the strokes, he recreated that murder that Sunday night – and went back to his friend Fitzmaurice's room to burn his apron in the grate. By Monday lunchtime he was back at his club. On Tuesday morning, the second of January, he will have read about the discovery of the body in the newspapers. On the Wednesday, from his club, he wired home to Yorkshire to tell his servants that their mistress had passed away and to report that he would be returning home with her body for the burial in due course.

'On the Saturday of the week of the murder, the sixth of January, he appeared at our friend George R. Sims' Twelfth Night party – in mourning, naturally, and there, having announced his wife's death in the columns of *The Times* the day before, received the sympathy of his friends – all of whom knew his poor wife had been in failing health and none of whom was surprised.

323

'What surprised me was his insistence that I should join him the following Monday for "a picnic lunch" to celebrate the birthday of Prince Eddy. I knew Sir Freddie, but I did not know him well. Why did he want me there? And with my friend, Dr Conan Doyle? I believe it was because he wanted to share his secret.'

'And did he?' asked Willie.

'Not in so many words, Willie, but the most interesting books are the ones where the truth is told between the lines. He told enough. He made it clear that he loved his wife and he loved Prince Eddy. He made it clear that his ultimate ambition was to the rescue the prince's reputation from the mire of suspicion. He made it clear that neither he nor his friend Fitzmaurice were long for this world.'

'Fitzmaurice was the bugger who was caught with the regimental goat?' queried Labouchere from out of the darkness.

'Careful, old man,' said Alec Shand. 'There's a lady present.'

'Ah,' said Oscar, 'you recall the story, Labby. So many of the best are remembered through the prism of their downfall. When Dr Doyle and I saw Festing Fitzmaurice last Monday he was no longer of this world – *sans* everything, save a curious sense of style – and I believed Sir Freddie when he told us that Festing was starving himself to death deliberately. I thought it would be tomorrow that Bunbury planned to take his own life – the anniversary of Prince Eddy's death and the day before he was due to return to Yorkshire for his wife's funeral when, of course, his story of her demise by natural causes might begin to unravel. But he chose to do it today . . .'

'At lunchtime,' said Macnaghten firmly from the far end of the table. 'He blew himself up with a home-made mortar, hours after savagely killing another woman in the same alley in much the same way.'

'No, Chief Constable, that wasn't Bunbury.'

'Can you be sure?'

'Quite sure. This morning's brutal murder – that was the work of Jack the Ripper.'

37

The promised end

In the distance the church clock struck one.

'Oh,' said Oscar, startled. 'It is the witching hour. And so soon. My time is up. I promised to release you all by one o'clock.'

'Don't be a damn fool, Wilde,' barked Henry Labouchere irritably. 'Just get to the point, man – with a little less of your flowery witching-twitching circumlocution.'

'For what it's worth,' said Walter Wellbeloved quietly, 'it is not yet the witching hour. In pagan ritual, the witching hour falls between three and four o'clock.'

Another voice spoke softly in the darkness:

Tis now the very witching time of night,
When churchyards yawn and hell itself breathes out
Contagion to this world: now could I drink hot blood
And do such bitter business as the day
Would quake to look on.

'I wish I'd seen your Hamlet, Mansfield,' murmured George R. Sims appreciatively.

Oscar laughed and, leaning forward, poured more port into his glass. 'Suddenly, after a long silence, all our Jack the Rippers speak at once!' He raised his wine to the figures in the shadows. 'Not that I'm accusing you of being him, gentlemen – but others have, as you know. Indeed, that's why you're here. And our doctors are here because two more of the accused have been consigned to their charge.'

Dr Rogerson spoke up: 'We're listening, Mr Wilde. We're here with rapt attention.'

'Which I appreciate,' replied Oscar, with a small bow. 'The more so, since my brother seems to be asleep.'

I glanced across the table. Willie Wilde had his hands folded comfortably across his ample stomach and his bearded chin was lolling on his chest. Whether or not his eyes were open, I could not see.

'He's not asleep,' said Sims. 'If he were, we'd hear him snoring.' A gentle chuckle rippled around the room.

'It's interesting,' said Alec Shand, 'how often we laugh when we are most afraid.'

'We'll give you fifteen minutes more, Wilde,' announced Labouchere, 'and then we're off to bed. We're all busy people.' I watched his silhouette turn to either side of him. 'The doctors have to get back to their lunatics, Salazkin's got to get to Paris—'

'And Labby has the Empire to run,' threw in George R. Sims.

'Very well,' said Oscar. 'I will be brief.'

'Who was this Jack the Ripper?' demanded Labouchere. 'Who is he? That's all we want to know.'

'I can tell you,' said Melville Macnaghten emphatically. 'The Whitechapel murderer was the doctor, Druitt, who killed himself after murdering Mary Jane Kelly. And the Chelsea murderer was Sir Frederick Bunbury, who took his own life today. I'm grateful to Mr Wilde and to Dr Doyle for unravelling the mystery of these latest killings.'

'And we are grateful to you, Chief Constable, for involving us in the matter and inviting me to bring what you charmingly called my "poet's eye" to the proceedings.' Oscar was full of energy once more. 'But Montague John Druitt was not a doctor. He was a barrister and a schoolmaster and he could not have been Jack the Ripper because there are reliable witnesses who will testify that he was nowhere near Whitechapel at the time of any one of the Whitechapel murders. His suicide came from quite another cause.'

'So who was Jack the Ripper?' demanded Labouchere. 'We've not got all night.'

Oscar breathed deeply as he lit another cigarette. 'Very well,' he said again. He considered the cloud of smoke as it filtered from his mouth and nostrils, as if the monster might appear from the miasmal mist. 'Who was he? Who is he? He seems to have been so many people since his arrival – and his christening – six years ago.'

He looked towards George R. Sims and then down at the slumped figure of Willie Wilde. 'To the gentlemen of the press – and to the public at large – he was whoever they could fix a name to. Who is interested in a murderer "name unknown"? But call him "Leather Apron" or, better still, "Jack the Ripper", and now there's a shivering up the spine and the papers start to sell. And bring in "celebrity" – a crass coinage for a noxious notion – and the whole kingdom is suddenly agog. Could it be Her Majesty's grandson, the heir to the heir to the throne? We've heard rum talk about him. It's a notorious crime, let's pin it on someone famous! What do you say? Lewis Carroll or George R. Sims?'

Sims chuckled obligingly.

'In the course of our investigation,' Oscar continued, 'with the help of Mr Wellbeloved and his friend Mrs Mathers, Dr Doyle and I took part in a séance. I was reminded then how often it is that when we try to contact "the other side" we expect to be greeted by an immortal of note. There must be millions of lost souls waiting out there in the ether, but when we come knocking we don't want any Tom, Dick or Harry responding to our summons. We want to find Joan of Arc or Charlemagne or Napoleon at the door.'

Oscar searched out Richard Mansfield in the gloom. The actor's monocle glistened in the candlelight. 'Mr Mansfield is playing Dr Jekyll and Mr Hyde in the Strand. He's been seen in Whitechapel after dark. He's famous. Let's make him Jack the Ripper.'

'Are you saying it's Mansfield?' interrupted Sims. 'That's preposterous.'

'Richard Mansfield has no alibis for the witching hours when the Whitechapel murders took place – though I acknowledge that he was on stage when the second of the bodies was left in the alley by Paradise Walk last week.'

'If your "poet's eye" has lighted on Mansfield, Oscar, you need to visit your oculist.'

'I'm merely saying, George, that – encouraged by the popular press – the public warms to the idea of a multiple murderer who looks the part. Richard III, Mr Hyde, Napoleon . . . these are monsters to reckon with.'

Mansfield said nothing. From what I could tell in the half-light, he appeared amused.

Oscar smiled. 'That's Jack the Ripper for the multitude,' he said. 'But, closer to home, nearer to the scene of the crime, he becomes a different character. According to the two policemen that Dr Doyle and I encountered as we walked the streets of

Whitechapel, whoever he was, the Ripper wasn't going to be a local man. There was too much blood and guts for that. He was going to be a stranger, an outsider, "a foreigner most like". Over many months the police collected hundreds of statements from so-called witnesses – people who had been in the vicinity at the time of one or more of the murders. Some thought they might have seen the man – but none was sure. Not one! They'd seen a figure near the scene of the crime on the night in question. Some said he was tall. More said he was short. Some called him swarthy, some called him pale. One was sure he had a limp. Few thought him clean-shaven. Most gave him a moustache; others a grizzled beard. But how could they tell in Whitechapel by night? It's darker than this room is now – and rolling up from the Thames there's invariably a mist and, as often as not, a pea-souper of a fog. Jack the Ripper could be anyone.'

'There needs no ghost come from the grave to tell us this, Oscar,' said Richard Mansfield, without rancour.

'Indeed not, sir, but I believe it was a ghost of sorts who told us where we should be looking – the ghost of Lizzie Stride.'

'Lizzie Stride?' repeated Dr Rogerson.

'Elizabeth Stride – the third of the Macnaghten victims. Dr Doyle and I encountered her sister, Stella, plying her trade in the very alley where poor Lizzie lost her life.'

I spoke – without thinking. 'Two Jacks for the price of one,' I said.

'Exactly, Arthur. "There might have been two of them." That's what Stella Stride said. One to watch and one to act. One to hold the lamp, one to do the deed. One to be the lookout, while the other wielded the knife. In all the reports of all the murders, very few cries for help were heard. Did one man cover the victim's mouth while the other began the butchery? And, as butchers, did they take it in turn to carve the joint? The police, led by Chief Constable Macnaghten, believe that only five of the Whitechapel murders can be attributed to Jack the Ripper because only five of the victims were slaughtered in the same way. But there were eleven brutal murders in Whitechapel between the summer of 1888 and the spring of 1891 and a further two, not-dissimilar ones, in Paradise Walk this past week. Thirteen in all. In some, the victims were slashed – mutilated and disembowelled. In others, the victims were stabbed – dismembered and decapitated. Thirteen murders. Two modus operandi. Two Jacks for the price of one.'

'But no witnesses spoke of seeing two men together?' said Melville Macnaghten.

'No one was looking for two men. Everyone was looking for Jack the Ripper.'

'Two men,' repeated Labouchere. 'Two men, hunting together – off and on over a period of almost six years. Could two men keep a secret for so long?'

'Yes,' said Oscar, 'I believe so, if they had a bond.'

'A bond?' queried Sims.

'If they were brothers, for example.' He glanced down at the slumped figure of Willie and smiled. He looked up across the table. 'Or felt they were brothers because they were both beleaguered Jews in a foreign land.'

'You mean Kosminski and Ostrog?' asked Dr Rogerson.

I spoke without considering my words. 'And Kosminski did the stabbing and decapitating while Ostrog slashed his victims and removed their internal organs with his knife.'

'Rather the other way around, I think,' said Oscar lightly.

'It's not possible, Mr Wilde,' said Dr Rogerson. 'You've seen Kosminski. He is an incapable imbecile. We keep him under lock and key. Even were he to escape, he hasn't the strength for barbaric crimes like these.'

'And five years ago?' asked Oscar.

'He was stronger then, yes,' said Rogerson, 'but I examined him on his admission – at length. There is nothing in anything he said that would suggest in any way that he was involved in murders such as these.'

'I can believe it,' said Oscar. 'Perhaps he did not know what he had done. Is it possible to wipe the memory clean?'

'Yes,' said Dr Gabriel, 'psychogenic amnesia is not unknown.'

'And what causes it?' asked Oscar.

'Severe abuse of alcohol, trauma to the head. It can be induced by hypnosis.'

'Never mind that,' said Dr Rogerson. 'Kosminski is not capable of the murders that have taken place this week. You have seen him with your own eyes. You must know that.'

'However,' said Oscar slowly, 'Ostrog might be.'

I looked up at Oscar. 'But Ostrog was in Paris last week when the second body was found in the alley off Paradise Walk.'

'Who told us that?'

'Mr Salazkin did,' I said. 'He told us Ostrog was in Paris on circus business, taking publicity material to the French printers or some such.'

'Indeed, Arthur, that's what we were told.' Oscar lit one of his Vestas. The flame flared and for a moment illuminated the table. The eyes I saw were all turned towards Salazkin. The ringmaster sat impassively at the far end of the table.

'Two Jacks – one King,' said Oscar. He lit his next cigarette and drew on it deeply. As he exhaled the blue-grey smoke, he set out his stall with the calm authority of an Old Bailey barrister. 'My friend Dr Conan Doyle once told me that the most difficult crime to track is the one which is purposeless. He is right, of course. He invariably is. But the first crimes – the Whitechapel murders – had a purpose – and a clear one.'

'Beyond the senseless mutilation of defenceless women?' asked George R. Sims.

'Oh, yes,' said Oscar. 'That was but the means to the end.'

'And what was the end?' asked Sims.

'Terror and confusion,' said Oscar. 'The Whitechapel murders were acts of terrorism.'

'Explain,' said Labouchere.

'Either acting on his own account or at the behest of his masters in St Petersburg, our country's "friendly informer", Ivan Salazkin, brought his Russian Circus to London and set about creating a little mayhem on the side. Whether he is a true revolutionary or an anarchist or, as I suspect, simply a monster with bloodlust in his veins – he is proud to claim descent from the countess who slaughtered young women by the score so that she could take baths in their blood – who knows? What I do know is that his circus was in London at Easter 1888 when Emma Smith was murdered. Before she died she said she had been the victim of two or three assailants. It could be that Salazkin was guilty of the crime or – more likely, in my estimation – it could be that the reports of her murder inspired his killing spree when the circus returned to London in August that year.'

'Is this possible?' hissed Labouchere. He turned to Salazkin. 'Say something, man.'

Salazkin said nothing.

'The dates all fit,' continued Oscar calmly. 'The Russian Circus was in London at the time of ten of the eleven Whitechapel murders. The exception is the twentieth of December 1888, when the circus was in Paris and Rose Mylett's body was found.'

'She died of strangulation,' said Macnaghten.

'As I recall,' said Oscar. 'Her death cannot be laid at Salazkin's door – except perhaps in the sense that every unexplained murder after the first few was heralded by our sensationalist newspapers as marking the return of Jack the Ripper. If the ringmaster's purpose was to spread terror in the streets of the capital, the gentlemen of the press certainly assisted him in his endeavour.'

Labouchere had his eyes fixed on the immobile Salazkin. Without turning towards Oscar, he asked: 'If terrorising the public at large was the object, why were the victims all prostitutes?'

'I am not sure that they were,' said Oscar. 'A torso was found under the railway arch in Pinchin Street in Whitechapel on 10 September 1889. No one had been reported missing. The victim was unidentifiable and unknown. And is so still. But at his Exotic Emporium in Whitechapel, Tom Norman told us that he had acquired a female head a few years ago – it had been washed up in the Thames – and later, when we saw that head preserved in formaldehyde, loosely disguised as the head of John the Baptist, Dr Doyle and I both noticed the young woman's Slavic high cheekbones. I don't believe she was a prostitute. I think it more likely that she was one of Salazkin's troupe of orphaned acrobats – killed on a whim and left in pieces in Whitechapel.'

'But most were prostitutes,' persisted Labouchere.

'Indeed,' said Oscar. 'Most were. Prostitutes were easy prey. And Ostrog and Kosminski were regular customers. They knew the territory. I doubt Salazkin went to Whitechapel himself on the nights his crimes were committed. He is a ringmaster, after all. He cracks the whip and the animals do his bidding.'

'They'd kill for him?'

'Without any difficulty. Have you not seen hypnotists at work at the fairground and the music hall? They can persuade almost anyone who is susceptible to do almost anything they command, however unlikely, however absurd, however evil – and, after the event, to have no recollection of what they have done.'

'But then the killing stopped,' said Labouchere.

'Yes,' said Oscar. 'The mischief had been done. Terror had been spread. It hadn't overthrown the government, to be sure, but it had unsettled the citizens and distracted the police. And now any unexplained murder was laid at the feet of the infamous Jack the Ripper. No further killing was required. Besides, Salazkin is no fool. He knows that in the circus you walk the tightrope. You don't fall off. He was never going to run the risk of getting caught. His creatures – his instruments of death, Ostrog and Kosminski – were recognised Whitechapel habitués and, by now, under suspicion. Nothing could be proved against them, but the authorities had them in their sights and contrived to have them put away. Each was committed to a lunatic asylum. Salazkin was content to let Kosminski go, but because he valued him, Salazkin found a way to save Ostrog from incarceration.'

'What do you mean?' asked Dr Gabriel.

'That the man you hold in your asylum, Dr Gabriel, is not Michael Ostrog but a substitute – a drink-sodden destitute found beneath the arches in Pinchin Street.'

'Where the blazes is Ostrog, then?' demanded Dr Gabriel.

'He was here, just outside in the vestibule, earlier this evening. He arrived with his master. I saw him.' Oscar glanced at his time-piece. 'By now I believe he will be in the custody of Major Ridout of the War Office.'

'And Kosminski?' asked Dr Rogerson.

'You hold him, Dr Rogerson. Yours is the genuine article.'

'You are making extraordinary allegations, Wilde,' said Labouchere.

'But why does not Mr Salazkin rebut them?' asked Sims.

In the darkness Salazkin raised a hand and waved it towards Oscar dismissively.

Oscar smiled. 'What can he say? Ostrog and Kosminski may not realise what they have done – what, through hypnosis, they have been made to do – but Salazkin knows the truth. He knows, too, that were it not for his hubris, he might have taken his dark secret to the grave. Instead, ten days ago, almost five years since the last of the Whitechapel murders, his arrogance got the better of him.' Oscar sipped at his port and smiled grimly. 'I fear that I am partly to blame for that.' He paused.

'Go on,' said Richard Mansfield. 'You're holding the house. Not a mouse stirring.'

Oscar continued: 'On New Year's Eve, Sir Frederick Bunbury "murdered" his wife just as Ostrog had murdered Martha Tabram. The story appeared in the paper. When I saw Salazkin at the circus shortly afterwards, foolishly I mentioned a detail that had not featured in the newspaper report. I spoke of the thirty-nine stab wounds and, I fear, in doing so, rekindled Salazkin's bloodlust. Why not bring Jack the Ripper out of retirement and have some fun with him once more? Sow some more confusion, spread a little terror in a different part of town – make some mischief in the street where my friend Oscar Wilde lives.

'Kosminski was no longer available to do Salazkin's bidding, but Ostrog was at his command as ever. And there was no need to travel to Whitechapel to find a victim. Salazkin could supply his own victims – girls from the circus would do. They often ran off without explanation. Dr Doyle examined the first of these new victims in the police morgue. She was young, well-nourished and strong. I imagine Salazkin – who liked to have his way with the girls – asphyxiated her during the act of darkness and left the rest to Ostrog. The circus yard contains two covered carts customarily used to carry and butcher the meat for the circus's wild animals. I imagine that's where Ostrog did his grisly work before driving the cart to Paradise Walk and dumping the poor girl's remains in the alley there.'

'Can this be possible?' asked Macnaghten in a hollow voice.

'Once you eliminate the impossible, Chief Constable, whatever remains, no matter how improbable, must be the truth.'

'This is so grotesque, Wilde,' said George R. Sims.

'Life imitates art, George. She always has. And lurid melo-drama has long been a staple of the English stage.'

Henry Labouchere had got to his feet. He stood over the motionless figure of Ivan Salazkin. 'Come, sir, Mr Wilde has made the most extraordinary allegations against you. Have you nothing to say?'

Salazkin pushed his chair back from the table, but made no sound.

'He does not need to speak,' said Oscar. 'His eyes have already told us all we need to know.' My friend looked around the room and raised his voice a little. 'You are all here tonight for a reason. Alec Shand is here for a particular one. He has written a book based on some remarkable research. He kindly sent me a copy and in it I read the details of an experiment that proved that if you show to someone a photograph of a young child smiling, it is impossible for the person seeing the picture not to smile them-selves. It is the natural, automatic human response. Only those with what the medical men now call "a psychotic personality" show no emotion in their eyes when confronted with a happy photograph of a happy child. Knowing of this experiment, I obliged my friend Dr Doyle to show a photograph of his two charming children to several of you – as you will recall. And all of you smiled – save one. Salazkin did not smile. Salazkin looked at the picture and showed no emotion. The eyes are the mirror to the soul. Everything you feel, they show. You cannot hide it. And if your eyes are dead it's because your soul is dead. Salazkin feels nothing. That may be why he is not even moving now.'

'Lights!' cried Mansfield. 'Give us some lights!'

Suddenly the room was full of movement. We had sat trans-fixed for an hour, caught in Oscar's spell. Now, at Mansfield's command, Macnaghten, Wellbeloved, the doctors, Shand – all were on their feet, reaching into their pockets for matches and striking them, lighting the candles around the table and in the sconces. In no more than a matter of seconds, the room was filled with light.

And all became clear at once. The immovable figure at the head of the table was not Ivan Salazkin: it was Michael Ostrog, dressed in the ringmaster's costume, hidden behind his master's beard and whiskers. Oscar began to laugh.

'What is the meaning of this?' cried Macnaghten.

'We've been gulled, Chief Constable,' roared Oscar. 'After we'd finished our meal and before I launched into my exposition, in a cubiculo in the gentlemen's lavatory, Salazkin and Ostrog must have changed clothes and changed places. We've been gulled by the oldest trick in the magician's handbook.'

'Where will he be now?' demanded Macnaghten angrily.

'Salazkin? Halfway to Dover, I imagine.'

'We must stop him!' cried Macnaghten.

'Will Major Ridout not have stopped him?' I asked.

'No. I warned Ridout about Ostrog, but Salazkin was our "guest of honour" tonight. He was Labby's "friendly informer", remember – a Foreign Office favourite. Major Ridout will doubt-less have saluted as he passed and waved him on his way.'

'Perhaps that's best, Wilde,' said Labouchere, looking down at the still motionless figure of Michael Ostrog. 'This is the man who committed the crimes. You've satisfied us of that. Dr Gabriel is here. Macnaghten can no doubt provide a police escort to accompany the doctor and his patient back to the asylum. That's where he should be. Kosminski is still under the charge of Dr Rogerson. We need say no more about whatever else you have disclosed to us tonight. What purpose would it serve?'

'The truth?' murmured Oscar.

Labouchere shook his head. 'Over the years Salazkin has done the state some service. He has brought us intelligence of value from other countries. He has alerted us to the existence of anarchists at work here in London. Something is being plotted even as we speak. We are aware of that, thanks to Salazkin. He has been an ally to our government. Do we want to reveal to the world that an ally of the government is Jack the Ripper? Besides, as you tell it, Wilde, he masterminded these crimes. He did not commit them.' Labouchere looked around the room and his steady gaze carried undeniable authority. 'Mrs Wilde, gentlemen, I hope we can be agreed: in the national interest, whether they are to be believed or not, tonight's revelations should not leave this room. They are for us to know and no one else.'

'So,' said Oscar softly, 'we all have secrets and these are to be ours. The world is not to know the true identity of Jack the Ripper?'

'You've established that Mansfield and Wellbeloved are innocent,' said Labouchere. 'That's enough.'

'And what you've told us about Druitt I accept as well,' said Macnaghten gravely. He was on his feet and, I now saw, holding a pair of iron handcuffs. He looked down at Ostrog. 'On your feet,' he ordered. 'Give me your hands.' Ostrog obeyed. Macnaghten slipped the handcuffs over the man's wrists. 'Case closed.'

'Who has the key to the room?' asked Labouchere.

'I do,' I said. I moved around the table and unlocked the door. Within a minute they were all gone. Labouchere, Macnaghten and the two doctors surrounded the unresisting Ostrog as they led him away. Wellbeloved and Mansfield followed, with George R. Sims and Alec Shand bringing up the rear.

'I'm glad the book proved useful,' said Shand. 'Did you notice that it was dedicated to Constance?'

'I did,' said Oscar. 'The eyes are indeed the windows to the soul. I see yours, Alec, and I notice that you love her still.'

'Goodnight, Oscar,' said Shand, smiling. 'Goodnight, Constance.' He kissed her hand and bowed and went on his way.

Martin the waiter came into the room. 'Is all well, sir?' he asked cheerily.

'Yes, Martin, thank you. Have they all gone?'

'They're getting into the carriages now, sir. None of them tipped me and they all looked a bit dazed, sir, if I'm honest. I hope the meal was to your liking?'

'It was all most excellent, Martin.' Oscar reached into his pocket and produced two sovereigns, which he handed to the boy. 'I think my guests were somewhat preoccupied.'

'Thank you, Mr Wilde. You're the best. I will begin to clear now, sir, if I may.'

'Give us just a moment, would you, Martin?'

'Of course, sir.' The waiter touched his forelock and left the room.

'Will you come home tonight?' asked Constance. 'I would be grateful.'

'Yes, my dear.' Oscar smiled. 'I rather think I'd better or, before I know it, you'll have left me for Alec Shand.'

'I shall read his book with interest,' I said.

'It won't disappoint you,' said Oscar. 'It cracked the case so far as I was concerned. When Salazkin looked at that photograph of your sweet children he showed no emotion whatsoever – though I imagine he recognised the delight the picture gave to others and resented it.'

'Can we drop off Willie in Oakley Street?' asked Constance.

'Oh no,' said Oscar. 'He'll wake up the whole house. He can have my room here at the hotel.' Oscar went over to his slumbering brother and shook him by the shoulder.

Willie opened his bloodshot eyes and looked up blearily. 'Is that you, Oscar?'

'It is, Willie. I trust you slept well.'

'Did I nod off? My apologies, old man. Did I miss the best of your performance? I so often do.'

'Oh no,' said Oscar, 'not this time. I have kept the best till last.'

'And what's that?'

'We were speaking of Jack the Ripper ...'

'I know.'

'You recall how the name of Jack the Ripper entered the public domain?'

'I do,' said Willie, rubbing his eyes and smacking his lips. 'It came from a letter and a postcard sent to the Central News Agency at the height of the killings in 1888 and purporting to come from the murderer himself.'

'But the letter and the postcard did not come from any murderer.'

'Did they not?'

'What murderer would think of sending a letter to a news

agency? A murderer would send it to a newspaper or to the police. Only a journalist would write to a news agency. Only a journalist would know the news agency's address.'

'Is that so?' said Willie, getting to his feet and stretching his broad shoulders as he did so. 'And do you know who that journalist was?'

'Yes, Willie, I do,' said Oscar.

'Oh, really?'

'Yes, really. It was you, Willie. It was you who gave Jack the Ripper his name.'

'And what makes you so certain, Oscar? Is this another poetic leap?'

'No, this comes from the evidence of my own eyes. Chief Constable Macnaghten gave me a file containing a photographic copy of the letter and the postcard. They were written in a deliberately awkward, childish hand, but I recognised it the moment that I saw it. We were boys together, remember, Willie. I knew at once that I had seen that hand before.'

AFTERMATH

1924

These events took place thirty years ago, in the first two weeks of 1894, and the discretion that Henry Labouchere demanded of us all that night in the Winter Room of the Langham Hotel each of us has shown in the intervening years.

On the morning after Oscar's night of revelations, the Russian Circus left London, never to return. Four weeks later, on 15 February 1894, an anarchist – one Martial Bourdin – was killed by his own bomb outside the Royal Observatory in Greenwich Park. Bourdin was a member of the Club Autonomie and his name was known to the authorities because it was on a list supplied to them by Ivan Salazkin.

Oscar was always fascinated by the power of names. 'Would that young man have turned to bomb-making,' he asked, 'if his name had not been Martial? Would I be as I am, were I not called Wilde?'

I saw much less of my friend in the months that followed and when I did see him I found him increasingly wild, gripped by a growing ego-mania that seemed to me to border on lunacy. He enjoyed a year of extraordinary theatrical success, culminating in the productions of *An Ideal Husband* and *The Importance of Being Earnest*, but these professional triumphs coincided with personal disaster. His young friend, Lord Alfred Douglas, returned to England and he and Wilde resumed their intimate relationship. Douglas's father, the Marquess of Queensberry, pursued them both to a bitter end. In the early summer of 1895, Wilde was tried for offences of gross indecency and sentenced to two years' imprisonment with hard labour. The presiding judge was Mr Justice Wills, who lived across the way from the Wildes and Melville Macnaghten in Tite Street, Chelsea.

Constance Wilde, one of the loveliest and most decent women I ever knew, stayed loyal to her husband to the last. She died in Italy, following an unsuccessful operation, on 7 April 1898, aged only thirty-nine. My own amiable and gentle wife, Touie, succumbed to tuberculosis in 1906, aged forty-nine. My second wife, Jean, whom I married the following year, has brought me all the comfort and joy I have known since.

Oscar found no such consolation. After his release from prison in 1897, he rekindled his friendship with Lord Alfred Douglas, but it was not as it had been before. Oscar died aged forty-six, alone and in debt, in a small hotel in Paris, on 30 November 1900. His nemesis, The Marquess of Queensberry, died at the beginning of the same year, on 31 January 1900, aged fifty-five. Lord Alfred Douglas is alive still. After Wilde's death, he married and fathered one son. He writes poetry which is admired by some.

Henry Labouchere died in 1912, aged eighty-one. As a member of parliament, Labouchere's principal legacy remains the amendment he introduced to Section 11 of the Criminal Law

Amendment Act 1885. This was the legislation that, for the first time, outlawed all male homosexual activity and enabled the successful prosecution of Oscar Wilde. Labby was a controversial and combative figure and I liked him, though many didn't. He operated *sub rosa*, partly because he enjoyed the excitement of secret operations, but, also, because he was denied formal public office. The prime minister, William Gladstone, wanted him in his Cabinet, but Queen Victoria vetoed the appointment on the grounds that Labouchere was disrespectful of royalty.

Royalty had no such reservations in the case of Melville Macnaghten. Chief Constable of the CID in 1894, he went on to become Assistant Commissioner of the Metropolitan Police in 1903, was knighted in 1907, created a Companion of the Order of the Bath in 1912 and awarded the King's Police Medal in 1913. He died quite recently, in 1921, aged sixty-eight. Shortly before his passing I read his autobiography, *Days of My Years*, and went to visit him in the mansion flat in Westminster where lived out his retirement. His book made no mention of the momentous events of the first two weeks of 1894. When I saw him, he said, 'You do understand why?'

'I think so,' I answered tentatively, hoping to coax more from him.

'What could I say?' he asked. 'Labouchere had called for our discretion and with good reason. Ivan Salazkin had undoubtedly been of use to the British government – he had been a "friendly informer" for several years – and his accuser was the unfortunate Wilde, who, while undeniably brilliant and probably correct in every conjecture regarding the Whitechapel murders, had few true friends in high places and was quickly engulfed in a scandal of his own that led to his disgrace and imprisonment.'

'Why did that happen?' I asked. 'London was awash with men

of a similar inclination to Wilde, but they weren't prosecuted and imprisoned. To avoid scandal, they were allowed – even encouraged – to leave the country. They weren't sent to gaol.'

Macnaghten shrugged. 'Wilde brought about his own downfall,' he said, sucking on his unlit pipe. 'Wilde was properly tried. He was guilty as charged.'

'But why was he charged?' I persisted. 'He could simply have been advised to flee to France – as others were.'

'Wilde had become unhinged. We were fearful of what he might do and say.'

'"We"? Who do you mean by "we"?'

'The authorities – the Metropolitan Police, the War Office, Labouchere . . . There was nothing to be gained by letting the world know that Jack the Ripper was a *quasi* secret agent who had supplied intelligence to the British government. *That* would have caused a scandal! In the months that followed Wilde's night of "revelations" at the Langham Hotel, he grew increasingly reckless. In one of his plays, he even included a mythical character called Bunbury! At large, he was a loose cannon. When the chance came to have him put away, we seized it. I'm sure you understand.'

I said nothing.

Macnaghten continued, reflectively: 'I was in court throughout Wilde's trial. On the final day, as he was sentenced, he looked up from the dock and called out to the judge, "And I, my lord, am I to say nothing?" My heart was in my mouth, I can tell you. What might he not have said? Fortunately, Mr Justice Wills silenced him at once and sent him down to the cells.'

'And in prison, of course, he could say nothing.'

'And once released he was a ruined man – who went into exile, drifted around Europe and drank too much. Whatever he said then would not matter. No one would be listening.'

'And what happened to Salazkin?' I asked.

'Salazkin and his circus left the country and never returned.'

'Do we know anything more of him?'

'I made some inquiries – discreetly, of course. From police contacts in France and Germany, I learned that while the circus continued to tour, Salazkin was no longer part of it. He appeared to have vanished into thin air – or at least to have returned to Russia. I heard nothing of him until much more recently – a few years ago, just after the end of the war. I was staying with a friend for the weekend – a former diplomat – and, leafing through his scrapbooks, I came across a newspaper cutting about the aftermath of the October Revolution in Russia. There were photographs of some of those who had been executed. One was named as Ivan Salazkin, Minister of Culture in the Russian Provisional Government of 1917. It was a small photograph, not distinct, but I think it was our man.'

'So, Jack the Ripper died in 1917,' I said. Macnaghten made no reply, but smiled. 'And what of Kosminski and Ostrog?' I asked.

'Kosminski died in the lunatic asylum, just recently. According to Dr Rogerson he was a virtual vegetable at the end. He is buried in the Jewish cemetery in East Ham. Rogerson and I were the only people to attend the interment. There was nothing to be gained from trying to prosecute him and Ostrog, of course. They could have given no evidence of value. Salazkin was back in Russia and Wilde was in Reading Gaol.'

'What of Ostrog?'

'I believe he is dead, too, but I cannot be sure. Officially, "Michael Ostrog" died in the Surrey County Lunatic Asylum sometime in 1904, but that "Ostrog" was the substitute – the vagrant from underneath the arches in Pinchin Street, not the real man. When we left the Langham Hotel that night, we took the real Ostrog directly to the asylum. Dr Gabriel agreed to keep him as a secure patient for the rest of his natural life, but on condition that he could invent a new alias for him. As Gabriel said, Ostrog had lived his life under a string of aliases: one more would make no difference. I didn't object, because Ostrog should have been inside the asylum in any event – he had been correctly committed there even if, initially, with Salazkin's help, he had managed to evade his incarceration. And I could understand that Gabriel – a good man doing a difficult job – did not want it known that for years he had had a patient who had been locked up in error and whose identity was unknown. He advised me to forget all about Ostrog. He told me that our lunatic asylums are full of people who don't know who they are or were. He said, rather amusingly, that at Surrey County hardly a month goes by without a new patient arriving claiming to be Jack the Ripper.' He laughed. 'Once all the lunatics wanted to be Napoleon. Now it seems it's either Jack the Ripper or Sherlock Holmes.'

I liked Macnaghten. He was a decent man whose instincts were sound. I enquired after the report he had prepared on the Whitechapel murders – the one that Oscar and I had been privy to in draft. He told me that in the final report, submitted to his superiors, he had removed the names of Richard Mansfield and Walter Wellbeloved from his list of suspects, but other than that had let it stand as it was.

Most, but not all, of those who were in that room at the Langham Hotel on that memorable night in January 1894 are dead now.

Richard Mansfield died in New London, Connecticut, in 1907, aged just fifty. The *New York Times* said of him: 'He was the greatest actor of his hour, and one of the greatest of all times.' His last major success was in the title role of *Ivan the Terrible*.

Mina Mathers is still alive, the head of the occult order, the Alpha et Omega, which she runs from a magic shop near the British Library, with the assistance of her devoted acolyte Walter Wellbeloved, now in his mid-seventies and still mourning his beloved mermaid.

Tom Norman is still alive, too. It seems that he did not leave England as he had planned, but moved across London from Whitechapel to Croydon, where he married a music-hall artiste named Amy and together, in short order, they had six sons and four daughters. The last I heard of him, he had opened an exhibition in the seaside resort of Margate, with, as his star attraction, Phoebe the Strange Girl.

Willie Wilde married his fiancée, Lily Lees, that January, as planned. Oscar did not attend the wedding. Oscar's friend, the writer and caricaturist, Max Beerbohm, said of Willie: *'Quel monstre!* Dark, oily, suspect yet awfully like Oscar; he has Oscar's coy, carnal smile & fatuous giggle, & not a little of Oscar's *esprit.* But he is awful – a veritable tragedy of family-likeness.' In July 1895, Willie and Lily had their only child, Dolly. Within four years, Willie was dead. He was aged forty-six. It was the drink that killed him.

'Do you think Willie died happy?' Oscar asked, when I saw him for the last time. This was in Paris, early in 1900. Before I could answer my friend's question, he did so himself. (Towards the end, that was his style.) 'Probably not,' he said, 'although perhaps he should have done. Giving a name to Jack the Ripper has turned a monster into a myth – and a myth that will last longer than any that I have created.' He looked up from his glass of absinthe and smiled at me. His teeth were green and jagged, but there was a sweetness to his smile. 'Now your Sherlock Holmes, Arthur, he will stand the test of time . . . What was there in the fog of London in those glory days of ours that enabled us to create these mythic figures? You conjured up Holmes – and Moriarty. People love a villain, don't they? Bram created Dracula. Robert Louis Stevenson produced Dr Jekyll and Mr Hyde – though, for the life of me, I never could remember which of the two of them was the evil one.' He laughed wheezily. 'I had a letter not long ago from your young friend James Barrie. He's writing a play about a boy who never grows up. I like the idea of that, don't you?'

'I do,' I said.

'Will you write the story of Jack the Ripper, Arthur? "It was the best of crimes, it was the worst of crimes . . ." That was to be the opening line, remember?'

'Perhaps,' I said.

'Oh do,' he pressed me. 'I told the story to another writer the other day – a Polish fellow I met here in Paris, shy but very charming. We had a pleasant evening, drinking together and exchanging stories. He said, with my permission, he might use parts of it one day.* Ours is a generation of myth-makers, Arthur – the last of a kind. You must write about Jack the Ripper, Arthur. Tell me you will.'

'Jack the Ripper is not a myth,' I said. 'He was real.'

'Yes,' said Oscar. 'And we knew him.'

For a few minutes, we talked about those January days and nights when we breakfasted together at the Langham and walked the streets of Whitechapel side by side – as Holmes and Watson might have done.

There was a question that I wanted to ask him, and I began to – but when I discovered that, until I reminded him, he had forgotten the names of Ostrog and Kosminski, I realised there was no point.

---

* He did. *The Secret Agent* by Joseph Conrad was published in 1904.

Besides, I knew the answer to my question. The last victim of Jack the Ripper, the girl who had been murdered on that fateful Saturday morning, the thirteenth of January 1894, was Olga – my Olga, my little Russian acrobat. At the time, Oscar told me that the victim had been beheaded because he could not bear to tell me the truth: he had seen her face. He knew that it was Olga.

Oscar told me, too, that when Salazkin had looked at the photograph of my children and had seen the delight the picture gave to Olga, he resented it. Olga was murdered because of the delight she showed in knowing me. I shall not forget her. Of all ghosts the ghosts of our old loves are the worst.

Gyles Brandreth

Gyles Brandreth is the President of the Oscar Wilde Society, the editor of the *Complete Fairy Tales of Oscar Wilde* (2008) and *Beautiful and Impossible Things: Selected Essays of Oscar Wilde* (2015), as well as the author of seven murder mysteries featuring Oscar Wilde, Arthur Conan Doyle and their circle – one of whom was George R. Sims (1847 –1922), kinsman of the Empress Eugénie, journalist, playwright and social reformer, who wrote the ballads *Billy's dead and gone to glory* and *Christmas Day in the workhouse*, and was the first journalist to claim to know the identity of 'Jack the Ripper'. Gyles Brandreth's great-grandmother was a first cousin of George R. Sims and the present volume owes its revelations to unpublished papers in the Sims archive.

Gyles Brandreth was born in 1948 in Germany, where his father, Charles Brandreth, was serving as a legal officer with the Allied Control Commission and counted among his colleagues H. Montgomery Hyde, who published the first full account of the trials of Oscar Wilde that year. In 1974, Gyles Brandreth produced *The Trials of Oscar Wilde* (with Tom Baker as Wilde) at the Oxford Theatre Festival and, in 2000, edited the transcripts of the trials for an audio production featuring Martin Jarvis.

Gyles Brandreth was educated at the Lycée Français de Londres, at Betteshanger School in Kent, and at Bedales in Hampshire, where the school's founder, J. H. Badley (1865–1967), provided him with a series of vivid personal accounts of Oscar Wilde's conversational style. J. H. Badley knew the Wildes, and their son Cyril was a pupil at Bedales at the time of Oscar's arrest. Like Montague John Druitt, Gyles Brandreth went to New College, Oxford (where he was a scholar, President of the Union and editor of the university magazine), and then embarked on a career as an author and journalist. His first book was a study of prison reform (*Created in Captivity*, 1972); his first biography was a portrait of the Victorian music-hall star Dan Leno (*The Funniest Man on Earth*, 1974). More recently, he has published a biography of Sir John Gielgud, an acclaimed diary of his years as an MP and government whip (*Breaking the Code: Westminster Diaries 1990–97*) and two best-selling royal biographies: *Philip & Elizabeth: Portrait of a Marriage* and *Charles & Camilla: Portrait of a Love Affair*. His diaries covering the years 1959 to 2000 appeared under the title *Something Sensational to Read in the Train* – a phrase borrowed from *The Importance of Being Earnest*. He is also the editor of the *Oxford Dictionary of Humorous Quotations* and the author of two *Sunday Times* bestsellers: *Word Play* and *The 7 Secrets of Happiness*.

As an actor Gyles Brandreth has appeared in pantomime and Shakespeare, and as Lady Bracknell in a musical adaptation of *The Importance of Being Earnest*. As a broadcaster, he has presented numerous series for BBC Radio 4, including *A Rhyme in Time*, *Sound Advice*, *Wordaholics* and *Whispers*. He has featured on *Desert Island Discs* and is probably best known as a regular on *Just a Minute* (Radio 4) and a reporter on *The One Show* (BBC 1). A regular on the Channel 4 word-game *Countdown*, his television appearances have ranged from being the guest host of *Have I Got News for You* to being the subject of *This Is Your Life*. With Hinge & Bracket he scripted the TV series *Dear Ladies*; with Julian Slade he wrote a play about A. A. Milne (featuring the young Aled

Jones as Christopher Robin); and with Susannah Pearse he has written a play about Lewis Carroll and the actress Isa Bowman. Gyles Brandreth is married to the writer and publisher Michèle Brown, and they have three children – a barrister, a writer and an environmental economist – and seven grandchildren.

Oscar Wilde died in a small, first-floor room at L'Hôtel d'Alsace, 13 rue des Beaux-Arts, in Paris, at approximately 1.45 p.m. on 30 November 1900. One hundred years later, at the same time, on the same date, in the same room, Gyles and Michèle Brandreth were among a small group who gathered to mark the centenary of his passing and to honour a most remarkable man, whose greatest play, according to Frank Harris, was his own life: 'a five-act tragedy with Greek implications, and he was its most ardent spectator'. In 2010, Gyles Brandreth unveiled the plaque commemorating the first meeting of Oscar Wilde and Arthur Conan Doyle at the Langham Hotel, London.

In 2015, at the Langham Hotel, Gyles Brandreth hosted a reception at which HRH the Duchess of Cornwall unveiled a bronze head of Oscar Wilde sculpted by the young English sculptor James Matthews. Before the unveiling, the actor Rupert Everett read from *The Picture of Dorian Gray* and Gyles Brandreth explained that everyone in the room had a connection with Oscar – some, like Merlin Holland, Wilde's grandson, obviously so; others, like the Duchess of Cornwall, less obviously.

In fact, the Duchess of Cornwall, born Camilla Shand, is the great-granddaughter of Alec Shand (1858–1936), whose intellectual legacy is his work as a pioneer in the field of social psychology. In 1914 he published *The Foundations of Character, Being a Study of the Tendencies of the Emotions and Sentiments*.

In her speech at the Langham Hotel in 2015, the Duchess of Cornwall began by quoting Wilde's line, 'There is only one thing in the world worse than being talked about and that is not being talked about', adding that it is one of the few maxims of his that she is not sure she would entirely agree with. She then explained her family connection with Wilde: 'My great-grandfather, Alec Shand, an intellectual who moved in both Bohemian and radical circles, was introduced by his sister, Bessie, to one of her friends, a beautiful, chestnut-haired, intellectually gifted woman named Constance Lloyd. They became secretly engaged, but, sadly, nobody knows why, or when, one of them broke it off. Constance went on to marry Oscar in 1887. The rest, as they say, is history.' She added, with Wilde's grandson in her line of sight: 'Oscar Wilde said, "The one duty we owe to history is to re-write it"; but if this particular piece of history had been re-written, I know that two people in this room would not be here today!'